01/24/14

Think you know what [...] isn't?
Think again...

D1041187

Resounding praise for
C.S. GRAHAM's bestselling thriller
THE ARCHANGEL PROJECT

Withdrawn/ASCE

"As current as today's headlines and as disturbing as your darkest nightmare. . . . Riveting, provocative, and enthralling . . . a debut not to be missed."

James Rollins, *New York Times* bestselling author of
The Last Oracle

"The pace . . . is blistering. . . . This moves at supersonic speed. . . . It'll keep you turning pages. . . . A very good book. . . . By the time you finish it, you'll be struck by how plausible the whole plot is and wonder if some of it might just be real."

Baton Rouge Advocate

"Fast paced fun! C.S. Graham mixes up careening action with compelling characters and fascinating research to create a roller-coaster ride of suspense."

Lisa Gardner, *New York Times* bestselling author of *Say Goodbye*

"A conspiracy that's as convincing as anything Dan Brown has given us. . . . [A] chase mystery you really want to catch."

Minneapolis Star Tribune

[A] riveting thriller, *The Archangel Project* might sound like science fiction, but it is based on fact."

New Orleans Times-Picayune

"Engaging . . . smart and exhilarating. An electrifying ride that rings with authenticity. No question, this is an auspicious beginning for C. S. Graham."

Steve Berry, *New York Times* bestselling author of
The Venetian Betrayal

By C.S. Graham

THE ARCHANGEL PROJECT
THE SOLOMON EFFECT

ATTENTION: ORGANIZATIONS AND CORPORATIONS
Most Harper paperbacks are available at special quantity discounts for bulk purchases for sales promotions, premiums, or fund raising. For information, please call or write:

Special Markets Department, HarperCollins Publishers, 10 East 53rd Street, New York, New York 10022-5299. Telephone: (212) 207-7528.   Fax: (212) 207-7222.

C.S. GRAHAM

THE SOLOMON EFFECT

HARPER

An Imprint of HarperCollins*Publishers*

3907504385375

This is a work of fiction. Names, characters, places, and incidents are products of the author's imagination or are used fictitiously and are not to be construed as real. Any resemblance to actual events, locales, organizations, or persons, living or dead, is entirely coincidental.

HARPER

An Imprint of HarperCollins*Publishers*
10 East 53rd Street
New York, New York 10022-5299

Copyright © 2009 by Two Talers LLC
Excerpt from *The Babylonian Codex* copyright © 2010 by Two Talers LLC
ISBN: 978-0-06-168935-2

All rights reserved. No part of this book may be used or reproduced in any manner whatsoever without written permission, except in the case of brief quotations embodied in critical articles and reviews. For information address Harper paperbacks, an Imprint of HarperCollins Publishers.

First Harper paperback printing: October 2009

HarperCollins® and Harper® are registered trademarks of Harper-Collins Publishers.

Printed in the United States of America

Visit Harper paperbacks on the World Wide Web at
www.harpercollins.com

10 9 8 7 6 5 4 3 2

If you purchased this book without a cover, you should be aware that this book is stolen property. It was reported as "unsold and destroyed" to the publisher, and neither the author nor the publisher has received any payment for this "stripped book."

To the Monday Night Wordsmiths—Pam Ahearn,
Rexanne Becnel, Elora Fink, Marie Goodwin,
Charles Gramlich, and Laura Joh Rowland—
with thanks for your encouragement, your
wisdom, and your friendship

THE
SOLOMON
EFFECT

1

Engines throbbing, the salvage ship slipped into the secluded cove by the cold light of a misty Baltic dawn. Stefan Baklanov stood at the *Yalena*'s prow, his hands clamped around the rusted rail, his gaze fixed on the empty docks of the dilapidated shipyard before them. He was sixteen years old and just beginning his fifth month working on the *Yalena*, a lumbering old diesel-powered catamaran. He heard his uncle, the captain, bark an order from the bridge, then felt the deck of the big ship shudder beneath him as the engines slowed. A shiver of excitement tingled up Stefan's spine, mingled with a stir of unease. He threw a glance over his shoulder at the barge that wallowed in their wake like a dead whale. On the barge's deck rested the ghostly wreck of a Nazi-era U-boat.

Even in the dim light of dawn, the huge submarine's long, low silhouette and upthrusting conning tower were unmistakable, its steel hull covered with accretions from the sixty-plus years it had lain beneath the waters of the sea, a silent tomb to the scores of Germans who'd once sailed her. The sailors were still there—or at least, their bones were still there. Stefan knew because last night he'd taken one of the dive lights and squeezed in through the sub's popped hatch for a quick look.

His uncle and a couple of the men had already spent hours crawling through the U-boat's narrow passageways and cramped quarters. Uncle Jasha emerged unusually silent and grim faced, but that only piqued Stefan's curiosity more.

At first it had been a grand adventure, squeezing through silent portals, gazing in wonder at the funny old glass and brass gauges in the control room and the cook pots still hanging over the galley range. But as the narrow golden beam of his light played over long-abandoned bunks and empty leather boots, Stefan grew more thoughtful.

He'd expected to crawl through a wet, rusted interior smelling of brine and the creatures of the sea. But nothing was wet. With a chill, he suddenly understood: for all these years, the sub's hull had held. He saw the pair of eyeglasses lying on a table and the trumpet clutched against the desiccated ribcage of the man who'd once played it, and the awful truth of what he was seeing hit him. These men hadn't died quickly in a fiery explosion. They hadn't even drowned. They'd suffocated. Slowly.

Stefan had grown up hearing his grandmother's stories of the Great Patriotic War, of the siege of Stalingrad and the deadly winters of 'forty-two and 'forty-three. He'd imagined the Nazis as demons, as somehow not quite human. He'd never thought of them as the kind of men who might set aside a pair of reading glasses to clutch a beloved musical instrument to their chest as they breathed in their last, dying gasps. Suddenly the narrow passageways and low ceilings seemed to press in on him, stealing his breath until he raced for the hatch again, not caring how much noise he made or who saw him.

Uncle Jasha had slapped his big hand against the side of Stefan's head for taking the dive light without asking. But when Stefan started ranting about how what they were doing was wrong—wrong and dangerous, for surely they were tempting the wrath of the ancient gods of the sea—Uncle Jasha had simply laughed and called him sentimental and superstitious. Yet the sense of foreboding lingered, even in the cold light of day.

Now, Stefan sucked in a breath of air tinged by the acrid stench of an old fire smoldering in the shipyard. A shout from one of the *Yalena*'s crewmen drew his head around and he caught the sound of an outboard motor cutting through the stillness. He peered into the mist, past the rocky point where a scattering of stunted, wind-twisted pines grew. It took a moment before he spotted the launch filled with six or eight men that skimmed across the flat pewter water toward the *Yalena*.

"Damn," muttered Uncle Jasha, coming to stand beside Stefan at the rail. A big, barrel-chested man with a salt-stiffened head of dark hair and a full beard, Jasha Baklanov still towered over Stefan by half a foot. For five years now, Uncle Jasha had been the closest thing to a father Stefan had. By turns gruffly affectionate and chillingly stern, Jasha lived by a looser moral code than Stefan's father. Which probably explained why Uncle Jasha was alive, whereas Stefan's father was dead.

Stefan glanced up at him. "Who is it? The men from the shipyard? Why are they coming out to meet us?"

Instead of answering, Uncle Jasha rubbed one work-worn hand across his mouth and down over his heavy beard, his nostrils flaring wide. "Get below."

"But I wanted to—"

"God damn it, boy. Do as you're told. For once."

Stefan threw a last look at the approaching launch, then pushed away from the rail.

But he didn't go below. Heading for the open stairwell, he ducked behind the tattered tarp that covered the lifeboats and their davits and doubled back so that he was some ten or fifteen feet away from the landing where the men would come aboard. Through a slit in the tarp he watched his uncle station himself beside the rail. A Russian bear of a man in a striped sweater and a Greek fisherman's cap, Jasha Baklanov stood with his legs splayed wide, his fingers combing through the wild disorder of his beard in that way he had whenever he was thoughtful—or troubled.

The whine of the outboard motor drew close, then suddenly died as the launch bumped against the *Yalena's* hull. Stefan watched the men come aboard—dark-haired, solemn-faced Slavs from the looks of them, with maybe a few Chechens. But the man who walked up to Uncle Jasha was subtly different. Dressed in a black sweater and loose overcoat, he was as dark-haired as the others, but tanned. When he spoke, his accent was strangely clipped, his phraseology awkward, like a man who'd learned his Russian as an adult or in school.

"This wasn't the plan," the man said.

Uncle Jasha's face darkened, and Stefan realized this must be the man who'd hired the *Yalena*, the man Jasha referred to only as "the Major."

"There were complications," Uncle Jasha lied. "We needed to move early."

A tight smile split the Major's face. "And you didn't notify us because . . . ?"

Rather than answer, Jasha Baklanov said, "You've been watching us."

"Did you think we wouldn't?"

From where he crouched behind the tarp, Stefan felt his

heart begin to pound. No, Uncle Jasha hadn't expected the men who'd hired him to be watching them. How had they done so?

The Major glanced toward the barge and its long, silent burden. Jasha Baklanov said, "The sub's cargo is intact."

"Good. Then you won't mind if my men take a look." The Major nodded to a couple of his men. Stefan could hear the tramp of their boots as they headed aft. When Stefan brought his attention back to the Major, he understood why the men wore loose overcoats. As he stepped away from Uncle Jasha, the Major's coat opened to reveal a machine pistol.

At his nod, the rest of the men—except for a big, red-headed Chechen—spread out over the ship in a way that made Stefan nervous. The minutes crawled past. Stefan watched, terrified, as the Major flipped open a sleek cell phone. He said something Stefan couldn't hear before glancing over at Jasha Baklanov, his eyes narrowing. "One of the sub's hatches has been blown."

The man beside the Major lifted his machine pistol so that the muzzle pointed at Uncle Jasha's chest. Jasha shrugged. "I was curious. What's the harm? I tell you, what you want is still there."

Again the Major said something into his cell phone. After a moment, he smiled. "You're right. It is." He nodded to the man beside him. "Kill him. Kill them all."

Stefan sucked in a gasp of air, the betraying sound lost in the rattle of submachine-gun fire. A line of bullets ripped across Jasha Baklanov's thick torso, his arms flying up, his body jerking repeatedly as a bloody spray filled the air. Stefan had to squeeze his eyes shut and sink his teeth deep into his lower lip to stop himself from crying out.

He heard another sharp, staccato burst of gunfire from somewhere below, followed by another and another. He bit down harder on his lip, his mouth filling with the metallic taste of his own blood as the killing went on and on.

When the quiet finally came, it sounded eerie, unnatural. Stefan could hear the gentle slop of the waves against the *Yalena*'s sides and the surge of his own blood pulsing through his veins. He had to force himself to open his eyes.

Uncle Jasha lay sprawled on the deck. As Stefan watched, the Major walked over to stand looking down at what was left of the *Yalena*'s captain. In a welling of raw grief and fury, Stefan willed himself to remember each detail of the man's full face, the thick lips that pulled into another tight smile. "Stupid greedy Russian," said the Major in his own language, a language that made Stefan shudder.

The Major glanced back at the man still cradling the extended stock of the machine pistol against his shoulder. "Search the ship. Make sure we have everyone."

Stefan flattened his hands against the cold steel behind him, not daring to breathe as the man brushed past. He was hideously conscious of his rough work boots visible beneath the loose edge of the tarp. When they searched the ship, they would find him. Christ, he thought; all they'd need do is stand still and listen, and surely they'd hear the pounding of his heart.

He watched, shivering, as the Major headed aft, his footfalls echoing on the silent deck. Dropping to his belly, Stefan wiggled out from under the tarp, darted across the deck, and climbed the rail in one frantic scramble. He heard a shout, but he was already pushing off, his body arching effortlessly into a long, flawless dive honed by years of practice. Once, it had been Stefan's dream to make Russia's Olympic swim team. Like so much else, that dream had died along with Stefan's father. But it had left him with the confidence to view the sea as an ally rather than another enemy—although in that, he had reckoned without the cold.

The water was an icy, cutting shock that drove the air from his body and all thought from his brain. Gasping with agony and fear, he surfaced more by habit than by conscious volition. He heard a shout, and dove again as bullets slapped into the water around him.

A pearlescent cave of icy soundless death, the sea cocooned him in crystalline suspension. He stayed down until his lungs burned and his vision dimmed and he knew he had to either risk being shot at again or die. He thrust his head up into the air, his body aching and shuddering as he drew breath. He was so cold his skin burned and his body jerked like a man caught in a hail of bullets. Swinging around, he realized with a new jolt of terror he'd become disoriented in the mist. Was he still headed toward the shore? What if he was swimming out to sea? Or what if—Oh, God—what if he was swimming back toward the *Yalena*?

Behind him, the outboard motor coughed to life, the sound magnified and distorted by the softly drifting fog. Kicking hard, Stefan struck out in the opposite direction, toward what he hoped was a rocky point crowned by the dark, twisted silhouettes of wind-tortured pines.

2

October Guinness stood in the small side yard of her Uptown cottage, her fists resting against the stiff white cotton of her *dobuk*. She could hear the chatter of the finches in the limbs of the old live oaks that lined the narrow street, feel the warmth of the honeysuckle-scented breeze against her cheek. Her breathing slowed, became even.

In some ways, Tae Kwon Do was like meditation and remote viewing: each in its own way came down to this, this ability to move into stillness, to connect with the vibrating energy of the universe. She opened her eyes and stepped left into a cat stance, arms flashing down into twin lower knifehand blocks in the beginning of the Taebaek third black belt pattern. She moved effortlessly through side kicks and thrusts, backhand strikes and reverse punches. Turning, she pulled her left foot back to her right and relaxed into the final stance with a smile. She was about to begin her practice again when she heard the first bars of *Anchors Away* floating through the open door from the kitchen.

Her cell phone. *Shit.*

If the call had been from anyone else, she would have ignored it. But that particular ringtone meant one thing and one thing only. Scooping up her bottle of water from the nearby garden bench, she raced up the steps to the kitchen stoop, banged open the screen door, and dove for the phone on the counter. "Hello?"

"Tobie. Glad I caught you." Colonel F. Scott McClintock's normally mellow voice resonated with barely contained excitement. "I just got off the phone with Washington. They're finally giving us a tasking."

She took a quick gulp of water and choked. "You're kidding, right?"

Under the patronage of Vice President T. J. Beckham, Tobie and McClintock had spent the last four months setting up a small remote viewing program at the Algiers Naval Support Facility across the river from the French Quarter. But up until now, their viewing sessions had all been training exercises. Not even the Vice President's patronage could keep the project from being regarded by the few people in the intelligence community who knew about it as a waste of money and an embarrassment, rather than as an asset. The assignments she and the retired Army Colonel had been hoping for had never materialized. Lately, the Navy had been making noises about closing down the program and transferring Tobie to a different assignment. In Iraq.

"It's no joke, Tobie. When can you come in?"

Yanking at the knot in her black belt, Tobie headed for the bedroom, the phone wedged between her ear and one shoulder of her *dobuk*. "Are you kidding? I'll be there as soon as I get changed."

Executive Office Building, Washington, D.C.

"I take it you've seen the Navy's report?" said T. J. Beckham, buttoning the neck of his dress shirt and turning up its collar. The reception at the White House for the Prime Minister of Australia was set to start in fifteen minutes, and the Vice President was not the kind of man to be late.

Once a simple pharmacist at a corner drugstore, he'd entered local politics almost by accident and advanced by what he privately considered a series of flukes, first to the state capitol, and then on to Washington, D.C. Even as the distinguished senior senator from Kentucky, Beckham had nourished no secret aspirations for higher office. But Beckham was a patriot, the kind of man who always did his duty, whether volunteering to serve in Vietnam, or rising from a sickbed to attend an important vote on the Senate floor. When the sudden death of the elected vice president left the office vacant, and his squabbling colleagues could agree on no one but the congenial Senator from Kentucky, Beckham saw his duty clearly and accepted the appointment.

"I've seen it," said the man who now stood in the middle of the Vice President's office. Tall and lanky, with the long, prominent bones of his New England ancestors, Gordon Chandler had been the DCI—the Director of Central Intelligence—for about as long as Beckham had served as vice president. But unlike Beckham, the DCI was a ruthlessly ambitious man.

Beckham looped his tie around his neck and swung to face the mirror. "Two days," he said, his voice gravelly with disgust. "It's been two days since the NSA intercepted a cell phone conversation linking some unspecified but impending terrorist attack on this country with a sunken Nazi sub. Yet it isn't until this morning that someone gets the bright idea to check on a U-boat I now learn we've been monitoring for years? *Christ Almighty*." Beckham raised his chin, stretching his neck as he looped the tie into a bow. "And that's not taking the Lord's name in vain, by the way. I'm asking for His help."

Glancing in the mirror, Beckham saw a muscle jump along the DCI's jaw, but he kept his mouth shut.

Beckham straightened the folds of his bow tie and tried to calm down. "Now that we know the submarine is gone, we can trace it, right? Seems to me, we find that U-boat, it ought to lead us straight to these terrorists."

"Theoretically. Unfortunately, it's not that easy, sir. We have a top team working on it. But you have to understand that by now, the terrorists will have removed the cargo from that sub and be long gone. We've determined that our resources are better allocated elsewhere."

"Such as?"

"Right now, the CIA is focusing most of its efforts on suspected links between homegrown radicals and known terrorist groups in Egypt and Pakistan, while the FBI and Homeland Security are rounding up anyone and everyone in this country who might possibly be involved."

Beckham frowned. "How many people are we talking about here?"

"Does it matter? If we put enough pressure on them, one of these guys is bound to crack."

Beckham studied the other man's smooth, complacent face. Chandler was one of President Bob Randolph's minions, and Beckham didn't trust him any more than he'd trust a crazy coon dog back home in the hills of Kentucky. "How many have already confessed?"

"A few. We're checking out their stories now."

"Most men will confess to anything under torture—"

"This country doesn't torture people, sir."

"—and in the meantime, the men who really made that

phone call are in all likelihood still out there, getting ready to implement their plans."

"I think you underestimate Homeland Security, sir. We know who our enemies are."

"Do we?" Beckham shrugged into his dinner jacket. "I think the key to all this is that U-boat."

Chandler buried a sigh of impatience deep in his throat. "I can assure you, sir, we've allocated every resource we can spare to tracing it."

Beckham gave a slow smile. "Not quite every available resource."

"Excuse me, sir?"

"I've asked Colonel McClintock to task October Guinness."

"You what?"

Beckham smoothed his lapels. "I know your opinion of remote viewing, Gordon. But you forget: if it weren't for that talented young lady, I'd be dead by now—and so would a lot of other innocent people."

"I'm sorry, sir, but every intelligence service in this country is already stretched to the breaking point investigating the *legitimate* leads we have. I can't in all conscience divert our resources to go chasing after some vision that could very easily be nothing more than the product of someone's overactive imagination."

"What about Division Thirteen?"

Beckham watched as a slow, malicious smile spread across the DCI's face. "I stand corrected. There is one man I could spare."

Alexandria, Virginia

Jax Alexander stuck the corkscrew in his back pocket, tucked a bottle of Shiraz under one arm, and scooped up two of the Senator's best crystal glasses. Through the open door to the townhouse's terrace, he could see the setting sun spilling a path of gold across the river's sparkling water and hear the screech of the gulls as they wheeled and dipped in the breeze.

"God I love this view," said Kelly Yardley, going to lean against the low brick wall that ran around the terrace.

Jax set the wine glasses on the ledge beside her and smiled. He hadn't had much luck with relationships lately, mainly because his job kept getting in the way. But he was hoping things might be different with Kelly. A long-legged Cornell graduate with a quick brain and a ready laugh, she'd been seeing Jax for almost a month now. They had a relaxing long weekend planned, starting with an early dinner and tickets to the National Symphony Orchestra at the Kennedy Center, followed by a couple days of sailing in the Chesapeake.

"Who'd you have to kill to get this place, anyway?" she asked as he peeled the foil off the top of the wine bottle.

Built of brick with white trim and louvered shutters, the elegant townhouse overlooking the Potomac River in Old Alexandria was way, way beyond the reach of most CIA operatives. Especially disgraced ones. He eased the cork from the bottle. "Senator James Herman Winston."

She gave a startled laugh, her nose crinkling in a way he liked. She was smart and funny without being at all pretentious, which was remarkable, considering that she was both gorgeous and a rising star with the biggest lobbying firm on the Hill.

She watched him pour the wine. "I'd heard a rumor your grandfather was Senator Winston, but I didn't believe it."

The Winstons were one of those venerable old New England families that could trace their eminently respectable lineage back to Colonial days. Which was why the Senator had never quite recovered from his only daughter Sophie's short, disastrous marriage to a guitar-playing hippie named

Aiden Xavier Alexander. Jax handed her a glass. "He had a hard time believing it himself."

"Good Lord," said Kelly, her eyes suddenly going wide. "That means your mother is Sophie Talbot."

"Well, her name was Talbot the last I checked. But she's had so many husbands I sometimes have a hard time keeping track." Sophie had divorced Jax's father when Jax was four, with a new husband—and a new name—appearing every few years since then. After the disaster of her first marriage, Sophie had made sure all her subsequent husbands were rich, powerful men.

Kelly laughed again. Then her smile faded. "That must have been tough, growing up."

"Nah. Growing up in the projects is tough. Being shunted off to boarding schools from the age of six is just . . ." He hesitated, searching for the right word.

"Lonely," she finished for him.

"Well, yeah."

They stood for a time watching the breeze billowing the canvas of a small sailboat as it headed toward shore. Jax felt his cell phone begin to vibrate. He ignored it.

"Mmmm," said Kelly, closing her eyes as she took a sip of the wine. "No one makes wine like the French."

Jax's cell stopped vibrating. He turned the bottle so she could see the label. "It's Australian. A McWilliams."

She choked on her wine, her laughter ringing out clear and uninhibited. "Oops."

He smiled, enjoying the way the setting sun brought out the subtle tones of auburn in her long dark hair . . . and heard the phone in the kitchen begin to ring.

"Sounds like someone's kinda desperate to get ahold of you," she said.

Jax set aside his wineglass. "I need to go check on the salmon anyway. Be right back."

Even before he saw that the number was blocked on his caller ID, Jax knew who it was. Cradling the phone between his ear and shoulder, Jax eased open the oven door. "I've got three days off, Matt. Remember? Leave me alone."

The voice on the other end of the phone gave a gruff laugh. "All leave has been canceled until after Halloween. Or hadn't you heard?"

Jax reached for the oven mitts. "All leave has been canceled for *essential* personnel. There aren't many advantages to being on the DCI's shitlist, but in this instance, being labeled 'nonessential personnel' is one of them."

"Looks like you're more essential than you thought. The DCI himself wants you in on this."

Jax set the hot poaching pan on the kitchen's marble-topped island with a soft *thump*. "That sounds ominous. Is he hoping it'll get me killed, or just humiliated?"

"Maybe both."

3

No one in the Central Intelligence Agency wanted to be trans-ferred to Division Thirteen. Any project or assignment with the potential to be either personally embarrassing or a career wrecker was handed down to the guys in the Division.

There'd been a time when Jax had been considered one of the Agency's hotshots. Then he'd lost his temper over American involvement with right-wing death squads in Colombia and slugged a United States ambassador in the middle of a diplomatic dinner party. Definitely not a good career move, although Jax might eventually have been able to live it down if the ambassador involved—Gordon Chandler—hadn't been named the new Director of the CIA.

"A phantom Nazi sub?" said Jax, staring at Matt von Moltke across the width of the basement cubbyhole that served as the Division's offices. "Please tell me this is a joke."

"I'm afraid not," said Matt, coming from behind a row of

filing cabinets with a sheaf of printouts in his hands. He was a big guy, with a wild head of dark curly hair streaked with gray and a bushy beard that covered most of his face. He'd earned his transfer to Division Thirteen long ago, back in the eighties, when he'd objected to some of the dirty arrangements that became known as the Iran-contra affair.

"U–114. We located it back in 2003, lying in about three hundred feet of water off the east coast of Denmark. A British destroyer sank it with depth charges just days before the Nazis surrendered." Matt paused. "I'm told it's what they call a Type XB."

Jax leaned against the doorjamb, his hands on his hips. "That's significant?"

"Very." Matt limped over to start assembling the books and papers scattered across the battered chrome-and-Formica table that took up most of the floor space in his office. The table looked like something out of the fifties, and the folder he was shoving the papers into probably hailed from the same era. "The XBs were the biggest subs used by the *Kriegsmarine* in World War II. Originally they were designed as mine layers, but because of their size they were eventually converted into transports. They hauled all kinds of shit to the Japanese in the Pacific, and brought back raw materials to Germany."

"What was this U–114 carrying?" said Jax, pushing away from the door frame.

Matt held out a black-and-white photo of a long, slim submarine lying on a sandy seabed. "They think it was gold."

"Nazi gold?" Jax took the photo. "Sounds like somebody's been reading too many paperback thrillers."

Matt didn't even crack a smile. "It's no joke. The Nazis were sending all kinds of shit out of Germany near the end of the war. Some of it was war material and research to help the Japanese. But some of it was just loot."

Jax came to perch on the edge of the sturdy old table. "So why is the CIA interested?"

"You've heard about the NSA intercept?"

"The latest terrorist threat? Are you kidding? Who hasn't?" The administration had deliberately leaked information on the intercept to the press. Terrorist threats were always good for the President's popularity ratings, and at the moment President Randolph needed all the help he could get.

"What isn't so well known," said Matt, "is that the bad guys made a passing reference to some old World War II U-boat. It didn't make any sense until the Navy checked on U–114 and realized it's gone."

Jax stared down at the grainy photo in his hand. He was no longer laughing. "What do you mean, 'gone'?"

"Just that. Gone." Matt handed Jax another photo. This one showed the same stretch of seabed, empty now except for a long depression in the sand and what looked like a few broken cables and chunks of rusting metal. "That image was shot this morning. Ever since we located the sub, we've been keeping an eye on it. Given its cargo, our government wanted to raise it, but the Germans refused. A lot of men went down with U–114. They consider it a gravesite and they didn't want it disturbed."

"Looks like somebody disturbed it," said Jax, studying the two photos.

"The guys running the task force at Homeland Security think the terrorists must be planning to use the gold from the Nazi sub to finance their attack."

"That's a stretch, isn't it? I mean, there must be a lot of easier ways to get money than to salvage a sunken U-boat."

"All I know is what I'm told."

Jax reached for one of the books on the table, an old hard-cover with a torn yellow-and-blue dust jacket that read, *Iron Coffins: A personal account of the German U-boat battles of World War II*. He wasn't exactly claustrophobic, but the thought of being trapped beneath the sea in an overblown sardine can wasn't something he cared to dwell on too long. "Just how hard is it to raise one of these suckers, anyway?"

"That depends on how deep it is, and whether or not it's still in one piece. There's a Monsoon lying in 500 feet of water off the coast of Norway with a cargo of weapons-grade mercury that's started leaking. The Norwegians don't know what the hell to do with it. It broke in half when it was sunk by a torpedo, and they're afraid it'll come apart completely if they try to lift it."

Jax nodded toward the photo of the missing U-boat. "This one looks like it's in pretty good shape." He squinted at the ghostly image. "Except for that raggedy bit at the end there."

"It is. And it was in fairly shallow water, so raising it wouldn't have been a big deal. Back in 2002, the Brits let out a contract to salvage the captured U-boats they sank off Ireland and Scotland after the war as part of Operation Deadlight. Those are scuttled war prizes, so the subs technically belong to the Brits rather than the Germans. And of course, there aren't any bodies."

Jax frowned. "I don't get it. What do they want them for?"

"The steel."

"Sounds like an expensive way to get steel."

"Yeah, but this isn't just any steel. This is pre–1945 steel."

Jax shook his head. "Am I missing something? What difference does it make when the steel was manufactured?"

"All steel manufactured since 1945 is radioactive."

"Radioactive?"

"That's right. Steel production involves a lot of air, and we've exploded so many nuclear bombs in the atmosphere in the last sixty-odd years that the air is radioactive. Steel picks it up."

"Now that's a scary thought."

"No shit. The problem is, we need clean steel for certain kinds of sensitive instruments. The only place to get it is from old ships."

"And subs," said Jax, staring down at the book in his hands. "Maybe terrorists didn't have anything to do with your missing U-boat. Maybe it was simply stolen by someone looking to make a quick buck salvaging the steel."

"You're forgetting the NSA intercept."

Jax huffed a soft laugh. "Right. You know as well as I do that most of the linguists the NSA has translating their intercepts would have a hard time ordering a cup of coffee in Cairo."

"Maybe. But these guys were speaking English. *Unaccented* English. Which is why Homeland Security thinks this operation is homegrown."

Jax reached again for the image of the empty seabed, and frowned. "Our satellite photos don't show anything?"

Matt shook his head. "We weren't targeting that area. It's open water. We're running computer checks to see if we might have picked something up by chance, but it's gonna take time. And time is one thing we don't have."

"What kind of timeline are we looking at here? Any idea yet?"

"These guys were talking about a terrorist attack going down on Halloween."

"A week? Shit." The administration hadn't leaked that, either. Jax was silent for a moment. "How long has it been since anyone saw this sub on the ocean floor?"

"It was there ten days ago."

"And Homeland Security thinks these guys have a terrorist attack scheduled for Halloween? No way. That's too tight of a timeline. Someone's not playing straight with us on something."

"If the bad guys had everything lined up, it could be done."

Jax wasn't so sure. "I assume we're already scrutinizing the gold bullion markets?"

"Yep. No one's admitting to knowing a thing. But then, if the bad guys are selling the gold to the Chinese or through some African outfit, we won't hear of it. We don't control things as much as we like to think we do."

"How about going at it from the other end? How many ships in the world are capable of salvaging a sub that size?"

"The DCI's got some guys drawing up a list." Matt glanced at the clock. "But we're hoping to have a different kind of lead coming in the next hour or so. It's going to be your assignment to follow up on it."

There was something airy about Matt's tone that set off Jax's warning bells. "A different kind of lead coming from where?"

Matt's gaze faltered away.

Jax picked up the pile of files and books, and slid off the edge of the table. "Out with it, Matt. What aren't you telling me?"

"The Vice President has asked Colonel McClintock to task Tobie Guinness."

A couple of books skittered off the pile of files in Jax's arms and clattered to the floor.

"Good idea," said Jax, hunkering down to retrieve the dropped books. "A phantom Nazi sub loaded with stolen gold probably isn't quite enough to get Division Thirteen laughed out of the Company. Why not add a touch of woo-woo?"

"Remote viewing is not woo-woo. It's science. And you know it."

"Right." Just because Tobie had managed to scuttle the

Keefe Corporation's nasty little scheme last summer didn't mean Jax bought into the whole "alternative states of perception" business. With every passing month, he'd found himself growing increasingly skeptical, increasingly convinced there must be some other explanation for what had happened. "Maybe we can find an astrologer and a tarot-card reader to consult while we're at it."

Matt made an incoherent noise deep in his throat, but said nothing.

Jax straightened. "This is why the Director wanted me assigned to this, right?"

"You got it."

4

Colonel F. Scott McClintock, United States Army, retired, stared through the one-way mirror at the small sound-proofed room before him. October Guinness sat at one end of the table, a pad of paper and a pencil on the surface before her, a microphone clipped to the collar of her shirt. She was a small woman with a boyish body and honey-colored hair, which she wore pulled back in a casual ponytail. Dressed in a polo shirt and jeans, she looked more like a college student than a Naval officer. She was also the best remote viewer McClintock had ever worked with.

Most people had an imperfect understanding of remote viewing, seeing it as a magical ability to transcend time and space in order to gather information about a "remote" target. Only, there was nothing magical about RV.

The U.S. government's awareness of the practice dated back at least to the end of World War II, when they'd cap-tured a bunch of documents detailing some interesting Nazi experiments in the application of extrasensory perception to intelligence work. But what really caught the attention of the guys in the Pentagon was when the Soviets started investing in "psychic" stuff big-time back in the seventies. All the U.S. intelligence branches—the CIA, the Army, the NSA—had sunk money into the procedure over the years, although they were very careful never to use the word "psychic."

The term "remote viewing" was a nice, sanitized expression coined by two of the physicists working on the phenomena for the government out at Stanford Research Institute. As they defined it, remote viewing required strict adherence to specific, controlled scientific protocol. Some of the guys working with remote viewing for the Army back in the nineties had gotten sloppy. But McClintock was always very careful to adhere to protocol; he didn't want anyone to be able to claim that their results were contaminated by leading questions and "frontloading."

He watched as his assistant, Peter Abrams, took the seat opposite Tobie. Normally, the Colonel was the tasker, the one who guided Tobie through her remote viewing sessions. But a clean session required the tasker to be kept ignorant of the target, and the Colonel had defined this exact target himself. He'd warned the Vice President that remote viewing didn't work well with this kind of target, but Beckham wanted to go ahead with it anyway.

McClintock had read about the impending terrorist attack in the press. He'd long ago learned to discount most of the sensationalism pumped out by the mainstream media, but according to Beckham, this threat looked like the real thing, and the government had virtually nothing to go on. They didn't know who was behind it. They didn't know what the terrorists were targeting. About all they did know was the date—Halloween—and that it was somehow linked to an old sunken U-boat.

McClintock felt himself tense with anticipation as he watched Tobie settle comfortably in her chair and close her eyes. Up until now, their viewing sessions had all been training runs. Remote viewing was a skill like anything else; the more you practiced it, the better you got. Now, finally, they were being given a chance to contribute to the defense of the country—and maybe show the doubters in D.C. what a good remote viewer could do, while they were at it.

The physicists out at Stanford who'd done some of the early research on remote viewing had demonstrated that most people can be taught to do it, the same way most people can be taught to dance or play the piano. But that didn't mean most people were particularly good at it. Remote viewing was a talent, and Tobie Guinness was a remarkably talented viewer.

Successful viewing required sinking down into what they called the Zone, which was basically the same state of relaxed reception achieved by deep meditation. Tobie was very good at reaching that state. McClintock could see her visibly relaxing, her breath coming deep and slow.

"Today is Saturday, 24 October," said Peter, the microphone system echoing his voice as it was fed to the Colonel and their taping system. "That's good, Tobie. Relax." Peter laid his open palm on the opaque manila envelope that rested on the table before him. "All right, using the information in this envelope, tell me what you see."

Like McClintock, Peter was watching Tobie's face. He saw her mouth open, her nostrils flaring as if she were gasping for air. "It's dark. Cold. It's like . . . I can't breathe. *Oh, God.*" Her voice broke, her face going slack with horror. "They're all dead."

Since Peter didn't know the target, he didn't understand what was happening. But McClintock understood only too well. "Back her out of there, fast," whispered McClintock, his fingers curling around the frame of the one-way mirror because he knew Peter couldn't hear him.

Peter might not understand what was happening in Tobie's mind, but he recognized the signs of distress. "Okay, Tobie," he said, keeping his voice calm. "I want you to back away from where you are a bit, maybe get above it. Now tell me what you see."

Tobie took another breath and shuddered, but McClintock could see the tension in her begin to ease. She licked her lower lip. "There's a long, rounded object. I think it's metal but it's . . . It must be old. It's rusted. Wet. It's resting on something bigger, something flat. I think it's also metal."

McClintock felt his heart begin to race. He'd been working with remote viewing for some thirty years. Yet every time he witnessed a successful viewing, every time he watched someone reach out with their mind and touch a distant place—he still felt the same chilling rush of excitement and wonder.

"Good, Tobie," said Peter. "Now I want you to move a little farther away."

"Okay."

"Tell me what you see."

"I get the impression of water. Lots of water. Rocks. Pebbles. It's a beach. A rocky beach. There's a rise of ground . . . here." Her pencil scratched across the pad as she drew a rough sketch. "A rise with trees." She paused. "I get a sense of cold. Clouds."

"Good," said Peter as she worked on her sketch. She barely glanced at what she was drawing. It was as if the image flowed directly from her mind to the paper. "Now look back at the long metal object. What do you see?"

"Wooden planks. It's . . . it's like a wooden platform or a dock. That's it. It's a dock. Wharves. A long stretch of wharves. But they seem old. Deserted. There's a big piece of machinery. Here." She added to her sketch. "It's yellow, and it sticks up in the air."

A crane? wondered McClintock, watching her.

Her pencil skittered across the page. She said, "I see a long row of something rectangular. I get the impression of storage, like warehouses, although they're mainly empty. And a road. Here."

"Can you follow it?"

"Yes." There was a pause. "It goes up a rise."

"Go to the top and tell me what you see."

"It's open, like a meadow. Maybe farmland. But it feels oddly empty, like it's . . . like it's abandoned."

McClintock knew a sense of frustration. Remote viewing worked best when the viewers were given specific geographical coordinates and simply asked to describe what was there. Back in the eighties, the Army remote viewers up at Fort Meade had successfully described secret Soviet submarine installations and the insides of enemy embassies. But there was a reason remote viewing had never worked well when it came to finding missing persons. The viewer could describe a room, maybe even a house or a ravine in the woods where the missing person was being kept. But where was that house? Where was that ravine?

Where was this beach?

McClintock had heard stories about how, back in the seventies, remote viewers at Fort Meade had helped the government find a Soviet plane that had crashed in the jungles of Africa. But that was a rare success story in the history of using RV as part of an attempt to find missing people or things. The Army viewers who had tried to trace kidnapping victims in Italy and Lebanon had been able to describe the captives; they had accurately described their physical health and mental states, the rooms in which they were being held, sometimes even the street outside. But they'd never been able

to provide the specific type of information that could enable
the Special Forces guys to go in and rescue anyone.

"Okay, Tobie," said Peter. "Go back to the wharves
and look again at the metal object. You said it was by the
water?"

"Not by the water. On the water." She worked on her
sketches some more, refining them, adding details. "There's
another building. Away from the warehouses, maybe halfway up the hill from the water."

"Tell me about the building."

"I get the impression of metal. A wavy metal. It's like another warehouse, but smaller. I can see cars parked behind
it. No, not cars. Vans. Blue vans. I think they all have the
same thing written on the sides."

McClintock felt a renewed surge of hope. Most remote
viewers couldn't read words or numbers. McClintock had
heard it had something to do with the way the two halves
of the brain process information. But Tobie—like Pat Price,
back in the seventies—could do it.

Her forehead crinkled into a frown. "It's in Greek. No.
Not Greek. Cyrillic." A talented linguist, Tobie knew Russian. But many other languages, from Macedonian and Ser-
bian to Belarusian and Ukrainian used the Cyrillic alphabet,
and she didn't know any of those.

"Militia," she said. "That's what it is. They're militia vans.
I think I can read . . . K . . . A . . ." Her frown deepened as she
slowly sounded the word out. "KALININGRAD," she said
suddenly. "That's it. Kaliningrad."

"Well, I'll be damned," said the Colonel, pushing away
from the window. He put in a call to Division Thirteen.
"Matt? McClintock here. I think what you're looking for is
at a shipyard on a rocky beach in Kaliningrad Oblast. That's
right. Russia."

5

Stefan Baklanov awoke in the grip of a blind terror. He felt his heart pound out one, two panicked beats before he realized the blackness that seemed to have swallowed him was merely the darkness of a cloud-shrouded night. It was another moment still before he remembered where he was.

He sat up, his arms wrapping around his bent knees, an ache pulling across his chest as he thought about Uncle Jasha and the others on the *Yalena*. There had been times during that long, seemingly endless swim to the shore when he'd come close to giving up and letting the sea take him. But he'd pushed on, even when his arms went numb and his legs felt so heavy he could barely move them. He still wasn't sure how he managed to drag himself up on the rocky point, gasping for breath and shivering so hard he didn't think he'd ever stop.

All he'd wanted to do was lie on the shore, close his eyes, and let exhaustion take him. But the throb of an outboard motor somewhere in the misty cove had driven him up and across a rutted, narrow road into the protective shelter of a copse of birch. His legs had felt as wobbly as a newborn calf's and his teeth chattered so hard he kept biting his tongue, but he knew he had to move or die.

He figured he'd covered maybe nine or ten kilometers, sticking to the fields and woods, hiding at the sound of every voice or approaching car, before he came upon the abandoned old German farmhouse. Built a century or more ago of good red brick, it sat well back from the main road in the midst of an overgrown field. There were tens of thousands of such houses scattered across Kaliningrad Oblast—entire villages whose inhabitants had fled west ahead of the conquering Red Army, or had been shot, or had disappeared forever into the frozen wastelands of Siberia.

The farmhouse door had long since been battered in and broken, but the old tile roof was still fairly sound and the stout brick walls kept out the cold wind that cut cruelly through Stefan's wet clothes. He thought about building a fire to warm himself, then realized that would be a mistake. Staggering up the stairs, he rummaged around until he found a tattered old blanket. Stripping off his icy clothes, he curled up in a leaf-littered corner and fell immediately into a deep, dreamless sleep.

He'd had a vague idea of sleeping until nightfall and then pushing on under the cover of darkness. But when he now looked at his watch he realized it was already past midnight. He'd slept far longer than he'd intended.

He pushed to his feet. Hugging the motheaten blanket around his shoulders, he lurched to the nearby window and peered through the broken panes at the dark, silent yard below.

He stared in helpless frustration into the blackness of the night. He could vaguely make out the looming outline of a collapsed barn and the distant, darker smudge of a copse of trees. But there could be a hundred men out there hiding in the shadows and Stefan knew he'd never see them. A sudden noise and a flurry of movement made him jerk back, gasping with terror. Then he let out a weak laugh as a barn owl landed on the rotting window casing, its eyes wide and staring.

The painful rumbling of Stefan's stomach reminded him that he'd eaten nothing all day except for a few scavenged wild berries he'd found in the woods. He couldn't stay here. Groping for his still damp pants, he reluctantly drew them on and reached for his shirt and sweater. He considered for a moment finding the nearest village and turning himself in to the militia. Only, he had no identity papers. Plus, going to the militia, now, would require him to admit his role in an activity that was not only illegal but could easily provoke an international incident. And what if the officials were corrupt? What if they were out there even now, helping the Major look for him?

Stefan turned toward the stairs, stumbling in his exhaustion and fear. No, he would avoid the militia, he decided; avoid the villages, avoid anyone who might betray him to the men who'd murdered Uncle Jasha and the others.

If he kept away from the main roads and villages, it ought to take him four, maybe five days to reach home. Until he'd started working with Uncle Jasha, Stefan had lived with his mother on the outskirts of a small hamlet near Yasnaya Polyana.

He'd grown up there, in a house much like this one, an old German farmhouse with a sweet-smelling hay barn and a pond and a flock of snowy white geese that honked imperiously for their dinner. At the thought, a wave of homesickness swept over him, so intense it brought tears to his eyes. He brushed them away, ashamed of himself.

At Yasnaya Polyana, he'd be safe. He told himself that once he reached home, everything would be all right.

At a small private airstrip near Primorsk, the man Stefan Baklanov knew only as the Major glanced at his watch. The Gulfstream was nearly loaded. In another moment the jet would be on its way and the most important segment of their assignment would be completed. All that remained, now, was to clean up a few loose ends.

Headlights stabbed the darkness and the Major turned. A black Durango braked at the edge of the field. A Chechen named Borz Zakaev climbed out of the car. He was a solidly built man of medium height with the red hair and scattering of freckles one sometimes saw in Chechnya. They were old comrades, Borz and the Major. Years before, they'd fought together in Afghanistan, when the Major had worn the *dish-dash* and long beard of a mujahideen.

"Did you find the boy's body?" asked the Major in his stilted Russian.

Borz blew out his breath in frustration and answered him in English. "No. We crisscrossed back and forth across the cove for hours. We searched the shoreline. We even searched the beaches to the west, in case the current carried him around the point. Nothing. The only thing I can figure is that the tide must have taken him out to sea."

"Or he made it to shore."

Borz shook his head. "That water can't be more than fifty degrees. He didn't make it to shore."

"Did you check the fishing village just up the road?"

Borz nodded. "Nobody's seen him. I tell you, he's dead."

"And if he's not? I'm not taking any chances." The Major reached into his pocket and drew out the identification papers he'd taken from the *Yalena*'s strongbox. "His name is Stefan Baklanov."

"Baklanov?"

"That's right. He's Captain Baklanov's nephew. According to the ship's records, his mother lives in the southeast, near Yasnaya Polyana." He flipped open the papers to the boy's picture. In the photograph, Stefan Baklanov was just a skinny kid with big eyes and a shock of dark hair. He didn't look hard to deal with. "Make copies of this. I want you and your men to cover every road out of the area. Offer a reward. Without his papers, he won't get far."

Borz glanced over at the Gulfstream, its cargo now safely stowed aboard. "Does the General know about the kid?"

"Yes."

Borz swore under his breath.

The Major slapped the side of the jet and stepped back, "I want this kid eliminated and I don't care what it takes. Either find him dead or make him dead. This operation goes down in a week. If you haven't found him in forty-eight hours, go to Yasnaya Polyana and take his mother hostage."

"Yasnaya Polyana? You think he'll go home?"

"If he's alive, he'll go home. Where else can he go?"

6

Tobie found the Colonel at his desk, his head bent over his key-board. "You wanted to see me, sir?"

He looked up, his eyes crinkling into a smile. A big man, still solid and upright despite his sixty-odd years, he'd spent most of his Army career as a psychologist working in intelligence. He was officially retired now, although he still saw a few VA patients on a volunteer basis, in addition to working with Tobie on the remote viewing project.

"Have a seat, Tobie. I just got clearance to tell you about the target for today's viewing."

She slipped into the straight-backed wooden chair on the far side of his desk. Feedback sessions were an important part of a remote viewer's training. Only, this hadn't been a training session; it had been a real tasking. She leaned forward, conscious of the same welling of dread she'd always experienced when a teacher started handing back tests. "And?"

"The target was an old World War II U-boat that sank off the coast of Denmark near the end of the war. U–114."

She drew a quick breath, then another, remembering the claustrophobic fear, the desiccated skulls of long dead men. "Oh, God," she whispered. "That explains it."

Then she frowned, recalling the images that followed, the endless stretches of deserted docks and empty warehouses, the barren, windswept trees. The first part of the viewing, obviously, had been right on target. After that, she must have veered seriously *off* target.

"I'm sorry, Colonel," she said, sinking back in her chair. "I don't know what went wrong after those first impressions."

"What? Oh." McClintock shook his head. "Nothing went wrong, Tobie. Someone salvaged the U-boat. From what you saw, we think it might have been taken to a shipyard in Russia."

She studied the Colonel's tanned, inscrutable face. "Why exactly is the U.S. Navy interested in an old German U-boat? Can you tell me that?"

He nodded. "It's part of why the base has been on high alert for the past forty-eight hours."

She listened, her heart racing, while McClintock gave her a quick briefing on the missing U-boat, the shipment of Nazi gold, and its connection to the NSA warnings of an impending terrorist attack on the United States. "I can't believe the CIA is really going to use what I saw," she said when he had finished.

He cleared his throat. "There's been some resistance, of course. But Vice President Beckham is backing us up. The DCI agreed to send one of his men to Kaliningrad."

She frowned. "Exactly who are they sending?"

"They didn't say."

Pushing up, she began to pace the room. "You know what'll happen, don't you? This CIA guy will take a quick look around, say it was all a waste of time, and go home."

"At this point, it's out of our hands, Tobie. We've done our part."

She swung to face him. "You know how you always had that theory, that one of the reasons remote viewers were never very successful at *finding* things as opposed to simply *describing* them is because in the past the viewers were never let out into the field?"

"Y-yes," he said slowly. "But I don't think I like where you're going with this, Tobie."

She flattened her palms on the surface of the desk and leaned into them. "Colonel, in the past, the military always kept their remote viewers at Fort Meade, and sent other people out into the field. The field guys had to try to interpret what the viewers had seen and it just didn't work. But what if—"

"No, Tobie."

She leaned forward. "Please, Colonel."

"Tobie, I'm not sending you undercover on a CIA mission to Russia."

"Colonel—"

"You have no experience with this kind of fieldwork."

"So? I won't be alone, right? I'll be working with this guy from the CIA."

The Colonel sat very still.

She said, "I even speak Russian. Fluently." It was one of the advantages of growing up with a father in the military and a stepfather in the oil industry—she'd lived everywhere from Dubai to Kuala Lumpur, and developed a knack for learning and remembering languages.

"I know," said McClintock. "But Tobie—"

"Please, Colonel. I know what I saw. But you and I are probably the only two people in the country who believe I actually saw it."

"You're forgetting Beckham," said McClintock quietly.

Tobie eyed him anxiously. "Will the Vice President support us on this?"

"I'm not sure *I'm* supporting you on this."

"Colonel—"

He held up one hand. "All right, all right. I'll see what I can do."

7

A powerful monument in marble and steel, the Walker Phar-maceuticals Tower thrust up directly from the shores of Miami Bay. More than just a corporate headquarters, the tower stood as a visible testimonial to the success of the man who had built it: James Nelson Walker III. Less than two decades had passed since Walker earned his Ph.D. in chemistry from MIT, but he'd long since taken the modest drug-manufacturing business he inherited from his grandfather and turned it into one of the most powerful pharmaceutical companies in America.

He stood now beside the softly tinted glass walls of his offices at the top of the tower, his gaze on the gleaming blue waters of the bay spread out below him. Small and wiry, he was in his forty-sixth year, his tightly curled, short dark hair little touched by gray, his body kept hard and lean by a vigorous regimen of diet and exercise. He wore a meticulously tailored navy suit and hand-sewn leather shoes, and he had just closed a new deal with the Chinese that would earn him a cool hundred million in the next twelve months.

"Miss Greenwald is still waiting to see you," said his secretary from the door.

"Tell her to come in."

"Yes, Mr. Walker."

"And Sherry?"

The secretary turned in silent inquiry. She was an attractive woman, intelligent and efficient and fiercely capable. As a wife or a lover, she'd make a man's life hell. But as an executive assistant, she was priceless.

He gave her a slow smile. "Go home, and enjoy what's left of the weekend."

Her face relaxed. "Thank you, Mr. Walker."

Walker stayed where he was, only shifting slightly as Judith Greenwald strode into the room. She was tall and unflatteringly slender, with straight brown hair and gaunt cheeks and an earnest expression that had etched frown lines in her high forehead. Years of exposure to the harsh sun and wind of Africa had fanned more lines into the delicate flesh beside her hazel eyes, making her look closer to forty-eight than to the thirty-eight he knew she was, for she'd been the college roommate of his ex-wife. Yet, for some reason Walker had never understood, she stubbornly refused to have any "work" done. She'd never even bothered to refashion the large beak of a nose she'd inherited—along with everything else—from her father, shipping magnate Max Greenwald. It wasn't as if she couldn't afford it. Her pink Chanel suit and strappy Jimmy Choo shoes cost enough to feed a good-sized village in Africa for a thousand years.

"Thank you for agreeing to see me on a Saturday like this," she said, shaking his hand.

"I had to come in anyway. Please. Sit down."

She settled onto one of the soft yellow leather sofas overlooking the bay and came straight to the point. "You've had a chance to look over our proposal?"

"Of course." In addition to the untold millions old man Greenwald had left his daughter, he'd also funneled another fifty million or so into a charitable trust that Judith now administered. Her *cause du jour* was AIDS in Africa, and she had come here, today, to see Walker because Walker Pharmaceuticals had recently released a new and highly promising AIDS treatment.

She gripped her Chanel purse in both hands. "And?"

"I'm afraid what you're asking is impossible."

"I don't see why. It's not as if we're asking Walker to *give* us the anti-viral drugs. Only to supply them to our operation at cost."

Walker let out a soft laugh. "What you're essentially asking for is a donation worth millions of dollars in lost profits."

"Profits you wouldn't have earned anyway."

Walker went to where an iced pitcher of acai and pomegranate juice stood on a tray with glasses. "Juice?" he asked.

"No, thank you."

He poured himself a glass. "It just so happens we do have a new product we're willing to supply to your organization at cost. It's showing promising results in the treatment of tuberculosis."

Tuberculosis was a growing problem amongst AIDS patients in Africa. She tilted her head, her eyebrows drawing together in a frown as she stared up at him. "I take it that when you say 'new,' what you really mean is, 'still under development'?"

"That's right."

"In other words, we pay you for the privilege of testing your drug for you. And if it turns out that it kills more people than it cures?"

"What difference would it make? They would have died anyway."

She pushed to her feet, two unattractive splotches of color riding high on her cheekbones. "I'll convey your generous offer to our board."

Walker raised his glass to his lips and took a sip. "You're sure you won't have some juice?"

"Thank you, but no. Good evening," she said, and swept from the room, leaving a cloying scent of *haute couture* and expensive French perfume and bleeding-heart-liberal hypocrisy.

Still sipping his juice, Walker went to stand again at the window, his gaze on the wind-ruffled expanse of blue water and the puffs of white clouds building on the horizon. If things went according to plan, Judith Greenwald and her kind would soon have far too many problems of their own to waste time worrying about AIDS and Africans.

The beep of his private line brought his head around. He reached for the phone. "Walker here."

The General's voice was abrupt, his usual Texas drawl clipped. "I'll be at your house by 2100 hours. There are things we need to discuss."

Walker drained his glass. "Good news, I hope."

"I think you'll be pleased."

8

Jax was at his desk skimming through an article on submarine salvage operations when Matt stuck his head around the edge of his cubicle.

"You're booked on the next flight to Berlin, with a connection tomorrow morning to Kaliningrad."

Jax looked up. "Please tell me this is a lead from one of our agents."

"Well . . ." Matt dropped a file folder on the desk in front of him. "I guess that depends on whether or not you consider Tobie one of our agents."

Jax sat very still. "Let me get this straight. We've got a terrorist attack about to go down in this country and the DCI is sending me all the way to Russia on the strength of some *remote viewing session*?"

Matt tapped one finger on the top of the folder. "Look at the report on her viewing. I think you'll find it impressive."

Jax didn't move.

Matt sighed and handed him another folder. "Then look at

this. After we got the Colonel's report, we checked with the National Reconnaissance Office. According to their latest satellite photos, there's something at an old shipyard near the Vistula Lagoon in Kaliningrad that wasn't there two days ago."

Jax flipped through the NRO report. "*Something*? What do you mean, 'something'?"

Matt scratched behind one ear. "Whatever it is, the Russians have set up camouflage nets over it. But it's about the right size and shape."

"'About?' Oh, that's encouraging."

"The Colonel's pretty sure about this, Jax."

When Jax still didn't say anything, Matt sighed again and handed him a bulky envelope. "Here's your legend."

Jax tipped the envelope to spill its contents across the surface of the desk: a well-used U.S. passport, credit cards and business cards, driver's license, and assorted pocket litter, all in the name of Jason Aldrich. "Aldrich? *Again*?"

"There wasn't a lot of time. Plus, it's a cover you're familiar with."

Jax gave a soft laugh. "Not only me. I suspect our friend Jason Aldrich has been blackballed by every car rental agency in the world with a computer system."

"If it makes you feel any better, I don't think car rental agencies in Kaliningrad have computers."

A tense silence fell. Matt shifted his weight and looked away again.

Jax watched him with a growing sense of unease. "Out with it, Matt; what else aren't you telling me?"

"Ensign Guinness has asked to be let out into the field on this one."

"They turned her down, right?"

"Not yet."

Jax shoved up from his chair so fast it went skittering across the floor. "Are they nuts? What the hell do they think she's going to do? Hold a séance on the beach or something?"

Matt snorted. "I think the idea is that she can help interpret what she saw in her viewing."

"Right. What's to interpret? I go there. I see there's no U-boat. I come home, and the taxpayers take another dredging picking up the bill for a wasted trip. End of story."

"And if U–114 is there?"

"Let's just say for the sake of argument that by some miracle the U-boat is there; what the hell would I need a *remote viewer* for?"

"It doesn't hurt to have a backup."

"A backup? *October Guinness*? You're kidding, right? She's not a field operative. She's a linguist . . . with a couple of screws loose."

"She's a Naval officer. *And* an Iraq War vet."

Jax gathered up his cover-story documents. "She went to Baghdad as an interpreter, Matt; not a SEAL. And she still managed to almost get herself killed—and earn a psycho discharge."

"She didn't deserve that and you know it."

"She can't shoot for shit—"

"True. But she does have a black belt in Tae Kwon Do—"

"And she can't run."

"She's got a bad knee!"

"My point exactly." Jax reached under his desk for the bag he kept packed and ready to go. "Tell her to forget it. I work alone."

"It isn't just Tobie pushing for this, Jax. The Vice President thinks it's a good idea, too."

"So?"

"So, you want me to tell the Vice President to forget it?"

"Yes."

Matt laughed and turned away. "You tell him. In the meantime, you'd better hurry. You've got a flight to catch."

9

Lieutenant General Gerald T. Boyd was the kind of general
American newscasters loved. Well-educated and articulate,
tall and broad-shouldered, he had the steely-eyed, hard-
jawed good looks of a born hero. Graduating first in his
class at West Point, he'd served his country with distinction
in theaters from Ethiopia to Iraq and half a dozen other
conflicts in between.

True, his frank, forthright speech could at times veer into
territory some considered racist, but in today's climate not
everyone considered that a liability. With his big, photogenic
family, his unabashedly devout Christian sentiments, and his
unstinting devotion to the men under his command, Gerry
Boyd could have had his party's nomination for president in
the upcoming election if he'd wanted it. He didn't.

Standing now on the stage of the freshly refurbished auditorium at MacDill Air Force Base, home of the Special Op-

erations Command, Boyd clasped his hands loosely behind his back and felt his heart swell with pride for the five brave young men who stood at attention beside him, their gazes fixed straight ahead as the Secretary of Defense pinned a bronze star to each man's chest.

This is what makes America great, thought Boyd as he stared out over the smiling, proud faces in the audience: parents, wives, children, sweethearts, all gathered to support the men being honored. *This, and the grace and favor of Our Lord Savior.*

Boyd himself had been just twenty-three years old when he earned his first bronze star. He'd been posted to Palawan province in the Philippines as an advisor when word came that a band of Communist guerrillas down in Basilan had kidnapped four American tourists from a resort on the coast.

Boyd was supposed to be in Palawan to train Philippine troops, not to lead them into action. In clear defiance of standing orders, he led his Philippine soldiers in a forced march through the jungles, tracked the guerrillas to their camp, and attacked at dawn. Not only were they successful in rescuing all four American hostages, they also killed every last one of those Commie sons of bitches. And then they cut off their private parts as a warning to all the other natives in the area: Don't fuck with the US of A.

His commanding officer, General Levenger, had wanted to court marshal Boyd for disregarding a direct order to stand down. But then the press got ahold of the story and started calling Boyd a hero, and the Defense Department was forced to backpedal. Rather than being cashiered, Boyd had earned a bronze star. He could still recall every detail of that award ceremony, how he'd been so flush with pride when the Secretary of the Army pinned the star on his chest that his ears stayed red for hours afterward.

That had been back in 1977, on the parade ground at Scofield Barracks in Hawaii. Not in a red-carpeted, oak-paneled auditorium like this one. In some ways, things were different today, Boyd thought as he studied the hard-chiseled faces of the five Navy SEALS standing at attention before him, heroes of the Global War on Terrorism. A different kind of ceremony, a different kind of war, but the enemy was still the same: a guy named Satan.

The fine young men being honored today were receiving their bronze stars from the Secretary of Defense. As Deputy Commander of SOCOM—the United States Special Operations Command—General Boyd could have awarded the medals himself. But the Secretary was in the area and only too happy to be of service. This kind of thing was good for the esprit de corps, and it was good for the politicians, too. The Secretary was getting great mileage out of it, meeting families and posing for lots of grip-and-grin shots, now that the ceremony was over.

"You've got a bunch of good people here, General," said the Secretary, clasping Boyd's hand. "Keep up the great work."

"Thank you, Mr. Secretary."

The Secretary's minder was already whispering in his ear, whisking him off toward Washington. Boyd worked his way down the line of proud young SEALS, shaking hands, pressing shoulders, saying, "We're proud of you. You did a great job." But all the while, his gaze was scanning the excited crowd for his own aide, Captain Syd Phillips. Boyd had a flight to Washington planned tonight himself, with a brief stop first in Miami.

For more than thirty years Gerald Boyd had played by the Government's rules. Time after time he'd had to watch while the girly men in Washington, D.C., let down the country and let down its troops because they didn't have the stomach to do what needed to be done to protect America. But Boyd was about to change all that. If he'd learned one thing from a lifetime of leading black operations, it was that a few dedicated men, working in the shadows, could literally alter the future of the world.

He was turning away from having his picture taken with the pretty, fair-haired wife of one of the SEALS when his aide, Captain Phillips, appeared and leaned in close to say, "Your plane is ready whenever you are, General."

"Good. I think at this point we can safely leave things to the unit commander."

"Yes, sir." Captain Phillips gave a quick glance around and cleared his throat. "Our friend at Langley just called."

"And?"

"Your activity in the Baltic has attracted attention. They're sending a man to Kaliningrad. He leaves tonight, traveling through Berlin."

Boyd pressed his lips into a thin, flat line. "Get the details to Rodriguez. I want someone in Berlin to stop this individual. And tell Rodriguez to have someone at the airport in Kaliningrad, too, just in case."

"Both?"

Boyd kept his voice low. "This thing is too close to going down. We can't afford any more mistakes. If we miss this guy in Germany, we nail him in Russia. Got it?"

"Yes, sir."

10

Tobie was at home, curled up on the sofa with her laptop and an orange alley cat named Beauregard when the call came through from McClintock.

"It's a go, Tobie. The DCI was dead set against it, but you've got Beckham solidly behind you."

"Yes!" She leaped up, unsettling the disgruntled cat and nearly sending her Apple flying.

At the other end of the line, the Colonel sighed. "I just hope I'm not making a mistake on this."

She sank back down on the sofa, her hand tightening around the phone. "I won't let you down, sir."

"That's not what I'm worried about, Tobie. How much do you know about Kaliningrad?"

"Not much. I was just Googling it."

McClintock huffed a soft laugh. "The province—Kaliningrad Oblast—used to be part of Germany. East Prussia. The Russians took it over at the end of World War II and split it with Poland. Just to confuse things, they renamed the main city Kaliningrad, too."

"What did it used to be called?"

"Königsberg."

"Königsberg? As in, Immanuel Kant?"

"That's right. Although there's not much of the old German city left anymore. Back in the days of the Cold War, the province was considered very important, militarily. But it's been hit pretty hard by the breakup of the Soviet Union."

"Why's that?"

"Because now that Estonia, Latvia, and Lithuania are independent, Kaliningrad is an exclave, cut off from the rest of Russia. The economy is worse than dead. This place doesn't have much in common with the rest of the New Russia. Life there basically hasn't changed in the last fifty years."

It was a description that fit in well with what she'd seen in her viewing. She said, "When do I leave, sir?"

"First thing in the morning, flying through Copenhagen. We'd like to have gotten you out of here tonight, but you know what connections are like out of New Orleans since Katrina. You won't actually be landing in Russia until Monday morning."

"When's the CIA guy getting there?"

"Tomorrow afternoon."

"That's not good. Any idea yet who they're sending?"

"Yeah. Jax Alexander."

"Jax? But . . . Jax doesn't believe in remote viewing."

"He saw it work last summer, right here in New Orleans."

"And he still thinks it's a bunch of New Age nonsense."

"Everyone at the CIA thinks it's a bunch of New Age nonsense. You knew when you asked for this that it wasn't going to be easy."

"You won't be sorry, Colonel."

McClintock made an incoherent noise. "Just . . . be careful, Tobie."

Later that evening, after she'd packed a bag and talked

to Ambrose next door about taking care of Beauregard, she stood in her darkened living room and gazed out at the ancient live oaks casting their gnarled shadows across the narrow moonlit street.

She could feel the tendrils of anxiety coiling tightly within her. She believed in remote viewing, and she knew what she'd seen. But she also knew that her viewings weren't always accurate. What if this was one of those misses? Or what if the viewing was accurate, but they'd misinterpreted what she'd seen? Looking at the full moon riding above the branches of the old oaks, she imagined she could already hear the clock ticking toward Halloween.

She felt Beauregard rub against her leg. Reaching down, she scooped the cat up into her arms. "Wish me luck, Beau," she whispered, and held him close.

11

The Major pulled into the darkened driveway in the leafy suburb of Mendeleevo and cut the engine. Once, this large stuccoed house with its expansive lawn and carefully tended garden had been the home of a German banker, or maybe an industrialist. Now it belonged to some Russian mafioso who rented it to those seeking a quiet, out-of-the-way property in a district where neighbors were hidden behind high walls and no one asked any questions.

A dog barked somewhere in the distance and was quickly hushed. The Major let his gaze rove over the building and its perimeter. Satisfied, he opened the door and stepped out into the chill of the Baltic night.

His name was Carlos Rodriguez. At forty-two, he was a leanly muscled professional soldier with olive skin and short-cropped dark hair. He wore the simple cotton trousers and closely knit sweater of a local, but he was not a local. The house served as headquarters for the team he'd assembled: two Americans, a Brit, four Russians, and the Chechen, Borz Zakaev. He needed the locals because they knew the geography and the people. But Rodriguez didn't like Russians, and he didn't trust them. He was glad to have Borz and the Americans there to watch his back.

It was the damned Russians who'd assured him the salvage ship captain, Baklanov, was reliable. Not honest—no honest man would have done business with them. But reliable. Instead, the man turned out to be an idiot. Only an idiot would try to cheat Carlos Rodriguez.

"What's the status on the U-boat?" he asked, letting himself in the house's side door.

The door opened into an enormous kitchen recently renovated with rich cherry cabinets and marble countertops and stainless steel industrial appliances. They'd set up their communications equipment in what was meant to be a nearby maid's room, a simple chamber with a single bed, a chair, and a low dresser.

The house was quiet, the rest of the men asleep. But Ben Salinger, the towheaded kid from Nebraska who served as Rodriguez's communications expert, looked up from his laptop, his eyes glazed with amphetamine-revved exhaustion. "We just got a report from Kirkpatrick. The sub still hasn't blown."

Rodriguez pulled the sweater off over his head and threw it on the maid's bed. "What the fuck?" After taking care of the *Yalena*'s crew, they'd rigged the U-boat's torpedo room with explosives. The first half-drunken Russian shipyard worker scrounging around for something to steal should have blown himself—and the sub—to perdition hours ago.

"The shipyard owner sealed off the U-boat and called the militia right away. They're keeping everyone out of it." Salinger stood up and stretched, his shirt hiking up to show the Special Forces tattoo on his side. In his late twenties, he'd done two tours in Iraq and one in Afghanistan before leaving the Army for a higher-paying job in the private sector.

Rodriguez had modeled his operation on a scaled-down Special Forces team, just the way he'd been taught. Salinger was their communications expert; Ian Kirkpatrick, a former SAS man from Liverpool, was their demolition specialist; an ex-SEAL from Arkansas named Clay Dixon was their weapons specialist. Borz was their linguist. Rodriguez had been doing this sort of thing for more than half his life, and he was very good at it.

He'd grown up in the nurturing warmth of a big, loving family of Cuban exiles. Back in the days before the revolution, his grandfather had been one of Baptiste's *jefes*. Rodriguez had seen pictures of the family's house overlooking the Plaza Vieja, the graceful arched windows shaded by louvered shutters, the cavernous high-ceilinged rooms filled with tables graced with crystal and silver, all kept gleaming by a legion of soft-footed, respectful servants.

All that had ended with Castro and his band of hooligans, with their big talk of providing free medical care for all, of getting rid of the Mob and the giant American companies they claimed oppressed the people. Because of Castro, Carlos was born in the charity ward of a Miami hospital, and his grandfather died in the surf at the Bay of Pigs.

Carlos had grown up on the streets of Little Havana, watching his dad and his friends train with the CIA. His dad had run scores of attacks against Cuba from their Florida bases, blowing up oil installations and movie theaters, shopping malls and tourist hotels. Carlos had even gone with them one glorious night, when they'd roared in close to shore on a motorboat and sprayed the crowds on the beach with machine-gun fire. He'd been just sixteen at the time. A year later, at the age of seventeen, Carlos joined the U.S. Army.

He'd breezed through Airborne, then moved into the

Rangers. It was his ambition to become the biggest badass in the Army. But in the Rangers, Rodriguez discovered it wasn't enough to be tough; it was also important to be smart. And Rodriguez was smart. Smart and ruthless. By the time he put in his twenty years and took to selling his skills on the private market, he'd managed to acquire a college degree and become an officer.

He watched Salinger twist the top off a bottle of water and drain it in one long pull. "We shoulda just blown the damn thing when we had the chance," said Salinger, wiping the back of one hand across his mouth.

Rodriguez shook his head. "No. We've already attracted enough attention with the hit on the *Yalena*. When that submarine blows, it needs to look like some idiot accidentally triggered one of the old torpedoes." He shoved a stick of gum in his mouth and went to stand at the rear window overlooking the darkened gardens below. "The militia are some of the worst thieves in the country. Eventually someone's going to go poking around in there. We just need to be patient. Why don't you get some sleep?"

The sharp ring of the satellite phone brought his head around.

"It's Phillips," said Salinger, holding out the phone.

Rodriguez frowned and took the receiver. Captain Syd Phillips was the General's aide de camp. "Rodriguez here."

Phillips came straight to the point. "I assume you have someone you trust in Berlin?"

"Yes. Why?"

"The General has another assignment for you."

12

The night was hot, the air thick with the scent of salt and the sea and a peculiar, pungent odor like old brass. Hurricane weather, the old-timers back home in Texas used to call it. General Gerald T. Boyd gazed at the twinkling lights of Miami spread out around the dark waters of the bay before them, and found himself wondering what would happen to this city of pastel-colored Italianate villas and glass-walled high-rises and extravagantly flaunted wealth the day a Cat Five plowed into it.

"Smells like a storm," he said, leaning his outstretched arms against the ornate stone balustrade that separated the flagged terrace from the sweeping floodlit lawns, the Olympic-sized pool, the private dock of James Nelson Walker's waterfront South Beach estate.

Walker shrugged. "I hear there's something out in the Atlantic. But it's too late in the year to worry about."

Boyd gave a sharp laugh. "Too close to Halloween."

Walker didn't crack a smile. He was a serious son of a bitch, all New England prep-school starch and boardroom business. While Boyd filled his leisure hours with fishing and hunting and all the rough-and-tumble of a boisterous family of six ranging in age from a twelve-year-old Little League dynamo to a daughter in her second year at Harvard Law School, Walker had only one daughter, whom he seldom saw and, apparently, never missed. As far as Boyd could tell, the man spent his days playing racquetball, running, and making money.

The two had met the previous winter, when Boyd presented the keynote speech at a CPAC conference here in Miami. Walker had listened to Boyd's thunderous address on the need to solve the never-ending economic and military bleed in the Middle East once and for all. A few days later, the business tycoon had approached Boyd with a very interesting proposal.

Theirs was a partnership of military and technical expertise joined with lots of good hard cash. The two men had little in common besides a profound hatred of Jews and Arabs, and a willingness to do whatever was necessary to make the world a safer and better place for Americans. That was enough.

Walker said, "I hope you're here to tell me everything is back on track."

"The shipment left Russian airspace an hour ago. It should arrive at your facility in St. Martin by nine o'clock."

"This is good news. I'll fly down to the island myself first thing in the morning." The sound of footsteps brought the man's head around. He waited while a slim, dark-skinned, dark-haired maid set a tray with glasses and a glistening pitcher of what looked like carrot juice on the heavy limestone top of a nearby table, then withdrew. "No more complications?" he said, going to splash juice into two glasses.

"Nothing to worry about."

"Oh?" Walker looked up, an eyebrow quirked in question.

"The CIA is sending one of their men to Kaliningrad."

Walker set down the pitcher hard enough to rattle the ice. "*Christ*. They know?"

"They don't know jack shit."

"They obviously know something."

Boyd felt a muscle jump along his tightened jaw. One of his boys had gotten sloppy a couple of days ago, blabbing on an unsecured line about the U-boat and dropping tantalizing hints about what they had planned. Boyd had taken care of the guy, but the NSA intercept had stirred up a hornets' nest at the FBI and with Homeland Security.

"They know someone salvaged the U-boat," he said. "But they're still convinced they're dealing with a bunch of ragheads. They're too busy raiding mosques from here to Timbuktu to cause us any trouble."

"Then why are they sending this guy to Kaliningrad?"

Boyd took the glass Walker held out, but made no move to taste it. Walker was always drinking this shit. When Boyd drank, it was either good Tennessee bourbon, or French cognac. "It doesn't matter. There's nothing there for him to find. It's all been cleaned up."

"You're sure?"

Boyd tamped down a spurt of annoyance. In the last thirty years, he'd faced down everything from rabid Sudanese tribesmen to hostile Congressional hearings and interfering presidents; he wasn't going to lose sleep over one lousy CIA agent. "Don't worry. It's under control."

The warm breeze gusted up, bringing them a faint burst of laughter from somewhere out on the water. Walker took a sip of his juice. "You keep saying that. What if he does find something?"

"He won't. He's being taken care of."

"Taken care of?"

"You have to expect casualties in any operation. The CIA is about to suffer one." Boyd glanced at his watch. "I've got a plane waiting to take me to Washington. Let me know when your people have had a chance to assess the shipment."

Walker frowned. "You've been called to Washington?"

"Not over this shit." Boyd realized he was still holding the glass of juice in his hand and set it aside. "I've been asked to testify before some Congressional hearings next week, and I'm flying up early for this reception the White House is giving tomorrow."

"You mean the one President Randolph is hoping will kick-start a new Middle East peace process?"

"Yeah. That one."

Walker drained his own glass and set it aside with a rare suggestion of a smile: "If they only knew. We're about to present them with the solution to that whole expensive can of worms, free of charge."

13

"I'm sorry, Mr. Aldrich," said the unsmiling young woman behind the check-in desk at the Berlin Royal Hotel. "We have no record of your reservation."

Jax slid the reservation number across the desk. "Yes, you do." He'd called Langley from the airport and had them book the room as soon as he heard Aeroflot was canceling their only flight of the day to Kaliningrad. It was standard procedure, but Jax should have known better than to follow it. Langley was always screwing up this kind of thing.

The hotel clerk pecked at her computer terminal with Teutonic efficiency and frowned. "The name on this reservation is James Aiden Xavier Alexander."

"That's it," said Jax. "The Company is always making that mistake."

"I'm sorry, sir, but I can't—"

He kept his smile in place. "Yes, you can. Call the number that made the reservation."

"But—"

"Just call it."

Ten minutes later, room key in hand, Jax crossed the lobby's polished marble floor toward the elevators. Out of habit, he was aware of the people around him without in any way appearing to be watchful. Two teenaged American girls in low-slung jeans walked toward him, their heads together, laughing. A svelte blonde with pouty lips hung on the arm of an aging Greek with a tanned, lined face who was waiting for his car to be brought around. A bony man in a tweed jacket read a newspaper in one of the upholstered chairs near the bar. When Jax passed, the guy in the tweed jacket folded his newspaper and stood.

As Jax waited for the elevator, the man in the tweed jacket came to stand beside him. Jax studied the guy's reflection in the elevator's shiny doors. He appeared to be in his early thirties, with dark hair, a prominent nose, and sharp features that might have been Slavic. He carried his newspaper tucked under his left arm and he wasn't looking at Jax.

The two teenaged girls, still giggling, pushed past Jax as soon as the elevator doors opened. Jax and the man in the tweed coat entered behind them. Jax pressed 6. The girls hit 10. The man in the tweed jacket maneuvered so that he was behind Jax and stood with his gaze fixed on the doors as they snapped shut.

It was one of the dictates they taught you in spy school: *always stay behind the man you're tailing.* Simple, useful information.

With a polite *ding*, the elevator whirled up to the sixth floor. Jax stepped out. The bony man in the tweed coat followed.

Jax felt his pulse beating in his neck.

The man followed Jax down the hall, dropping back slightly.

Setting down his carryon bag outside room 615, Jax inserted his key card in the lock and heard it buzz open. Pushing down the handle with one hand, he was reaching for his bag when the man in the tweed coat closed on him, a suppressed Walther in his hand.

Jax felt the man's left hand in the small of his back and understood how the next few seconds were meant to play out: the assassin would shove Jax into his room and then shoot him in the back.

But Jax was already bending for his carry-on bag. He closed his left hand around the handles of the bag and just kept bending, reaching between his ankles with his other hand to grab a fistful of the guy's pant leg and jerk it up. The assassin had two choices: he could either let Jax dislocate his knee, or go down.

He went down. Jax heard the man's breath leave his chest in a little huff as his back slammed into the carpet. Jax spun around, the guy's ankle clamped between his two legs. The gunman swore, his body rolling involuntarily to one side, gun hand down.

He squeezed off two suppressed shots. The first went wild, shattering an overhead light and raining down broken glass. The second round thudded into the wall beside them.

"You sonofabitch," swore Jax, slamming his carry-on bag into the guy's right hand. The gun clattered away, spinning some two or three feet.

The killer rolled onto his stomach, scrambling after the gun. Jax dropped with a knee in the guy's back and grabbed a fistful of dark hair. Yanking the guy's head up with one hand, he closed his left hand on the guy's chin, jerked his head back—

And heard his neck snap.

"Shit," whispered Jax.

For a moment he stilled, his knee in the guy's back, his breath coming in quick pants. If he'd kept the guy alive, he could have asked him some very important questions. Like,

Who sent you? And, *How did you know I was here?* Instead, he had no answers to his questions and a dead body to deal with.

Looking up, he stared at the security camera at the far end of the hall and said, "Shit," again.

Pushing to his feet, Jax opened the door to room 615. Propping open the door with his bag, he grabbed the body by the feet and dragged it into the room. He ducked back out into the hall for the Walther and the guy's newspaper, then quickly shut the door.

Jerking out his phone, he went to sit on the edge of the bed and punched in the number for the American embassy.

"I'd like to speak to Peter Davidson, please," he said. "Peter Davidson" was the code name for the CIA Operations Officer on duty at the embassy. The CIA loved to play these little cloak-and-dagger games.

There was a pause as the person at the other end of the phone drew in a quick breath. "Did you say, 'Peter Davidson'?"

"Why? Did they change the code?"

There was a clucking noise. The voice said, "Just a moment, please."

A minute ticked past. Two. A woman came on the line. "This is Petra Davidson. May I help you?"

Jax squeezed his eyes shut. "Jason Aldrich here. I've just flown in from Washington and I need a list of agricultural contacts in Bavaria." You had to wonder who came up with this stuff. "I need a list of agricultural contacts in Bavaria" was code for *There's a dead body I need you to make go away.*

The other end of the phone went silent.

"Hello? Miss Davidson?"

"I'm here," she said in a heavy Bronx twang. "I think I can come up with that. Where would you like it delivered?"

"The Royal Berlin. Room 615."

"You should have it in a few hours."

"*Hours?* How many hours are we talking about here?"

"What you're asking for is complicated," she snapped.

"Complicated, but urgent," he said patiently. "There's a security camera that needs to be taken care of."

"Where?"

"In the corridor."

"At the Royal? Those suckers haven't worked for months."

"You're sure?"

"It's my job."

"But complicated."

There was a long pause. She said, "You want the list of agricultural contacts in Bavaria, or not?"

Jax looked at the guy in the tweed coat sprawled in an ungainly heap across the hotel-room floor. "Yes, please."

"Then I'll see you in a few hours," she said and hung up.

"Great," said Jax, his gaze still on the silent corpse. "Looks like you and I are going to be keeping company for a while." He reached for the folded newspaper, curious to see which edition Tweed Coat had been reading. As he picked it up, a printout of a photograph of Jax fluttered to his feet.

Jax froze. This was no anonymous snapshot captured with a telephoto lens. This was an official photograph taken shortly after Jax's incident in Colombia for inclusion in his file at Langley.

Jax's gaze traveled from the photograph to the dead assassin's impassive face. The implications were beyond ominous.

"How the *hell* did you get that?"

14

The massive doors of the airplane hangar rolled open, filling the cavernous space with a suffocating blast of tropical heat and the deafening roar of the approaching jet.

From the air-conditioned comfort of his limousine, James Nelson Walker watched the Gulfstream roll inside. Ten months of careful research and planning—not to mention a substantial investment of funds—had brought him to this moment.

Up until now, Walker's role had been largely financial, with Boyd drawing on his years of special operations, and his many contacts, to provide them with the paramilitary expertise they needed. But the next segment of the operation would be under Walker's control.

The jet pivoted smartly, and a blessed silence fell over the hangar as the engines shut down. Absently kneading his lower lip with one thumb and forefinger, Walker waited while the pilot and copilot removed their headphones. They had no knowledge of their cargo, or the use to which it would be put.

He waited while the two men casually joked with each other, then left the hangar without a backward glance at either the limousine or the white van that waited at the other end of the hangar.

At a nod from Walker, his driver pressed the remote control, closing the big hangar doors and shutting out the bright tropical sunlight with an echoing bang.

"Now," said Walker to the small, olive-skinned man with a hawklike nose and acne-pitted face who sat beside him.

Dr. Juan Garcia nodded. At his signal, the back doors of the waiting van opened. Two technicians in hazmat suits leaped out.

"How long will it take before we know if the shipment is still viable?" Walker asked while the two technicians opened the jet's cargo hold.

Garcia shrugged. "We should have a preliminary report within twenty-four hours."

Walker's eyes narrowed as he watched the guys in hazmat gear carefully lift the first of the decades-old canisters between them. "We have three days to get this ready to go."

"If it's still viable, that won't be a problem," said Garcia, turning toward the van. "We'll be ready."

Washington, D.C.

Sunday morning dawned clear and sunny and wickedly cold, with a blustering wind that scuttled the small puffy white clouds across the deep blue sky over the nation's capitol. General Gerald T. Boyd went for a three-mile run along the Potomac, then showered and changed into his dress blues in preparation for the reception being held that morning at the White House.

"Any word on the shipment yet?" he asked his aide, Phillips.

"Not yet, sir."

Boyd reached for his hat and slipped it on. "The instant something comes through, I want to know about it."

"Yes, sir."

Half an hour later, the General was standing beneath the portico overlooking the White House Rose Garden watching the President of the United States try to coax a scowling New York senator in a skullcap into conversation with the Palestinian Archbishop of Jerusalem when the DCI, Gordon Chandler, walked up to him.

"Our commander in chief doesn't appear to be having much success there," said Chandler, dropping his voice so that only Boyd would hear.

"I don't know about that. At least they're not killing each other."

"Not yet. Although rumor has it the reason we're freezing our collective nuts off out here in the Rose Garden is because half of today's honored guests have sworn never to be in the same room with each other."

Boyd kept his gaze on the two men beside the President, and smiled. *One more week, you bastards*, he thought. Some men hated Jews; others hated the Arabs. Boyd had no use for either side. In the last fifty years, the sons of bitches had collectively cost the United States trillions of dollars and thousands of lives. Thanks to Boyd, all that was about to end.

But all he said was, "I don't care if they can't stand to be in the same room together. I just wish they'd learn to be in the same country together." He let his gaze drift over the dozens of extra Secret Service personnel. "I don't think I've ever seen security at the White House this tight."

"You haven't. And the closer we get to Halloween, the tighter it's going to be." Chandler cleared his throat. "I hear you advised the President against canceling either today's reception, or the Children of the Book Conference in Miami next weekend."

"That's right."

"Was that wise?"

Boyd huffed a rough laugh. "You know as well as I do how many terrorist threats we get every day. They're always bullshit. The President leaks a few choice ones to the press, the people get nice and scared, and no one complains the next time Randolph wants to ram a special defense-spending bill through Congress. It's a win-win situation all around."

"I have a nasty feeling this one's different."

Boyd studied the long New England face of the man beside him. Gordon Chandler might be a ruthless son of a bitch, but like so many of the idiots down at Langley, he was still an effete Ivy League blueblood. "You got any new intelligence to back that up?"

Chandler dropped his voice again. "You've heard about U–114?"

Boyd shrugged. "Nazi subs are valuable commodities these days. I'll be surprised if there are any left in shallow waters by the end of the decade."

"I hope to God that's all there is to it."

Boyd was aware of his aide, Phillips, hovering a few feet away. Boyd gave the DCI a hearty clap on the shoulder. "I'll tell you what, Chandler. Come next Sunday, if no crazy A-rabs have treated us to some nasty Halloween surprise, I'll suspend my lifelong prohibition against imbibing on the Lord's day, just so you can have the privilege of buying me a drink."

"And if you're wrong?"

"Then you can send a case of Jack Daniel's to my funeral."

Captain Phillips waited until the DCI had laughed and moved off. Then he took a step forward and said, "There've been some developments."

Boyd drained his glass and set it aside. "It's about time. Let's go."

15

The newspaper was the latest edition of the *International Herald Tribune*, which told Jax nothing.

Tossing it aside, he searched Tweed Coat's pockets, the lining of his jacket, the soles of his shoes. But the assassin was obviously a professional. Jax found a handful of euros and rubles, but no ID.

He started checking clothing labels. The guy's jacket had come from London. His shirt was French. His shoes, Italian. A European, perhaps. Judging from the rubles, possibly a Russian. But not necessarily.

Jax sat back on his heels, his gaze going to the dead man's gun. A Walther P99. The Russian mafia liked Walthers. But so did a lot of other people. Jax knew guys in the Company who liked to carry Walthers.

He pushed to his feet. He was getting hungry. Unwilling to take the chance of having Tweed Coat accidentally discovered by some room-service personnel, he rummaged around until he found a spare blanket on a shelf in the closet.

Rolling the dead body up in blue polyester, he dragged the corpse into the closet and shut the door before dialing room service. Then he put in a call to Matt.

Matt's voice was gravelly with concern. "I heard your flight had been canceled," he said. "This isn't good, Jax. It means you won't be in Kaliningrad to meet October when she lands."

"At the moment, babysitting Beckham's remote viewer is the least of my problems." The phone was encrypted, but Jax still chose his words carefully. "I had an unexpected visitor."

There was a moment's pause. Matt said, "Was this someone we know?"

"One of our competitors' representatives. Fortunately I managed to convince him we had this market all sewn up, so he's moved on to greener pastures."

Matt groaned. "Oh, jeez; not again. Did you call Peter Davidson?"

"Petra. Petra Davidson." Jax glanced at the closed closet doors. "My concern is, there are indications the competition found out that I was going to be working this market from our own home office. You might want to check and see if there's been any interest in my being assigned to this area."

"Shit. I'll look into it." Matt drew a deep breath. "In the meantime, be careful, okay?"

"I'm always careful."

Matt laughed and hung up.

Jax sat for a time staring unseeingly at the phone in his hand. Then he went to pull the folder with October Guinness's remote viewing session out of his bag. He'd been so convinced it was all a bunch of woo-woo bullshit that he hadn't even bothered to look at the report. The arrival of Tweed Coat changed things.

He thumbed quickly through the Colonel's report, then

read the transcript of the viewing itself. Jax had witnessed one of October's viewings last summer, and he'd done enough research on the subject to understand how RV worked . . . just not enough to believe in it.

He flipped to the drawings at the back of the report and felt a faint chill run up his spine. October's sketches were rudimentary but detailed enough that Jax had no doubt he was staring at a picture of a World War II-era U-boat resting on a long, flat barge. The barge was tied up at a wharf beside a line of what looked like warehouses. To the right she had drawn a smaller corrugated metal building located about halfway up a hill; an office, perhaps. Beyond that he could see a rocky point covered with wind-stunted pines.

Jax thumbed back through the report. He wanted to think the Colonel must have given her some indication of the target, but Jax knew McClintock was too careful, too professional, to have frontloaded the viewing that way. There was little doubt that October had "seen" a U-boat. The only question was, how accurate was their interpretation that the target location was Kaliningrad? The arrival of Tweed Coat seemed to suggest that it was pretty damned accurate.

It was nearly ten o'clock, long after Jax had finished his trout amandine and put the tray outside the door, when he heard a desultory *squeak, squeak* coming down the hall toward his room. He'd been reading Herbert Werner's *Iron Coffins*. Now he lifted his head and listened.

The squeaking stopped outside his door. He heard a murmur, followed by a knock. A female voice with the unmistakable intonations of the Bronx said, "This is Petra Davidson. I've got your agricultural reports."

Setting aside his book, Jax went to open the door.

The woman standing in the corridor was short, probably no more than five foot two. She had thick dark hair she wore cropped boylike in a style that might have given her a gamin

look when she was in her twenties. Now that she was in her
mid-thirties, the effect was somewhat different. Her body had
begun to thicken with the approach of middle age, although
she still looked solid. Jax had no doubt she ran her three to
five miles every morning with the same determination as she
practiced regularly at the shooting range. Her dark synthetic
pantsuit was eminently practical, her low-heeled pumps sensible. She was a short woman in a man's world, which meant
she had to try twice as hard and be twice as tough.

She snapped, "Jason Aldrich?"

"That's right." He looked beyond her, to the two burly
guys in buzz haircuts pushing a big maid's cart covered in
canvas. "And these, I take it, are the Marines?"

The Marines were obviously anxious to get out of the
hall. They shoved past Jax and into the room, the wheels on
their maid's cart shrieking with each revolution. Jax glanced
down at the large briefcase Petra carried. Since she hadn't
known if she was being called to the scene of a shooting or
a knifing or something worse, procedure called for her to
bring along first-aid equipment, luminol, and a black light.
If necessary, the luminol and black light would be used to
find blood traces she'd then corrupt to prevent DNA analysis, while the first-aid kit was to patch up Jax.

"You won't need the kit," he said, shutting the door behind
her. "There's no blood. I broke the guy's neck. This is going
to be simple."

She whirled to face him, her face tight. "Simple? You
think this is simple? I've got a body to dispose of. That's
never simple, especially these days. This isn't the Cold War
anymore, you know. The Germans aren't as understanding
about these things as they used to be."

Jax held up his hands, palms outward. "I only meant you
won't need to worry about trace evidence. He didn't even
leave prints in here."

Her frown deepening, she glanced around the room. "Where is he?"

"In the closet."

At her nod, the two Marines opened the closet doors. Blue polyester cocoon unfurling, Tweed Coat flopped out. "Who is he?" she asked as the Marines moved to lift the body between them, one at the head, the other at the feet.

"I don't know."

She brought her gaze back to Jax's face, her eyes narrowing. Her name wasn't Petra, of course. Probably something like Gina Guiliani or Maria Centrello. She had that Sicilian look about her. She said, "I called Langley. They told me you're just passing through here. So you—what? Had some time on your hands and just decided to kill someone?"

Jax tried to clamp a lid on his temper. "I take it you'd have preferred I let the guy shoot me? You'd still have had a body to deal with, you know—only it would have been mine."

She shrugged. "We'd have just passed you off as some stupid dead tourist. We deal with dead tourists all the time. This—" She pointed to Tweed Coat, now being stuffed into the maid cart. "This is a political disaster waiting to happen. What do you think the Germans are going to do if we get caught with this dude? The boys here in Berlin don't like it when we treat the place like it's an American colony. It'd be different if we were in Cairo or Seoul or someplace like that."

He gave her what was supposed to be a disarming smile. "I have confidence in you, Petra."

It was a lie, of course. Until he found out how Tweed Coat came by that official photo, Jax wasn't trusting anyone associated with the Company except Matt.

She was neither disarmed nor charmed by Jax's smile. She walked right up to him with a bandy rooster kind of strut, her hands on her hips as she leaned forward, head tilting back. "I've heard about you, Mr. Jax Alexander." She said his name slowly, just in case he missed the fact she wasn't using his alias anymore. "You've caused trouble every place from Guatemala to Indonesia and back. You don't play by the rules. You're a loose cannon. I don't understand why you're even still with the Company."

Jax picked up Tweed Coat's gun and handed it to her. "Here. You might as well get rid of this while you're at it."

He watched a dark tide of anger sweep up her face. "When do you leave?" she asked.

"Tomorrow morning."

"Good." She shoved the Walther in her bag and turned toward the door. "See if you can get out of here without killing anyone else, will you?"

"I'll try."

She waited for the Marines to open the door, their cart going *squeak, squeak* as they pushed it out into the hall. She followed them, only looking over her shoulder long enough to say, "And don't come back."

16

Stefan forced himself to concentrate on putting one foot in front of the other. Each step had become an act of will, every mile a penance of pain. At first the salt-stiffened trousers chafing his inner thighs had been an inconvenience. Then soreness turned to raw agony. By now, he was forced to admit that if he didn't find clean clothes somewhere, he was never going to make it back to Yasnaya Polyana.

He drew up at the top of a small rise, his breath ragged with pain. There was a cold wind blowing from the north, and he shifted into the shelter of a sturdy pine, his eyes narrowing as he studied the hamlet that straddled a stream at the edge of the wood below.

He could see a string of dilapidated cottages with a few shops, a power line, and a half-renovated church. A horse pulled a cart loaded with apples and driven by an old woman in a shawl.

The banging of a door drew his attention to the back porch

of a frame cottage on the outskirts of the village. A woman wearing a thick gray sweater and a nondescript skirt, a basket balanced on one hip, strode across the hard-packed yard to where clothes hung up to dry flapped in the frigid air. As Stefan watched, she started to unpin a dress, then paused to run her hand down the cloth to the waistband. Frowning, she reached out to feel the cuffs of a nearby shirt. With a shake of her head, she stomped back toward the house. Stefan, watching her, let out his breath in a small sigh.

If he could, he would gladly pay the woman for the blue work shirt and trousers he could see hanging at the end of the line, near a weathered old shed. But he only had ten rubles in his pocket. If he wanted a change of clothes, he was going to need to steal them.

He felt his stomach roil with shame and despair at the thought. Five years ago, Stefan's father had been faced with a choice: cooperate with a corrupt scheme to skim electrical components from the shipments his small trucking company ferried to the port, or die. Uncle Jasha always called his brother a fool, a martyr to an outmoded system of honor. But Stefan had been proud of his father, proud of his choice. Now, Stefan realized he had more in common with his uncle than he'd ever wanted to admit.

He crept painfully down the hill, his gaze on the cottage's back door. His breath bunching up in his throat, he darted across the muddy road. Ducking behind the shed, he stood for a moment, hands splayed against the rough boards of the outbuilding, heart pounding. Swallowing hard, he threw one last, quick glance at the light that now flickered in the cottage window, and sprinted toward the clothesline.

He snatched the trousers and a clean shirt on the fly. With every step, he kept expecting to hear a shout, a cry of *Stop! Thief!* Trousers and shirt clutched to his chest, he ducked back behind the shed. He waited, trembling and listening.

But all he could hear was the breeze rustling the autumn-shriveled leaves of a nearby birch and the lowing of a cow somewhere in the distance.

Hunkering down, he shucked off his sweater, stiff trousers, and shirt. The cold air bit his bare skin. He shivered and quickly scrambled into the purloined clothes. The trousers were a little damp around the cuffs, but blessedly soft. He pulled his own sweater back over his head, turned up the too-long trouser legs, and carefully transferred the contents of his pockets to his new clothes. He didn't have much—the ten rubles, a piece of amber shaped like a horse's head he'd picked up on the beach and kept for good luck, and the penknife his father had given him for his tenth birthday.

His heart was still hammering so hard his chest hurt, but he forced himself to roll up his own clothes and dash back into the farmyard to leave them as a kind of trade on the back stoop. He was just tucking the clothes roll under the step's unpainted railing when the door jerked open and the woman in the gray sweater took a step out onto the porch.

She drew up abruptly, her eyes going wide, her jaw slack. She looked to be somewhere in her thirties, rail thin and bony, her straw-colored hair fading toward gray. Her gaze locked with Stefan's. She swallowed convulsively and let out a shriek.

"Victor!" she screeched, whirling back into the house. "Victor. Come quick. Someone's stolen my washing!"

Dropping his clothes bundle, Stefan bolted across the yard and down the rutted drive. It wasn't until he reached the muddy road and threw a quick glance over his shoulder that he noticed the blue militia van parked out front.

Idiot! he thought, arms pumping and legs stretching out as he dashed up the street. *What kind of imbecile steals clothes from a policeman's wife?*

Gasping with fear, he pelted over the arched bridge and

into the hamlet. A bent old man in suspenders appeared at his doorway as Stefan streaked by. From the far side of the creek came Victor's furious shout, "Stop that boy! He's a thief!"

Stefan caught the sound of running footsteps pounding the dirt road behind him. His jaw clenched with concentration, he veered to his left, dodging another man in a butcher's apron who made a grab for him. He could see a line of trees ahead, the beginnings of a patch of ancient forest that stretched across the next hill. The temperature was falling, the light cold and flat. It would be dark soon. If he could just make it to the trees . . .

He heard another shout from the militiaman behind him. Then a second man's voice joined with his, the pounding of footsteps drawing nearer. Stefan could smell the sharp scent of the pines, the deep earthy humus of the forest floor rising up to beckon him on. Lungs aching, legs shaking with exhaustion and fear, he gave one last desperate spurt. Ten meters. Five. Then the darkness of the woods closed around him, like the embrace of a loving mother drawing a penitent son to her breast.

Monday morning dawned cold and overcast, the air pregnant with the scent of wood smoke and the dampness of coming rain. Rodriguez was up early, his feet pounding the pavement as he ran down a tree-lined avenue past an ancient graveyard with lichen-covered stones engraved with German names. Looking at the sturdy old houses and the red brick Gothic church, he could easily have imagined he was in Hamburg or Potsdam—except for the jarring reminder offered by the Cyrillic street sign at the corner.

He circled around the rusty iron fence enclosing the half-ruined church and started back. This place gave him the creeps. It reminded him of his grandparents' house in

Havana—lost, like these houses, to the spread of Communism.

Rodriquez had taken a night class in twentieth-century history in college, but it had left him more confused than anything else. He'd always been told that France and England declared war on Germany because Hitler invaded Poland. But the problem with that explanation was that the Russians had invaded Poland at the same time, in alliance with the Nazis. The Russians had also invaded Finland, although nobody declared war on the Russians. And when the war was supposed to be over, the Russians were still in Poland—and a hell of a lot of other places, too. So it seemed to Rodriguez that if the war had been fought to free Eastern Europe from invaders, then the whole thing had been a failure. Sure, it had gotten rid of the Nazis. But the Nazis had always been a lot more interested in fighting the Communists than they were the Western Allies—which was why they'd let the Brits escape at Dunkirk, and why they kept resisting Roosevelt's repeated efforts to drag them into a war with the States. Only, for some reason, people seemed to forget that.

Rodriguez was breathing hard now, legs pumping as he sprinted down a quiet lane, his wet T-shirt sticking to his back despite the chill. He passed a park with a statue of Lenin staring straight ahead, as if he could see all the way back to Moscow, and he found himself wondering what would have happened if the West had just let the two motherfuckers fight it out. Hitler and Stalin. Nazis and Commies. He had a feeling the world would look a lot different today.

He slowed to a walk as he neared the house, then did a hundred push-ups and a hundred crunches in the yard before heading inside.

"Heard from our guy in Berlin yet?" he asked Salinger as he let the kitchen door slam behind him.

"Nothing yet."

Rodriguez grabbed a liter of water and downed it in one long pull. "Something's gone wrong."

"Could just be a delay."

Rodriguez shook his head. After years of running operations, he'd learned to trust his gut. "Get onto our source at Aeroflot."

Salinger tapped at his computer for a few minutes, then looked up. "The representative from Langley checked in for his flight to Kaliningrad twenty minutes ago."

"Fuck." Rodriguez glanced across the kitchen to where the other men were clustered around a big oak table and eating breakfast out of takeout containers from a local inn. "Dixon, you and Salinger come with me. We'll get the son of a bitch when he lands."

17

Burrowing deep into her jacket, Tobie stepped off the flight from Copenhagen into an icy Baltic wind and found herself staring into the muzzle of a machine gun.

A stony-faced circle of guards herded the flight's passengers across the nearly deserted tarmac to an ugly Soviet-era terminal. A row of battered booths controlled the passage from the immigration hall to customs, but only one booth was manned. Waiting in the endless line with her bag clutched to her side, Tobie had plenty of time to watch the way the tall, thin guard was subjecting each passenger to a ruthless scrutiny.

Something was wrong.

Despite the frigid atmosphere of the room, she suddenly felt hot. CIA personnel were typically assigned to embassies, a position that conveniently provided them with diplomatic immunity. Intelligence personnel without diplomatic passports were said to be under "unofficial cover." In this case, "unofficial" basically meant *exposed*.

Without the immunity afforded by a diplomatic passport, Tobie was just an ordinary foreign national. And while the Cold War might be over, some things hadn't really changed in Russia. If the Russians knew or even suspected her connection to the CIA, she could disappear into a system that would treat her like—well, like the U.S. treated the guys they sent to Guantanamo Bay and Abu Ghraib and a couple dozen other secret prisons scattered from Afghanistan to Rumania to Morocco. When the guard finally raised his head and called out, "Next," Tobie jumped.

"Sdrasvytye," she said with a smile as she stepped up to the booth.

The guard stared at her passport, his dark bushy eyebrows drawing together in a frown. She expected him to say, "And what is the purpose of your visit?" But he didn't say anything. His frown deepening, he swung away to peck at his computer's keyboard.

"You will wait to one side," he said, jerking his chin toward the cinderblock wall behind him.

Tobie stopped breathing. "Is there a problem?"

"You wait," he told her, already motioning to the next person in line.

A stirring at the edge of the room drew her around. A barrel-chested man with short-cropped dark hair, full lips, and a crooked nose strode across the chipped linoleum floor, his face set in harsh lines as he walked up to her. He was casually dressed in a black turtleneck and jeans, but there was no doubt from the way everyone deferred to him that this was one seriously scary individual.

"Ensign October Guinness?" he snapped.

Ensign? Holy shit. How did he know that? Tobie's voice shook. *"Da."*

He said in Russian, "Come with me, please."

Andrei Gorchakove had graduated from the Academy and joined the KGB in the dying days of the once-mighty Soviet empire.

Like most Russians, he remembered those chaotic years with bitterness and shame. Ironically, both the Americans and Osama bin Laden liked to take credit for the collapse of the Soviet Union. Andrei himself thought the fault lay with the slow bleed of the Afghan War and the environmental disaster at Chernobyl. But whoever or whatever the cause, there was no denying that the breakup of the Soviet Union had brought terrible hardship to them all—or at least, to most of them.

Bereft of the ideology that had guided them for nearly a century, the Russian people had stumbled through a dark and terrible period as the millennium drew to a close. The state collapsed. Hordes of ruthless oligarchs calling themselves capitalists gobbled up the wealth of the country and brought a once-proud nation to her knees. KGB men like Andrei were forced to take jobs as bodyguards and day laborers, just to stay alive.

But they had a saying in Russia: *There's no such thing as an ex-KGB man*. In the end, the men of the KGB decided they'd had enough. The oligarchs were thrown into prison, or fled to places like England and Israel. A new war against the Chechens united the people and fired them with patriotism; the downward slide into poverty and despair was brought to an end. Once again, Mother Russia was beginning to stand tall.

Now, thanks to the Americans' own misadventures in Afghanistan and Iraq, it was the United States that was feeling the strains of overreach, while the revenues from soaring oil prices gushed into Russia's coffers. There had been a time, Andrei knew, when the Americans had made the mistake of thinking that Russia was finished—that they could treat their erstwhile rival like a conquered nation. In that, they had erred. Andrei had no idea why they had sent this young woman, this Naval ensign, to Kaliningrad, now. But by the time he was finished with her, he would find out.

He ushered her into a frigid, windowless room with a steel table and one metal chair. Her checked bag lay open on the table, the clothes strewn across the metal surface. "*Pazhalista*," he told her. "Sit down."

She sat, her face ashen and drawn with fear, her gaze following him as he went to stand on the far side of the table. She was young, no more than twenty-five, dressed like most Americans in jeans and sports shoes, with a navy V-necked sweater pulled over a button-down shirt.

He tossed a file on the table before her. "I see you're a linguist. You speak Russian, Arabic . . . many languages."

She swallowed hard, but said nothing.

He pressed his palms flat on the tabletop and leaned into them. "We have computers, too, you know. And according to our records, you were given a psychological discharge from the Navy a year ago. Yet, this past summer, you were recalled to active duty and given a promotion to ensign. This is correct?"

"Y-yes."

"Why?"

"You mean, why was I recalled?"

He nodded.

"I—" Her voice cracked. She swallowed and tried again. "I don't think it's a secret that the United States military has a hard time making their recruitment quotas these days. They needed me back."

"Despite the fact they'd decided you're crazy?"

Her eyes narrowed, and he had the satisfaction of knowing he'd hit a raw nerve. "I'm not crazy," she said in a tight voice.

Andrei allowed a hint of a smile to touch his lips. He pushed away from the table to wander the room. "I ask myself, Why is this attractive young American woman traveling alone to Kaliningrad Oblast?"

He was aware of her watching him closely. She said, "You don't get a lot of tourists?"

"Some. Mainly Germans who come to see the lost homes of their parents or grandparents, or to visit the beaches and sand dunes of the Curonian Spit. Tell me, Miss Guinness; are you German?"

She shook her head. "Irish. Among other things."

He nodded. "Your father was Patrick Guinness?"

He saw the confusion in her eyes. Confusion and fear, as she wondered how he knew about her father. A decorated Vietnam vet, Lieutenant Colonel Patrick Guinness had died when his daughter was still in kindergarten. Andrei suspected he knew more about what had happened to her father than she did.

She swallowed again. "Yes."

"You are to meet someone here?"

The sudden shift in topic obviously disconcerted her. She hesitated, uncertain how to answer. Despite the frigid temperature of the room, he saw a sheen of perspiration form near her hairline.

He said, "There is another American arriving this morning on a flight from Berlin. A man calling himself Jason Aldrich. You wouldn't know him by any chance, would you?"

Her eyes widened, but she said nothing. As he watched, a bead of sweat rolled slowly down the side of her face. She had dark brown eyes and honey-colored hair. An unusual combination—especially for someone who claimed to be Irish.

Andrei leaned his shoulders against the wall, his thumbs hooked in the pockets of his black designer jeans. "You're not very well trained, are you?"

"I'm a linguist."

The sound of the door opening behind her jerked her head around. A man walked into the room, flanked by two armed soldiers. Just above medium height and leanly built, he wore a pullover cashmere sweater and a black leather jacket that had the effect of making him look European rather than American. But then, that was one of the things they taught you in spy school—how to blend in with the natives.

He drew up just inside the doorway, his expression inscrutable as he gazed first at the woman, then at Andrei. "Jesus Christ," said Jax, smoothing the cuffs of his jacket as the soldiers stepped back. "What the hell is going on here, Andrei? The Cold War is supposed to be over."

Rodriguez was at the Kaliningrad airport when the call came through from Borz Zakaev.

"We may have something. Last night, at a village near Ayvazovskaya, a kid matching Stefan Baklanov's description stole some clothes. A militiaman chased him, then lost him in the woods."

Rodriguez shoved a stick of gum in his mouth and watched as a baldheaded Dane pushed open the battered doors from the Customs and Immigration hall. "Where is this Ayvazovskaya?"

"Southeast of Kaliningrad."

"Could be him." Rodriguez glanced at his watch. The passengers on the Aeroflot flight from Berlin would be coming out at any moment. He said, "We should be done here soon. Let me know when you have something positive. Once we get the little shit, all we need is the U-boat's big boom, and we're outta here."

Borz gave one of his deep laughs. "You don't like Kaliningrad?"

"I don't like Russia."

"Neither do I," said Borz, and hung up.

18

Jax let his gaze travel from Andrei Gorchakove to October Guinness's white, strained features, and thought, *Sonofabitch.*

When it came to delicate international situations, Jax didn't like dealing with unknowns, and at the moment he was facing a shitload of them. Not just, *What did the Russians know?* But, *How much had they managed to wheedle out of October?* She wasn't a field operative, and she'd never been trained to handle interrogations, and Washington should never, ever have sent her on an assignment like this.

"You took your time getting here, Jax," said Andrei, pushing away from the wall. "We were expecting you last night."

"Blame Aeroflot."

Andrei made a sound deep in his chest that might have been a laugh. Dismissing the two soldiers with a nod and a snap of his fingers, he led them to a more comfortable room with a desk and a couple of upholstered chairs set before a window overlooking the bleak runway.

"Please, have a seat." He glanced at his watch, said, "Excuse me a moment," and left the room.

Jax watched October sink down on the edge of one of the upholstered chairs. From the looks of things, she was sweating and shivering at the same time—never a good sign. He frowned. "You all right?"

She glanced up at him, a lock of loose hair falling across her face. "Aside from being scared shitless, I'm great."

He gave her a crooked smile. She might be untrained and way too far into woo-woo for his taste, but she wasn't stupid, and she wasn't weak.

She jerked her head toward the door and lowered her voice. "Who is that guy?"

Jax went to lean against the window overlooking the tarmac, his arms crossed at his chest. "You do realize this room is bugged—and probably set up with a video camera, too?"

She blinked, and he knew from the expression on her face that no, that hadn't occurred to her. God help him.

"Okay," she said slowly. "But I think they already know who he is. And you know who he is. So the only person who doesn't know who he is, is me."

Jax said, "How much do you know about the KGB?"

"I thought it didn't exist anymore."

"Not technically. After the collapse of the Soviet Union, the KGB basically split into two organizations. There's the FSB, or Federal Security Service, which is like a combination of our FBI, Secret Service, Customs Agency, and DEA, all rolled into one. And then there's the SVR, or Foreign Intelligence Service. They're the Russian equivalent of the CIA."

"Let me guess; this guy Andrei is with the SVR?"

"You got it."

"So how do you know him?"

"The first time we met, we were in the jungles near Mandalay and I was right out of the Farm." Jax glanced out the window at the heavy gray clouds pressing down on the runway and surrounding fields. A few drops of rain had begun to fall, beading on the glass to run down in long rivulets. "Andrei saved my skin."

"So you owe him."

"At the moment, we're even. I saved his ass last year in Niger."

"So does that make you friends or something?"

"Hardly. Don't let him fool you. Andrei Gorchakove is a dangerous sonofabitch. He's fiercely loyal to Russia, and he can be utterly ruthless when he needs to be."

"I'd figured that part out myself," she said dryly.

"That's reassuring. Now I need you to tell me exactly what you told them—and nothing more," he warned her.

She sat for a moment, as if running the last hour or so through in her head. "They already knew I was a linguist with the Navy. They even knew about my psychological discharge." Her forehead crinkled. "How could they know any of that stuff?"

"You think we're the only ones with spies? Their intelligence network is a hell of a lot more effective than it used to be. Back in the days of Communism, the Soviets were so insular the only spies they could run in the West were assigned to their embassies or with Aeroflot, which made them really, really easy to watch. Now the West is overrun with millions of expat Russians. And a big chunk of them report to the SVB."

"He even knew about my father."

Jax frowned. "Anything else?"

"No."

It was time, Jax decided, to end Andrei's little listening game. He said, "How's your cat?"

The question obviously disconcerted her. Her face went almost comically blank. *"My cat?"*

"Your cat. What's his name?"

"You mean, Beauregard?"

"That's it. Beauregard." Jax could practically hear Andrei sighing with frustration at the other end of the mike feed. A minute later, the door opened and the SVB man walked back into the room.

"Sorry about that," he said in his precise English, shaking out a packet of British cigarettes. He held them out to October. "You smoke?"

"No, thank you," she said with painful politeness.

The Russian went to perch on the edge of the desk, his attention all for the task of lighting his cigarette. It was a moment before he spoke. "You asked what's going on, Jax." He exhaled a stream of blue smoke. "I'll tell you something: *I'd* like to know what's going on."

He pointed the tip of his cigarette at them. "A couple of days ago, the Kaliningrad militia reported a curious incident at a shipyard near the entrance to the Vistula Lagoon. When the manager stopped by to check on a shipment Saturday morning, he found his night watchman with a slit throat and a salvage ship called the *Yalena* floating in the cove. Everyone on board was dead."

"A shipyard?" said Jax incredulously. He looked at October to find her sitting forward, her lips parted. He didn't want to believe she had "seen" U–114 simply by reaching out with her mind, but the evidence was starting to stack up. "Did you say a shipyard? And a salvage ship?"

Andrei flicked the ash from his cigarette and frowned. "That's what I said, Jax. A shipyard, a salvage ship, and thirteen dead men—fourteen, counting the night watchman. That's an unusually high body count, even for Russia. And then I hear that Jason Aldrich has booked a flight to Kaliningrad." He paused to look at Jax. "Don't you ever change your cover identity?"

"There wasn't a lot of time."

"Evidently." Andrei inhaled deeply, his eyes narrowing against the smoke. "I ask myself, what has happened, is happening, or is about to happen in Kaliningrad Oblast that's unusual? I think about that incident near the Vistula Lagoon, and I find my curiosity piqued."

His gaze shifted to October. He said, "So I leave my nice, comfortable office in Moscow and travel down to this god-forsaken place, expecting to meet my old friend Jax Alexander at the airport and show him a good time in Kaliningrad. And what happens? A beautiful young American Naval officer flies in that same morning."

October squirmed uncomfortably, but said nothing.

Andrei spread his arms wide, then dropped them to his sides. "So, here I am. I have a salvage ship with thirteen dead bodies, a dead night watchman, a live CIA agent, and an American Naval officer with an interesting past, all showing up in Kaliningrad Oblast at roughly the same time. So now I ask you, Jax, what is going on here?"

Jax leaned back against the window, his gaze on his old adversary's battle-scarred face. His options were severely limited, and he knew it. If he tried to stonewall Andrei, the Russian would have them both on the next flight out of Kaliningrad—or worse. There were times when the truth was the best option. "It's about Nazi gold."

October threw him a quick, incredulous glance, while Andrei—caught with a lungful of cigarette smoke—fell into a coughing fit. "*What*?" he said when he was able.

"The militia didn't by any chance find an old German U-boat at this shipyard, did they?"

Andrei's eyes narrowed. "How did you know about that? We haven't even notified Berlin yet."

"We saw it," said Jax. He was aware of October giving him another look. But Jax knew what Andrei would think—that the Americans had "seen" the sub on a satellite image.

Andrei cupped his hand around his cigarette to scratch behind his right ear. "What is your interest in the U-boat?"

Choosing his words carefully, Jax laid it all out for him—the missing sub, the Nazi gold, the link to a looming terrorist hit on the United States.

At the end of it all, Andrei blew out a long stream of smoke, his eyes twinkling with silent laughter. "And you expect me to believe this?"

Jax shrugged. "It's what they told me."

Andrei's smile widened. "I take it you're still in Division Thirteen?"

"What do you think?"

The Russian swung his head to fix October with a hard stare. He was no longer smiling. "And you?"

She froze, her eyes widening in a deer-in-the-headlights look.

Jax answered for her. "The CIA didn't anticipate me receiving such a warm and personal reception from the SVR. Since my Russian's no better than it used to be, they sent Ensign Guinness along as a translator."

"Her command of the language is certainly better than yours ever was," said Andrei, his gaze still on Tobie. "Tell me, Ensign, did you learn Russian before or after your psychiatric discharge from the Navy?"

"Before."

She said it calmly enough, although Jax knew that psychiatric discharge was a sensitive subject with her. Which was, of course, why Andrei mentioned it. Andrei was very good at finding sore points and pressing on them.

"That's the only reason you're here?"

Jax said, "What other reason could there be?"

Rather than answer, Andrei said, "You do realize, of

course, that if there ever was any gold on that U-boat, it's not there anymore?"

It was common knowledge among Russians that when the militia investigated a robbery, anything the thieves missed, the militia took. Jax said, "It's not the gold I want. I want the guys who hired that salvage ship in the first place."

"You mean, your terrorists?" Andrei blew out a lungful of smoke, his eyes narrowing with what looked like amusement. "I think there's something on that U-boat you need to see."

Jax pushed away from the window. "If you'll just point us to the local rent-a-car people, we'll be on our—"

"You forget; I know you, Jax." Andrei took a final drag on his cigarette and ground it out on the ashtray beside him. "Which means you go to the shipyard in my car, or you don't go. It's that simple."

19

"You didn't expect it to really be here, did you?" said Tobie, shouting to be heard over the roar of wind and rain. "The U-boat, I mean."

They were standing beneath a short overhang at the rear of the terminal, waiting for Andrei to bring up his car. Jax squinted at the angry gray clouds roiling overhead. "Stop gloating."

"Why? Gloating is fun." She cast a quick glance around and lowered her voice. "Can we talk here?"

"Carefully."

"I'll be careful. Can you tell me why in God's name the Russians are being so nice and cooperative?"

"It has nothing to do with being nice, and everything to do with the fact they think we know something they don't, and they want to find out what that something is."

"But you already told them everything."

"You don't actually think Andrei believed me, do you?"

"Why wouldn't he?"

Jax snorted. "The first lesson you need to learn in this business is, Don't believe anything you're told."

"By anyone?"

"Anyone. Including your own government." He thought about it a minute. "Make that, *especially* your own government."

"So how do we know what we've been told about this U-boat is true?"

"We don't. I was told it's true. That doesn't mean it's not bullshit."

"Well, that's comforting." She burrowed her cold hands deeper into the pockets of her jacket. "So what's the second lesson?"

"The second lesson? Don't expect anyone to believe anything you tell them."

She stared across the parking lot to where Andrei was talking to a guard. "You think that could be why he's taking us to look at the U-boat? Because he doesn't think you'll believe him if he just tells you about it?"

"Partially."

She watched the Russian step off the curb and walk briskly toward them, his leather jacket flaring open to reveal the Makarov pistol in a shoulder holster beneath it. She said, "I don't think I'd like to cross that guy."

"You don't. Not if you want to live to tell about it. People who cross Andrei have a nasty habit of turning up dead."

She was silent for a moment. "You said that to scare me."

"Yeah. But that doesn't mean it isn't true. Just remember: you're here as the woo-woo specialist. I do the talking. Understand?"

She ducked her head and pulled an imaginary forelock. "I'll try to remember my place, Sahib. You want I should walk three steps behind you, Sahib?"

A big silver sedan swung in close to the curb and stopped. Gone were the days of Zhigulis and Ladas; Andrei's car was a shiny new S-Class Mercedes, with a stocky, round-faced driver who looked like he might have come out of the steppes of Asia with the Golden Horde.

Jax reached to open the door for her. "Just let me do the talking, okay?"

But she just gave him a wide smile and slid into the car.

Rodriguez stood with eyes narrowed against the strengthening rain and watched as the target from the CIA ducked into the Mercedes across the street. Beside him, Clay Dixon lowered the visor on his motorcycle helmet and started his Kawasaki 750ii.

"Salinger and I will stay behind you," said Rodriguez. "Keep the tail loose. When we figure out what's going on, then we can decide when and where to make the hit."

Dixon nodded.

Rodriguez waited until the Mercedes pulled out into the light traffic, then stepped back. "Go."

Sliding into the passenger seat of the Range Rover, he said to Salinger, "Follow Dixon. But keep your distance."

"Who the hell is this Russkie?" said Salinger, dropping in three cars behind the Kawasaki.

"I don't know. But whoever he is, he's damned important. You should have seen the way everyone in the airport was scrambling to do what he told them."

"So why's he with our CIA guy?"

"Because life is never easy." Rodriguez unwrapped a new piece of gum and shoved it in his mouth.

They followed Dixon out of the airport and onto the hopeless excuse for a road that passed as a highway in Kaliningrad.

"Shit," he said as the Mercedes turned away from the city, toward the northwest. "The sonofabitch is taking them to the shipyard."

Beside him, Salinger grunted. "Maybe we'll get lucky and

they'll trip the booby trap on the U-boat and blow themselves to hell."

"What part of 'life is never easy' did you miss?"

"You never know; we might get lucky."

Rodriguez laughed. "We might." He checked his watch, figured out the time difference in Washington, then put in a call to Boyd anyway.

"What is it?" said the General. His voice was low and icy, but he sounded instantly awake.

"Things are not going as well as we'd expected. The representative from Washington arrived in Kaliningrad this morning."

"I thought someone was dealing with this guy in Berlin."

"We haven't been able to contact our man in Berlin to ascertain exactly what went wrong. It's not a problem; we'll deal with him here. There's just one detail that requires clarification."

"Yes?"

"The representative from Washington has joined up with another individual who flew in from Copenhagen. A woman. You didn't tell us about her."

"I didn't know about her."

"Her name is October Guinness," said Rodriguez. The information had been easily obtained from the sulky, green-eyed woman with spiked hair and well-developed capitalistic instincts who worked behind the Scandinavian Airlines counter. In the New Russia, anything and everything was for sale.

"I'll see what I can find out about her," said Boyd. "Where are these individuals now?"

"They were picked up by a Russian escort. An *official* Russian escort. We're following them."

"I want this guy taken care of by nightfall. Even if you have to take out a few Russians to do it."

"Understood," said Rodriguez, closing his phone with a snap.

Salinger threw him a quick glance. "We really going to kill the Russians?"

Those guys? Not if I can help it. But if we have to . . ." Rodriquez clipped his phone onto his belt and shrugged. "People don't disappoint Boyd and live."

Washington, D.C.

General Boyd pushed up from the edge of his bed at the Willard Intercontinental Hotel and went to pour himself a drink. He stood for a moment, his gaze on the dark and quiet streets of the city spread out below. Then he reached for his phone and punched in a number.

It rang four times before a colonel named Sam Lee picked it up, his voice slurred by sleep and confusion. "Hello?"

"Lee? Boyd here. I need you to do something for me."

20

Jax noticed the Kawasaki behind them as they were pulling out of the airport. It might not mean anything—after all, there weren't that many roads in Kaliningrad, and the rider wasn't exactly being careful about keeping close to them. Then again, he could be part of Andrei's escort. Chase riders were no longer as necessary in Russia as they had been in the wild, lawless days after the breakup of the Soviet Union, but they were still common. Jax noticed Andrei casting one or two glances behind, before looking away.

They drove through thick, desolate pine forests interspersed with flat empty fields that lay dark and sodden beneath the leaden sky. Turning sideways in the passenger seat, Andrei shook a cigarette out of his pack and said, "So where exactly did you learn your Russian, Ensign?"

Jax was aware of October casting him a questioning glance, but he only raised his eyebrows. She cleared her throat and said, "I spent a semester in Moscow, when I was nineteen."

"A semester only? And you learned our language so well? No wonder the CIA finds you useful."

She wisely let that slide, saying only, "I've never been to Kaliningrad Oblast, though."

Andrei stuck a cigarette between his lips and fumbled in his pocket for his lighter. "Until recently, no one was allowed in Kaliningrad Oblast. It was a closed military area. Kaliningrad is the only ice-free port in Russia, you know."

"Not to mention the fact that it's within such easy striking distance of so many European capitals," said Jax.

Andrei laughed, his eyes narrowing against the smoke as he drew on his cigarette. "That, too. I'm afraid the breakup of the Soviet Union has been hard on Kaliningrad Oblast. Military expenditure used to be the mainstay of the economy, but no longer. And when you add to that the fact that Poland and Lithuania have both closed their borders to us, making the Oblast an exclave . . ." He shrugged his shoulders again. "Many of the people here have been forced to turn to smuggling, just to survive."

"And to salvaging U-boats?" said Jax.

"So it would seem."

He gazed out the window at the ruins of an old brick farmhouse. Beyond it he could see the skeleton of a barn, its rafters etched stark against the white sky and bare except for a couple of giant storks' nests. They had passed many such abandoned homes—entire villages even—their walls crumbling, a tangle of trees growing up from within the ruins of houses, castles, ancient churches.

"Look, there's another one," said Tobie. "Why do I keep seeing all these empty villages and farms?"

Andrei took a deep drag on his cigarette and exhaled slowly. "They are old," he said. "From before the war."

"What you're seeing," said Jax, "is one of the twentieth century's dirty little secrets. Until the end of the Second World War, this used to be part of Germany. Then Churchill and Roosevelt gave it to Russia, and Stalin 'cleansed' it of its original Prussian inhabitants. The ones who were lucky managed to flee west, ahead of the Red Army. The rest were either shot or sent to slave labor camps in Siberia. Stalin brought in Russians to replace them, but the population today is still under a million—which is less than a third of what it once was. And they're all Russians."

He was aware of October staring solemnly as they swept past another overgrown field with a jumble of collapsed walls beyond it. It was one thing to read about "border adjustments," and something else entirely to look at the ruins of what was once someone's home.

"I can see you're shocked, Ensign," said Andrei, his voice rough. "You think we are butchers. Inhuman. Yet you Americans did it to your Native Indians, just as the Israelis are doing it today to the Moslems and Christians of Palestine. If history teaches us one thing, it is this: ethnic cleansing works."

They topped a ridge, and the flat, silver waters of the Baltic Sea opened up suddenly before them. In the lee of the slight rise lay a sheltered cove lined with the weathered docks of an old shipyard, its vast wharves stretching out eerily empty beneath the cloud-filled sky. A shabby metal office building stood just below the crest of the hill, fronting a narrow, rutted road that wound down to the row of warehouses lining the docks. Jax could see three blue and white militia vans parked next to a dusty white pickup behind the office.

He felt a disconcerting chill run up his spine. Everything was much as October had drawn it, except that the office and rocky point were on the left, when she'd drawn them to the right.

"It's backwards," he whispered, leaning in close to her.

She sat forward, her gaze riveted on the scene below. And he found himself wondering what it must be like, actually seeing in person what she'd previously reached out and touched with her mind. "That happens sometimes," she said softly. "The brain gets so used to reversing the images we get from our eyes that it sometimes reverses what you 'see' in a viewing."

Andrei frowned. "You've seen this place before?"

Jax shook his head. "Only in pictures."

They turned in through the ratty, ten-foot-high wire fence that ran along the road and surrounded the shipyard complex. A dilapidated guard post stood beside the gate, unmanned now. Behind them, the Kawasaki slowed, then continued on up the road. Jax watched it, his eyes narrowing.

Not a chase rider, after all.

"It's an old military facility," Andrei was saying, "privatized after the navy gave it up ten or fifteen years ago. Now it's used mainly for unloading shipments of frozen chickens and pork from Brazil—and for smuggling, of course."

The Mercedes bumped and swayed over the rutted road that wound down to the wharves. At the far end of a distant jetty, out in deeper water, Jax could see a large, rusty catamaran that rocked gently with the motion of the waves. Rigged with a lifting boom and giant orange buoys, it was obviously a salvage ship. His Russian was just good enough to enable him to spell out the word *Yalena*, painted in a fading Cyrillic script along the side.

"Why didn't you see *that*?" he said to Tobie in a whisper.

But she just frowned and threw a warning glance at the back of Andrei's head.

The barge bearing U–114 had been pushed in next to the nearest stretch of wharves that fronted the line of warehouses along the shore. The U-boat was much bigger than Jax had expected, a mammoth hulking thing hundreds of feet long, its once sleek hull rusted and thick with the accretions of sixty years beneath the sea. The small tugboat that had been used to push the barge up to the inner docks was still berthed nearby, beside the rigging for the camouflage netting. As they neared the docks, a small yellow crane at the end of the wharf swung into action, lifting a crate from the sub's open hatch and depositing it onto the back of a nearby flatbed truck. Jax remembered seeing the crane in Tobie's drawings, but not the tugboat. Why had she seen some things, he wondered, and not others?

"Pull up here," Andrei told his driver. With a crunch of gravel, the big Mercedes rolled to a halt behind the nearest warehouse.

"You're unloading the U-boat?" said October, her expression solemn as she watched the crane swing back toward the submarine's deck.

A militiaman ran forward to open Andrei's door and saluted smartly. Andrei tucked a bulky file under one arm and stood. "Until the cargo has been inspected and inventoried, we won't know what we have."

Jax thrust open his own door. "And when exactly is Moscow planning to notify Berlin about the sub?"

The cold wind off the sea swirled a fine white dust around them. Andrei smiled. "When we know what we have."

The tide was low, the waves splashing against the exposed supports of the pier and filling the air with the scent of salt and seaweed and rust. Cutting between the warehouses, they walked out onto a weathered wharf littered with stacks of barrels and cargo containers, some so oddly shaped they looked as if they must have been especially built to fit beneath the U-boat's floor plates or in its torpedo tubing. Every one of the containers showed signs of having been ripped open.

Jax said, "Were any of these broken into before the militia arrived?"

"A few, yes. But not many."

"So what is all this stuff?"

"So far we've found everything from a disassembled Messerschmitt jet fighter to diplomatic mail and technical drawings."

"A fighter?" October had been staring at the rusted hull of the old U-boat, its aft section caved in by depth charges. Now she turned. "Why would the Germans have been sending a fighter to Japan?"

"So the Japanese could copy it," said Jax, hunkering down to get a closer look at one of the barrels. "Ever hear of Operation Caesar?"

"No."

"It was a project the Nazis started in late 1944 or early 'forty-five. By that point even Hitler had to admit the war was not going well. Someone in Berlin got the idea that if they could prop up the Japanese, then maybe the Allies would be forced to put more effort into the War in the Pacific—and take some of the heat off Europe."

"Prop them up how?"

"The Germans had made some incredible advances in technology during the war—way ahead of where we were at the time. They started sending the Japanese everything from armor-piercing shells to design plans for missile guidance systems and rockets."

"I've even heard of Hitler shipping out German scientists and engineers," said Andrei. His eyes crinkled into what might have been a smile. "But I've never heard of the Nazis sending Japan any gold."

"Not to Japan," Jax admitted. He pushed to his feet, his gaze shifting to the old U-boat. The submarine's wooden decking had long since rotted away, leaving a rough, pitted surface. The original ladder on the conning tower was gone, too. Someone had propped a new one in its place.

"Come," said Andrei, leaping the distance to the U-boat's deck. "I think you'll find this interesting."

Jax jumped after him, then turned to hold out his hand to October.

"That's okay," she said, her face held oddly tight. "I think I'll wait here."

"What's the matter? Claustrophobic?"

She looked down, her attention all for the task of buttoning her jacket against the sharp wind. "Not exactly. Just . . . take my advice and watch where you step."

"What's that supposed to mean?"

"You'll see."

"What do we do now?" said Dixon, drawing the Kawasaki up beside the Range Rover.

They were parked in the shadows cast by a copse of beech at the crest of the hill. Looping the loose strap of his binoculars around the fist of one hand, Rodriguez watched the Russian and their target drop through the conning tower's open hatch. Then he swung to focus on the girl.

She was small and slim and young, probably no more than twenty-four or -five. As he watched, she hunched her shoulders and shivered, as if she were cold—or afraid.

He had a VSSK Vychlop sniper rifle with an integrated bipod and silencer in a case on the floor of the backseat. The 12.7mm VSSK had been developed by the Russian Design Bureau at the special request of the FSB. Designed for counterterror and high-profile anti-crime operations, it offered silent firing and superior penetration. Even at this range, he could blow her to pieces with a single shot and be long gone before anyone below figured out what had happened.

On the downside, the hit would not only leave their main target—Alexander—alive, it would also warn him.

"We watch," said Rodriguez, shifting his gaze back to the U-boat.

"We should have blown the fucking sub when we had the chance," said Salinger for something like the tenth time.

"It'll blow," said Rodriguez. "It'll blow."

21

Swinging through the open hatch, Jax felt the thick, dank air of the U-boat close around him. He set his jaw and slid down the aluminum ladder to land with a light thump beside what he realized too late was the grinning, mummified skull of a long-dead German submariner.

"Jesus Christ!" he yelped, hopping to one side and making a grab for the ladder to keep his balance. "What the hell is he doing still here?"

Andrei shrugged. "Moscow's supposed to be sending over a team of anthropologists. They told us to leave the bodies alone."

Jax studied the cadaver's sunken body cavity, the tattered uniform, the dark, leathery flesh stretched across the cheekbones and clawlike fingers. "I could have landed on him."

Andrei's eyes creased with quiet amusement. "The Ensign did warn you to watch your step."

Jax turned in a tight circle, his gaze taking in the control room's jumble of ducts and valves, hand wheels and switches, gauges and wires. The militia had rigged up a string of electric lights that ran toward the bow, casting ghostly shadows around the tight compartment. He could hear a faint hammering coming from the bow, the vibrations reverberating down the length of the hull.

He brought his gaze back to the desiccated body sprawled at their feet. "You didn't tell me the hull had held all these years."

"Most of it," said Andrei, leading the way forward. "The two aft compartments were torn apart by depth charges, which flooded the diesel and electric engines. That's why she sank."

Jax glanced back at the closed, watertight hatch that had sealed the control room off from the aft compartments, and felt the hairs rise along the back of his neck. "Sonofabitch," he said softly. "They suffocated."

Andrei nodded. "Poor bastards."

Stepping over two more bodies, they ducked through the open round hatch in the front bulkhead and pushed toward the bow in silence. They passed the radio room and the listening room, the captain's corner with its faded green curtain still in place, the men's quarters with their bunks stacked four high on each side of the passageway.

Not all the bunks were empty.

"So exactly what did you bring me down here to see, Andrei? It must be good."

Andrei ducked through another bulkhead, then stopped abruptly beside a small WC. "You Americans. Always so impatient. It's here."

Jax peered through the gaping door beside them. "We're here to look at an old German toilet?"

"Not the toilet. That."

Jax shifted his gaze to the shattered storage compartment that lay just beyond the WC and fell silent.

"How's your German?" said Andrei.

Reaching out, Jax ran his fingers across the broken wood, where boldly stenciled letters warned ACHTUNG! GEFAHR! Danger. "A hell of a lot better than my Russian. It was like this when you found it?"

"Yes."

"What do you think was in here?"

"That, we do not know. But it doesn't look like it was designed to hold gold, now, does it?"

Jax hunkered down to study the floor plates, searching for some clue as to what the space might once have contained. "No," he said. "No, it doesn't."

A loud metallic clang, followed by a burst of laughter and men's voices speaking in Russian, sounded from nearby.

"What's up there?" said Jax, pushing to his feet.

"The forward torpedo room. The militia has just started clearing it."

Pausing at the next bulkhead, Jax peered into the rank gloom and counted four fat sausage-shaped cylinders. "Jesus. The torpedoes are still here, too?"

"Live torpedoes," said Andrei, stepping over another mummified submariner, "and dead Germans."

"That ought to tell us something profound," said Jax. "I'm just not sure what."

"Herzlich willkommen." A militiaman lurched toward them, stumbled, and raised another round of laughter.

Jax said, "Why do I smell vodka? Somehow, I don't think vodka and old torpedoes are a really good mix."

Andrei gave another of his shrugs. "The militia doesn't tend to attract the best men."

They headed back toward the control room and climbed the ladder to the conning tower. Jax paused at the top to draw the sweet, misty air deep into his lungs.

"Find anything?" said October, scrambling up from where she'd been sitting at the edge of the dock.

"Just a broken wooden storage compartment stenciled with danger warnings." Jax leaped the gaping three feet of choppy gray water that separated the U-boat's deck from the wharf. "It was great in there. You should have come."

"That's okay," she said, then dropped her voice to add, "Once was enough."

Jax laughed softly, and turned as Andrei landed beside them. "So, do we get to see the salvage ship, too?"

"It contains nothing of interest."

"I'd still like to take a look."

Andrei glanced at his watch. "You can have five minutes."

"I don't get it," said October as they turned to walk along the dilapidated docks that stretched toward the outer harbor. "Why would the Nazis store gold in a wooden compartment and label it 'Danger'?"

"They wouldn't," said Andrei. "That's the point. If that submarine had been carrying gold, it would have been under the floor plates with a reinforced steel hatch welded shut." He tore the cellophane off a new pack of cigarettes and let the wind carry it away. "Exactly what gave your government the idea U–114 was carrying gold, anyway?"

Jax watched October catch the wrapper and shove it in her pocket. He said, "You know that kind of information is classified, Andrei."

Andrei huffed a soft laugh. "In other words, they didn't tell you where the information came from, did they?" He shook out a cigarette. "You know as well as I do that such a scenario makes no sense. That's not how these things work. First, one plans an operation and secures funding. Then, one recruits the necessary personnel and material and sets the date for the attack. It doesn't happen the other way around. What does your government think these so-called terrorists have been doing? Charging everything on their American Express cards? Now the bill is coming due, so they decide to go salvage a sunken U-boat and steal its gold?"

A fine mist hovered over the heaving gray surface of the water, like smoke drifting from an invisible grass fire. Jax said, "Maybe these guys are new at this."

"Or maybe someone in your government is being less than honest with you."

Jax was aware of October's gaze upon him, but all he said was, "The one undeniable fact in all this is that *someone* salvaged that U-boat and took something off it. There wasn't a manifest among the U-boat's papers?"

"If there was, we haven't found it."

Jax squinted at the *Yalena*, riding the gentle swell of the incoming tide. "What does the shipyard manager have to say about all this?"

"As little as he thinks he can get away with." Andrei let the unlit cigarette dangle from his lips as he searched for his lighter. "At first he claimed he was as surprised as anyone to find the *Yalena* floating in his cove with a German submarine in tow. It wasn't until the militia confronted him with his telephone records that he admitted Baklanov had contacted him about using his wharves."

"Who's Baklanov?"

"Jasha Baklanov. Captain of the *Yalena*." Andrei struck his lighter, his chin jerking toward the big catamaran. "According to the militia, he was not exactly what you'd call a good, upstanding comrade."

"Smuggling?"

"Among other things." Andrei tucked away his lighter and flipped open the thick file he carried beneath his arm. "He was found on deck, his body practically cut in half by machine-gun fire."

Jax tried to peer over Andrei's shoulder, but the Russian snapped the file shut again. "Uh-uh," he grunted. "You're forgetting how this works. I give you something, then you give me something. It's your turn."

"I already told you everything I know. All we have is the interception of a careless cell phone call linking some sunken U-boat to a terrorist hit."

"On Halloween."

"On Halloween."

Andrei swung around to stare back at the sub. Following his gaze, Jax saw that one of the militiamen had appeared at the conning tower. As they watched, the man dropped down onto the wharf and climbed into the passenger seat of the loaded truck. They could hear the truck's engine laboring as it shifted gears, the sound carrying clearly across the quarter mile or so of open water. The weathered wharves and jetties of the shipyard stretched out between them, silent and deserted beneath the cold gray sky.

"Is that supposed to be a joke?" said Andrei.

"If it is, no one in Washington is laughing. They may have got the U-boat's cargo wrong, but at this point, I'm thinking maybe—" Jax broke off as a low rumble reverberated across the cove. He saw a geyser of fire shoot out the hatch in the submarine's upper deck, just above the bow torpedo room.

"Holy shit," he yelled. "Get down!"

From where he crouched within the shelter of the birch grove at the top of the rise, Rodriguez swore softly under his breath. He'd set up the Vychlop with a clear line of fire. But every time he got the CIA agent lined up in his sights, the girl would move in the way, or the Russian.

He finally had a clear shot and was just squeezing the trigger when all hell broke loose in the cove below. The asshole from Langley hit the deck, and the solid bronze pointed-nose high-penetration bullet that should have blown him to smithereens smacked into the water with a splash that was lost in a shattering roar. The old U-boat heaved out of the water and turned into a fireball. Smoke roiled over the harbor, obscuring visibility.

"Fuck!" said Rodriguez, pushing to his feet. "Now? The fucking sub blows *now*?"

Moving quickly, he disassembled the Vychlop's silencer and shoved it in its case. "This place is going to be crawling with militia in minutes," he said, throwing the rifle in the backseat. "Let's get out of here."

22

Tobie let out a startled yelp as Jax slammed into her, knocking her off her feet. She rolled onto her stomach, her arms wrapping around her head as a second explosion ripped from one end of the U-boat's frame to the other, obliterating it in a huge fireball. She felt a wave of searing heat wash over her. Even from this distance, the percussion was deafening.

"Jesus Christ," said Jax, stretched out flat beside her. "You all right?"

"I think so." Fighting to catch her breath, she turned her head to meet his gaze. "What happened?"

"One of the old torpedoes must have blown and set off the rest."

She ducked her head again as flaming debris began to rain down around them, hissing as it hit the water.

A jagged piece of charred wood landed on Andrei's back. He thrust it away and scrambled up to take off running back along the docks, only pausing long enough to turn and point a warning finger at Jax. "*You stay here.*"

Tobie sat back on her heels. She was trembling, her breath coming in fast, wheezing gasps. She knew she was hyperventilating and fought to bring her breathing under control. But it wasn't easy.

Both the barge and the sub had simply disappeared, leaving an oily sheen on the churning, debris-filled water. Most of that section of the wharf was gone, too, the tugboat flipped on its side and almost completely submerged. Flames engulfed the shattered warehouses, filling the air with black smoke. The twisted remnants of the flatbed truck stood out stark against the flames, the two men inside black, unrecognizable silhouettes.

"My God," she whispered.

Pushing to his feet, Jax brushed off the front of his jacket, then bent to pick up the file Andrei had dropped.

"What's in it?" she asked as he flipped through the pages.

"The militia report." He raised his gaze to the *Yalena*. The salvage ship was still pitching in the aftermath of the explosion, but she hadn't been thrown over. "Come on," he said. "We need to move fast."

Tobie rose shakily to her feet. "I thought Andrei told us to stay here."

"Since when do you ever do what you're told?"

"What's that supposed to mean?" she demanded, sprinting down the dock after him.

"I saw the reports filed by your shrink in Wiesbaden. The one that says, 'Has trouble with authority.' "

She leaped from the dock to the still-pitching deck of the *Yalena*. "The shrink in Wiesbaden was a stupid ass."

Jax let his gaze travel around the salvage ship's dilapidated deck. "I still don't understand why this wasn't part of your vision."

"I don't have *visions*. It was a remote viewing session." Reaching out, she let her hand trail along a tattered tarp that covered the nearest lifeboat davits, and felt an odd terror seize her chest.

"What is it?" he said, watching her.

She shook her head and turned away. "Nothing. What exactly are we looking for?"

"Anything that can lead us to the bad guys. Although at this point, I'd settle for some indication as to what was really on that U-boat."

"Are you so sure it wasn't gold?"

"Sure? Hell no. I'm not sure of anything. But in my experience, governments tend to store gold behind things like reinforced iron plates. Not in wooden storage lockers stenciled with words like 'Attention' and 'Danger.'"

A fine cold mist blew off the sea, smelling of brine and pungent smoke and bringing them the distant sound of shouting and the wail of sirens. The morning rain had washed away much of the blood from the deck. But an ugly pattern of splatters and smears were still visible on the bullet-pocked bulkhead and rigging. She said, "You think the people who hired Baklanov are the same people who did this?"

Jax went to hunker down beside the stained, splintered bulkhead. "Maybe. Maybe not."

Opening the file, he flipped through the militia photographs of the *Yalena's* dead crew. Tobie cast one glance at the eight-by-ten shots of blood-soaked, bullet-torn bodies, and turned away to stare out over the smoke-swirled waters of the cove.

He pushed to his feet. "Come on. I want to check the captain's quarters."

The captain's cabin lay at the top of the ship, just beyond the blood-splattered bridge with its bullet-shattered gauges and splintered woodwork. At the hatch leading to the small cabin beyond it, Jax paused and let out a low whistle.

Tobie drew up beside him. The bunk's mattress had been pulled askew, the drawers yanked from the desk and dumped, clothes strewn across the floor. "Did the militia do this?"

"Some of it, maybe." He reached over to pick up a waste-basket filled with ashes. "But not this. Looks like whoever killed Baklanov and his crew burned every piece of paper they could get their hands on."

"But . . . why?"

"Because if you've just committed mass murder, you don't want to take the time to sort through everything just to find what you're looking for."

"Which was . . . what?"

"Presumably, anything that might lead back to our terrorists." He handed her Andrei's file. "Here. Your Russian is a hell of a lot better than mine. Take a look."

Perching on the edge of the bunk frame, she flipped through page after page of forms, all filled out in a tiny, nearly illegible Cyrillic scrawl. "Jeez. You'd think they'd have typed up the report before sending it to Moscow."

"This is Kaliningrad, remember? They still store their potatoes in earthen burrows and haul hay to market in horse-drawn carts."

"Listen to this," she said, pointing to a cramped paragraph on the next page. "According to the shipyard manager, this isn't the first German U-boat the *Yalena* salvaged."

Jax crouched down to look at a smashed strongbox. "I wonder if the shipyard was planning to buy it."

"The U-boat?" She glanced up from the report. "But . . . why?"

"For the steel. Our terrorists might have hired Balkanov to raise the sub for its cargo; as a salvage operator, Baklanov would know that U-boats are valuable in and of themselves, for their pre–1945 steel."

She ran through the rest of the report, then shook her head. "I get the impression this Captain Baklanov was just planning to unload and store the sub here for a while."

"Until when?"

"It doesn't say."

Andrei's gruff shout drifted up from below. "Alexander! Get the hell off that ship."

Jax threw a quick glance through the porthole. "Does the report list the address of this Captain Baklanov?"

Tobie flipped back through the pages.

Andrei shouted again. *"Alexander. I told you to stay put!"*

"Here it is. The salvage company's offices are in some place called Zelenogradsk. But Baklanov himself lived in Rybachy. Looks like he had a wife. Anna."

"That's good. She might—"

"Alexander!"

"Come on," said Jax, pulling her to her feet.

"So how are we going to get rid of your buddy Andrei so we can talk to this widow?"

"First of all," said Jax, heading for the companionway, "Andrei is not my buddy. Secondly, you don't *get rid of* an SVR officer. Thirdly, Andrei just lost I don't know how many militiamen and a stolen Nazi U-boat that Moscow hadn't gotten around to telling Berlin about, which means he's going to want to get rid of us."

"That doesn't sound good."

"It's not."

23

General Gerald T. Boyd was halfway through his morning work-out routine in one of the Pentagon's weight rooms when a slim, half-Asian colonel in his early forties sat down on the bench beside him.

Boyd braced his forearm on his thigh and curled the dumbbell up in a slow, controlled motion, his attention all for his breathing and the careful execution of form. Only then did he glance over at Colonel Sam Lee, noting the officer's bloodshot eyes, the slack jaw of a man roused urgently and too early from his sleep.

"You have something for me?" said Boyd.

A computer geek, the Colonel had been assigned to the Directorate of Operations of the Central Intelligence Agency for the past two years. It was a plum position for a man close to putting in his twenty years; from here, he'd be able to walk into any one of a number of high paying jobs with the private sector when he retired. And he owed it all to Gerald T. Boyd.

"Not as much as I'd hoped," said Colonel Lee. He was a small man, with short-cropped dark hair and the gentle features of his parents, who had fled Vietnam after the fall of Saigon.

Boyd watched his own bicep flex and relax, flex and relax. "There's a problem?"

Lee reached for a fifteen-pound dumbbell. "This Guinness woman is the problem. I started by looking at her passport file."

"And?" Boyd didn't really care how Lee got the necessary information on October Guinness, as long as he got it—and was careful to cover his tracks.

"Turns out she's in the Navy."

Boyd frowned. "The Navy?"

"An ensign. I thought it would be a piece of cake, accessing her files."

Boyd waited.

Lee cast a quick glance around and leaned in closer. "Instead, that's when everything went to shit. The Navy doesn't have her file." His voice dropped to a whisper. "She's been detailed to the CIA."

"That's a problem?"

"I don't know what she's doing, but whatever it is, it's a deep dark secret. Special Access shit."

"So why is she in Russia?"

"I don't know."

Boyd switched the dumbbell to his left hand. He didn't like this. He didn't like it one damned bit. But all he said was, "I need for you to stay on this. I want to know exactly who she is, and why she's involved."

A muscle twitched beside the other man's small mouth. "I'm afraid I may have already stumbled across a trip wire."

Boyd pushed to his feet and dropped the dumbbell on the rack. "I'll take care of the Agency. Just get me the information I need."

Sam Lee glanced down at the dumbbell in his hand, then up again, his shoulders drooping with fatigue and a touch of fear. "Yes, sir."

24

The Tatar kept a heavy foot on the gas all the way back to the
city of Kaliningrad, his shoulders hunched, his hands clutching
the wheel. Sheltered by the row of warehouses, he'd survived
the explosion with only a few scrapes and bruises. But the Mercedes he'd been sitting in had been pretty badly pummeled by
debris. They drove back to Kaliningrad in one of the blue-and-
white militia vans with the siren wailing and Andrei shouting
into his cell phone for so long that, by the time they thumped
over one of the bridges crossing the Pregel River and onto the
island of Kneiphof, the Russian was hoarse.

"I'm supposed to be at a meeting that started ten minutes
ago," he said as the van swooped in next to the curb. "You
get out now."

"Here?" said Jax, looking around. Once, Kneiphof had
been the island heart of old Königsberg, a jewel of medieval
and renaissance architecture and learning. But the graceful,
ancient university buildings were long gone, bombed to dust

by the Allies, while the Russians had dynamited the city's famous castle back in the 1960s and replaced it with a concrete governmental monstrosity frequently described as the ugliest example of Soviet architecture in existence—which was really saying something. Even the cobbles from the surrounding lanes had been taken up and relaid in Moscow's Red Square. Only the cathedral had survived, as a hollowed-out shell that was now being restored.

"The car will be back for you by seven. You're both booked on tonight's flight to Berlin."

"Berlin?" October froze in the act of scooting across the seat. "But my ticket is through Copenhagen."

Andrei lit a new cigarette from the embers of his old one, his cheeks hollowing as he inhaled. "I want you out of here tonight, and the next flight to Copenhagen isn't until later this week. You're going to Berlin. And Jax—"

Jax paused with his hand on the edge of the door. "Yes, Andrei?"

"Be here. If I have to make other arrangements to get you out of the country, you really aren't going to like them."

"Got it," said Jax, and closed the door.

"I guess he doesn't want to play nice anymore," said October, her brows drawing together as she watched the militia van speed away.

"No. But that doesn't mean he's not still playing."

She glanced over at him. "What does that mean?"

Jax put his hand under her elbow, drawing her across the square toward the looming red brick nave of the cathedral. "Don't look, but there's a guy in a black leather jacket and a visored helmet who just parked his Kawasaki down the street. He was following us when we left the airport this morning."

Jax watched, amused, as she struggled really, really hard to keep from staring down the street. "You think he's one of Andrei's men?"

"There's only one way to find out."

She dug her fists into her pockets and kept her head down as they walked rapidly across the park. "Is he still following us?" she asked as they skirted the newly roofed sidewalls of the old German cathedral.

"Yes."

They cut around behind the towering red brick nave, to where the still waters of the river reflected an autumn riot of golds and rusts.

The guy from the Kawasaki stayed behind them, one hand creeping to the small of his back as a tall rose-colored portico closed off by a wrought-iron fence loomed before them.

"What's that?" said October, her head tilting back as she stared up at the soaring columns.

Jax turned so that he could keep one eye on the guy from the Kawasaki. "It's the tomb of Immanuel Kant. He was an atheist, so they buried him out here. Which is kind of ironic, when you consider that his tomb is the only reason the Russians didn't tear down the cathedral—Marx being a big fan of Kant, you see."

She glanced over at him. "How do you know all this stuff?"

"I majored in history at Yale."

She started to laugh.

"That's funny? Why is that funny? Because I majored in history, or because I went to—" Out of the corner of his eye, Jax saw the Kawasaki rider's hand come up. "*Look out!*" he shouted, shoving October to one side.

He heard a whine, and a corner of the worn old sarcophagus disappeared into dust.

"Shit," said Jax, gravel rolling beneath his loafers as he dragged her behind one of the slender columns.

October lost her footing and almost went down. "He's shooting at us? Why is he shooting at us?"

"Because he's not Andrei's guy." Jax yanked her up. "*Come on!*"

As they sprinted around the side of the cathedral, October stumbled and almost went down again. "Ah, *shit*," she cried, one hand on her knee.

He knew she had an old knee injury dating back to the same incident in Iraq that earned her a psycho discharge. "Here," he said, wrapping an arm around her waist. "Lean on me. Can you make it?"

She straightened, her jaw set hard. "I can make it."

Up ahead, a side door opened to disgorge two middle-aged women wearing heavy handknit sweaters and plastic rain caps over their coiffed gray heads. Jax yanked the door open wider and pushed October inside.

"*Ey! Prikratitye!*" bellowed a red-faced guard with a sagging belly and a walrus mustache. "This is an exit. You are not allowed to enter this way!"

"Sorry," October shouted back at him.

October limping badly, they pelted down the soaring nave of the cathedral, the guard blowing hard on his whistle. She glanced sideways at Jax. "What's the penalty for crashing a museum in Russia?"

"I don't know," said Jax. "But it can't be worse than getting shot."

They heard the door bang open behind them again, streaming natural light into the dim nave. The guard let out another bellow.

She threw a quick look over her shoulder and said, "Shit. It's him. What do we do now?"

Up ahead, a clutch of tourists choked the main door from the porch. "We mingle."

They slowed to a walk, shoving their way through the tight-knit group, eliciting stern frowns, disapproving hisses. Jax could hear the tour guide's stentorian voice saying in heavily accented English, "Over one hundred children sought refuge here, beneath the tower, on the second night the Allies bombed the city. The cathedral took a direct hit. All were killed."

As Jax pushed toward the tall arched entrance, the tourists—a bunch of British pensioners, from the looks of them—turned mulish, refusing to budge. He was aware of the Kawasaki rider skirting the edge of the group, positioning himself to close on Jax as he neared the top of the main entrance steps.

"Excuse me," said October, seizing a furled black umbrella from the hands of the pudgy, balding man beside her. "Can I borrow this?"

"I say," sputtered the tourist.

As the Kawasaki rider lunged forward, the muzzle of his suppressed pistol coming up toward Jax, October reached out to thrust the handle of the borrowed brollie between his legs. Hooking one ankle, she gave it a sharp yank.

The man staggered, hunching forward as he fought to regain his balance. But by then, October was close enough to aim a downward chop at his extended right wrist, followed by a snap kick that spun the man around and sent him stumbling backward to pitch down the short flight of steps to the pavement below.

Wheels clanging, a tram trundled up the cobbled street before the cathedral, its windows filled with curious faces pressing forward. A chorus of gasps and *tut-tuts* arose from the tour group as a flock of helping hands descended on the man sprawled at the base of the steps.

"Thank you," said October, restoring the umbrella to its rightful owner.

"Nice job," said Jax. He grabbed her hand. "We have a streetcar to catch."

Dashing down the steps, they leaped onto the back platform of the streetcar as it clattered past. On the pavement behind them, the Kawasaki rider struggled to his feet, still surrounded by a clucking, smothering horde of concerned British tourists, all talking at once.

"You okay?" Jax said, glancing at her.

She nodded, her breath coming hard and fast. The tram picked up speed, rattling over the bridge just as the cathedral clock began to chime the first notes of Beethoven's Symphony Number Five, the somber tones ringing out to drift across the river and down the mist-filled valley.

Rodriguez watched Clay Dixon swing his leg over the Kawasaki's seat, his hands clenching around the motorcycle's handlebars, his body rigid with rage and frustration as he stared at a rusty barge floating past on the river below.

Rodriguez walked over to stand beside him, his gaze on the pigeons swirling around the clock tower of the cathedral.

"You okay?"

Dixon hawked up a mouthful of bloody spittle and shot it at the gutter. "Fucking bitch. We should have hit them on the road when they were with the Russians."

"That would not have been wise." Rodriguez kept his gaze on the cathedral's red brick façade. "We can deal with this. There are two places our targets will logically go next: Baklanov's house in Rybachy, and the salvage company's office in Zelenogradsk. I'll send Lysenko and Saidov to Rybachy. You go to Zelenogradsk."

Dixon gunned the Kawasaki to life. "Fucking assholes. I want her. I want them both."

"I don't care who gets them, as long as we get them."

25

They rented a beat-up old Lada from a shady outfit in a grimy lane just off a wide avenue the Soviets had renamed Moskovsky. The white-haired, wizened Russian behind the counter insisted they pay cash in advance, but magnanimously threw in a free Cyrillic map of the province.

"It's a little out of date and not particularly accurate, but—" He broke off to toss a quick glance over his shoulder, then leaned in closer to add in a whisper, "Accurate maps are considered military secrets, so you might be in for a few surprises. Still, it's better than nothing." He hesitated. "Usually."

"This doesn't sound promising," said October, spreading the map open across the dashboard.

"Can you find Zelenogradsk and Rybachy, or are they still military secrets?"

"Here's Rybachy. It's on the Curonian Spit." She drew her finger along the thin bar of sand dunes that stretched from the Oblast to Lithuania and divided the Baltic Sea from the Curonian Lagoon. "I don't see Zelenogradsk."

"It must be around there somewhere." He turned the key, and on the third try managed to get the Lada to turn over.

He wrestled it into gear, and the car lurched forward. "We'll try Rybachy first."

Keeping one eye on the rearview mirror, he spent about ten minutes weaving in and out of city traffic, driving randomly around first one block, then the next.

"See anyone?" she asked, craning around to look back.

"No."

"Maybe there's no one else."

"Maybe," said Jax, unconvinced.

They drove through dark fallow fields and sodden bogs, the road a narrow tunnel between avenues of elms that met overhead and stretched on for miles and miles across the countryside. In another week or two the tree limbs would be bare, but now they were clothed in brilliant shades of yellow and rust that drifted softly down around them. Occasionally they'd see the broken spire of an abandoned church in the distance, or pass through villages of three to five houses huddled around the inevitable statue of Lenin. More often they found place-name signs whose villages were slowly disappearing.

"Why hasn't anyone ever heard about what happened here?" said October, staring at the crumbling ruins of a medieval church marooned in a plowed field.

"It didn't just happen in East Prussia, you know. The Allies massacred huge German-speaking populations in the provinces taken over by Poland and Czechoslovakia, too."

She turned to look at him. "How many people are we talking about?"

Jax shifted down to swing out around a lumbering farm wagon that nearly blocked the road ahead. "No one ever bothered to do an accurate, detailed reckoning, but the most unbiased estimates put the number of German-speaking civilians expelled from Eastern Europe at around sixteen million."

"Sixteen million people?"

"Give or take a few million." He swung back into the right lane. Glancing in the rearview mirror, he could see the plodding wagon, then the narrow road stretching out straight and empty behind them. "The lucky ones managed to make it across the new German borders. But a lot of the women and children were just herded into concentration camps and left to die of starvation and disease, or killed outright. And then there are the tens of thousands of Germans that the Russians sent to slave labor camps in Siberia. Only a handful of those survived to make it back to the West."

"How many?" she said softly. "How many died?"

He glanced over at her white, tightly held face. "No one knows for sure. A U.S. government study in the late forties put the number of dead at between two and three million—most of them women and children. And the very old, of course."

"I don't believe it," she said.

Jax blew out his breath in a long sigh. There had been some revisionist attempts to drastically lower the death figures. But most historians without a political agenda tended to agree that the original estimates were probably conservative. He said, "We all think we know what's true and what isn't. You think the U.S. could never have been complicit in something like this, while I think it's impossible for someone to sit in a room on a Naval base in New Orleans and somehow 'see' a Russian shipyard in her mind."

She was silent for a moment, watching a stork rise from its nest on the rafters of a ruined barn. "That's different."

"Is it?"

By the time they reached the coast, a brisk wind had blown away all but a few wisps of the low-hanging clouds that had made the morning so bleak. The sky that arched above them now was a vast, pastel blue reflected by the waters of the Curonian Lagoon to their right and the Baltic Sea to the north.

They followed a narrow road that cut through vast dunes ranging from thirty to sixty feet high. Most had been planted with pine forests in an effort to overcome the dunes' habit of swallowing entire villages. But some were still wind-sculpted, shifting mounds of bare golden sand.

They found the village of Rybachy just a few kilometers short of the Lithuanian border. Seagulls wheeled, screeching, above rows of wooden fishing boats rocking beside a pier that stretched far out into the waters of the lagoon. Nearby, the ruins of an old Teutonic Knights' castle stood guard over a few hundred houses, many of them still showing the carved wooden fronts of a different age and different inhabitants.

"There," said October, pointing to a white stucco house with a red tiled roof about halfway down a leafy street. "That's where Captain Baklanov's widow lives."

Jax pulled into the shelter of a spreading elm and killed the engine. The curtains at the house's windows were all tightly drawn, the neatly tended yard deserted.

"I wonder if she speaks English," said October, thrusting open her car door.

"Probably not. Why?"

A soft smile touched her features. "I was just trying to figure out how I'm supposed to let you do the talking if she only speaks Russian."

"Oh? Like you let me do the talking with Andrei?"

"I did."

"You didn't."

They walked up a brick path to the house's shallow front steps. Jax noticed her limp was getting better. She said, "What if she doesn't want to talk to us?"

"We tell her we're from her husband's insurance company. She'll talk to us."

October stopped in the middle of the walk. "But that's mean. What if Baklanov didn't have any insurance? We'd get her hopes up for nothing."

He groaned. "You have way too many scruples to work for the CIA. Tell her we're journalists from the AP doing a story."

"On what?"

"Crime? Modern pirates?" He rang the bell. "Make something up. It's what spies do, you know. We lie."

Heavy footsteps sounded on the other side of the door. "But—"

The door swung inward to reveal a stout woman with graying hair and a full, puffy face, her features blurred by grief. "Yes?" she said, her eyes narrowing with suspicion.

"Dobrih dyen," said October, giving the woman a wide smile. "Uhhh . . ." For a moment, she froze. Then she cleared her throat and said in her flawless Russian, "We're journalists with the Associated Press."

She chose the modern Baltic pirates angle. Jax's Russian was just good enough to enable him to follow most of what was being said. When Anna Baklanov turned her watery gray stare from Tobie to Jax, he slipped out his wallet and presented her with his press card.

While October stared at him in wide-eyed wonder, the captain's widow took the card between two fingers and scowled. He had no way of knowing if she could read it or not, but her jaw hardened and she started to close the door. "There's nothing I can tell you."

Jax stuck his foot in the rapidly closing gap and said to Tobie, "Tell her we'll pay."

October translated.

The widow sniffed. "I've no time for this. I'm on my way to stay with my mother-in-law."

"A thousand rubles," said Jax. In a province where over half the population made less than four thousand rubles a month, a thousand rubles was a lot of money. In the States, it would buy you a tank of gas.

Anna Baklanov sniffed again and opened the door.

She led them into a bizarrely furnished sitting room that looked more like Arabian Nights than Russian Revolution. Massive *mansaf* trays a meter wide, made of copper coated with tin, hung above olive wood chests inlaid with mother of pearl. There were scimitars from Turkey and Syria, daggers from Yemen and Saudi Arabia, colorful thick carpets from the land of the Hindu Kush. This was a side of Jasha Baklanov they hadn't been expecting. At the far end of the room, dominating it all, stood an easel proudly displaying a framed black-and-white photograph of a little girl with wild hair presenting President Brezhnev with a bouquet of white roses. If Jax squinted, he could see the ravaged remnants of that little girl in Anna Baklanov.

"I had the militia here two days ago," she said, fumbling with a pack of cigarettes. "Wanting to know who hired Jasha to raise that old U-boat. As if I knew."

October nodded sympathetically. "Jasha didn't talk about his business much, did he?"

"What man does talk about business when he comes home? Hmmm? That's why he comes home, to get away from business. Eat his dinner, drink his vodka." She paused to light her cigarette and drew hard. "You'd like some vodka?"

"No, thank you," said October.

Jax smiled, "One glass."

Anna Baklanov heaved to her feet and disappeared through a door.

October whispered, "I hate vodka."

"Russia runs on vodka. You'll never get her to talk if you don't drink with her."

The widow was back in a moment bearing a tray with three glasses, a bottle of vodka, and slices of dark bread. She filled their glasses to the brim.

"It must be tricky raising an old submarine," said October, taking her glass with care.

"Jasha was the best." Vodka in hand, Anna Baklanov leaned forward and lowered her voice. "He'd done it before, you know. Sold the sub itself for the steel, and auctioned everything from Kraut helmets to belt buckles and gas masks on eBay."

October took a sip of her vodka and choked. "Someone hired him for that?" she asked, her voice a raw rasp. "Or was it his own plan?"

"Of course it was his plan." Anna Baklanov upended her own glass and let the vodka slide down her throat in an easy motion that made Tobie's eyes widen. "He got the idea from something he read on the Internet, about the British salvaging the old German U-boats they sank off the coast of Ireland."

"Smart man," said October.

Jasha's widow nodded and fumbled for a handkerchief to blow her nose.

October said, "So he had experience raising World War II submarines. I suppose that's why these men came to him."

Anna Baklanov tucked her handkerchief out of sight, lit another cigarette, and nodded. "They'd heard about him."

"They were Russians?"

She shook her head. "Two of them spoke Russian, but they weren't Russian."

"Ah. Foreigners."

The widow filled their glasses again. "There's no point asking me where they were from because I don't know. Jasha was always secretive. Why, just last month he left on a trip for four days without telling me a thing. If I hadn't found the receipt from that Beirut restaurant in his pocket when I was washing his trousers, I'd never have known where he'd been."

October's hand jerked, nearly spilling her vodka. "He went to Lebanon?"

"He goes there a couple of times a year." The widow paused, then corrected herself. "Used to go."

"Do you still have the receipt?"

"For the restaurant? No. Why?"

"Do you remember the name?"

"No." She polished off another vodka and sniffed. "Poor Jasha. The militia keeps refusing to release his body to me. Can you imagine? They haven't let any of the families see the bodies."

Jax thought about the condition of the bodies he'd seen in those big glossy militia photographs, and figured that was probably a good thing.

Anna Baklanov dabbed the pad of one finger at the corner of each eye. "It's so hard on Jasha's poor old mother, losing the two of them."

"The two of them?"

She nodded. "Jasha's nephew was on the *Yalena* with him, you know. Jasha'd been like a father to the boy, ever since his brother died. And now Stefan's dead, too."

"I'm so sorry," said October. "I had no idea."

Lurching to her feet, the widow reached for a snapshot in a cheap brass frame that rested with a collection of others atop a nearby piano. "This was taken last year," she said, holding it out.

"But he's so young," said October, holding the picture in both hands.

Peering over her shoulder, Jax found himself staring at a skinny, dark-haired boy of maybe fourteen or fifteen. The picture was taken on a rocky beach on a cold, overcast day, the sea a sullen gray in the background. But the boy was rosy-cheeked and laughing, with one arm thrown affectionately around the shoulders of the big shaggy mutt panting happily beside him.

"Nice dog," said Jax.

Anna Baklanov sniffed. "Stefan's father got him for Stefan when the boy was just a little thing. Broke the poor boy's heart when the dog died, not more'n a month after this picture was taken."

She took the photograph back and stared at it soulfully before carefully returning it to its place on the piano. "He could sing like an angel, you know. Sang in the church choir from the time he was small. Jasha used to say it made him weak, like his father. But then, Jasha had no use for the church. Russia might not be Communist anymore, but Jasha was a member of the Party until the day he died."

Jax lifted his vodka in a silent toast. To Jasha Baklanov. Smuggler. Thief. Proud Party member. He had the glass halfway to his lips when a thought occurred to him. "How old was the boy?" he asked in his fractured Russian.

He obviously got it wrong because Anna Baklanov's bleary eyes squinted into a frown. "Excuse me?"

October repeated the question for him.

Anna Baklanov blew a stream of blue smoke out her nostrils. "Just sixteen."

They wavered back to the car in a haze of vodka fumes.

"What are you doing with a press card?" said October.

Jax frowned at two big Kawasakis parked at the end of the lane. "It comes in handy sometimes."

She was silent for a moment. "Funny, I never thought about it, before."

"About what?"

"How much spies lie."

He gave a sharp laugh. "Don't like it, do you? See, there are some advantages to letting me do the talking."

"When you know the language."

"When I know the language," he agreed, his attention drawn again to the men at the end of the block. Both riders had the visors on their helmets down. He could hear the motorcycles' powerful roar as they revved their engines impatiently.

She said, "It's sad about the boy."

"Baklanov's nephew? Maybe more curious than sad." Jax opened the door for her. "I looked at the photographs of every man killed on that salvage ship. I could be wrong, but I didn't see anyone who looked like young Stefan. In fact, I'd say none of those men was under twenty-five."

Closing her door, he went to slip behind the wheel, aware of the Kawasakis pulling away from the curb. He thrust the key in the ignition and listened to the old Lada grind painfully over and over again without catching.

"Shit," he whispered under his breath.

"What's the matter?"

He threw a quick glance in the rearview mirror. "See those two motorcycles behind us? I think we're in trouble."

26

The Lada coughed. Caught.

Jax threw the old car into gear and stepped on the gas as the motorcyclists came up behind them. October skewed around in her seat to watch them out the back window. The Kawasakis were nearly identical, one dark blue, the other black.

"I don't get it," she said. "What are they doing?"

"At the moment, they're just following us. It's when we get out of town we'll need to worry."

She cast a quick glance around at the dwindling houses. "This is a very small town."

"I'd noticed."

Leaving the last straggling houses behind, they cut through wild dunes of soaring sand that disappeared beneath a thickly planted pine grove. But beyond the trees the sandy dunes reemerged, untamed and windblown. Deserted.

"Shit," said Jax as the leather-jacketed men gunned their engines, roaring right up on his ass. He already had the accelerator floored.

"Why are they getting so close?" she shouted over the whine of the engines.

He tightened his grip on the steering wheel as the bumps and dips on the pavement bounced the old car wildly from side to side. "Because this road's so bad, they're going to need to get close to get a good shot at us." Glancing in the rearview mirror, he saw one of the riders reach beneath his coat. He jerked the steering wheel violently to the left and yelled, "Get down!"

The rear windshield shattered in a rain of glass.

Tires squealing, he spun the wheel to the right again, careening back and forth across the centerline to keep the motorcyclists from getting a steady shot. He heard a ping, then another as bullets buried into the Lada's metal frame.

"*Sonofabitch*," he swore. "Brace yourself!"

He stood on the brakes. The Lada's backend broke loose, sending the heavy car into a sideways skid that filled the air with the screech of tires and the stench of burning rubber.

Too close to stop, the thug on the blue motorcycle jerked to the right, laying down a line of black rubber as he shot off the side of the road to crash head-on into a massive pine tree. They heard a whooshing explosion, and rider and bike disappeared in a ball of fire.

The black biker's reactions were a split second slower. Hitting his brakes, he slammed into the Lada's left rear fender with a tearing shriek of metal and a jarring thump that reverberated through the heavy old car. And then he was airborne, a black leather blur that sailed over the Lada's trunk to land in a sprawling skid that carried him far down the old blacktopped road and ripped off his helmet. When he finally slid to a halt, he didn't move.

"Oh, my God," whispered October.

Jax was out of the car almost before it stopped. The air was thick with the black smoke from the burning bike down the road. A sickly sweet stench of charred flesh mingled with the smell of the pines and the briny breeze blowing in off the sea.

Crouching down, he stared into the second cyclist's wide, unseeing eyes. He glanced up and down the narrow deserted road and pushed to his feet. Walking back to the Lada, he straightened the rear fender enough to be sure the wheel would turn. Then he got back in the car, threw it into gear, and hit the gas.

They drove on in silence, the Baltic a sun-struck shimmer of endless water on their right. Finally, Jax glanced over at October and said, "You all right?"

She pushed the loose hair out of her face with a hand that wasn't quite steady. "Yeah."

She was quiet for another moment, then said, "Someone seems to be pretty serious about making sure we're dead. How can you be so positive it isn't your buddy Andrei?"

"Andrei is not my buddy. But if he wanted us dead, he'd do it quietly, in a basement, or an abandoned quarry somewhere, with a single shot to the back of the head. He wouldn't send someone to hit us in the middle of the city or ambush us out on an open road."

"So who are these guys?"

"Someone who thinks we're getting too close for comfort."

"You're kidding, right? We don't know jack shit."

"Yeah. But they don't know we don't know jack shit."

She put her head down between her knees. After a moment, she said, "Do you ever rent a car without wrecking it?"

They found the town of Zelenogradsk near the tip of the Sambian Peninsula, where the dunes of the spit just began to rise. It wasn't on the map, and they'd driven right past it on their way to Rybachy.

"I don't see how an entire town can be a military secret," said Tobie as they rolled down weed-choked streets nearly empty except for the inevitable stalls selling amber. "The map makers must have left it off by mistake."

Once a thriving resort, Zelenogradsk did not appear to have fared as well under the Soviets as Rybachy. Most of its elegant, prewar seaside villas had been reduced to rubble by the fighting of 1945, while the few old houses that remained were largely abandoned and covered in moss.

"I don't know," said Jax. "I think I'd be tempted to keep this place a secret, too."

Jasha Baklanov's office lay on the second floor of a seedy, two-story Soviet-era concrete block a few hundred feet from the water. Leaving the car parked in the rubbish-strewn square out front, they entered the open street door and climbed a set of dirty concrete steps to a frigid second-floor hall lined with rows of battered slab doors. A small, chipped sign on the door at the end of the hall read BAKLANOV SALVAGE.

"Why did he need an office?" she whispered, hugging herself against the chill of the concrete building. "A small-time operator like this?"

Slipping a silver pen from his pocket, Jax quickly disassembled it into a set of picks and eased a slim tension wrench into the lower portion of the keyhole. Applying a light torque to the wrench, he thrust a pick into the top of the keyhole, his eyes closing with concentration as he deftly eased each pin out of the way. There was a faint click, then the cylinder turned and the door opened. "I suspect the people our Jasha was doing business with weren't exactly the type he wanted visiting his family."

Tobie watched him pack away the lock-pick set. "They teach you to do that in spy school?"

"Yes." He put a hand on the door and pushed it inward.

The hinges squealed in protest. A single, uncurtained dirt-encrusted window on the far wall let in just enough light to show them a square cubbyhole sparsely furnished with a desk, a table with a couple of chairs, and a battered filing cabinet that looked as if it had been salvaged from an old ship. A chessboard, a half-empty bottle of vodka, and a couple of glasses littered the tabletop. But the chess pieces had been knocked into disarray; a glass lay on the floor, shattered. The drawers of the filing cabinet and desk hung open, their contents spilling out onto the floor.

"Looks like whoever hit the *Yalena* beat us here," said Jax, quietly closing the door behind him.

"How do you know it wasn't the militia?"

"Because the militia would have taken the vodka."

"Ah." She reached to turn on the light, but he put out a hand, stopping her. "Better not."

Her gaze met his, and she nodded.

While she started on the files, he went to hunker down beside the shattered drawers of the desk. After ten minutes of searching, she let out an exasperated sigh. "If there ever was anything here to find," she said, picking up another handful of scattered papers, "it's gone. You know that, don't you?"

But all he said was, "Just watch out for broken glass."

They worked in a tense silence punctuated by the rustle of paper, the thump of furniture being righted. She was gathering up the last of the scattered files when she found a half-spilled box of business cards, printed on cheap stock. They looked new.

She pulled one out and held it up to the fading light.

BAKLANOV SALVAGE
Baltiskaya 23b
Telephone: 7-4112-21352
Fax: 7-4112-31698

She started to put the card back, then stopped to look around. "Do you see a phone?"

"There isn't one," said Jax, nodding to the fax machine that sat at a drunken angle on the edge of the desk. "Looks like he just had a dedicated fax line."

"Who has a fax these days?"

"People who do business with the Third World."

"But if he only had a fax, then why is there a telephone number on his business card?"

"Let me see that." Reaching out, Jax took the card between his thumb and forefinger. "It's a cell phone." He gave her a grin. "See. You did find something."

"This is good?" Tobie pushed to her feet. "Why is this good?"

"Because even as we speak, the geeks at the NSA are busy snooping on the telecommunications of the world. We like to think we're the only ones doing it, but the truth is, every country with a good tax base does it, too."

She took the card back and stuck it in her bag. "Which means?"

"Which means, now that we know Baklanov's cell phone number, Matt ought to be able to pull his records." He glanced toward the patch of smudged sky visible through the window. In the fifteen minutes they'd been in the office, the sky had grown significantly darker.

"It's getting late," said Tobie, following his gaze.

"No shit. We've got just enough time to make it back to the cathedral before Andrei turns us into pumpkins."

It was when they were backing out the door that Tobie noticed the sheet of paper that had slipped beneath the desk, one small white corner protruding from the edge.

"What's that?" Jax asked as she reached over to pick it up.

"It's a fax. And oh, look; you're in luck. It's in English."

"Very funny," he said, pulling the door shut behind them. "When was it sent?"

She frowned. "According to the dateline, it came through less than an hour ago. From somebody named Kemal Erkan. In Turkey."

"Turkey? Let me see that."

He scanned it quickly, then grunted. "Listen to this. 'Been trying to reach you for two days now. Have buyer lined up for steel from U-boat. Great price. Let me know when to expect arrival.'"

"Nothing ominous-sounding about that," she said. She was walking ahead of him and had almost reached the stairs when she felt the hairs rise on the back of her neck, and slowed.

"What is it?" said Jax, just as a black-leather-gloved hand appeared around the corner from the stairwell with a Glock 17 held in a professional grip.

She lunged forward, grabbing the unseen assailant's wrist with both hands to yank the gun up just as he fired off three suppressed shots in quick succession.

Sounding like muffled pops, the percussions filled the narrow hall with the stench of burnt powder and a film of blue smoke, and knocked chunks of plaster off the dingy walls. The man let out a roar of rage, swinging around to knee her, hard, in the small of her back. She went down on all fours.

The black-jacketed motorcyclist was pivoting toward her, the Glock leveled at her head when Jax's fist caught him under the chin, snapping his head back. Jax pounded him again and again, knocking the Glock flying and sending him stumbling backward toward the top of the stairs.

"You sonofabitch," said Jax, landing a roundhouse kick that caught the assassin just above the ear. He wavered a moment, then tumbled back, falling heavily against the wall before pitching awkwardly down the rest of the concrete steps.

"That guy needs to learn to stay away from stairs," said Jax, breathing heavily. He swung back to Tobie. "You all right?"

"Yeah. Just winded," she said, wincing slightly as she tried to straighten.

Picking up the Glock, Jax went to stand at the top of the steps and brought the knuckles of his right fist to his mouth. "The sonofabitch," he said again. "I hope this time he broke his neck."

Andrei Gorchakove's voice drifted up to them from the bottom of the stairwell. "From the looks of things, I'd say he did."

27

"How did he find us here?" whispered October.

Jax threw her a warning frown and shook his head. "Just let me do the talking, okay?"

"I don't know what it is you're always so afraid I'm going to say," she hissed as they walked down the stairs to where Andrei stood leaning against the grimy concrete wall, the dead man at his feet.

At their approach, Andrei reached inside his jacket and came up with a half-empty pack of cigarettes. "Must you always leave a trail of bodies wherever you go, Jax?"

"Body. One body."

"What about the two motorcyclists the militia found on the road from Rybachy?"

"Motorcyclists?"

"The ones who shot up your Lada."

"Ah. Those guys." Jax hunkered down to study the dead man's ruddy-cheeked face. Wide and sightless blue eyes stared up from beneath straight, sandy-colored brows. It was the motorcyclist from the cathedral.

Andrei stuck a cigarette between his lips. "Ever see him before?"

"No," lied Jax, pushing to his feet. "Any idea who he is?"

"You tell me. He's not carrying ID, but I checked the labels on his clothes. They're American. If this is one of your terrorists, Jax, I'd say Washington needs to rethink some of their suppositions about what's going to happen come Halloween."

Jax stared beyond Andrei, to where the blue-and-white militia van waited, its Tatar driver beside it, beefy arms crossed at his chest. "I must be losing my touch. I'd swear I wasn't being followed. Either by you or" —he jerked his head toward the dead motorcyclist sprawled at their feet— "by him."

Faintly smiling, Andrei pushed away from the wall to saunter outside. He reached beneath the Lada's right front fender to come up with a small black box with an antenna.

"Shit," said Jax. "How did that get there?"

"After I dropped you at the cathedral, I had every car rental agency in the area notified that you might be coming. They were told to give you the 'special.' "

"It's nice to be predictable."

Andrei struck his lighter, his eyes narrowing against the cigarette's harsh blue smoke. "Did you find anything?"

"Not really."

Andrei nodded to his driver. "You won't mind if we verify that?"

The Tatar patted down Jax's pockets and drew out the fax from Turkey. "Well, there was that," said Jax.

His jaw silently bunching and flexing, the Tatar grasped October's bag and upended its contents across the hood of the Lada.

While Attila pawed through her iPod, passport wallet, lip balm, and sunglasses case, October said, "The tracking device explains how you found us." She jerked her head toward the dead man in the stairwell. "But what about him?"

"Perhaps he was here waiting for you." Andrei took one last drag, then dropped his half-smoked cigarette to grind it beneath the sole of his boot. "Come. You have a plane to catch."

"Are you done with my bag?" said October. When Andrei nodded, she scooped up her things and shoved them back inside.

No one had even glanced at Jasha Baklanov's business card.

Jax stared out the wide plate-glass window at the darkened runway below. The window was filthy, streaked with water marks on the outside and smeared by children's sticky fingers on the inside. Andrei had personally escorted them to the departure section of Kaliningrad's decrepit airport, and he didn't seem to be going anytime soon. Jax had been reduced to calling Matt from the men's room to ask him to look up a guy named Kemal Erkan in Turkey, and to pull Baklanov's cell phone records.

Standing now beside Jax, the Russian lit another cigarette and blew out a long stream of smoke, his gaze on October. "So tell me about the woman," he said quietly.

Jax cast a glance at where she sat on one of the departure lounge's hard chairs, her head bent over a Chinese textbook. "What about her?"

"She's pretty, but she doesn't seem like your type."

"What's my type?"

"Tall, long-legged. Very high maintenance."

Jax gave a short laugh. "We're just working together."

"I thought you liked to work alone?"

"I do."

Andrei's eyes narrowed with amusement as he drew on his cigarette. "We might get further if we cooperated on this, you know."

"I am cooperating."

"You just forgot about the fax in your pocket, did you?"

Jax kept his gaze on the runway, where a plane was slowly

taxiing in, its landing lights winking out of the darkness. "According to Anna Baklanov, the captain's sixteen-year-old nephew was supposed to be on the *Yalena*. But I don't remember seeing a boy in the militia photos of the dead crew."

Andrei frowned. "You think the boy was cooperating with the terrorists?"

"I suppose it's possible, but I doubt it. According to his widow, the captain was like a father to the boy."

"The killers could have thrown his body overboard."

"True. But, why him?"

"Maybe he went over the rail when he was shot." Andrei ground out his cigarette. "Why are you so interested in this boy?"

"If he's alive . . ."

"He's not alive."

There was a stirring amongst the assembled passengers as a uniformed woman appeared at the gate. "You're in luck," said Andrei. "Only an hour late."

He stood for a moment watching Jax shoulder his carry-on bag. Then he said, "You're going too easily, Jax. I think you found something else—something you're not telling me. What happened to détente? Glasnost? International cooperation and the New World Order?"

"I don't know anything you don't know."

Andrei glanced at October. "Are you kidding? I still don't know why she's here. Her Russian is better than yours, yes. But yours isn't as bad as you like to pretend. So why is she with you?"

October shoved her textbook in her bag and stood up. "His Russian is terrible."

"See?" Jax nudged her toward the gate. "Go."

"I will find out, you know," Andrei shouted as they started down the ramp. "This is what's wrong with the world today. You Americans, you all think you're still cowboys."

Later that night, Rodriguez stood in the backyard of the old German house in the exclusive enclave in Mendeleevo, his legs splayed wide, his thumbs hooked in his hip pockets, his head tipped back as he watched a wind-whipped stream of clouds scuttle across the cold face of the full moon.

In the last twenty-four hours, he'd lost four men—three dead, one missing. He didn't care about the Russians; they were expendable. Cannon fodder. But Dixon was a good kid. An American. He had a wife back home in Arkansas and a baby girl just two months old. That was tough.

He heard the back door of the house open and footsteps cross the terrace. He was aware of Salinger coming to stand beside him, but he didn't turn. "Any word yet from Borz on the little shit?"

"Not yet," said Salinger. He hesitated. "We just got a confirmation from our contact in Turkey. They have someone to make the hit on Kemal Erkan."

"Good." They had no way of knowing how much Baklanov might have told the Turk, but Rodriguez wasn't taking any chances. He glanced at the man beside him. "We need that guy shut up, and we need him shut up fast. How much do they want?"

"The usual."

"Tell them to move. I want Erkan dead by this time tomorrow."

The night had turned so cold they could see the exhalation of their breath hanging like a white fog in the darkness. Salinger still hesitated. Rodriguez said, "What is it?"

"According to our contact at Aeroflot, Alexander and the Guinness woman were on the last flight to Berlin. The General's not going to be happy we missed them."

Rodriguez pressed his lips into a thin line and said nothing.

Salinger said, "You think they found anything?"

"Nothing that's going to do them any good."

Salinger nodded. "When do we leave here?"

"When we get the kid," said Rodriguez, and headed for the back steps.

28

The call from Rodriguez came through when Gerald T. Boyd was
in his room at the Willard, sipping a glass of Jack Daniel's
and reading over his notes for the testimony he'd be giving
to Congress over the next few days.

He listened to the mercenary's report in a tight silence,
then said, "You fucked up," his voice as sharp and lethal as
a wire twisted around a man's throat.

"Yes, sir. The targets are on their way to Berlin. I can leave
my men to finish up here and go after them myself."

"Negative. You focus on getting this fucking kid. I need
you back stateside by Friday."

"I'll be there, sir."

"Don't disappoint me again, Carlos."

"I won't, sir."

Boyd sat for a time, the satellite phone clutched in one
tight fist. Then he put in a call to Lee.

"The representative from Washington is moving. If he's
not headed back here, I want to know where he's going."

There was a tense silence. "That information won't be easy to obtain, sir."

"I didn't ask for an evaluation of the assignment's level of difficulty, Colonel. I'll expect your report first thing tomorrow morning."

"Yes, sir."

Grand Case, St. Martin: Monday 26 October 3:15 P.M. *local time*

James Walker strolled through the shadowy, echoing house, throwing open one set of French doors after the other to let the warm Caribbean breeze sweep through the big high-ceilinged rooms.

Walker believed in fresh air. Fresh air, fresh fruits and vegetables, and lots of regular exercise. Let the rest of the world pop the pills that earned Walker Pharmaceuticals billions. Walker himself had long ago learned the real secret to health and longevity, and it couldn't be put in a gelcap.

He'd bought the estate on the outskirts of Grand Case, St. Martin, at the urging of his ex-wife, Catherine. But over the years he'd discovered a fondness for sun and blue skies and palm trees that would have shocked his dour New England forebears. When he finally decided marriage to Catherine was more trouble than it was worth, he'd insisted on keeping the St. Martin house, along with the houses in Miami and St. Tropez. She'd have given him anything, as long as Walker let her keep her precious daughter. Walker saw his daughter at Christmas and for two weeks in the summer, which was more than enough for both of them.

Lately, though, he'd been thinking about redoing the house in St. Martin. The place had far too much in common with his villa on South Beach: terra-cotta floors, white sailcloth-covered sofas, arcaded galleries framing achingly blue water. The architecture had seemed elegant and sophisticated when Catherine first found the place fifteen years ago. But with the proliferation of millionaires in recent years, Italianate villas had become so . . . common.

At one point, he'd considered building something new, something in the local style of the island, with carvings and fretwork like the old houses down in Grand Case. But no one knew better than Walker that the next few years would not be a good time to invest in expensive properties. An extraordinary number of luxury homes were about to be thrown onto the market. And there were going to be a lot less people alive to buy them.

In the end, the world would be a better place. No more endless Middle East crises. No more suicide bombers. No more money-grubbing Jews, siphoning off billions in foreign aid, competing with American arms manufacturers, and wrecking havoc on the world financial scene. But Walker was, at heart, a businessman, and he had no doubt that the coming events were going to shake the world economy. Like any good businessman, he'd been reviewing his portfolio, making adjustments to certain key stock holdings. His financial advisors found these changes baffling, now. But in the days to come his actions would be seen as fortuitous. The world was about to change drastically, and Walker had given considerable thought to how a man could capitalize on those changes. It was as if he had been given a crystal ball in which he could see the future. Only a fool would fail to act on that knowledge.

Pouring himself a tall glass of liquefied wheatgrass sweetened with apple juice, he wandered out onto the gallery overlooking the sun-struck sea below and put in a call to Boyd.

"I just got the report from my lab guys," said Walker, settling into an upholstered bamboo chair framed by a garden of wind-ruffled palms and dark tropical foliage.

Boyd's voice was a low growl. "And?"

Walker let the moment draw out, enjoying the suspense. He took a sip of his juice. "The shipment was still 60 percent viable."

"That's good."

"Good?" Their best-case scenarios had been 40 percent. "It's great."

"When will it be ready?"

"We should be able to sail with it Wednesday morning." They were transporting the shipment to the mainland on Walker's private yacht. "We'll make Miami by Friday."

There was a pause. Boyd said, "It's come to my attention you've been making some unusual financial transactions."

Walker sat forward. *How the hell had Boyd found out about that?*

"This isn't about money, Walker. It's about doing what has to be done to save this country."

Walker let his head fall back, his eyes squeezing shut as he enjoyed a moment of quiet amusement. The General Boyds of this world never could seem to grasp the fact that, in the end, everything always came down to money. *Of course* this was about money—money that should be going to education, to rebuilding America's crumbling roads and collapsing bridges, to fixing a medical system that was a disgrace to the Western world. The country was flushing itself down the toilet, wasting billions and billions of dollars every month for—what? To wipe the noses of a bunch of ungrateful ragheads in Afghanistan and Iraq? To prop up Israel? And why? Because that pissant little country was strategic to American interests? Hardly. Walker supposed there were some people who might actually believe that. Much easier to swallow the standard line than to admit that certain individuals with divided loyalties had grown so powerful that they had every politician in America falling all over themselves to kiss their asses—while all the gullible, Armageddon-obsessed Christians just stood around singing hallelujah and waiting for the Rapture. Walker had learned a long time ago that the world revolved around money. It was only dinosaurs like Boyd who thought life was about honor, and loyalty, and service.

"Don't worry," said Walker. "No one's going to notice."

"Someone might see a pattern."

"You mean, like the interesting financial transactions that occurred right before 9/11?" Walker took another sip of his juice. "So some conspiracy nut notices and puts up an Internet site. So what? Americans only believe in conspiracies if they're hatched in a cave in Afghanistan. If you were smart, you'd make some adjustments of your own."

"I will not profit from what is about to happen."

"Well, I'll tell you what: I'm sure as hell not going to suffer because of it."

"If you jeopardize the mission—"

"I'm not jeopardizing anything. I'm just recouping my costs." *With a little extra*, Walker thought. He let his gaze linger on the stretch of turquoise water before him and felt its calming influence. "Relax, Boyd. Things are going better than we ever expected. In less than a week, it will all be over."

"Really? I'd say that by this time next week, it will have only just begun."

29

The flight from Kaliningrad to Berlin smelled of raw onions and vodka and hot, closely pressed bodies. Tobie leaned back in her seat and closed her eyes, but she was too exhausted and jittery to sleep.

Jax passed out before the flight even pushed back from the terminal.

Watching him sleep, she knew a welling of frustration that only seemed to grow with each passing minute. In less than a week, an unknown group of terrorists would launch a deadly attack on the United States. She had successfully located the U-boat the men had salvaged. But the true nature of its cargo had turned into an enigma, while the identity of the terrorists themselves remained a mystery.

No one knew better than Tobie the limits of remote viewing. Anything she tried to view from here on out could be dangerously influenced by what she already knew about the case. And tasking herself was always tricky. Without the protocol of an official viewing in place, no one in the intelligence community would give credence to anything she "saw." But she had to try.

Taking a deep breath, then another, she willed herself to relax, sinking slowly down into her Zone. Her target was a person: the leader of the force that attacked the *Yalena* Saturday morning and killed its crew. Her target time: now.

The first images were, as always, indistinct. She saw a man. Dark hair. Dark skin. A flat nose. Full lips. Dark jeans. A heavy pullover sweater. She could feel the anger seething within him, combined with a lethal determination that sent a chill down her spine.

She pulled back from him, trying to get a sense of place. She was aware of the pinch of cold. Smelled damp earth and wet leaves. He stood outdoors, in the country, perhaps, or in a garden. In the darkness, trees and bushes were all reduced to indistinct shadows buffeted by the wind.

Pulling back further, she saw the faint glow of a lamp spilling through an uncurtained window. The sulfurous haze of a streetlight shining on wet pavement. A city, but not a crowded city.

What city?

Patiently, she returned to the man standing in the shadowy garden. The house behind him began to come into focus. High gables. Jutting dormers. Steep roof. Mullioned windows. A large house, well cared for, yet quiet.

She shifted her perspective to the street, the images of the neighboring houses becoming increasingly cleaner, stronger. If she were ever to find herself on this street, she would recognize it in an instant. But when she tried to move beyond the darkened houses, to the city itself, her impressions became less distinct and dangerously susceptible to "overlay" by her imagination.

With a sigh, she opened her eyes to stare out the plane's

small window at the darkness beyond. She felt the vibrations of the jet's engines thrumming through her, and she knew it again, that sense of frustration combined now with a growing urgency. She had seen the man they sought; she was sure of it. She had felt his anger and his dark purposefulness. But who was he?

And *where* was he?

It wasn't until their flight hit the runway, bounced, then rattled to a shuttering halt that Jax opened his eyes.

She said, "How do you do that?"

He glanced over at her and yawned. "What? Sleep? Practice."

"I'm beginning to think I might kill for a bed and a shower."

"You should be able to get both at the station."

"The station? What station?"

He got that look on his face, the one he always got whenever she reminded him just how little she knew about espionage or the world of spycraft. "The CIA station at the embassy. Every embassy has one. They'll probably debrief you there before sending you back to the States."

She paused in the act of leaning over to pick up her carryon bag and straightened slowly. "The States? But . . . I thought we were going to follow up on Baklanov's contacts in the Middle East."

"No. I'm following up on Baklanov's contacts in the Middle East. Your role in this assignment is over."

She felt a pulse of anger throb through her, making her fingers tingle and her face grow hot. She said, "Why? The U-boat was in Kaliningrad, just like I said it would be."

"And what did you see in Turkey?"

She looked at him blankly. "I didn't see anything in Turkey."

He unbuckled his seatbelt and stood. "Exactly. The woo-woo part of this mission is over." He didn't say it, but she knew what he was thinking: *Thank God.*

She followed him down the narrow, crowded aisle. "You're going to *Turkey*?"

"Yes."

"But . . . why?"

"Because Kemal Erkan is in Turkey."

"But Erkan was interested in buying the submarine, not the cargo; I think we should go to Lebanon. That's where Baklanov was planning to sell the cargo."

He glanced back at her over his shoulder. "Did you see that in your crystal ball, too?"

"I don't have a crystal ball and you know it." She waited, but when he still didn't say anything, she said, "I vote we go to Lebanon."

He went to stand in one of the long immigration lines. "This isn't a democracy. I'm going to Turkey. And you're going to New Orleans."

They'd just cleared Customs and were pushing their way through the crowd waiting outside the wide double doors when a female voice with a pronounced Bronx twang said, "You can stop right there."

Tobie turned to find a stocky woman with short-cropped dark hair descending on them, a manila envelope clutched against her brown pantsuit jacket.

"Why, Petra," said Jax with a smile that didn't exactly ooze charm and good cheer. "You didn't need to put yourself to the trouble of meeting us."

The woman's dark brown eyes narrowed down into hostile glints. "Believe me, meeting you is a lot less trouble than cleaning up after you." She slapped the manila envelope against his chest. "This is for you. Don't even think about leaving the airport. You're both booked on the red-eye flight to Izmir."

"*Both* of us?"

"Both of you."

Tobie poked him in the ribs with her elbow. He ignored her.

Petra said, "You got a report from Division Thirteen headquarters. It's in the envelope with your e-tickets."

Jax's hand tightened around the envelope. "You're very efficient. Thank you, Petra."

Her frown darkened. "You haven't asked, but I'm going to tell you anyway: we cleaned up your little mess."

Tobie looked from one to the other. "What mess?"

For the first time, Petra's gaze shifted to her. "What mess? He was in Berlin less than eighteen hours and he still managed to find the time to kill someone."

Tobie blinked.

Jax said, "Did you ever find out who the guy was?"

"No." Petra turned to leave. "The tickets to Izmir are one-way. Make sure that however you come back, it's not through Berlin."

"Thanks, Petra. You're a champ."

She spun back to face him. "Catalano. My name is Rita Catalano."

Jax gave her a smile that showed his teeth. "You'll always be Petra to me."

"You're gloating again," he said as they pushed their way into the waiting area for the flight to Izmir.

"I'm not gloating."

"You're gloating."

Tobie allowed her smile to spread a little wider. "Okay. Maybe just a little." She dropped her voice and threw a quick look around. "You didn't tell me you killed someone in Berlin on your way to Kaliningrad. Who was it?"

"Some jerk with a big nose and a gun he intended to use on me."

"You think he's connected to our friends on the Kawa-sakis?"

"Probably."

"But . . . how did they know you were going to be in Berlin?"

"That's the troublesome part. I was only in Berlin because my Aeroflot connection was canceled. And the Company made my hotel reservations."

Tobie was silent a moment, considering this. "You think that CIA woman had something to do with it? Is that why you were kinda funny with her?"

"Petra? Nah. She's just a pain in the ass."

They found a couple of seats squeezed in between a wall and a green-eyed woman, dressed in dark slacks, a tunic, and a headscarf, who was nursing a toddler on her lap. Jax opened Petra's envelope and pulled out the report from Matt.

Tobie peered over his shoulder. "What's all that?"

He thumbed through the pages. "Matt checked with Interpol. Oh, look. Surprise, surprise: Baklanov Salvage seems to have been involved in low-level smuggling."

"Let me guess. Cigarettes and vodka?"

"You got it. But that's not all. There's also strong suspicion that our friend Jasha was into gunrunning."

"To Lebanon?"

"Right again."

"See. I keep telling you we should be going to Lebanon."

"Did the guy on the Kawasaki look Lebanese to you?"

"No. But he didn't look Turkish, either."

Jax flipped to another printout, this one with columns of phone numbers. Some of the numbers had names associated with them, but most were only identified by location—if that.

"Those are Jasha's cell phone records?" she said, eying them.

He nodded. "The last three months' worth. Looks like this guy was in contact with people in Beirut, Spain, Florida, Finland . . . a real international businessman." He ran his finger down the list. "Here's our friend Kemal Erkan. He lives in some place named Aliaga, wherever that is. In the last two days, he's called Jasha six times."

"Aliaga is just north of Izmir."

He looked up at her. "How did you know that?"

She glanced away, to where a steady stream of passengers was unloading through a nearby gate. "My dad was stationed at Izmir when I was a kid."

"So you speak Turkish?"

"Yes. Do you?"

When he said nothing, she leaned in close to say, "I guess it's a good thing you're going to have me along after all, isn't it? So I can do all the talking."

"Don't let it go to your head." He flipped to the transcript of Erkan's voice-mail messages. "Ah. It's all coming together. This guy Kemal Erkan owns a shipbreakers yard."

"A what?"

"A shipbreakers yard. They tear old ships apart for scrap. It can be done right, with good environmental controls and safety procedures for the workers. But doing it right is expensive, so most companies sell their aging ships to countries like India or China. They cut the ships apart right on the beach and just burn or dump whatever they can't sell."

Tobie rubbed the bridge of her nose between one thumb and forefinger. "I'm confused."

The toddler next to them began to cry, its face screwed up in a wail of exhaustion. The mother stood, jiggling him up and down as she walked him back and forth.

Jax said softly, "I have a hunch our mysterious friends heard Baklanov Salvage had experience raising old World War II-era submarines, and hired Jasha to raise U–114. Only,

Jasha got greedy. He decided he could make more money selling the sub to Turkey for the steel and hawking its cargo on the black market . . . and on eBay, of course."

"So they killed him?"

"And took whatever it was they wanted from the sub."

"Which may or may not have been gold."

"Which probably was not gold." Jax thumbed back through Baklanov's cell records and sucked in a hissing breath.

"What is it?" she said.

He pointed to the last two entries on the list. "Look at this. Someone accessed Baklanov's voice mail on Sunday morning, then again this afternoon."

"I don't get it. Baklanov was killed early Saturday morning. How is that possible?"

"Easy. You kill a man. You take his cell phone. And then you check his cell records to see who he's been calling."

"And who is calling him." Tobie watched the woman in the headscarf swing her son up to her shoulder and pat him softly on the back. "I think Mr. Kemal Erkan might be in trouble," she said.

"No shit."

30

Early the next morning, Stefan was crouched down on his hands and knees, digging for carrots in an overgrown field near the half-collapsed barn where he'd spent the night, when the dog came to him.

Black and tan, with floppy ears and a waggy tail, it looked like some kind of a shepherd mix, half grown and skinny. Panting hopefully, it leaned against Stefan's legs and looked up at him with softly pleading brown eyes.

"Go away," said Stefan, throwing a frightened glance about. "Go home."

But all the villages and farms around here were deserted, inhabited only by storks and ghosts. The dog whined, its head dipping.

Stefan reached out a tentative hand to scratch behind the pup's ears. It flopped down beside him, its tongue flicking out to lick his wrist.

He ran his hands down the dog's bony sides and flanks.

"What's the matter, boy? Hmm? You lost? Or don't you have a home at all?"

The dog whined again.

Stefan stared down at his small pile of hard-won carrots. He hesitated, then broke one into quarters and held it out in the palm of his hand. "You hungry?"

After Sunday night's disaster near Ayvazovskaya, Stefan had vowed once again to avoid all villages and towns. But the dog didn't seem to care for carrots, and it kept whining. After two hours of walking, the pup was lagging, its head drooping. Drawing up at the top of a low rise, Stefan hunkered down to loop an arm over the pup's shoulder as he eyed the town below.

It was a cheerless place, its ugly concrete houses dating back to the Soviet era. Built on the edge of a stretch of marshland, the town's only reason for existence seemed to be the railroad tracks that ran on an elevated embankment along the edge of town. Stefan could see a freight train coming in the distance, the dirty brown smear from its diesel engine stretching out across the marsh.

He brought his gaze back to the town center, where a line of shops fronted a small rubbish-strewn square with the inevitable statue of Lenin at its center. He wasn't going to try stealing again—he'd learned his lesson. But surely ten rubles would be enough to buy the dog some scraps from a butcher?

Trying desperately not to attract anyone's attention, Stefan walked down the hill to the town's desolate windblown main street, one hand clutching his lucky amber horse head, the dog limping at his heels. They had almost reached the looming statue of Lenin when he glanced up and saw a big black Durango parked at the edge of the dusty square.

Stefan's mother had a saying: *Honest men drive Russian cars.* In Kaliningrad, only New Russians, thieves, and whores drove Durangos and Mercedes.

Dropping his hand to the dog's neck, Stefan swerved sideways into a narrow rutted lane choked with weeds and broken clumps of concrete. Flattening himself behind an old garage, he listened to the buzzing of insects in the grass, smelled the drift of cooking onions from a nearby house, and tried to stop trembling. Beside him, the dog whined. Stefan whispered, "*Shhh!*"

It was a full minute before he summoned the courage to peek around the corner of the garage. Two men in turtleneck sweaters and dark trousers were working their way down the row of shops on the far side of the square. They had something in their hands—a piece of paper? a picture?—that they kept showing to everyone they came to. The townspeople would look at the paper for a moment, then shake their heads. Stefan could imagine them saying, *This boy? No, I haven't seen this boy. What has he done?*

Then one of the men turned, and Stefan recognized the big Chechen with red hair and a ruddy complexion who'd shot Uncle Jasha. With a gasp, Stefan drew back his head, his heart pounding so hard his chest hurt.

"We'll find another village with a butcher," he told the dog, turning. "Come on."

The dog gave a low *woof* and darted out into the square.

"*No!* What are you doing?"

Sniffing the Durango's tires, the pup swung around and calmly lifted its leg.

Stefan's gaze flew to the men across the square, but both were turned away. He brought his gaze back to the SUV.

Against such men and their guns, Stefan knew, he could do nothing. But that didn't mean he was helpless.

The dog came bounding back, its tail wagging proudly. Stefan closed one hand convulsively around the lucky amber in his pocket, then reached out and touched the dog's shoulder. "You stay."

The dog sat down and cocked its head.

"Good dog. Stay."

The dog lay down, its head on its paws.

Hunkering low, Stefan sprinted across the alley to crouch behind the Durango's big fender. Over the broad, shiny expanse of the car's black hood he could see the men on the far edge of the square, still busy working the shops. Jerking his penknife from his pocket, he dropped to his back and wiggled underneath the SUV.

The familiar, pungent scent of hot oil from the Durango's engine engulfed him. Stefan had grown up working with his dad on truck engines; it took him only a moment to locate the Durango's brake line. Breathing a small prayer of thankfulness that the line wasn't made of metal, he started hacking at the rubber.

He could feel the sharp stones of the roadway digging into his back and rump as he sawed the small blade back and forth. His arms began to ache from the effort of working over his head in the cramped space, but he kept cutting, desperately aware of the passage of time.

The blast of a train's whistle, sounding unexpectedly close, distracted him. He jerked his head out of the way just as the line finally broke, sending a stream of brake fluid squirting out into the dirty road. He was tempted to leave it at that, to run while he had the chance. But a cut brake line could be quickly dealt with; a missing section of line was a lot harder to fix. Biting his lip, he started a second cut some six inches from the first.

Glancing over his shoulder, he realized the men were now standing together at the corner, talking. Just as the big redheaded Chechen stepped off the curb to cross the square, the section of hose came loose in Stefan's hand.

Scooting out from beneath the Durango, he pushed to his feet . . . and heard a shout go up across the square.

"Mother of God," gasped Stefan.

He pelted down the alleyway, the black-and-tan dog leaping up and yelping with joy at the sight of him. "Come on, boy!" he shouted. "Run."

"Get the car!" the Chechen yelled. "Cut him off at the street."

The dog bounding at his heels, Stefan ran down a rutted weed-grown lane hemmed in by high fences of vertical weathered boards. He could hear the pounding of running feet behind him, the loud gunning of the Durango's engine in the square. He risked a quick glance over his shoulder and saw the big Chechen, red-faced and gaining on him fast. Then the driver of the Durango floored the gas, and Stefan heard a horrendous tearing crash.

Whooping with delight, he swerved to his right and squeezed through a gap where a board had broken off one of the fences. The dog wiggled in behind him.

The Chechen was too big to slip through the hole in the fence. As Stefan darted across the overgrown yard and down the gravel drive leading to the street, he could hear the big man grunting and swearing as he heaved himself up over the tall, jagged fence. He hit the ground on the other side hard. But by then Stefan was already flying down the street toward the railway embankment.

He was aware of the train thundering closer, its whistle now a loud shriek of warning. And he realized that if he didn't make it across that embankment before the train cut him off, he'd be trapped.

He heard a whimper and looked back. Its head drooping, the pup faltered, stumbled.

"*No!*" Reaching down, Stefan scooped the dog up against his chest. Staggering beneath the weight, he stumbled across the street, tripped over a rock buried in the rank grass of the elevated rail bed. He could hear the Chechen drawing nearer, his breath coming in determined grunts. Gritting his teeth against exhaustion and pain, Stefan raced up the embankment, his legs reaching, his arms hugging the pup tight.

Big and black and deadly, the engine bore down on them, its shrieking whistle a painful physical blast. Lungs bursting, Stefan sprinted across the tracks. He felt the sucking vacuum as the train roared past behind him, the earth trembling beneath him as he half fell, half slithered down the far side of the embankment, the pup at his side.

At the base of the slope he paused, his heart pounding, his hands shaking as he drew the dog to him and buried his sweaty face in the animal's thick, warm coat. Then he pushed up, the rhythmic *clickity-clack* of the train's wheels loud in his ears.

Looking back he could see an endless line of boxcars stretching out across the marsh, and he smiled. "Come on, boy," he said to the dog. "Let's go."

Salinger parked the silver Range Rover in the shadow of a ruined Teutonic castle and cut the engine. "That's it."

Rodriguez studied the tidy stucco house halfway down the street. "Wait here," he said, pulling on his gloves. He was opening the car door when the call came through from Borz Zakaev.

"There's been a new development," said Borz in his deep, gravelly voice. "We were near Znamensk, showing the kid's picture to some townspeople, when he cut the brake line on the Durango."

Rodriguez glanced over at Salinger. "You're sure it was the kid?"

"We chased him," said Borz. "The little shit ran across the railroad tracks right in front of a train. By the time we got around it, he was gone." Borz hesitated. "We're going to need a new car."

"You can't get the Durango's brakes fixed?"

"We didn't know about the brakes until Zoya crashed into a cement wall. He's okay, but the SUV's a wreck."

"Fuck," said Rodriguez. How much trouble could one fucking little shit be?

A movement overhead drew his gaze to the cold expanse of northern sky, where a dozen or so ducks flew in a perfect *V* formation, their wings beating the air as they fled the coming ice and snow. Rodriguez smiled.

"This kid, he thinks he's smart. He thinks he just bought himself some time. But he's not smart, he's stupid. He let us know he's alive." He reached for the map, spread it open on the Range Rover's console. "Where is this Znamensk?"

"Just south of E77 and A229, on the railroad line."

Rodriguez followed the route with his finger. Most maps of Kaliningrad were shit. But this one had come from the Russian army. The town lay about a third of the way between Kaliningrad and Yasnaya Polyana. He smiled and folded the map away. "Looks like our little pigeon is flying home."

"So what do we do?"

"Keep checking the towns along the route. You may flush him out. When we're finished here, the rest of us will move operations to Yasnaya Polyana."

Nodding to Salinger, Rodriguez closed the car door quietly behind him and started down the walk toward Anna Baklanov's well-kept little house.

31

Serene and sun-kissed, the city of Izmir stretched out in a graceful arc around its wide Aegean bay. Once, the city had been called Smyrna, birthplace of Homer and site of more than three thousand years of Greek civilization. Then came the devastation and ethnic cleansing that followed World War I, and this new city, Izmir, had risen from the ashes as a symbol of modern Turkey, with wide tree-lined avenues and—for more than half a century now—a strong U.S. military presence.

As they circled in for their landing, Jax was aware of October leaning forward beside him, her shoulders set in a straight, tense line as she stared out the window.

"For some reason, I thought your father was a petroleum engineer," he said, watching her.

She shook her head, her gaze still on the city wedged between the mountains and the sparkling blue sea below them. "My stepdad's in the oil industry. My real father was in the Navy."

"Then if he was stationed at Izmir, he must have been in intelligence."

She turned to look at him. "How did you know that?"

"Maybe I'm psychic," he said teasingly.

She wrinkled her nose at him, and he laughed and said, "Most Americans stationed in Izmir are Air Force personnel assigned to the air base. But there's also a huge listening station here that's been operational since the fifties. So if your dad was in the Navy, and here, I figured he must have been in intelligence."

"Ah."

"How long was he stationed in Turkey?"

"Two years." She was silent a moment, then said, "He died here. His plane crashed in the Aegean."

"I'm sorry."

"What's strange is that your buddy Andrei mentioned my dad when we were in Kaliningrad."

"Andrei is not my buddy."

A glint of amusement lit her eyes, but all she said was, "How could he have known about my dad?"

"The Russians have always kept files on U.S. military officers, especially intelligence personnel. They get their information from everything from open sources like the *Army Times* to reports fed back to them by their own people."

"But my dad died when I was a kid."

Jax shrugged. "Andrei started out in the KGB. They might have run into each other."

She fell silent, her gaze returning to the city that now rushed toward them, its whitewashed walls turned to gold by the light of the rising sun.

They stepped off the plane into a soaring, ultra-modern glass-and-steel airport terminal to find a tall, lanky man in a United States Air Force uniform waiting for them.

He had the short-cropped sandy hair, tight jaw, and rigid bearing of a career military man. "Jax Alexander?" he said, assessing Jax with a flinty gaze and obviously finding him wanting. "Rita Catalano suggested I meet you."

"Ah. Dear Petra," said Jax.

The Captain frowned. "Petra?"

"Never mind."

The Captain's gaze slid past Jax to October, and an amazing transformation came over his face. His eyes widened. His sneer faded. Jax squinted at her, trying to see her through the Captain's eyes. Sure, she was an attractive woman. But after two long flights and a day spent being chased around Russia, she was looking more than a little ragged.

"*You're* Ensign Guinness?" said the Captain, shaking her hand with cheerful enthusiasm. "I'm Lowenstein. Tom Lowenstein. I've got a car waiting for us out front. If you'll follow me, your bags should already be on their way down."

He ushered them toward a nearby stairwell, where a uniformed guard toting a machine gun stepped forward menacingly. Lowenstein flashed his ID. The guard saluted and stepped back.

"It's always so nice operating in countries where the military keeps a tight hand on the reins," said Jax as their footsteps echoed down the enclosed stairwell. "Little things like customs and immigration are just inconveniences, easily dispensed with in the right circumstances."

Lowenstein's eyes narrowed. "Catalano wasn't kidding about you, was she?"

"Why? What did she say?"

But Lowenstein turned his back on Jax and said to Tobie, "Is this your first time in Turkey?"

She shook her head. "I was here as a kid."

He gave her a smile that showed two rows of straightened white teeth. "So you travel a lot, do you?"

Jax turned a snicker into a cough and buried it in his fist.

They walked out of the air-conditioned terminal into a

blast of dry heat just as a black Mercedes driven by a Turkish policeman slipped in next to the curb and stopped. Jax drew up short.

"This is your car?"

"That's right. I've already arranged an appointment for you with the owner of the shipbreaking yard up in Aliaga. He's expecting us this morning."

"Us? Hang on. I don't suppose it occurred to you that Mr. Erkan might be a lot more open to talking to the Ensign and me if we arrive without a uniformed policeman and a U.S. Air Force captain as escorts?"

"Maybe. But it's not happening. Things aren't as cozy between Washington and Ankara as they used to be. The last thing we need is some cowboy coming in here scattering dead bodies all over the place. I have orders from the station chief not to let you out of my sight." He opened the back door for Tobie and said to Jax over his shoulder, "You can have the front seat."

Jax indulged in a fantasy that involved wringing Petra Davidson's neck and tossing her lifeless body in the wine-dark Aegean Sea. Then he slid into the seat beside the driver.

The driver's name turned out to be Mustafa. He was lean and short, with the bushy dark mustache that seemed a requisite badge of manhood in this part of the Middle East. As they swung in an arc around the city's sweeping bay and headed north, he chain-smoked a series of short, foul Turkish cigarettes that made Jax's eyes water.

In the backseat, Lowenstein leaned in closer to October and said, "Do you ski?"

"Some."

"We have a great trip planned to Oberammergau this—"

"The shipbreakers yard," said Jax, slewing around in the seat so he could face him. "Tell me about it."

There was a moment's pained silence, then Lowenstein

said, "It's owned by a man named Kemal Erkan. His cousin is the Minister of the Environment, which is how he gets away with what he does. You usually see operations like this in places like India or China. They used to do it in Europe, but the costs of meeting health and safety standards got too high. Workers here have no health and safety standards, no Tyvek suits or breathing apparatus. Asbestos, dioxin—you name it, it doesn't matter to these guys."

"It's a big business?" said October.

"It's huge. Thanks to the Chinese, there's a boom in the world's steel industry. Only about two thirds of today's steel comes from iron ore; the rest is recycled from stuff like cars and washing machines—and ships. You can get over a million dollars out of an end-of-life vessel."

"So this guy's rich."

"You better believe he's rich."

Jax said, "Does he do much business in pre–1945 steel?"

"It's one of his specialties."

They were driving along the coast now, through dry rocky hills covered with fragrant olive groves and rows of grapevines withering with the shortening of the days. Many of the villages along this part of the Aegean had become tourist destinations, attracting overseas visitors to their sandy beaches and clear blue waters. Not Aliagra.

They came upon the shipbreaking yard just before the outskirts of town, its dirty gravel beach dominated by the looming half-dismantled hulk of what looked as if it might once have been a cruise ship. Jax eyed the mustachioed Turkish driver beside him. "How about the two of you stopping at a taverna for a *raki*, and letting the ensign and me take it from here?"

"Not a chance," said Lowenstein as the Turk turned in through the gates and drew up next to a pile of rusty barrels and stained old urinals. "I'll stay with the car. But I'm not letting you out of my sight until I put you back on that plane."

32

The ship—or what was left of it—had been dragged a quarter of the way out of the water and up onto the beach. Someone had made the token gesture of casting booms around the worksite, but a spreading sheen of oil and debris fouled the water that lapped a nearby sandy beach. A haze hung over the site, the pungent smoke from old fires mingling with the fumes from a droning diesel engine.

The ship's superstructure had already been removed. Now, men with blowtorches were cutting into the sides of the hull. Two huge 150-ton cranes loomed nearby. One stood idle, but as they watched, the second crane rattled into action, lifting a slice of the hull and swinging it toward the beach. The din was horrendous, the hiss of the blowtorches punctuated by the reverberations of a sledgehammer at work someplace out of sight within the bowels of the ship. Jax could see one man wearing an orange hard hat. The rest were bareheaded, many stripped to the waist, their work-hardened bodies browned by the sun and smudged with black grease and carbon and gleaming with sweat.

The office was in a battered construction trailer set on a

weedy patch of high ground. Beyond it spread a vast open dump site where half a dozen barefoot kids were scrambling around, scavenging for anything they might be able to sell. Jax was turning toward the trailer when October touched his arm.

"I think that might be our Mr. Erkan, there," she said, nodding to where a balding, middle-aged businessman in an exquisitely tailored Italian suit, white shirt, and tie was wading in the dirty surf beside the idle crane. A passel of shouting, gesturing workmen splashed around him. "Something must be wrong."

Jax squinted against the gleam of sunlight reflecting off the oily water, his gaze on the silent crane. "Looks like one of the cables broke."

Switching directions, they crossed the dirty shoreline past a bizarre assortment of refuse that ranged from sinks and copper piping to rusty metal bunks and old filing cabinets. White and brown clumps of what looked like asbestos were everywhere. As they approached, the man in the expensive suit swung to face them.

"*Merhabe*," called October from the water's edge.

Kemal Erkan was not in a good mood. Letting loose a stream of incomprehensible—to Jax—Turkish illustrated by energetically waving arms, he waded toward them, fine navy Italian wool dragging in the dirty salt water.

October answered him with a fluency that seemed to take the man by surprise. They jabbered back and forth, Erkan breaking off to shoot a glance at Jax, along with an obvious question. *Who is this guy?*

Jax caught his name in the reply.

Kemal Erkan said to him in heavily accented English, "You don't speak Turkish?"

"No."

"Then we will speak English." He nodded toward the idle

crane. "One of the cables broke, dropping a load of steel and nearly toppling the damned thing over. I'm afraid it might have put a strain on the tower. You have five minutes. Why did you wish to see me?"

Jax and October exchanged glances. Jax said, "I wanted to talk to you about a business arrangement you had with Jasha Baklanov."

Kemal Erkan turned to walk with them along the dirty beach, away from the ship. "Which one? Jasha and I have been doing business for more than twenty years. He's a good salvage operator."

Jax wondered how the captain of a salvage ship all the way up in Kaliningrad got to be on such good terms with the owner of a Turkish shipbreakers yard, but all he said was, "Did you know he's dead?"

The animation in the man's swarthy, fleshy face slowly collapsed. "Dead? But . . . when did this happen?"

October said, "Saturday. Someone murdered the *Yalena*'s entire crew."

Erkan stood very still. A gaunt, smoke-blackened man walked past, carrying a load of pipes on his shoulder. Erkan didn't even turn his head.

Jax said, "When was the last time you talked to him?"

Erkan seemed to gather himself together. "Jasha?" He shrugged. "Last week. Maybe the week before. I don't know. Why?"

"What can you tell us about the World War II U-boat he was salvaging?"

Erkan cast a glance at the U.S. Air Force officer waiting in the distance beside his car. "A German submarine? I don't know what you're talking about."

Jax narrowed his eyes against the sun and gazed out over the milky, oil-fouled water. "That's the problem with modern technology, you know. It makes it so hard to keep things private. In the last two days, you've left three messages on Baklanov's voice mail. And you sent him a fax."

The Turk's head jerked up and back as he let out a hissing noise that sounded like *sssk*. "You'll have to excuse me," he said, turning back toward the ship. "I have work to do."

Jax fell into step beside him. "What was on that U-boat that was so valuable? It wasn't just the steel Baklanov wanted, was it?"

The Turk swung to face him again. "Since I don't know anything about this submarine, how could I know about its cargo?" He gestured toward the idle crane, the Rolex watch on his wrist shining in the hot sun. "I have a serious situation here that I must deal with. You'll have to excuse me." He nodded to Tobie. "Miss Guinness."

Jax stopped at the water's edge. He was wearing a four-hundred-dollar pair of Forzieri handmade Italian leather loafers. No way was he getting those suckers wet. "If you change your mind, I'll be at Pasaport Quay," he called after the Turk. "Just don't wait too long."

Erkan waded deeper.

Jax raised his voice over the reverberations of hammers striking steel and the throb of the diesel engine. "Think about this: whatever was on that U-boat cost your friend and his crew their lives. Baklanov was involved with some seriously scary people. And when you're dealing with people like that, even a little bit of knowledge can be a dangerous thing."

"Erkan obviously doesn't know anything," said Lowenstein, thrusting a piece of pita bread in his mouth and chewing heartily.

They were eating *meze* at an outdoor café near Pasaport Quay, looking out over the wide sweep of the Gulf of Izmir. The sun sparkled on an achingly blue sea, the salty breeze blowing off the water was fresh, and Captain Lowenstein was still trying to hit on October.

Jax raised his Perrier to his lips and drank deeply. "He knows."

Lowenstein's sandy eyebrows went up in two contemptuous arcs. "So why aren't you doing something?"

"I am."

"Really? What?"

"I'm waiting for Erkan to change his mind."

"I can't believe you."

"Got a better idea?"

Lowenstein leaned back and grunted in disgust, just as a passing waiter in a white dinner jacket discreetly slipped Jax a note.

Turning his back on Jax, Lowenstein said to October, "So where exactly are you stationed?"

"The Algiers Support Facility, in New Orleans."

"Really? That's fascinating."

Quietly amused, Jax glanced down at scribbled writing. MEET ME AT 3:00 AT THE AGORA. COME ALONE.

Lowenstein said, "What do you do there?"

Before October could come up with an answer, Jax said, "How about you, Captain? Surely you have more important things to do than babysit a couple of people from Washington. Maybe go help the Turks bomb the Kurds or something?"

Lowenstein shifted his frosty blue stare back to Jax. "Right now my job is making sure you don't kill anyone on my turf."

Jax glanced at his watch. It was already a quarter past two.

He was aware of October staring at him in that still way she had. He met her gaze. He'd have sworn no one saw that adroit delivery of Kamil Erkan's message. But she must have, because she suddenly gave Lowenstein a wide smile and said, "Walk out on the quay with me, will you?"

The Captain's face broke into a grin that fell as he threw an uncertain glance at Jax.

Jax leaned back in his seat and yawned. "Don't look at me. I've got a great view of the bay from right here."

Lowenstein hesitated, torn.

"We won't be long," she said, cupping her hand beneath the Captain's elbow and drawing him up with her.

Jax would have sworn she was a woman without an ounce of subterfuge or feminine guile. But as he watched her walk away with the Captain, he realized that in that, he had erred.

33

The two men walked along the Reflecting Pool in the Mall.
A cold wind ruffled the waters beside them, splintering the
image of the Washington Monument mirrored by the pool's
surface. Gerald T. Boyd clasped his hands behind his back
and fixed his gaze on the towering obelisk before them. "So
what have you managed to learn, Colonel?"

Colonel Lee cleared his throat. "I'm getting a little uncomfortable with this, sir."

"Oh? How's that?"

"I saw the station's report on what happened in Berlin."
Lee hesitated, then pushed it out. "I didn't realize I was setting Alexander up as a target."

"Alexander made himself a target."

"But . . . he's CIA, sir. He's one of ours."

"You need to remember, Colonel: this operation is more
important than one man. The very future of America is at
stake here. We're talking about the survival of our entire

way of life. Freedom, democracy—everything we hold most dear. You do understand that, don't you?"

"Yes, sir."

A gust of wind buffeted the grass as a cloud half obscured the rising sun. Lee turned to stare down at the choppy waters beside them. Most people thought of the CIA and the Pentagon as two distinct organizations, and in many ways they were. But there were always a significant number of military personnel assigned to the CIA. In fact, by tradition either the Director of the Agency or his Deputy was always a general. Sam Lee might work for the CIA, but he was still an Army colonel. Which meant he not only owed his plum job at the Agency to Boyd; Boyd could destroy Lee's entire future in a heartbeat, if he wanted to. And they both knew it.

Boyd said, "Where is Alexander now?"

A muscle began to tic beside the other man's left eye. "Turkey, sir. Izmir. But I don't think he's planning to be there long."

"Where's he going next?"

"I don't know."

"Well, keep on him. Is the Guinness woman still with him?"

"Yes, sir."

"What have you found on her?"

"I'm working on it, General."

Boyd grunted and turned toward the Capitol Building. "Work faster, Colonel."

"Yes, sir."

34

The ruins of the ancient Greek agora lay on the slopes of a fortified mount known as Kadifekale, overlooking the city and the bay beyond. Once, this had been the commercial, judicial, and political heart of the ancient Greek city of Smyrna. Refounded in fine style by Alexander the Great, the grand municipal buildings had been toppled by an earthquake, only to be rebuilt again by Marcus Aurelius. But that was nearly two millennia ago. Now it was just a collection of broken columns and underground vaults baking in the hot Mediterranean sun.

Jax wandered along the western stoa, his watchful gaze roving continually over the area. The message from the Turkish shipbreaker was welcome, but vaguely ominous. Men like Kemal Erkan didn't frighten easily.

A fly buzzed Jax's ear. Swatting it away, he turned to look out over the old Greek site. From here he had a clear view of the courtyard and its surrounding portico of fragmented marble columns standing up stark and white against the vivid blue sky. The ancient basilica lay beyond that, while over it all loomed the dark crenulated battlements of the fortress begun by Alexander the Great and expanded many times down through the centuries.

The agora was nearly deserted. The hordes of tourists from the cruise ships that docked in the port below tended to prefer day trips to better-known sites like Ephesus, to the south. Jax understood why Erkan had selected it as a meeting place.

The purr of an expensive engine drew Jax's attention to the parking lot. A dark blue Mercedes SLK-Class Roadster pulled up outside the simple guard's hut. Kemal Erkan got out of the driver's side and walked through the gate with a nod to the attendant. That the shipbreaker had come alone, without either driver or bodyguard, was significant.

Jax stood at the edge of the ancient stoa and waited for the Turk to walk up to him. Erkan said, "I called Anna Baklanov."

"And?"

"I got some old woman. She said Anna is dead. Someone broke her neck this morning."

Jax thought of the little girl proudly presenting that bouquet of roses to Brezhnev, and felt a pain pull across his chest.

The Turk pursed his lips. "The old woman said Jasha is dead, too."

"You didn't believe me?"

Erkan raised one eyebrow. "Why should I?"

They turned to walk along the colonnade. After a moment, Erkan said, "Why is the American Government interested in the murder of a simple Russian ship's captain?"

"We think he was involved with terrorists."

"Terrorists." Erkan huffed a soundless laugh. "You Americans. Always going on about *terrorists*. Which terrorists? The ones your government pays to blow up mosques and pipelines in Iran? Or maybe the ones you've been sending against Cuba for the last forty years?"

"Not those. The ones who don't like us. I'm hoping something you can tell me will help us figure out which ones—and help us find the men who killed your friend."

Erkan sneered. "You don't care about Jasha."

Jax didn't deny it. "But you do. Our motives might be different, but our objective is the same. We both want the people who killed Jasha Baklanov . . . and his wife."

Erkan stared off into the distance, to where the once grand stadium was now no more than a depression in the grass. His thick, dark eyebrows drew together in a frown. He hesitated, then said, "Jasha contacted me two, maybe three weeks ago. He said he had a contract to raise some Nazi sub that sank off the coast of Denmark at the end of the war."

"Did he say who hired him?"

Erkan jerked his head up and back, his eyebrows lifting in that peculiarly Turkish way of saying *no*.

Jax said, "There was something on the sub they wanted?"

Erkan gave him a sideways glance. "You know the kinds of things the Nazis were sending out of Germany at the end of the war?"

"You mean gold?"

The Turk laughed. "That was my first assumption as well. But not Jasha's. He thought the U-boat might have been carrying uranium or something equally as dangerous."

Jax could feel the heat of the sun baking his shoulders and the top of his head. He said, "Yet he agreed to raise it anyway?"

"They showed him the submarine's original manifest."

"Not a copy?"

"No. The original."

Jax studied the man's fleshy, sweat-sheened face. "So what was the sub carrying?"

Erkan's gaze slid away. The agora was virtually deserted, an open space of weed-grown paving stones and row after row of white marble columns. A Scandinavian couple were exploring the water channels and reservoirs of the western stoa. Two boys on the other side of the chain-link fence were playing a jumping game. Jax could hear the lilting sound of their laughter carrying on the breeze as a large man in a light blue windbreaker crossed the courtyard, his hands in his pockets.

"Jasha was a great one for running schemes," Erkan was saying. "Once he learned what was on the U-boat, Jasha knew he could find a buyer for it."

"You mean, another buyer?"

"That's right. The men who hired him planned to be there when the *Yalena* raised the submarine. They were going to remove the cargo and just sink the U-boat again, so no one would know it had ever been raised. But Jasha, he got the idea to raise the old submarine a day early. He was going to take it back to Kaliningrad, remove the cargo, and then sell the U-boat to me for the steel. You know about pre–1945 steel?"

"Yes." The man in the windbreaker was getting closer. He was taller than Lowenstein's driver, and darker, but he had that same swooping handlebar mustache. "In other words," said Jax, "Jasha was going to double-cross the men who hired him."

"He planned to hide the U-boat at the shipyard, then go out with the men who'd hired him the next day and pretend to be as surprised as anyone when they discovered the sub already gone. He thought he was just dealing with thieves." Erkan exhaled sharply through his nostrils. "Not killers."

"What was the cargo?"

Erkan paused in front of one of the massive columns. He'd changed suits, Jax noticed. A fine lightweight gray wool rather than the navy he'd worn that afternoon. He fiddled with the jacket's top button, buttoning and then unbuttoning it.

"What was the cargo?" Jax said again. "If it wasn't gold, what was it?"

"You think—" Erkan began, just as the man in the windbreaker walked up to him, pulled a big Heckler and Koch from beneath his jacket, and shot Erkan point blank in the chest.

35

The Heckler and Koch was a massive model 23. The mustachioed man in the light blue windbreaker squeezed off three rounds, one after the other. The big hollow-point through-and-throughs tore through Erkan and blew out his back. Blood splattered the white marble column behind him as shattered shards of stone exploded into the air.

The man in the windbreaker shoved the H&K beneath his jacket again and kept walking.

For one suspended moment, Erkan wavered, still on his feet, his white shirt blooming a charred scarlet. He opened his mouth to speak and a torrent of blood spilled down his chin. Then his eyes rolled back in his head and he collapsed.

He fell backward in an ungainly sprawl, arms flung out at his sides, his exquisitely tailored gray suit falling open to reveal a small Walther PPK in a holster clipped inside the waistband of his slacks. Jax snatched it up.

Walking quickly, the killer had almost reached the gate. Jax shoved Erkan's Walther under his shirt and followed him, also at a walk. It was never a good idea to run away from a dead body. It tended to attract attention.

Other people were running—running *toward* Erkan. Jax kept walking. At the gate, the man in the pale blue windbreaker threw a quick glance over his shoulder. He saw Jax and began to run.

"Shit," said Jax, and sprinted after him.

They pelted down a crooked lane between narrow whitewashed houses that loomed up to cast the worn paving stones into shadow. This was an old part of town, one of the few areas that had escaped the Great Fire of 1922. Jax dodged café tables, scarlet geraniums spilling out of clay pots, a sleeping gray cat.

The killer hung a quick left, into a shady, stone-paved passageway so steep it soon gave up and became steps. Jax tore after him, the soles of their shoes clattering on the broad ancient stairs, the scent of damp stone and ancient decay wafting up around him.

The steps emptied into a winding street filled with market stalls hung with baskets and brass pots that glinted like gold in a shaft of early-evening sunlight. The driver of a green van laid on his horn, its brakes screeching as the man in the blue windbreaker darted across in front of him.

Jax ducked around behind the van, his gaze on the dark mouth of an alley opening up on the far side of the street. The killer bolted down it, Jax twenty steps behind. The air here was cool and dank, the houses shuttered, silent, the only sounds the pounding of their feet and the rasp of their breath and the swish of traffic from the street ahead.

As he cleared the alley, the man seemed to come to some kind of a decision. He whirled, his hand reaching beneath his jacket to close on the handle of his gun. But the sidewalk here was narrow, his momentum so great that he took a step back off the curb into the street as he brought up the big H&K.

Jax heard a squeal of brakes, saw the man's head turn, his eyes widen the instant before a battered white delivery truck slammed into him with a heavy, fatal thud.

36

Tucking Erkan's Walther out of sight beneath his sweat-soaked shirt, Jax pushed his way through the excited, jabbering crowd of shoppers gathered around the front of the truck. Jax took one look at the man's blood-smeared face, the wide and sightless eyes, and turned away.

A couple of blocks down the hill, he paused long enough to wipe down Erkan's gun and drop it into a convenient trash receptacle. Then he turned his steps toward the blue waters of the bay below. From somewhere to his left came the low, melodic notes of the afternoon call to prayer. *Allah Akbar . . .*

One after the other, the muezzins of the city's mosques joined in, until their voices rose up in a wave of sound that rolled across the bay. *Allah Akbar. Ash-hadu alla ilaha illallah. God is Great. There is no God but God.*

Captain Lowenstein was not going to be happy.

Jax called Matt from the shade of a plane tree overlooking the Gulf of Izmir. His truncated conversation with Erkan had raised some serious questions, and Jax had doubts about

Langley's ability—or maybe its willingness—to give him straight answers.

"Where are the German military archives from World War II kept?" Jax asked.

"The military archives?" There was a pause while Matt digested this. "I think they're still in Freiburg im Breisgau. Why?"

"Then that's where I'm going."

"You know, we do have people in Freiberg. I could ask them to—"

"No. I want to find out for myself exactly what was on that damned sub."

"Did something happen I need to know about?"

"Kemal Erkan is dead."

"Shit. Listen, Jax. I've got a contact in Freiberg I can set you up with. A historian by the name of Walter Herbolt, at the university."

Jax stared across the broad avenue, toward the water. From here he could see Tobie and Captain Lowenstein. Tobie was calmly sipping a bottle of Evian at a shady table overlooking Pasaport Quay. But Lowenstein was pacing up and down, his cell phone plastered to his ear with one hand, his other hand gesturing wildly through the air as he talked. Jax said, "Thanks, but I'm getting kinda tired of these station people."

"Herbolt isn't part of the Company. He's a personal friend. I'll tell him to expect you." There was a pause. Matt said, "It doesn't sound like that U-boat was carrying gold, does it?"

"No. No, it doesn't."

"You're feeling pretty cocky, aren't you?" Jax said to Lowenstein as the captain escorted them through Izmir's crowded, gleaming airport toward their concourse.

So far, news of the shooting in the agora had yet to wend its way through Turkish police channels to the base, and from there to field personnel. Pausing at the sign that warned in four languages, TICKETED PASSENGERS ONLY BEYOND THIS POINT, the Captain rocked back on his heels and grinned. "You may have given me the slip there for a while, but I think I made a pretty good recovery. And in another forty-five minutes, you'll be gone."

"And without a single international incident." Jax slapped the big Air Force captain on the back and turned to leave. "You did a heckuva job, Lowie."

"I don't like the sound of that," whispered October as she put her carry-on bag on the conveyer belt at security. "Who did you kill?"

"Not here, October." Jax kept a smile on his face as he glanced back at Lowenstein. As he watched, the Captain answered his cell phone, his expression changing ludicrously as he listened to the voice at the other end. Across the crowded security area, the two men's gazes met. Jax brought one hand to his forehead in a wry salute and turned away.

He gave October a full briefing as they sat by the gate, waiting for their flight to Istanbul to board.

"What I don't understand is why that gunman in the agora didn't shoot you, too," she said when he finished. "I mean at first, when he had the chance."

"Probably because no one paid him to kill me. He looked like he came from the local rent-a-thug crowd, which means that whoever hired him to kill Kemal Erkan had no way of knowing I'd be there when he made the hit. And guys like that don't do freebies."

"You think he was hired by our friends in Kaliningrad?"

"Or at least by the same outfit that hired our friends in Kaliningrad."

A rustle of movement wafted through the waiting crowd as a uniformed attendant appeared at the gate. "Now it's your turn," said Jax, studying her through narrowed eyes.

"What?" she said with a half laugh. "Why are you looking at me like that?"

"When we were at Pasaport Quay, how did you know I wanted you to distract Lowenstein?"

She leaned into him teasingly as a droning voice began to announce their flight's boarding pattern. "What's the matter? Are you afraid I read your mind or something?"

"The thought did occur to me."

Still smiling, she sat back and shook her head. "Just because I'm good at remote viewing doesn't mean I'm psychic, Jax. I saw the waiter hand you the note."

He continued to stare at her, unsure whether to believe her or not. She said, "Do you think Lowenstein will ever connect you to what happened at the agora?"

"Officially? Not if he's smart."

37

By the time their connecting flight from Munich swooped down over the mountains of the Black Forest to land at Freiburg im Breisgau, it was early the following morning.

"These overnight flights are going to kill me," said October as they caught a cab directly from the airport to the philosophy faculty of the university. "I must look like shit."

"Lowenstein obviously didn't think so."

"Enough about that, already." Settling into the cab's backseat, she rummaged around in her bag for a brush and used it to draw her hair back into a clip. "I don't even know what day it is anymore."

"It's Wednesday."

She looked up at him, her arms stilling at her task. "The twenty-eighth?"

"That's right."

"Christ," she whispered. Halloween was three days away.

"Be thankful for overnight flights."

They drove past undulating renaissance facades of red

sandstone and white plaster, past gently flowing canals that gurgled with the fresh waters of the Dreisam River. By the end of the Second World War, Jax knew, American and British carpet-bombing had reduced this elegant university city to a burned-out shell. But there was no sign of that now. The historic heart of the city had been painstakingly and lovingly restored.

They found Professor Herbolt stuffing papers into a battered brown-leather briefcase in his office. He looked up, his straight, pale blond hair falling forward to frame a soft, plump-cheeked face.

"Ah. There you are," he said. Somewhere in his late thirties or early forties, he had gentle gray eyes and the slightly stooped shoulders of a man who'd spent too many years of his life hunched over books. "I'm on my way to a meeting at the Historisches Kaufhaus." He buckled the straps of his briefcase and swung it off his desk. "Walk with me."

The briefcase in one hand and a lumpy paper-wrapped package tucked under his arm, the professor led the way through a warren of restored university buildings to the Bertoldstrasse. "Matt told me something of what you're looking for. How much do you know about Germany's military records?"

Jax shook his head. "Nothing, really."

The professor nodded, as if he'd been expecting as much. "The Allies seized all the German military and government archives they could find after the war," he said, ushering them up the noisy, crowded street. "At first, the archives were held in Washington and London. But eventually most of the material was microfilmed and the originals were returned to us in the fifties. Since Germany was still an occupied, partitioned state, there was a reluctance to create a central archives at Bonn, so various archives were established in different parts of the country. The Bundesarchiv-Militararchiv was set up here, in Freiburg."

"All the Naval records were sent here?"

"Most of them. The U-boat war journals weren't declassified and returned to us until the late seventies. But then they came here, yes. The Naval records are by far the most complete. The Army, less so. The Air Force holdings were heavily destroyed and are very fragmentary."

"So how complete are the U-boat records?"

"Not as complete as one might wish, I'm afraid, especially with regard to the later period. The archives have no material at all on nearly three hundred U-boats that were commissioned into service at the end of the war. The last months of the war were very chaotic, you know. The Allies carpet-bombed our cities virtually every night, killing hundreds of thousands—some say millions. Many records were lost. Some U-boats were commissioned that we don't even know existed."

Jax stared down the length of the Kaiser-Joseph-Strasse, to where one of the old medieval gates of the city was still visible. "Let me guess: U–114 is one of those."

"I'm afraid so. Until the wreckage was found off Denmark, we had nothing on it. Your government originally identified it as a Type XB submarine, but as far as we know, only eight Type XB submarines were built. Two survived to surrender at the end of the war, and six are known to have been sunk. Because they were so large, they were very useful for carrying cargo long distances. But their size also made them disastrously slow and difficult to maneuver."

"What do you mean, the wreckage was 'originally' identified?"

The professor was silent as they cut between two tall, narrow buildings to emerge in the Münsterplatz, the open marketplace surrounding the ancient cathedral. "I've been studying the photographs Matt sent of U–114 on the seabed," he said, "and I don't believe it was a Type XB. They were originally designed as minelayers, you know; when they were used as transports, they carried most of their cargo in their mineshafts. The XB was unique in that it only had two torpedo tubes, at the stern."

Jax drew up short. "But U–114 definitely had a forward torpedo room."

The German paused to look back at him. "You're certain?"

"Yes." He'd seen it himself.

Herbolt nodded. "Then I suspect we're dealing with a Type XI-B U-cruiser."

October said, "That's significant?"

"Very," said the professor, leading the way across the open square, "when you consider that there are no official records of any of the Type XI-Bs ever becoming operational. We know that four keels were laid down in the shipyards of Deschimag AG Weser, in Bremen. But it was assumed they were all scrapped prior to completion."

Jax said, "They were big?"

"Oh, yes. Over one hundred sixteen meters long, and some nine and a half meters wide. They were quite large."

"The XB class subs were—what? Three hundred feet long?"

"Eighty-nine meters, yes."

Jax tried to picture the U-boat they'd seen resting on a barge in the shipyard in Kaliningrad. Had it been three hundred feet, or closer to four?

"There have been persistent rumors that at least one class XI-B was completed near the end of the war," said the professor, "and sent out on a secret mission."

"As part of Operation Caesar?"

Herbolt paused before a colorful renaissance hall with a ground-floor arcade and fancifully decorated gables. "It's possible."

"What kind of rumors are we talking about?"

"Reports from dockworkers, mainly." The professor glanced at his watch. "I'm sorry I couldn't help you more." He started to turn away, then hesitated. "There is one other place you might try. The official archives are here, in Freiburg. But there is something called the Deutsches U-Boot Museum-Archiv, in Altenbruch. It began as a private collection held by a former submarine officer named Horst Bredow, but it eventually grew so large he turned it into a nonprofit foundation run by volunteers. They have gathered everything they can find on Germany's U-boats, not just copies of the official records, but also things like letters, memoirs, transcriptions of firsthand accounts by survivors. If anything does exist on this U–114, that is where you'll find it."

Jax stared off across the old German square, filled that morning with market stalls piled with buckets of sunflowers and shiny pyramids of apples and trays of fresh pastries. "Do you think U–114 could have been carrying gold?"

Herbolt shrugged. "It is possible. After Stalingrad, many here in Germany knew the war was lost. Corporations such as I. G. Farber and Krupp Industries were converting their holdings into gold and sending it out of the country, to places like Portugal and Argentina. But if what I believe is true—that one of the XI-B class U-boats was rushed into commission and sent on a special mission—then I think it was carrying something more important than rich men's gold."

"Something like—what?"

The German shrugged again. "I'm not going to speculate. Talk to the people at the Deutsches U-Boot Museum-Archiv. I'll tell them to expect you."

October said, "Where is Altenbruch?"

"In Cuxhaven, on the North Sea." Setting down his briefcase, he held out the bulky brown-paper-wrapped package. "I almost forgot. Matt wanted you to have this."

"What is it?" said Jax, taking the parcel.

"Something he seems to think you may need." The professor picked up his briefcase again and turned to leave. "Just be careful to open it in private. We have very strict rules on firearms here in Germany."

38

The farmhouse lay on the edge of a desolate glen, just beyond the outskirts of Yasnaya Polyana. Sturdily built of red brick and stout timbers by some long-vanished German, it now boasted a statue of Lenin that stood surrounded by flower-beds like a Kaliningrad version of a garden gnome, thought Rodriguez. As he watched, a cold wind ruffled the surface of the nearby duck pond and rattled the yellowing leaves of the elms that sheltered an old black-and-white cow.

They'd pulled off into a rutted track surrounded by a tangled growth of birch and oak in what might once have been a field, sixty years ago. Leaning against the trunk of a gnarled oak, he swept his field glasses across the farmyard to the ancient barn and henhouse, and then back. Stefan Baklanov's mother was on the porch, a big basin clamped between her knees as she shelled a mound of peas with quick, practiced movements.

Salinger said, "Looks like she's alone. We can take over the place in a minute. She'll never know what hit her."

"No. This kid knows we're after him. We don't do anything that might spook him. We leave the place alone and wait. Let him come to us."

Salinger watched, his eyes narrowing, as an old Lada crept down the nearby narrow road to disappear around a bend. "When's Borz supposed to get here?"

"Tonight."

Rodriguez watched the woman below stand up and stretch, the basin of peas balanced on one hip. She was built long and bony, with dark hair just beginning to go gray and a face lined by worry and hard work. She walked into the house, the door banging behind her. He said, "I want a tap put on her phone. Can you do that?"

"Easy."

The woman reemerged. They watched her walk down the steps, a bucket in one hand.

"Think the kid'll be stupid enough to call her?"

"He'll call, or he'll come. One way or the other, we nail him."

Freiburg, Germany: Wednesday 28 October
10:35 A.M. local time

They unwrapped Herr Herbolt's package in a shadowy, out-of-the-way pew of the *münster*.

"God bless Matt," said Jax, quickly clipping the holstered Beretta inside the waistband of his chinos.

"Somehow it doesn't seem right to be fawning over guns in a church," whispered Tobie, eyeing the compact Beretta 9000 Matt had sent for her.

"I like guns a lot better than funerals—especially my own." He picked up the small Beretta and held it out to her.

She made no move to take it. "You've seen my marksmanship records, right?"

He grinned and dropped the gun into her shoulder bag. "What marksmanship records? The military loves to hand out marksmanship medals. You're the only person I've ever heard of who didn't manage to score some kind of marksmanship commendation."

"There are a few of us." She slipped the strap of her bag over her shoulder and stared up at the brilliant jewel-toned stained-glass window beside them. "So how do we get to Altenwhatever?"

"Altenbruch. We take an InterCity Express train to Bremen, and then rent a car."

She turned to look at him. "I didn't think Jason Aldrich could rent a car anyplace that has computers."

"He can't. Which is why you're renting the car."

"Me?" A nearby group of tourists turned to frown at them. She realized she was shouting, and dropped her voice again. "On my own credit card?"

He pushed to his feet. "I'll make sure the Company reimburses you."

"And if we run into a bunch of bad guys and wreck it?"

"We won't."

"Right."

She followed him down the nave and out into the weak autumn sunshine. "There's no other way to do this?"

"Nope."

She thought about it a minute, then sighed. "Okay. But I drive."

"Fine. You drive."

"I mean it. I drive."

He laughed. "I get it. You drive. As long as you drive better than you shoot," he added, then ducked when she swung her bag at his head.

St. Martin, Caribbean: Wednesday 28 October
9:00 A.M. local time

One of James Walker's favorite toys was a gleaming one-hundred-and-ten-foot fiberglass Hargrave with a raised pilothouse. It was Catherine who'd christened the yacht the *Harlequin*. She'd wanted to keep it in the divorce, too, but all he'd had to do was whisper those magic words, "joint custody," and she'd backed off in a hurry.

Carrying an aluminum case containing a carefully padded secret, Walker climbed aboard the *Harlequin* just after breakfast and nodded to his captain. "Ready to sail?"

"Yes, sir."

Walker turned toward his stateroom. "Then let's do it."

Washington, D.C.

Boyd's second day of testimony before Congress received a standing ovation. It was all bullshit, of course. But Boyd had learned early in his career that officers who told politicians what they wanted to hear got promoted; the fools who told the truth found other jobs.

He was smiling and shaking hands with the members of the Senate when Colonel Sam Lee leaned in close and whispered, "We need to talk."

Boyd paused to acknowledge the congratulations of some grinning idiot who said, "You've convinced me, General. If the President can get this appropriation bill to the floor, it's got my vote."

"Why thank you, Senator. It's good to know the military can count on your support." Boyd clapped the Senator on the shoulder, then added quietly to Lee, "The coffee shop around the corner. Wait for me."

Half an hour later, he found Lee sipping a cappuccino in a booth near the back of the shop, a half eaten muffin abandoned on the plate before him. Boyd ordered good old-fashioned coffee, black, then slid into the booth. "What have you got?"

"It's about Ensign Guinness, sir."

Boyd took a sip of his coffee, grimacing as the bitter, hot liquid slid down his throat. "What about her?"

"She was given her commission at the direction of Vice President Beckham himself."

"Beckham? What's that left-leaning son of a bitch got to do with anything?"

"She saved his life."

Boyd frowned. "Are we talking about that incident last summer?"

"Yes, sir." Lee leaned forward. "But this is where it gets interesting: she was recalled to active duty after getting a psycho discharge over some incident in Iraq."

"So what's she doing in the CIA?"

Lee dropped his voice even lower. "Remote viewing, sir."

"What?" Boyd made a rude noise. "I think someone's jerking your strings, Colonel. The Government got out of the hocus-pocus business more than ten years ago."

"Yes, sir. But this isn't a formal program; it's a small project Beckham is running through Division Thirteen." The Colonel paused. "She's supposed to be very good at it, sir."

Boyd threw back his head, his laughter coming loud and long. "You don't really believe in that bullshit, do you?"

"I managed to access her viewing report."

Boyd wasn't laughing anymore. "And?"

Lee drew a folded sheaf of papers from his pocket and slid it across the table. "I printed it out, sir. I think you'd better look at it."

Boyd hesitated a moment, then reached to close his fingers around the report. "Where are they now?"

The tic beside Lee's eye was back, worse than ever. "Germany, sir."

39

The *U-Boot Archiv* lay on a narrow street not far from the
deep blue waters of the North Sea. By the time Tobie parked
her rented red Jetta outside the small, steeply gabled yellow
archives building, the sun had already slipped low enough in
the sky to throw long shadows across the pavement.

The archives had officially closed hours before. But at their
approach, a wizened face appeared at one of the windows. A
moment later they heard the lock on the front door turn.

"Velcome," said the ancient, white-haired wisp of a woman
who opened the door for them. Neatly dressed in a white
blouse with a round collar, a spruce green cardigan, and a
plaid wool skirt, she stood about five feet high and couldn't
have weighed more than ninety pounds. In age, she might have
been anywhere between eighty and a hundred. "I am Marie
Oldenburg. I've been vaiting for you. Please, come in."

She led them to a small office crowded with shelves and filing
cabinets, all neatly ordered and gleaming with fastidious cleanliness. "Herr Herbolt tells us you are interested in U–114."

"You know something about it?" asked Tobie, taking one of the seats the woman indicated.

"Yes, and no." She sat behind a lovingly polished old desk, her gnarled hands folded before her. "I have been vorking in the archives for twenty years now, ever since Herr Bredow turned what vas once his private collection into a foundation. My husband, Hans, was a submariner, you see. He vas on U–648 when it disappeared on a mission in 1943. Ve haven't yet discovered what happened to U–648. But ve have solved many riddles. Many riddles."

Jax glanced at Tobie, but said nothing.

Marie Oldenburg cleared her throat. "You know that the numbers U–112 to U–115 vere to be assigned to four type XI-B vessels whose keels vere originally laid down before the war, but that there are no Kriegsmarine records of the submarines ever being finished or commissioned?"

"We heard there are no official records," said Jax.

She nodded. "Germany had over a thousand U-boats in World War II. Ve have records here on nearly all of them. Some of our collections are so extensive that it is possible to trace the entire history of a submarine, from the laying of its keel to the day of its loss. Up until six months ago, I vould have told you no XI-B class boats ever existed."

"So what happened six months ago?"

"A man named Karl Wertheim came to see us. I spoke to him myself. It seems his grandfather had vorked at the docks at Bremerhaven. After his death, the young Wertheim found a number of papers and other memorabilia in a trunk in his grandfather's attic that he thought ve might be interested in purchasing. Amongst those papers vas the manifest of a U–114, dated March 1945." She hesitated. "Or so he claimed."

"The archives didn't buy the papers?"

She spread her hands wide. "This is a nonprofit venture. Everything you see here and in the museum has been donated. I tried to convince the young man to contribute his grandfather's papers to the archives, but he refused. He vouldn't even let me copy them—he said it vould reduce their sale value."

"But you saw them?"

"Some of them. Not, unfortunately, the manifest of U–114. The young man vas very secretive about it. He claimed that amongst its other cargo, U–114 carried a secret veapon—what you Americans like to call a veapon of mass destruction."

Tobie felt a tingle of fear run up her spine. "You mean an atom bomb? Is that possible?"

Marie Oldenburg laced her fingers together on the desktop before her. "There is much debate concerning how far the German atomic program had actually progressed at the time of the surrender." She paused. "Are you familiar with the vork of Wolfgang Palmer?"

Tobie glanced at Jax, but he shook his head. "I'm sorry, no."

"Herr Palmer is a journalist. He has spent years researching the German atomic program, and he tells me it is indeed possible that the Nazi government tried to send an atomic bomb to Japan—or at least the material to make such a bomb. But at the moment, ve have only young Wertheim's vord that the XI-B even existed. Whereas for its cargo . . ." She let her voice trail away.

Jax said, "Where can we find this Karl Wertheim?"

Marie Oldenburg sighed. "Unfortunately, he is dead. Two of our members—both former submarine officers themselves—vent to see the young man, hoping to persuade him to donate the items in his grandfather's name. But he told them he'd already listed them on eBay and had located an interested buyer. Two days later, his house caught fire and Karl Wertheim was found dead."

"He died in the fire?"

"No. Someone had slit his throat."

40

The closer Stefan drew to Yasnaya Polyana, the more skittish he became. He had slept most of the afternoon, snuggled up next to the black-and-tan pup for warmth, emerging only at dusk to walk along the edge of the fallow, frost-covered fields.

They kept well back from the pavement and the occasional darting beams of passing headlights, but he'd given up trying to go overland. Once, he'd blundered into a patch of stinging nettles; another time, the pup strayed into a bog and got stuck. Plus they kept getting lost, going off in the wrong direction or unwittingly circling around on themselves. He'd finally decided to stick close to the main roads and travel only at night. He and the pup were both footsore and hungry and desperate to get home. '

The problem was, it had occurred to him that going home might not be safe.

With a whine, the dog flopped down on the grassy verge,

his tongue hanging out as he panted heavily. Stefan dropped beside him. "What's the matter, boy? Tired?"

He lay back, his eyes blinking as he stared up at the dark sky. The night was cold and overcast, allowing only faint glimmers of starlight to peek through. Stefan felt a lump rise in his throat, and resolutely squeezed his eyes shut against an upwelling of tears.

Sleep came by stealth. He awoke with a start, shivering, unsure at first what had roused him. He heard a snort and a jingle of harness, and raised his head to find a decrepit farm wagon pulled by a pair of graying mules drawn up beside the verge.

A hunched figure wearing a woolen cap perched on a hard wooden seat high above the wagon's great iron-banded wheels. "You all right, boy?"

Stefan scrambled to his feet, ready to run. "How'd you know I was here?"

The man laughed. "I saw you. What'd you think? I may be old, but there's never been anything wrong with my eyes. I bet I can see better at night than you."

Stefan wiped the back of his fist across his nose. "You must have eyes like an owl."

The man laughed again. "How'd you like a ride?"

Stefan dropped his hand to the pup's head. "And my dog?"

"The dog's welcome, too."

He lifted the pup up onto the floor of the wagon, then swung himself up using an old iron step. The farmer made a clucking sound and danced the reins on the backs of the mules. Stefan breathed in the pungent, earthy smell of potatoes, and sneezed.

The old man laughed. "Where you headed?"

"Chkalovo," said Stefan, naming a hamlet just beyond Yasnaya Polyana.

"You can go back to sleep, if you want. I'll wake you when we get there."

Stefan shook his head.

"What's your dog's name?"

"He doesn't have one."

"Everyone should have a name. Man or beast."

"So what're your mules' names?"

"Karl and Marx."

Stefan laughed so hard he had to grab the side of the wagon seat to keep from falling off.

The old man shrugged. "They're old mules."

They talked for a time about mules and farming and the price of grain. They were easing down a dark wooded slope when they came around a bend and saw the glow of flares. Against the dancing flames of a fire stood two silhouettes in uniform.

The dog sat up and gave a low growl. Stefan put a warning hand on its head. "*Ssshh*, boy. What's that?"

"Looks like the militia've set up a roadblock. I went through another checkpoint just like this one, maybe ten miles back. They were looking for a young man. That wouldn't be you, would it?"

Stefan curled his hand over the edge of the seat, ready to jump. The old man said softly, "You jump now, they'll see you."

Stefan drew in a quick breath, trying to ease the sudden pain in his side, but it didn't help. "What do I do?"

The old man pursed his lips. "Get in back. You'll find some empty gunnysacks beneath the seat you can pull up over you."

"And if they search the load?"

The old man was silent for a moment. "Then I'll take care of your dog."

41

Crouched in a narrow space between the seat and the mounds of potatoes, Stefan pulled the scratchy pile of dusty sacks over his head and shoulders, clutched his lucky piece of amber in one tight fist, and tried not to breathe.

As the wagon drew up at the checkpoint, he heard the old farmer shout, "Another roadblock? Don't you young men have wives whose beds need warming?"

One of the militiamen laughed. "What you doing out so late, old man?"

"Axle broke. This wagon's getting too old. Like me." Stefan heard the clink of glass against wood, then smelled the strong familiar pinch of alcohol. The farmer said, "Like a drink to chase away the chill?"

"Well . . . I guess a swallow won't hurt."

Through a crack in the slat back of the wooden seat, he caught a glimpse of firelight on a man's ruddy face. Then he squeezed his eyes shut, afraid the militiamen might somehow sense that he was watching them.

"Who're you looking for?" said the farmer.

"A boy. Sixteen. Dark. Skinny."

"What's he done?"

"Murder. Up near the Vistula Lagoon."

From his place beside the farmer, the dog began to whine. Stefan thought his heart would stop.

"I'll be sure to keep a lookout for him," said the farmer, reaching out to scratch behind the dog's ears. "Can't be too careful these days."

The militiamen pulled the barrier out of the road. "Watch yourself, old man."

The farmer gave a *cluck-cluck*, and Stefan felt the wagon jerk as the mules leaned into their collars.

"I didn't kill anyone," said Stefan, emerging from beneath the sacks when the checkpoint had been left far behind.

"I didn't think you did."

Altenbruch, Germany: Wednesday 28 October
7:05 P.M. local time

"I wish I could have been of more help," said Marie Oldenburg as she followed them out to the sidewalk. The setting sun had slipped beyond the horizon, taking with it the lingering warmth of the evening.

"You've been very helpful," said Tobie. A strengthening breeze rattled the dying leaves on the trees and made her wish she'd pulled on her jacket before they left the car.

Jax said, "Any idea where we might find this Wolfgang Palmer?"

Marie Oldenburg eased the door of the archives shut behind her and turned the key in the lock. "Actually, I gave him a call when Professor Herbolt told me you vere interested in U–114. He says he's villing to meet with you this evening, if you like. At a Gasthaus to the northeast of Bremen. A place called Mumbrauer, near Breddorf. At half past seven."

"We are very interested. Thank you."

"Good. I'll tell him to expect you." Slipping the archives key into the pocket of her skirt, the old woman moved to where a sturdy green bicycle leaned against the trunk of a nearby elm. "You should know that Herr Palmer's vork is very controversial. He has made many enemies, both here in Germany and in America."

"Is he reliable?" said Jax.

Marie Oldenburg mounted her bicycle, her gnarled hands gripping the widespread handlebars. "Oh, yes. No one questions what he has found. It's his conclusions that are debatable."

"Do you believe him?"

She thrust out her lower lip and glanced downward in a characteristically German gesture of thoughtfulness. "I believe the true story of those six tragic years of war has never been told, and probably never vill be." She nodded her head briskly and shoved off. "*Auf Wiederschen.*"

Tobie watched the slight figure pedal into the gathering gloom. "Wow. I hope I'm that alert and agile when I'm her age."

"How good are your genes?"

"Not that good."

"Mine neither." Turning toward the car, Jax took out his phone and punched in a number.

"Who are you calling?" she asked, watching him. "Matt?"

He shook his head. "Andrei."

"You know Andrei's number? Right off the top of your head?"

"Yeah. Why?"

She went to lean against the side of the Jetta. "And you say he's not your buddy."

"He's not my buddy."

She watched him frown. Andrei obviously wasn't answering. She said, "And why exactly are you trying to call the Russians?"

He put his phone away. "Because I want to know if they ever checked that damned U-boat for radiation."

She felt her heart lurch uncomfortably in her chest. "Oh, Jesus. I never thought of that. And you were crawling around in there forever. Do you think you could have been exposed to radiation?"

"Don't you mean, 'we'? You think you were that much safer standing on the wharf?"

When she simply stared at him in horror, he said, "Come on. Unlock the car. There's no point in worrying until we're sure exactly what kind of material we're talking about. You never know—it could have been well shielded."

She fumbled for the Jetta's key and hit the remote button twice to unlock all the doors. "I don't think they knew too much about shielding that stuff sixty years ago, did they?"

He opened the door. "No."

As she tossed her bag onto the backseat, he made another call. "Hey, Matt," he said, sliding in beside her. "You know that shipment of Nazi gold? Well, it wasn't gold."

42

The Mumbrauer turned out to be a rustic old Gasthaus on the outskirts of a sleepy half-timbered village. Inside, it was all dark aged oak and an atmosphere scented by wood smoke and beer.

They found Wolfgang Palmer waiting for them in a paneled booth overlooking the tree-lined parking lot. A big, hairy bear of a man somewhere in his late fifties, he stood up to grasp first Tobie, then Jax in a hearty handshake. "Call me Wolfgang," he said in an accent that sounded more like Texas Panhandle than the Black Forest. "Please. Sit."

Sliding in beside Jax, Tobie studied the man's ruddy-cheeked, open face and plaid shirt. He was wearing jeans with cowboy boots and a big brass belt buckle in the shape of the Lone Star State. She was still trying to push aside every assumption she'd made about this man when Jax said, "Marie Oldenburg tells us you're a journalist."

Wolfgang nodded. "I used to be with the AP, but I'm semi-retired now. I'm working on a book."

"On the Nazi atomic program?"

"You guessed it."

"You don't sound nearly as German as your name."

He laughed. "My daddy's from Lubuck, and my mama's from Wichita Falls. My dad was a career Army man. Warrant officer. They were stationed at Wiesbaden back in the fifties, when I was born, which is how I ended up being called Wolfgang."

A waitress came to take their order. After she left, Jax settled back into a corner of the booth and said, "What can you tell us about the German atomic program in World War II?"

Wolfgang hunched his shoulders and laid his hands together, edgewise, on the scarred wooden surface of the old table. "The first thing you need to understand is that the Germans never had a military industrial complex like we developed at Los Alamos. The U.S. had literally thousands of scientists working on the Manhattan Project, with billions of dollars in funding pouring into it."

"So what did Germany have?"

Wolfgang paused while their waitress set three enormous beer steins in front of them. "Initially they called it the Uranium Club," he said, wrapping his big hands around his stein. "Uranverein. It was just a small group of no more than a few dozen scientists—mainly physicists, but also a few chemists and mathematicians. When the war broke out, they ended up under the German Army Ordnance Office. Basically they were looking into three things: uranium isotope separation, uranium and heavy water production, and building what they called a Uranmaschine, or a nuclear reactor."

"How far did they get?"

"We-ell," he said, drawing the word out into two syllables, "that depends on who you talk to. By 1942, the German high command came to the conclusion that their nuclear energy project was unlikely to advance fast enough to make a decisive contribution to the war effort."

"So they moved away from it?"

"In a sense. At that point, the research became more fragmented. There were something like nine different institutes working on it. The main center for everything was at Berlin, of course, but toward the end of the war even those people were scattered all over, because of the heavy Allied bombing runs. The scientists from the Kaiser Wilhelm Institute for Physics—men like Werner Heisenberg—moved to Hechingen and Haigerloch, near the Black Forest, while Nikolaus Riehl shifted his operations to Oranienburg."

"What was he working on?"

"Riehl? He tended to concentrate on the large scale production of high-purity uranium oxide."

Wolfgang leaned back in his seat and waited while their waitress set their plates on the table before them. "Up until recently, there were basically two schools of historical thought on the subject. Some writers, like Thomas Powers, came to the conclusion that German scientists like Heisenberg and Riehl were deliberately dragging their feet—that they didn't believe an atomic bomb should ever be built by anyone."

"Do you think Powers got that right?"

The Texan had ordered bratwurst and potatoes. Picking up his knife and fork, he cut a big chunk of sausage. "It's certainly true that Heisenberg was no Nazi. He was good friends with Jewish scientists like Einstein and Niels Bohr, and he refused to join the Party, even at first when it looked like Germany had won the war. He always remained firmly against the war with the West, although he didn't oppose the war with Russia."

Wolfgang chewed for a moment in silence, then said, "Heisenberg was a complex man. He hated Hitler and the

Nazis, but he was a patriot. You have to remember that most of the men who fought for Germany in the War fought for *Germany*, not for Hitler. Not for the Nazis."

Tobie picked at her own omelet and salad. "So was he dragging his feet, or not?"

"I honestly don't know. We know he warned his colleagues that the Americans were working on an atom bomb. If the war hadn't ended when it did, the Allies would have dropped their two bombs on Berlin and Hamburg, rather than on Hiroshima and Nagasaki. How could any man knowing what his country faced not work to avert that?"

Tobie said, "So what's the other school of historical thought?"

Wolfgang raised his beer stein and drank deeply, then swiped the back of one meaty hand across his mouth. "In the late nineties, another historian came out with a book arguing that the only reason the Germans failed to develop an atom bomb was because they didn't understand how it could work. Basically, he said Heisenberg was a bumbling idiot."

"Was he?"

"*Werner Heisenberg?* Are you kidding? You've heard of the Heisenberg Uncertainty Principle, right? That's him. The guy won the 1932 Nobel Prize in Physics for his work in quantum mechanics. Yeah, he made some mistakes, but they all did—even Oppenheimer." Wolfgang leaned forward. "Among other things, the author of this new book claimed the Germans failed to appreciate the potential of plutonium to be a nuclear explosive."

"You don't think he got that right?"

"Hardly. We've since found a preliminary patent application for a plutonium bomb written in 1941 by Carl Friedrich von Weizsäcker."

Jax frowned. "Where did that come from?"

"The Russian archives." Wolfgang laid down his knife and

fork. "You've heard the expression, 'What's not in the files didn't happen'?"

"Yes."

"Well, up until ten years ago, most of the historical research into the German nuclear project was limited to the Uranium Club, mainly because they're the only ones whose documents we had. But you see, under the Reich Research Council, the Army was also involved in atomic research—as was the Navy and the Air Force. Like I said, it was all very diversified."

"So what happened to their documents?"

"All the files from the Kaiser Wilhelm Institute for Physics were grabbed by the Soviets when they took over Berlin in April and May of 1945."

"They took them back to Moscow?"

Wolfgang nodded, his mouth full. "That's right," he said, swallowing hard. "They weren't made accessible to the West until 2002."

"Have you seen them?" asked Tobie.

"I have." Wolfgang drained his beer stein and set it down with a thump.

"And?"

"And I believe that a team led by Kurt Diebner actually tested a nuclear device in Germany, in Thuringia, right before the end of the war."

Tobie dropped her fork, the handle clattering loudly against the side of her plate.

"When?" said Jax. "When was this?"

"On the third of March, 1945."

43

Jax quietly ordered three more Beck's beers, although Tobie had barely touched hers. "What kind of nuclear device?" he asked, his gaze on the Texan's hairy face.

"It's difficult to say now, although evidence suggests it was not a standard nuclear weapon powered by nuclear fission."

"So what was it?"

"Maybe a hybrid-nuclear fusion weapon."

Tobie picked up her fork. She didn't have a clue what the difference between nuclear fission and nuclear fusion even was.

Jax said, "Where in Thuringia did this happen?"

"At a place called Ohrdruf. The blast was carried out under the supervision of the SS. Anywhere from several dozen to several hundred prisoners of war and concentration-camp inmates are said to have died in the blast."

Tobie said, "But surely there would still be evidence of that kind of explosion, even today?"

"There is. Recent test results from the site show elevated levels of radioactive isotopes. The problem is, there's no way to know for certain if it came from the 1945 blast, or if it's contamination from the Russian disaster at Chernobyl."

Jax and Tobie exchanged quick glances. Jax said, "Where does the evidence for this device come from? From the Russian archives, too?"

"A lot of it." Wolfgang wiped his napkin across his mouth and tucked it beneath the rim of his empty plate. "The thing is, only a small group of scientists was involved, and all relevant documents were immediately classified top secret when they were captured by the Allies."

When Jax remained silent, the Texan looked from him to Tobie, and gave a wry half smile. "You don't believe me, do you?"

Jax reached for his new beer. "You have to admit, it is hard to believe."

"You think I don't know that? But there's more. Along with the patent for a plutonium bomb, the Russian archives also contain a report from a Russian spy in Germany. The report was considered significant enough that it was sent on to Stalin. According to their guy, 'reliable sources' described two huge explosions in Thuringia on the night of three March."

"It could have been anything."

"It could have," Wolfgang agreed. "Except the East German authorities interviewed a number of eyewitnesses around Ohrdruf in the early 1960s. They reported a bright light followed by a sudden blast of wind. And they all said they suffered from nosebleeds, headaches, and nausea for days afterward."

Ducking his head, the Texan rummaged around in the tattered knapsack that rested on the bench beside him. "Here. Look at this," he said, holding out a photocopy of a sketch rendered in blue and red ink.

Peering over Jax's shoulder, Tobie found herself staring at a drawing of what looked like a big teardrop, or what might almost have been an elongated mechanical bug, with a small head framed by two projecting arms. In the belly of the "bug" was a big blue circle surrounding a smaller red inner circle.

"What is it?" asked Jax, looking up.

"It's a diagram of a primitive nuclear weapon. It's a schematic, mind you; not a practical blueprint. But what's significant is that it was part of a newly discovered report."

"Written by whom?"

"We don't know. The title page of the report was missing when it was found in the archives." Wolfgang pointed one of his thick fingers at the bulging end of the teardrop. "It's a fission device, based on plutonium. The report even goes on to discuss a theory for a hydrogen bomb."

Jax looked up. "I thought the Germans didn't have a working reactor to produce plutonium."

"That's what we used to think. But recent industrial archaeology on the remains of the experimental German reactor in Berlin suggests it did work—in fact, it might have been up and running for several weeks."

"Long enough to make the material for a bomb?" said Tobie.

"For at least one." Wolfgang leaned forward. "Some people believe the device exploded at Thuringia was a hybrid—fission and fusion. Others think it was a 'dirty bomb,' using enriched nuclear material with conventional explosives." He lowered his voice even further. "And then there are those who think the bombs the U.S. dropped on Japan were actually German made—seized by the Allies when they overran Germany."

"That's ridiculous," said Tobie.

"Is it? Ever hear of U–234?"

"No," she said, while Jax nodded.

"It was a Type XB submarine. One of those big mothers."

"One of the ones originally designed as a minelayer?"

"That's right. It left Kiel on 25 March 1945, headed for Japan and loaded with everything from a dismantled Me–262 jet fighter to V–2 missile components, and experts on rockets and jet engines."

"Operation Caesar," said Tobie quietly. The cargo of U–234 sounded much like the material they'd seen stacked on the wharves in Kaliningrad.

"You know about it?"

"We've heard of it."

Wolfgang nodded. "Well, along with everything else, U–234 was also carrying 550 kilograms of uranium."

"How many bombs would that make?" Jax asked.

"Of the size we dropped on Japan? Two. Some people think that even if the U.S. didn't drop German-made bombs on Japan, they used the uranium from that U-boat."

Tobie said, "What happened to it? The U-boat, I mean."

"They were still in the Atlantic when the order came through from the German High Command, saying the war was over and that all U-boats were to surface and fly a black flag from their periscopes."

"So they surrendered?"

Wolfgang nodded. "An American boarding party escorted them to New Hampshire."

Jax said, "The uranium oxide—where was it stored?"

"You mean, where in the U-boat was it? I don't know. All I know is it was packed in ten metal containers. When the Americans cut them open with a blowtorch, they found them full of smaller containers, shaped like cigar boxes. A quarter ton of uranium oxide, altogether. J. Robert Oppenheimer himself was supposedly there when they opened it."

Jax was silent for a moment. Tobie noticed he hadn't eaten much of his jaeger schnitzel. Finally, he said, "Marie Oldenburg told you about the cargo manifest of U–114?"

"Yes."

"Do you think it's possible that submarine could have been carrying an atom bomb?"

"I'd say so, yes."

Jax sat back in his seat and let out his breath in a long, slow sigh that sounded like "*Fuck*."

Tobie leaned forward. "You said there were other files—files the Allies seized after the war and that are still kept top secret?"

"That's right."

"But why? Why would they do that?"

"Keep them secret, you mean?" Wolfgang pressed his full lips into a thin, flat line. "World War II might have ended over sixty years ago, but it's still a very controversial topic. A lot of people say Truman and his generals should have been tried as war criminals, for dropping the A-bomb on Japan."

"It was horrible, yes," said Tobie. "But it actually *saved* lives, by helping to end the war sooner."

Wolfgang gave a wry smile. "That's the argument you always hear. The problem is, Japan was trying to surrender *before* we dropped the bomb on them. They were willing to accept every single U.S. demand, except they wanted to be allowed to keep their emperor."

Tobie frowned. "I thought in the end we let them keep their emperor."

"Exactly."

"But what does that have to do with the Germans developing the bomb?"

The Texan drained his beer stein and set it aside. "Think about what it would mean, if Germany had the bomb but didn't use it. I mean, the Nazis are supposed to be the biggest baddies the universe has ever seen, right? So what does that say about us Americans, if we dropped a weapon even the Nazis were reluctant to use?"

"I don't believe it," said Tobie.

"I have to admit," said Wolfgang, pushing to his feet, "I don't want to believe it, myself."

44

"You didn't eat much," said Jax after the big Texan had shaken hands again and left.

Tobie stared down at their plates. "Neither did you."

"No."

They sat in silence for a long moment. Jax said, "It never made any sense, the idea of terrorists raising that U-boat for gold. Not with this attack supposedly planned for Halloween. The timing was just too tight."

"It's still tight, isn't it? Even if what they were after was an old German A-bomb."

Jax glanced out the window, to the darkened parking lot lit only by the faint flicker of gas lamps. "If there really was an old German A-bomb on that sub, anyone going after it would deliberately have planned the operation to be tight. Whoever these guys are, they'll want to move as fast as they can. The longer they have that bomb in their possession, the more likely it is to be detected."

She studied his half-averted profile, with its high cheekbones and lean jaw line. "You believe Wolfgang, then? That the Germans not only developed a small nuclear bomb, but decided in the last days of the war to send a prototype to Japan?"

"Somebody obviously believed it enough to go through the trouble of raising that U-boat."

"But would the thing still be viable? After sixty years?"

"Viable enough to cause considerable damage, whatever kind of device we're talking about."

She pushed away her plate. "What I don't understand is how anyone even found out about that bomb in the first place. They would need to have known about it before, right? Before Karl Wertheim advertised his grandfather's papers on eBay."

"You heard what Wolfgang said. New information has been turning up all over the place in the last twenty years. Not just in the Russian archives, but in the personal papers of men whose families were living in East Germany when the Iron Curtain came down. Someone could have found out about it that way." He was silent a moment. "I also have an ugly suspicion the honchos in Washington know more about that submarine's cargo than we've been told."

"What makes you say that?"

"Because according to Matt, the Navy has been keeping an eye on U–114 ever since they located it. That hit a sour note with me. I just can't see them doing that if all they thought she was carrying was gold."

She was aware of him watching the scene outside the window, although he'd been careful not to look directly that way again. She glanced toward the parking lot, and saw nothing except silent rows of cars.

"What do you keep looking at?"

"Don't stare."

She obediently looked away. "Why? What is it?"

"There's a black Mercedes GL-Class parked beside the Jetta. See it?"

She threw a quick sideways glance at the shadowy rows of vehicles. "The SUV?"

"That's it."

"So?"

"So, they pulled in about ten minutes ago. Only, no one got out of the car."

"Could be a coincidence. They could be waiting for someone."

"It's possible."

Tobie reached for her beer stein and took a long, bitter swallow. "What do we do?"

Jax signaled their waitress for the bill. "I've got an idea."

After they paid their tab, Jax walked up to the middle-aged man at the inn's front desk and said in flawless German, "I'm afraid we have a problem. My friend here"—Jax nodded toward Tobie—"is being stalked by her ex-husband, and he's out in the parking lot right now, waiting for us."

The desk clerk, a small man with fair, receding straight hair and a long, thin nose, threw a nervous glance toward the front of the inn. A worried spasm crossed his nipped features. "Where?"

"The black GL-Class. Next to our red Jetta."

He cleared his throat. "You would like me to phone the police?"

"I don't think we need to do that." Jax laid the Jetta's key on the desk, along with a hundred marks. "The last thing we want to do is disrupt your patrons with an unpleasant incident. Perhaps you could simply bring our car up to the front and leave it running for us?"

The man's thin nose quivered. Germans hated scenes almost as much as the British. His hand closed around the key—and the hundred-mark note. "Yes. It would be better. I'll get it right away."

"And leave both doors open, would you?" Jax called after him.

They stood just inside the door and watched the man walk briskly across the shadowy lot toward their car. "As soon as he pulls up in front," Jax told Tobie, "we run out and jump in the car. I'll drive."

"But it's rented in my n—" she began, then broke off. She'd never seen anyone who could handle a car the way Jax could. "All right. But please, please don't wreck it."

"I'll try." They watched the Jetta's reverse lights come on, just as the big SUV beside it roared to life. "Here he comes." Jax slapped open the gasthaus door. "*Now.*"

They sprinted down the short walk to the curb. Tobie dove in the Jetta's passenger door, pulling it shut behind her just as Jax hit the gas. They were halfway out the parking lot before Jax's door slammed shut.

He spun the wheel, the Jetta's backend fishtailing as they screeched out onto the narrow country road. "What's he doing?"

Tobie swung around to stare out the back window. Careening out of the parking lot on two wheels, the big Mercedes barreled after them. A second GL-Class roared after it.

"Shit. There's two of them!"

45

Jax floored it, the engine whining as he shifted rapidly up through the gears.

They tore through a darkened countryside of flat farmland edged with hedgerows, the road curving around shadowy groves of silent trees. As they pulled clear of the last straggling houses of the village, the first SUV swung out into the opposite lane, hit the gas, and laid on his horn. Jax yanked the wheel to the left and swerved into him.

Tobie let out a yelp. "What are you doing? He's bigger than we are!"

Jax flashed her a grin. "Yeah. But is he braver?"

She made a grab for the armrest. "*Oh, my God.*"

At the last possible nanosecond, the Mercedes chickened out and dropped back, horn blaring.

"See?" said Jax, spinning the wheel again.

"You're crazy."

Tires squealing, he rocked the Jetta back and forth across the centerline, weaving from side to side, cutting off the SUV each time it tried to creep up beside them.

Suddenly, the headlights of an approaching car pierced the

darkness, bearing down on them. Tires screeched. Jax cut back into his own lane the instant before a sleek BMW convertible whipped past, its angry driver leaning on his horn.

The Mercedes swung back out into the other lane again, moving up fast. Jax hit the gas, crowding him over.

Tobie said, "Uh . . . curve coming!"

"I see it." Shifting down, Jax cut back into his own lane.

The SUV stayed in the other lane, pulling abreast of them as they swung around the bend.

"Oh, shit!" cried Tobie as a glare of lights hit her in the eyes. She heard the blast of a horn, the squeal of brakes. The driver of the SUV swerved to the left, careening off the far side of the road and down a small embankment to crash into a darkened stand of shrubs as a panel truck tore past in the opposite direction.

"What's the second SUV doing?" said Jax, shifting rapidly back up to fifth.

Tobie craned around to stare at the twisting road behind them. "He's staying with us. But it doesn't look like he's trying to crowd us."

They raced through the dark night, past a farm with a looming old barn and a neat white picket fence that glowed out of the darkness. "I don't get it," she said, just as Jax's phone began to ring.

He unclipped the phone from his belt and hit Speaker.

"What the fuck are you doing, Alexander?" demanded a man's gruff voice. "You were supposed to pull over."

Jax cast a quick, incredulous glance at the phone. "Excuse me?"

"You heard me. You just ran my guys off the road."

Jax raised his gaze to the rearview mirror. The second Mercedes was still there, its headlights two bright unwavering points of light racing after them. "Who the hell are you?"

"This is Agent Farnsworth, with Homeland Security."

Jax kept his foot on the gas. "Like that explains anything?"

"You're in trouble, smartass."

When Jax said nothing, the voice barked, "Pull over, damn it. We need to talk."

Jax smiled and feather-edged a corner, the Jetta's engine purring. "We are talking."

"Just pull the fuck over."

Jax said, "I'll pull over when I can see you in a well-lit area with lots of people around."

"Are you crazy?"

"No. Just careful."

There was a moment's fuming silence. Farnsworth said, "There's a village about a mile up ahead. Will that do?"

"Probably."

The houses whizzing past on either side were growing closer together. Jax eased up on the gas. They thumped across a narrow old stone bridge, into a main street where the curtained windows of close-packed stuccoed houses glowed brightly with light. A man in a raincoat and hat looked up as they passed, the little wire-haired dachshund at the end of his leash letting out a halfhearted *woof.*

"It's well lit, with lots of people," barked the voice on the phone. "What are you waiting for?"

"I'll know it when I see it."

Near the far outskirts of the village they came upon a closed market, its small lot well lit by a high bank of sulfurous lights. Rolling into the lot, Jax threw the Jetta into reverse and backed into a slot just in front of the market's closed doors, his headlights stabbing out into the lot.

"I want you to park directly across from me and turn off your lights," he said into the phone.

"You got it, asshole."

Jax watched the big Mercedes back into the row across from them. Turning the phone off Speaker, he covered the mike and whispered to Tobie, "Get out your gun and cover me."

She dug the compact Beretta out of her bag. "You know I can't shoot, right?"

"You've got twelve bullets. If anything goes wrong, just point it in these guys' direction and let it rip."

Tobie eased off the safety with trembling fingers. "Right."

"Now open your door, slowly, and stand behind it," he told her quietly. "Keep your gun out of sight, but ready."

She nodded and cautiously lifted the handle of the door.

On the far side of the parking lot, the driver of the Mercedes killed his lights. Jax could see two tall figures silhouetted against the streetlamp behind them.

Agent Farnsworth said, "What now, asshole?"

"Now get out of your car. Carefully. If you've got an ID, I want it in your hands. And that had better be all that's in your hands. Hold your ID up to your chest with both hands and walk across the lot toward me. Your friend stays in the car."

"You got it." The passenger door of the Mercedes swung open. A tall, lean man slid out carefully and began to walk toward them.

Jax opened his own door and slowly straightened, his Beretta in his hand. He waited until the guy was maybe three feet away, then said, "That's far enough."

Agent Farnsworth drew up, the muscles of his clenched jaw working furiously. He was a lean, hard-muscled man with dark eyes and darkly tanned skin and a sharp-featured face that ended in a pointed goatee.

"Keep your hands where I can see them and hand me the ID," said Jax, the car door still between them.

"What's your fucking problem?" said Farnsworth, holding out his badge. "It's a fucking Homeland Security ID. It's real."

Jax gave a soft laugh. "Yeah. I had FBI credentials myself just two weeks ago."

He glanced through the guy's credentials, then tossed it back. Farnsworth caught it with one hand. Jax said, "What do you want?"

Farnsworth started to put his ID away, then froze when Jax said quietly, "Don't."

The muscles along the man's jaw bunched again. He said, "This is a Homeland Security operation from here on out. You've done your job. Now it's time for you to back out."

Jax stared at the idiot. "That's what this stunt was for? So you could tell me *that*?"

"You're the one who decided to play cute by taking off."

"I've got people trying to kill me."

"We'd have identified ourselves if you'd have just given us a fucking chance."

"Give the wrong people a chance, and you end up dead."

The guy was practically grinding his teeth. "It's not your problem anymore. Now that we know for sure what we're dealing with, we can take it from here."

Jax hooked one elbow over the top of the Jetta's open door. "You know, I hate to tell you this, but I don't take orders from you guys. I work for a whole different outfit."

"We're all on the same team, remember?"

"That's what I keep hearing. I tell you what: you go back and pull your guys out of that ditch, and just go on with whatever you were doing. When my boss tells me to quit, I'll quit."

Farnsworth jabbed the air between them with a pointed finger. "You'll be hearing from him," he said, and turned back toward the Mercedes.

Jax said, "By the way—"

Farnsworth swung around again. "What?"

"Where'd you get my phone number?"

Rather than answer, Farnsworth just turned his back and walked away, one finger raised in a backward salute.

Jax called after him, "Next time you want to talk to me, use the damned phone."

Farnsworth kept walking.

"Well, that was all very adult and highbrow," said Tobie, sliding back into the car and slamming her door.

Jax shut the driver's door with a click. "Hey, I didn't hurt the car, did I?"

She stared across the parking lot. "I don't get it," she said as they watched Farnsworth jerk open his door. The Mercedes' powerful engine roared to life, tires squealing as the agents peeled out of the parking lot and raced back up the road.

Jax turned the key and eased the Jetta into gear. "It's just a bureaucratic turf war. Homeland Security grew big and fast after 9/11, which meant they hired a lot of arrogant assholes who don't really know what the fuck they're doing. And thanks to the Patriot Act, they think they can do anything they want."

"But what are those guys even doing here? I didn't know we had Homeland Security people in Germany."

"Are you kidding? We have Homeland Security people everywhere. Even the NYPD has 'anti-terrorist' guys over here. It's supposed to make everyone feel safer." Jax thrust the Jetta into gear and hit the gas. "Bankrupt, but confident."

She was silent as he rolled slowly back through the quiet village. As they hit the outskirts and he began to pick up speed, she said, "Do we back off?"

"Not until Matt tells us to."

"Do you think he will?"

Jax shifted rapidly into fourth, then fifth, the Jetta's engine purring through the dark night. "Not a chance in hell."

They took a room in Bremen, at a small guesthouse beside the Weser River. While October took her first shower in four days, Jax called Matt.

"I take it you passed on my information about the possible atomic nature of U–114's cargo to Homeland Security?"

"Share and share alike; you know our new motto. But their reaction was interesting."

"How's that?"

"I got the feeling it wasn't exactly a big shock to them."

Jax was silent for a moment. "Are we the only ones who thought this whole thing was about Nazi gold?"

· "Probably. You know what Washington is like. No one ever levels with anyone else."

"Share and share alike."

"Right." Matt was silent a moment before blowing out a harsh breath. "This is serious shit, Jax. If these terrorists really have got their hands on an atom bomb—even an old one . . ."

"We'll find them, Matt."

"You're running out of time."

"I know."

After he got off the phone with Matt, Jax sat at a small, round table overlooking the Weser. The thick bank of clouds building overhead hid the moon and turned the water sliding past into something black and cold. After a moment he got up, rummaged around in his bag, and found a sweater to pull over his head.

Halloween was just over forty-eight hours away. Somehow, knowing exactly what kind of attack they were facing made that date seem to loom even closer. And they still had no idea where the attack was going down, or who was behind it.

Twisting the top off a bottle of springwater, he went to lean against the window frame, his gaze on the river below. Somehow, it all kept coming back to the Russian connection. The *Yalena*. Kaliningrad. The Russian archives that had kept the German scientists' records buried for the last sixty years. If only there were some way—*some* way to . . .

Reaching for his phone, he put in a call to Colonel McClintock. "Colonel? Jax Alexander here. I want October to do another remote viewing."

46

Vice President T. J. Beckham stood behind his wide, well-polished desk and waited for the Director of Central Intelligence to walk up to him.

Beckham liked to think of himself as a down-home kind of guy, easy and approachable. Normally, he went out of his way to make folks feel comfortable, to keep from overawing people with the authority of his position.

Today, he wanted to reinforce it.

"You asked to see me, Mr. Vice President?" said Gordon Chandler.

"Yes, Gordon; I did." Beckham waited while Chandler settled in the comfortable leather club chair on the far side of the desk, then he rubbed his nose with his knuckles and eased out a perturbed sigh. "I've just received a somewhat disturbing report, Gordon."

Chandler's eyebrows rose in a parody of innocent inquiry. "Sir?"

"About U–114. It seems that submarine wasn't carrying gold, after all. Word is, it had a real live atomic bomb on it. And you knew about it."

Chandler blinked, but kept silent.

Beckham flattened his palms on the surface of the desk and leaned into them. *"Why wasn't I told?"*

Chandler cleared his throat. "Up until now, it was just a theory, and not one we tended to give much credence to."

"A theory. Where exactly did this theory come from?"

"Some of the files we seized from Germany at the end of the war—combined with reports from certain captured scientists—suggested that Germany was actually farther along in their atomic program than is generally believed."

Beckham studied the other man's smooth, handsome face. "You obviously had more than that. Something that led you to focus on U–114."

Chandler shrugged. "We knew the Nazis had secretly commissioned one of their XI-Bs. It seemed reasonable to assume they were using it for something important. And the timing was right—March of 1945."

"So we knew U–114 was an XI-B, rather than an XB?"

"Yes, sir."

"And how did we know that?"

Chandler's complacent expression never slipped. "We've returned most of the archives we seized to the Germans, but not quite all of them. Some sensitive material is still classified. We knew U–114 sailed for South Africa and Japan as part of Operation Caesar, and we knew that amongst its other cargo it carried an unidentified weapon referred to only as 'die Klinge von Solomon.'"

Beckham frowned. "What's that?"

"It's German for 'the Sword of Solomon.'"

Beckham felt a chill run up his spine.

Chandler said, "It all seemed to fit."

Beckham pushed away from his desk to stand and look out the window. It was a moment before he spoke. "None of this explains why I wasn't told the truth."

"The President made a strategic decision to limit the number of people with access to the intelligence."

Beckham swung to face him again. "Why?"

"Why?" Chandler huffed a soft laugh. "If this information gets out, it'll rewrite the history books—and not in a way that would reflect well on the United States."

"My God, man. You think that's more important than preventing some terrorist outfit from detonating an atom bomb on our soil?"

A muscle tightened along Chandler's jaw. "We have over fourteen hundred crews fanning out all over the country, sir. If those sons of bitches have brought that device into the States, we'll find it."

Beckham studied the other man's smooth, handsome face. "Your confidence is inspiring. But I can't help thinking that, thanks to you, I sent two brave young people into danger without even knowing what I was asking them to face."

Chandler pushed to his feet. "We plan to bring them home tonight, sir."

Beckham shook his head. "I don't think so. They've done pretty darn good, so far. I say, let 'em run with it."

"Sir—"

"You heard me. I want Guinness and Alexander to keep following this thing wherever they think it's leading them. At least for now."

Chandler's jaw tightened. But he simply inclined his head and turned toward the door. "Yes, sir."

47

"This isn't going to work," said October. Wrapped in one of the guesthouse's big, fluffy white bathrobes, she sat on the edge of the bed, her wet hair hanging straight about her shoulders.

"Why not?" said Jax.

"There's a protocol—"

"I know. I talked to the Colonel. I've selected the target myself. It's written down, here." He laid a folded square of paper on the table before him. "When we're ready, I'll give the Colonel a call. He doesn't know what the target is, so he can do the tasking from New Orleans, over my speakerphone."

"This isn't something you can do over a speakerphone."

"Why not?"

She ran the splayed fingers of one hand through her wet hair, raking it off her forehead. "I don't know. It just isn't."

"I don't see why it should make a difference."

She stared at him with wide, luminous brown eyes. "I thought you didn't believe in remote viewing."

"I don't. But, for some reason I can't begin to understand, it works." He hesitated. "Sometimes."

"See. You don't believe in it."

He pushed away from the table. "You saw that U-boat in Kaliningrad. I don't know how or why, but I can't deny the fact that it was there, right where you said it was." He went to put his hands on her shoulders. He could feel the tension thrumming through her like fine little tremors. "You need to do this, October," he said more gently. "We have just over two days left until Halloween. Right now, we don't know who these guys are, or where they're going to hit. About all we do know is that if we don't stop them, a lot of innocent people are going to die. Horribly."

She gazed up at him. "What if it doesn't work? Then what will we do?"

He shifted his hands to her neck, kneading the tight muscles. The truth was, they'd reached a dead end, and time was running out. But all he said was, "We'll figure out something. But we need this viewing, October. Will you do it?"

He felt her draw in a deep breath that shuddered her small frame. "Let me get dressed."

While he dimmed the lights, she pulled on a turtleneck and a pair of sweatpants, then went to sit cross-legged in a darkened corner of the room, her hands resting on her knees, her eyes closed. Part of her success as a remote viewer came, he knew, from this—this rare ability to sink so easily and deeply into the required state. Her vegetarian diet, and the years she had spent practicing yoga and meditating, all helped. But the last few days had been chaotic and frightening; how would that affect her ability to reach her "Zone"?

He watched her lips part, her chest rising and falling with her even breathing. There was a peace about her, a calm grounding, that he both admired and—he was ashamed to realize—vaguely envied.

She opened her eyes and gave him a soft smile.

"Ready?" he asked.

She nodded.

He reached for his phone.

"The target is written on the folded piece of paper Jax laid on the table," said the Colonel, his voice sounding vaguely hollow as it came through the speakerphone. "It's a location. I want you to tell me what you see."

October sat silently. She had shifted to a comfortable chair, a pad of paper and a pen on her lap. From the table near the window, Jax watched as a slight frown twitched her forehead. Her lips parted, but she said nothing.

After a moment, the Colonel said, "Just take your time, October."

She closed her eyes. Jax had only seen her do a viewing once before, but he could sense the tension in her. Something was wrong.

The Colonel said, "Tobie?"

She shook her head. "It's not working. I'm not getting anything."

The Colonel's voice was soothing. "That's okay, Tobie. Just try to relax. Describe what you see."

She took another breath. "I see . . . darkness."

The Colonel waited patiently, but after a few minutes of continued silence, he said, "Describe some sensory elements, Tobie."

Her pen was moving across the paper now, in slow looping circles. "I sense . . . a void. It's like the dull moan of a blowing wind. It's . . . I've never experienced this before. It's . . ."

She thrust up suddenly from the chair, both hands coming up to pull her still damp hair away from her face. "*It's not working.*"

The Colonel's voice was low, calm. "It's all right, Tobie."

She spun to face Jax. He stood beside the window, watching her. She said, "No, it's not."

"Yes, it is."

"Without this viewing—without the information we need from it—we don't have anything."

"We can try again, later," said McClintock.

Jax picked up the phone and took it off Speaker. "I'll get back to you, Colonel. Thanks." He looked at October.

She said, "The target. What was the target?"

He shook his head. "If we're going to try it later, that kind of frontloading—"

"No. What was the target?" She snatched up the piece of paper that still lay on the table. He'd folded it into thirds, and then again in half. Spreading it open, she stared down at what he had written.

The current location of the atomic device taken from U–114.

"Maybe I worded it wrong," said Jax.

She shook her head. "No. It should have worked. I should have seen *something*, even if it wasn't enough to tell us exactly where the bomb is."

His hands closed over hers, crushing the sheet of paper she still held. "It's okay."

She jerked away from him. "I don't understand what went wrong. I've never had a complete miss like this. It was as if I reached out with my mind and touched . . . nothing."

"How often are you wrong?"

"It depends on how you define 'wrong.'" She thought about it for a moment. "I get details wrong. I miss things that are there—sometimes important things, like the *Yalena* at the shipyard. And sometimes I'll see things that aren't there—or I'll interpret some of what I see wrong. Then other times, my attention will waver from the intended target to something nearby that's more interesting."

"Like what?"

"Well . . . one time I described a church, when the target was a bicycle shed across the street. And then sometimes I'm off in time."

He frowned. "In time?"

She nodded. "Once, McClintock ran me against a target I described as a swimming pool, when it was supposed to be a warehouse. At first we thought it was a complete miss. Then we discovered that the site used to be a public swimming pool, before it was abandoned during the Civil Rights movement in the sixties."

Jax studied her smooth-skinned face. "Are you telling me you can remote view *different time periods*?"

She gave him a wry smile. "Why is that so much harder to believe than remote viewing across distance?"

"Because—" He broke off. The truth was, he didn't know why it was harder to believe. Hell, both should be impossible.

"One of the reasons quantum physicists have always been at the forefront of research into remote viewing is because they *know* that our ideas about time and space are just mental conveniences that don't actually describe the fundamentals of reality at all. The problem is, it's a concept the rest of the scientific community has a hard time grasping—mainly, I suspect, because it threatens so many things we all believe in."

He went to stand at the window, his gaze on the dark river sliding silently past below. His own knowledge of quantum physics—of things like string theory, or M-theory–was at best vague. Not something he'd ever felt a compelling need to understand. Now, it had suddenly become vitally important.

After a moment, he said, "So why do you think it didn't work tonight? Because the setup was wrong?"

She shook her head. "No. That shouldn't really have made a difference. The constructs McClintock and I use—always having an independent tasker, always keeping the viewer ignorant of the target—are important in training, and to provide clean quantifiable results for statistical purposes—or for intelligence work. But the truth is, experienced remote viewers are capable of tasking themselves."

"How do you know you're not just accessing your own imaginations?"

"We don't. That's part of the problem. It's why I wanted tonight's setup to be as structured as possible—to reduce the chance I would simply tap into my own imagination."

He looked at her over his shoulder. "But you didn't access your imagination. All you got was . . . nothing."

She pursed her lips and blew out a long sigh. "It could be because I'm tired. Because I'm tense. Because I know so much is riding on this." Reaching down, she snatched up the crumpled paper from the floor. "And it's not like I was really ignorant of the target. I had a pretty good idea what you were setting me against—either the atomic device, or the men who have it."

"So you can still try it again, later?"

"I can try."

The rattle of his phone vibrating against the table drew his attention. He picked it up without even glancing at the caller ID. "Jax Alexander."

A heavily accented voice said, "You wanted something?"

Jax met October's questioning gaze. "Hey, Andrei," he said lightly. "Just the man I wanted to talk to. Did your guys ever do a radiation check on that U-boat?"

"What do you think? We're stupid? We know about U–234. Of course we did a radiation check."

"And?"

"And, nothing. It came up clean. Why do you ask, Jax?"

"Just wondering."

"Right, Jax. It doesn't have anything to do with the interesting rumor I heard this evening?"

"Rumor? What rumor?"

"That U–114 was carrying some kind of atomic device."

Sonofabitch. Wolfgang Palmer obviously had a big mouth. Aloud, Jax said, "The Nazis never developed an atom bomb, Andrei."

Andrei gave a soft laugh. "Just because the West has been ignorant of the contents of our archives for the last sixty years, Jax, doesn't mean we were."

Jax looked out the window, at the cold stars glittering from out of the black northern sky.

Andrei said, "I checked into your suggestion about the boy, Stefan Baklanov."

"And?"

"And his body was not among the thirteen dead found on the *Yalena.*"

"So he is still alive."

"Perhaps. Or perhaps he was somehow involved in the killings."

"I find that hard to believe."

Andrei grunted. "One more thing. It seems the captain of the *Yalena* was in contact with a mutual friend of ours."

"We have mutual friends?"

"Call him a business acquaintance. Azzam Badr al'Din." He gave the name its proper pronunciation, *Bed-ra-deen.*

"Shit." Jax was aware of October's frowning gaze upon him. He said, "We'd heard Baklanov was into gunrunning."

"This was more than gunrunning. We're not talking about a bunch of Kalashnikovs here, Jax. Whatever was on that ship was big. Baklanov was asking a million euros for it."

Jax leaned back against the edge of the table. "Why are you telling me this, Andrei?"

"Because this is your problem, Jax, not mine. Besides . . ." Jax could hear the malicious smile in the Russian's voice. "What are friends for?"

48

As far as Gerald T. Boyd was concerned, remote viewing belonged in the same category as sun signs and chakras and all the other New Age nonsense embraced by the credulous fools of the world. He knew about the Army's decades-long flirtation with the phenomenon, and had always found it a source of profound professional embarrassment. So it was with a sense of anger mingled with disgust that he settled at the desk of his room at the Willard that evening and spread the report on Ensign Guinness's "viewing" session across the leather blotter.

It's some kind of a fraud, he thought. No one could "see" images with only their minds. Someone had obviously leaked the location of the *Yalena* and its illicit cargo. The problem was, who? Baklanov? Rodriguez?

Impossible.

As he flipped through the pages, anger bled slowly into disquiet and, ultimately, into doubt. Pushing up from the desk, he paced the room, his mind testing and rejecting one hypothetical explanation after the other. He poured himself a glass of Jack Daniel's and drank it down in one long pull. Then he splashed another two inches into the bottom of his glass and went to flip open his laptop.

The convictions of a lifetime are not easily overturned. But as he worked his way through the publicly available literature and then on to the material that was still classified, he found himself eventually confronted with more evidence than he could deny. In the end, he was inclined to agree with the general who'd once said that if you didn't believe in remote viewing, you hadn't done your homework.

Whether October Guinness's ability was a gift from God or the devil, it was not Boyd's place to judge. He knew only one thing: the woman was dangerous, and she needed to be located and eliminated.

Quickly.

Bremen, Germany: Thursday 29 October
12:10 A.M. local time

They went for a walk along the Weser River, where a wide paved path ran between the embankment and a looming stone wall that protected the red brick buildings above from floods.

"So who is Azzam Badr al' Din?" October asked, huddling deep in her jacket. A cold wind was blowing in off the North Sea, fluttering her hair around her face and bringing a rosy glow to her cheeks.

"A Druze gunrunner," said Jax.

She glanced over at him. "A what?"

"A Druze. It's a kind of offshoot of Islam, with a heavy influence from Gnosticism and neo-Platonism thrown in.

Most of the Druze live in Lebanon and Syria, although there are about a hundred thousand of them within the borders of pre–1967 Israel, with maybe another twenty thousand in the Occupied Territories and Jordan. Sometimes they side with other Muslims, but they've been known to form alliances with the Maronite Christians and the Israelis, too."

"So who does Badr al'Din sell his guns to?"

"Basically, anyone who can afford them. As far as Azzam is concerned, if you've got a Swiss bank account, then you're in business. He doesn't care where your money comes from, just as long as it converts."

"And how exactly do you and Andrei know this guy?"

"I'm not sure about Andrei. But I first ran into Azzam in the Horn of Africa. He was selling guns to my people, and to Andrei's people, and cheating both of us."

She walked along in silence for a moment, her hands thrust into her pockets. "You think he's the one who hit the *Yalena* and set the U-boat to explode?"

Jax shook his head. "Azzam Badr al'Din is a liar and a cheat, but I've never known him to have blood directly on his hands. Don't get me wrong—I'm sure he's caused the deaths of tens of thousands of people, indirectly. But what we saw on the *Yalena* . . . That isn't his style."

"So what is his part in all this?"

"I don't know." Jax reached for his phone. "But I intend to find out."

She watched him. "You know Badr al'Din's phone number, too?"

Jax paused at the edge of the stone embankment leading down to the river. "No. I'm calling Matt. It's not going to be easy, setting up a meeting with this guy."

She tilted back her head, her breath showing white in the cold as she stared up at the pointed spires of the cathedral, thrusting tall above the roofs of the ancient buildings lining the quay. "Let me guess; we're going to Lebanon."

He grinned. "If I remember correctly, you wanted to go to Lebanon when we left Russia."

She sighed. "At least I get to sleep in a bed tonight."

Jax glanced at his watch. "If you hurry."

Matt called back about an hour later.

"I got a fix on your Azzam Badr al'Din," said Matt. "He's in the Chouf region of Lebanon. You're booked on the six-A.M. Lufthansa flight from Bremen to Beirut."

Jax glanced over at Tobie, who had fallen asleep, still dressed, on top of the covers. "How do I contact him?"

"We're working on that. We should have something by the time you land in Beirut."

"How many people know we're going to Lebanon?"

"The usual channels. But don't worry. I told the station people at the embassy there to give you a wide berth."

"I was thinking more about the file photo my friend in Berlin was carrying."

"Ah." Matt blew out his breath in a long sigh. "We're still trying to get a fix on that. Whoever's accessing your file is good, Jax. We can't trace them."

"What is it you're saying? That they've done it again?"

"About half an hour ago. Your file, and October's, too."

49

By one o'clock that afternoon, Jax and Tobie were in Beirut, standing in front of a seedy falafel stand known as Chez Mahmoud. A fierce Mediterranean sun flooded the narrow street with golden waves of dusty heat as a steady stream of sleek Mercedes, honking Fiats, and diesel-belching trucks thundered past.

"He's late," said Tobie, glancing at her watch. They had been told to wait here, in South Beirut. Azzam Badr al'Din would contact them.

Jax gave a soft laugh. "Of course he's late. This is Beirut, not Berlin."

Tobie's gaze drifted to the bullet-pocked walls of the buildings around them. Once, Beirut had been called the Paris of the Middle East, back in the days when Lebanon had been held up as a shining example of how people of different religions could coexist peacefully for centuries. Then came the creation of Israel in 1948, and hundreds of thousands of Christian and Sunni Muslim Palestinians poured across the border to escape the fighting. The delicate balance teetered. Collapsed. By the 1970s, Lebanon had descended into a brutal civil war that killed tens of thousands; repeated Israeli invasions and bombing raids killed tens of thousands more. Now, in the wealthier areas along the Corniche, rebuilding efforts were once again underway. But here, in the poorer sections, debris and bomb-shattered buildings were everywhere.

"What is it?" she asked, as she watched Jax's eyes narrow.

"The tan Range Rover. See it?"

She saw it. Swooping in close to the curb, the driver hit the brakes. The SUV skidded to a halt; two men toting Skorpion machine pistols spilled out of the car.

"Shit," she whispered, taking an involuntary step back.

One of the men was big and brawny, maybe mid-thirties, his complexion olive, his hair dark and wavy. His companion was both younger and fairer, no more than a boy, with green eyes and a wide smile. He held the muzzle of his machine pistol against Jax's cheek and said in rapid Arabic, "Get in the car, please."

They got in the car. The brawny, olive-skinned guy took the seat next to the driver, while his younger companion squeezed into the back with Jax and Tobie.

Jax, she had discovered, spoke fluent Arabic. He said, "No blindfold?"

The boy beside them laughed. "You've been watching too many Hollywood movies. Everyone in Beirut knows where Dr. Badr al'Din lives."

Tobie whispered to Jax, "Doctor?"

"He has a Ph.D. in psychology. From Berkeley."

"You didn't tell me that."

They took off in a swirl of dust. It occurred to her, looking back, that no one on that crowded street seemed at all shocked or disturbed by what had just happened. The guy in the falafel stand hadn't even looked up.

They headed south, past the sports stadium, past a squalid ghetto of tiny shacks built of concrete blocks hideously crowded together. As she stared at the grim, crooked alleyways lined with wretched half built, half destroyed houses crisscrossed by sagging lines of tattered wash that drooped in the dusty heat, she realized what she was looking at. A refugee camp.

"That's Sabra and Shatila," said the boy, following her gaze.

For some reason she couldn't explain, she felt a brush of cold air against her cheek, like the whisper of an unseen, unhappy ghost that was there, then gone.

She was glad when they broke free of the city, passing through olive groves and scattered villages of whitewashed houses with flat roofs and shutters rolled down against the heat of the day. The sea was a swath of vivid sparkling blue on their right. Then the road they followed swung toward the mountains, and thick stands of sweet-smelling cedars rose up beside them until the sea only appeared in surprising glimpses when they rounded a bend or crested a ridge. The driver punched a CD into the stereo, and the wail of a popular Lebanese singer filled the car.

Gradually, the road narrowed, deteriorated. Chickens scratched at the rocky soil beneath scented orange groves; goats lifted their heads to watch as the dusty Range Rover roared past. They were stopped at one checkpoint, then another. Looking ahead, Tobie saw a fortresslike compound rising above them.

With its high stone walls and massive corner guard towers, the compound reminded her of the castle of some medieval robber baron. Only, instead of being surrounded by a moat, this fortress rose from amidst rolling fields of some leafy green crop she couldn't identify, and the guards in the towers had heavy 50 caliber machine guns. She had no doubt that the men standing on the roof of the tall sandstone house in the center of the complex had Stinger missiles.

Waved through by the guards at the gate, the Range Rover swept into a courtyard softened by hanging vines of bougainvillea and sweetly scented jasmine. Two men in fatigues reached out to yank open the car doors.

Stiff from the long, cramped ride, Tobie clambered out.

"Marhabah. Welcome to my home."

She turned to see a man somewhere in his late thirties or early forties descending the shallow stone steps from the house's broad veranda. He was slim and fit, with an open tanned face and a rapidly receding hairline. He was also, she realized, quite short—probably no more than five-four or –five.

"Jax, my dear old friend," said Azzam Badr al'Din, engulfing Jax in a fond embrace. "It's been too long."

"If I remember correctly, the last time we met, you said if you ever saw me again you'd shoot my balls off."

Azzam took a step back. "I said that?"

"You did."

Assam laughed and threw a questioning glance toward Tobie.

Jax said, "This is Ensign Guinness."

Azzam's eyebrows rose at the "Ensign," but he shook her hand in warm welcome and said, "I hope you don't believe everything he's told you about me."

"How much of it should I believe?"

Azzam laughed again. "No more than half." He spread one arm wide in an expansive gesture toward the house. "This way, please."

"Let me do the talking," Jax whispered to Tobie as they followed the arms dealer around the house, to a broad, stone-flagged veranda shaded by a grapevine-draped pergola.

For once, she wasn't inclined to argue. This guy was seriously intimidating.

Azzam said, "Please, sit. You'll have tea?"

A slim brown boy of maybe twelve appeared from the house bearing a tray with tea and flatbread and a yoghurt-and-cucumber dip. The drinking of either mint tea or a vile, thick Turkish coffee was an inescapable part of any social or business interaction in the Middle East. At least it wasn't vodka, Tobie thought as they seated themselves on a set of rattan chairs with floral cushions.

"So," said Azzam when the tea had been served and the boy withdrew. "What is so important that you'd risk having your balls shot off by coming here?"

Jax tore off a piece of flatbread and dipped it in the yoghurt sauce. "A Nazi U-boat."

Azzam gave one of his sharp laughs. "What do I know of Nazi submarines?"

"Just one sub. An XI-B Type that went down off the coast of Denmark near the end of the war. A Russian by the name of Jasha Baklanov talked to you about selling part of its cargo."

Azzam took a slow sip of his tea and said nothing.

Jax said, "I know he came to you."

Azzam held his cup with both hands. He was still faintly smiling, but his eyes were hard and bright. "What is your interest in Jasha?"

"Jasha is dead. His entire crew was massacred five days ago and the U-boat destroyed."

"Surely you don't think I'm responsible?"

"No. The way I see it, Jasha was planning to double-cross the men who hired him and sell the sub's cargo through you. That's why they killed him."

"So, what is it you think I can tell you?"

"I want to know who hired him."

Azzam leaned back in his chair. "That, I can't tell you."

"Can't, or won't?"

"There are certain kinds of information men like Jasha keep to themselves. You know that."

"So tell me about the cargo."

Azzam's smile widened into something less than pleasant. "You of all people should know I don't give anything away, Jax."

"Not even for old times' sake?"

"Especially not for old times' sake."

Jax tore off another piece of bread and chewed it slowly. "Jasha was planning to sell the U-boat to a Turkish ship-breaker by the name of Kemal Erkan. Erkan is dead, too."

"If you mean to imply that I myself might somehow be in danger, I suggest you take a look around. Everyone from the Israelis to the Phalangists and Hezbollah have been trying to get me for years. I'm not an easy man to kill, Jax."

At this rate, thought Tobie, they were going to be here all week. She set aside her teacup with an impatient clatter. "How about a trade?" she said. "You give us what we want, and we give you something you want."

Both men turned to stare at her: a female interrupting a time-honored demonstration of macho strut. She was aware of Jax giving her a warning frown. She ignored him.

Badr al'Din shifted in his seat. She was an unknown quantity, and he wasn't sure where she was going with this. He said, "What are you offering?"

"The information we need really isn't important to you, is it? The only reason you're not telling Jax what we want to know is because you need to feel like you're getting the best of him."

Azzam let out a surprised bark of laughter. "Now that's a novel approach." He leaned forward. "I tell you what, Ensign. I'll give you what I know, as a gift. But at some time in the future, you"—he pointed to Tobie—"will owe me a favor."

There was no accompanying leer to suggest any kind of sexual innuendo. She said, "It's a deal."

The Druze sat back, his elbows propped on the wide arms of his chair, his hands folded before him. "All right. What do you want to know?"

It was Jax who answered. "We want to know exactly what Jasha told you."

A hot breeze ruffled the vine leaves overhead and brought them the scent of garlic sizzling in olive oil. Azzam chose his words carefully. "He said he had an item for sale—an item that would be of great interest to an enemy of Israel."

"He didn't say what it was?"

Azzam shook his head. "He wanted me to arrange a direct meeting with a potential buyer."

"With you earning your usual finder's fee?"

"Of course."

"And did you find a buyer?"

"I arranged a meeting, but the buyer wasn't interested."

"Who was it?"

"That, I can't give you. But I can ask this individual if he's willing to talk to you. If he is, he'll contact you."

The Druze pushed to his feet. The interview was over. "My men will drive you back to Beirut. Get a room at Hotel Offredi, near the stadium."

"And?" said Tobie.

"And wait."

50

Borz Zakaev kept a heavy foot on the gas as he headed east toward Yasnaya Polyana. It was only late afternoon, but already the light was beginning to fade from the white, cloud-laden sky.

This entire oblast gave him the creeps, with its dark bogs and empty, silent houses. He'd heard it said that before the war, East Prussia had been one of the most intensely cultivated and heavily populated regions in Europe, second only to the Netherlands. No one would believe that now.

He put his foot down harder and heard the *blip* of a siren. Casting a quick glance in the rearview mirror, he saw a militia van with flashing red and blue lights coming up behind him, and swore.

The snow began to fall late in the afternoon.

Stefan stood in the soaring doorway of the abandoned granary and watched the big, fluffy flakes float down to cover the world in a hushed wonder.

It had been sometime before dawn when the old farmer reigned in to let Stefan and the pup down some two kilometers before Yasnaya Polyana. "You're going home, aren't you?" said the farmer.

When Stefan only stared up at him, the old man laughed, displaying a scant collection of stained, gaping teeth. "If someone's after you, home's the first place they'll look. You know that, don't you?"

Stefan tried to swallow the sudden lump in his throat, failed, and simply nodded, his lips pressed tight together.

"You take care, you hear?" said the farmer, and spanked the reins against his mules' rumps.

The old man had only confirmed Stefan's worst fears. And so, even though he was so close to home that he imagined he could practically smell his mother's freshly baked bread and hear the honking of the geese as she walked down to the pond at feeding time, Stefan and the pup had come here, to the vast ruins of what had once been the royal stables of Trakehnen.

The stud farm was the birthplace of the famous warm-blooded Trakehner horses, begun back in the eighteenth century by the Prussian King Friedrich Wilhelm I. Stefan had heard it said that at one time the village of Yasnaya Polyana had been called Trakehnen, too, back in the days when Kaliningrad had been a German land and the stud farm had housed more than twelve hundred horses and three times that many people.

Now, the horses and their handlers were all gone. The dilapidated old mansion, with its towering stucco walls and moss-covered red-tiled roof, had been turned into a school. But the rest of the vast stud lay deserted beneath the falling snow, a crumbling ruin of brick stables and grain silos and overgrown, empty pastures.

Stefan felt the dog's cold nose thrust against his hand.

Hunkering down, he threw an arm across the pup's shoulders and drew it close. From here he could look out across the fields to the old riding ring and the school beyond. "What do we do now? Hmmm, boy? Any suggestions?"

But the pup only gazed up at him with silent, trusting brown eyes.

51

Hotel Offredi was built into the side of a dusty, weed-strewn hillside scarred by piles of broken rocks and bulldozed raw earth. Cheap aluminum-framed windows reflected the glare of a pitiless hot sun that wilted the fig tree growing in a cinderblock container near the front door. Rows of rusting rebars thrust up from the walls at the roofline, as if in anticipation of another story that might or might not be built someday.

Inside, they found a thickset woman in a long dress and headscarf seated behind a desk with a simple sign that said in Arabic, Rooms To Let. English and French-speaking patrons didn't usually make it into this part of town.

"I wanted to ask you," October whispered to Jax as they followed the woman up a set of bare stairs to a narrow hall. "What exactly was the crop growing around Badr al'Din's compound?"

"You didn't recognize it?"

The hall was starkly bare, the floor paved with cheap tile

inexpertly grouted by someone in too much of a hurry to wipe up stray blobs of mortar.

"No," said October. "What was it?"

"Cannabis."

"Cannabis? You mean—" She broke off. "Oh."

Wordlessly, the woman leading them thrust open the door to a small room with a hard bed covered in faded red chenille. A battered, fifties-style blond-veneered chest of drawers and bedside table, and an orange plastic chair completed the room's furnishings. Everything was worn and cheap but meticulously clean. Mohammed had taught his followers that cleanliness is next to godliness, and they still struggled valiantly against dust and sand and poverty to please God.

"*Shukran*," said October.

The woman nodded and withdrew.

Jax went to stand at the window overlooking the mean street below. A withered old man, his head down, pushed a wheelbarrow loaded with propane tanks past a handful of noisy, half-grown boys playing what looked like a version of *Star Wars*. Otherwise, the street was quiet in the mid-afternoon sun. Yet, Jax's palms were damp, and he could feel waves of heat rising from his stomach to his throat. He didn't like this setup. He didn't like it at all.

"It's beginning to sound more and more as if there really was an atomic bomb on that sub," said October, dropping her bag on the floor with a thump. "Or at least, the material to make a dirty bomb."

Jax glanced back at her. She sank down on the hard plastic chair, hooked her heels on the edge of the seat, and drew her knees up so she could clasp them to her chest. He said, "Maybe. Maybe not."

She tossed her head to shake the loose strands of honey-colored hair away from her face. "So what exactly are we hoping to get out of this mysterious contact of Azzam's?"

"Confirmation." Jax pushed away from the window.

"Is that really necessary at this point?"

"It's always necessary. Remember the run up to the Iraq War? How certain individuals cherry-picked unconfirmed intelligence suggesting Iraq still had a WMD program and was in contact with al-Qa'ida? It was all bullshit."

"Yeah, but that was deliberately planted bullshit, designed specifically to trick the American people into supporting a war. This is different."

A dusty old white Mercedes crawled down the street, scattering the laughing children. Jax watched it through narrowed eyes. "I keep coming back to that remote viewing session you tried in Bremen."

"You mean the one that didn't work?"

"Yeah. That one."

She pushed up from the chair. "It didn't work because it was just too weird and distracting, having the Colonel task me over the phone. And because I knew too much about the target. When a viewer knows too much up front, their conscious, analytical mind can kick in and block out access to—"

Jax held a finger to his lips. She fell silent.

He heard it again. The scruff of footsteps on the stairs. The light treads of two men in the tiled hall.

The footsteps stopped outside their room. He saw her eyes widen.

"Mr. Alexander?" A light knock sounded on the door.

Jax moved to open it carefully.

Two young men pushed into the room. Lithe and clean shaven, they wore fatigue pants and T-shirts with black-and-white kafiyas draped rakishly around their necks. Both carried MAC–10 machine pistols.

"Kaif halak," said the one in a white T-shirt decorated with a portrait of Che Guevara. He looked slightly older than his companion, perhaps twenty-four or twenty-five. "This is

Abu Elias," he said, nodding to his companion. "You can call me Amin." His gaze flicked to October, one eyebrow cocking in inquiry. "You're Ensign Guinness?"

Jax didn't like the way the Arab used her Naval rank. She nodded, her throat working visibly as she swallowed.

The one called Abu Elias couldn't have been more than nineteen or twenty. He said something in a low voice to Amin that Jax didn't catch.

Amin nodded and said, "You will both take off your watches and empty your pockets, please. Very slowly and carefully."

Jax piled up change, wallet, phone, and keys on the scarred dresser top. The only thing October had in the pockets of her chinos was a small yellow Burt's Bees lip balm.

"Now hold your arms out at your sides and stand very still."

Tucking his machine pistol under one arm, Abu Elias reached into his pocket and came out with a small black box with steady red and green LED lights. He carefully passed the box over each of them in turn, like an FTA employee checking suspicious-looking airplane passengers.

"What is that?" asked October.

"It's a radio frequency detector," said Amin. "It detects anything that emits an electronic impulse—hidden transmitters, tape recorders, tracking devices—whatever."

"We're not hiding anything."

Amin flashed her a smile that showed his teeth. "You'll excuse me if I don't take your word for it. You"—he nodded to Jax—"will sit. But I must ask you, Ensign, to take off your shoes."

Aware of Abu Elias's narrowed gaze upon him, Jax settled carefully onto the hard plastic chair. He now had a really, *really* bad feeling about all of this.

October said, "My shoes?"

"Min fadlik." Amin turned to survey the two bags standing just inside the door. "Which is yours?"

"The green one."

Hunkering down beside it, the Arab laid the bag on its side and unzipped it. "Excuse me," he said as he rummaged through her things, "but it is necessary."

"Why?" she asked, kicking off her tennis shoes.

"It's too easy to hide things in the soles and heels of shoes." He came up with a pair of navy-and-white-striped flip-flops. "Here. You will wear these."

She slipped on the flip-flops without argument. "I'm not carrying a weapon."

"Nevertheless, I'm afraid I must also check your hair."

"My hair?"

"My apologies." Reaching out, he systematically ran his fingers through her shoulder-length, honey-colored hair. "Women have been known to hide razor blades in their hair."

She cast an uncertain glance to where Jax sat in the orange plastic chair, his hands resting carefully on his thighs. They were both painfully aware that no one was checking his hair or making him take off his shoes.

As if conscious of the train of Jax's thoughts, Amin said to him, "You are to stay here, with Abu Elias. Only the girl can come."

"But—" Jax started to push out of his chair, then froze when the younger man made a *tssk*ing sound and jerked his head back, his finger twitching on the machine pistol's trigger.

"Laa. Khalleek hawn!"

Jax sank back very slowly.

"Don't worry," said Amin. "She will come to no harm." He glanced at October. "Are you ready?"

52

They walked together down the narrow set of concrete stairs to the hotel's small, spartan lobby. Tobie noticed that the older woman in the long dress and headscarf who had been behind the desk when they arrived was no longer there.

Outside, the evening was hot and dry, with a warm wind blowing out of the east that sifted dust over the stark, stone-faced facades of the neighborhood's buildings. The sidewalk here was made of swirled tiles of alternating red and yellow clay, some cracked, some missing entirely. They dodged piles of builders' sand, a battered wheelbarrow encrusted with dried concrete, a spindly olive tree struggling to survive. Tobie was aware of two women chatting beside a doorway who fell silent as she drew abreast, the women's heads turning to watch her pass.

Amin touched her arm. "This way."

They ducked down a narrow passage kept shaded and dank by tall apartment blocks hung with laundry drying limply in the fetid air. The passage emptied onto a street similar to the one they'd just left, although with more small shops, their front windows displaying their wares. They passed a bakery with stacks of fresh flatbread and a tray of croissants, and a tiny shoe store with boxes of children's plaid slippers in a range of sizes. A man in a dark sweater stood at the corner, near a grocery selling Digestive biscuits and bananas, bottled water and yoghurt. As they passed, Tobie noticed he had a Bluetooth in his ear, his eyes narrowing as he scanned the street.

"Why just me?" said Tobie.

Amin shook his head and kept walking.

They made three or four such turns, winding back on themselves, passing more men—and one young woman—wearing Bluetooth earpieces and quietly watching the street behind them. As they drew abreast of the woman, she nodded to Amin and said quietly, "You're clean. No one is following you."

Halfway down the next block, Amin drew up in front of an ancient stone building with a bullet-scarred facade. Staring through the dusty windows, Tobie could see a small restaurant crowded with aluminum tables and chairs with seats covered in dark green plastic. More tables and chairs spilled outside onto the narrow sidewalk.

This was the time of day when such places were typically filled with old men smoking hubble-bubbles, drinking coffee, and playing backgammon. But Tobie could see only one man, sipping tea by himself at a table near the kitchen door.

Amin nodded toward the restaurant's entrance. "You go in. He's waiting for you."

She hesitated a moment, then pushed open the door. Her escort stayed outside.

Inside, the air was heavy with the scents of cinnamon and allspice and coffee. From his table at the rear of the restaurant, the man watched her approach. His features were sharply formed, his nose aquiline, his eyes large and deeply set, his brows heavy and straight. At first she supposed he must be somewhere in his forties, with a heavy dark mustache and dark hair he wore clipped short. But as she drew closer, she realized he was older than she first took him to be, his hair touched by gray at the temples, the skin beside his eyes creased by years of staring into a hot Mediterranean sun. He wore gray chinos and a well-cut black polo shirt, and he might have been mistaken for a French businessman if it weren't for the MP5 that rested casually across his lap.

"Please," he said in heavily accented English. "Sit."

Tobie pulled out the chair opposite him and sat.

A thickset middle-aged woman appeared with fresh tea and another cup from the kitchen. After she had left, the man said, "Do you know who I am?"

Tobie took a quick swallow of the tea and burned her tongue. "No."

One eyebrow rose in polite incredulity. "You're not with the CIA?"

"No. I'm in the Navy."

"Why have they sent you?"

"I'm a linguist."

He switched to Arabic. "You speak Arabic?"

She answered him easily. "I lived in Dubai as a child."

A wry smile curled his lips, lifting the edges of his mustache. "You speak Arabic like a Beduin."

"And you speak Arabic like a Palestinian."

He tipped his head to one side, acknowledging the point. "My family is originally from Gaza."

"You're with Hamas?"

He blinked and took a slow swallow of his tea before answering. "My apologies for not introducing myself. My name is Farrah. George Farrah."

"Ah. So you're a Christian," she said. Arab men named George were always Christians.

"We Palestinians were the first Christians, you know," he said softly. In Arabic, the word for Christian was Masihi, from the Aramaic word for Messiah. He leaned forward, his hazel eyes watching her face. "A hundred years ago, Arab Christians made up 40 percent of the population of Palestine. We are the descendents of the Jews who followed Jesus, of the Canaanites and Philistines who were here before the Jews but followed Christ, too, and of the Romans and Crusaders who came to the Holy Land and stayed. Now . . ." He spread his hands wide. "Now we are scattered all over the world in our own diaspora."

He had unexpectedly graceful hands, with fingers that were long and lean and finely tapered, like a musician's or an artist's. As she watched his hands, he took another sip of his tea and said, "Why are you interested in Jasha Baklanov?"

"I'm interested in what Baklanov tried to sell you."

"I didn't buy it."

"I know. I'm trying to find out who has it now."

"That, I can't help you with."

Tobie leaned forward, her palms pressing flat against the aluminum tabletop. "The people who originally contacted Baklanov found out he was planning to double-cross them, and they killed him."

George Farrah nodded. "I had heard he was dead."

"Do you know who hired the *Yalena* to raise the U-boat?"

"Jasha never said."

Tobie wasn't sure whether he was telling the truth or not. She said, "You can't tell me anything about them?"

Farrah rolled one shoulder in a typically Mediterranean shrug. "He said something about a Chechen, but he didn't mention any names."

"Chechens?" Tobie drew in a quick breath. "Could Baklanov have been dealing with al-Qa'ida?"

Farrah's heavy brows drew together. "What would al-Qa'ida want with this?"

"Everyone says they've been trying to get their hands on a nuke for years."

He sat back with a bark of laughter that ended abruptly. "Is that what you think Baklanov was selling? A nuclear weapon?"

Tobie shook her head, not understanding. "If it's not a bomb, then what is it?"

Farrah sat very still. When he spoke, his voice was a harsh whisper. "Something worse. Something far worse."

Tobie stared at him. "What could be worse than an atom bomb?"

"What could be worse?" He leaned forward, one hand coming up to punctuate the air between them, his lean musician's fingers delicately curled. "I'll tell you what would be worse: a biological weapon with the potential to kill two hundred million people or more."

53

In the sudden silence, Tobie became aware of the fans slowly circling overhead, moving the hot air, ruffling the edges of the napkins on the tabletop before her. She tried to think back to that conversation in the Deutsches U-Boot Museum-Archiv, in Altenbruch. What had Marie Oldenburg said? *"He claimed that amongst its other cargo, U–114 carried a secret veapon—what you Americans like to call a veapon of mass destruction."*

Had anyone actually used the word "atomic"? She didn't think so. They'd heard those dreaded words—weapon of mass destruction—and simply assumed they were dealing with an atom bomb.

George Farrah said, "It's the ultimate threat Hollywood loves, isn't it—terrorists armed with a nuclear bomb? Do you know why?" He leaned forward, answering his own question. "Because we all grew up with Cold War tales of an all-out war between the Soviets and the Americans that would obliterate life on earth as we know it. The thought of terrorists with such a weapon taps in to those fears."

"I don't know about you, but I find the idea of terrorists setting off an atom bomb in New York or San Francisco pretty scary."

Farrah sat back in his chair. "Of course it's scary. The sudden death of thousands is always scary—not to mention the radiation sickness, the contamination. But is it really the worst that could happen?"

When Tobie kept silent, he said, "You Americans killed—what? Two hundred thousand people when you dropped your bombs on Hiroshima and Nagasaki. A sixty-year-old bomb would be even less deadly. It might kill a few thousand—maybe ten thousand. Horrible, yes. But it would be one event. Over. Finished. Whereas, this . . ." He paused, his arms spreading wide, only to drop listlessly to his sides.

Tobie forced herself to keep her voice calm and even. "What kind of biological weapon are we talking about?"

Farrah shrugged. "According to Baklanov, it was something the Nazis discovered at Dachau—a disease that strikes only those of Semitic origin."

"What? But that's impossible." She hesitated. "Isn't it?"

"You think so? Look at what European diseases did to the American Indians half a millennium ago."

"But that was because they had no built-up immunity."

"True. But there are some diseases, such as sickle cell anemia or alcoholism, that still strike those with certain genetic backgrounds. You are familiar with the story of the Passover?"

Tobie said softly, "On the night of the Tenth Plague, the Angel of Death passed over the houses of the Israelites and spared their firstborn."

Farrah nodded. "If this disease is let loose upon the world, it will be like the original Passover, only in reverse. And it won't simply kill each family's firstborn. It will kill everyone of Semitic origin. Millions of people. Tens of millions."

She sat very still, torn between disbelief and the hideous realization that he might—just might—be telling the truth.

He said, "There have been many attempts in the last

eighty years to develop such things, you know—bioweapons that will target only specific ethnic groups. The Israelis and South Africans have tried it. So have you Americans."

"I don't—" She broke off.

A ghost of a smile crinkled the edges of his green eyes. "You don't believe your government would do such a thing? Look into it. I think you'll be surprised by what you find."

She wrapped her hands around her now cold teacup. "When Baklanov offered you this weapon, what did you tell him?"

"What do you think? I want my homeland back, yes. And I want revenge. For the tens of thousands of Palestinians who have been killed in the last sixty years. For the millions more who are dispossessed and homeless. But this weapon?" The man's eyes were so wide with fear, she could see the milky whites surrounding the irises. "That stupid Russian. He didn't know Arabs are Semites, too. If this disease gets loose, it won't just kill the Jews. It will kill the Arabs as well. All of us."

Farrah's voice dropped to a whisper as he leaned closer. "Think about it. All across the Middle East, across Europe, across the United States and Latin America, anyone with Middle Eastern ancestors—Jew, Christian or Muslim . . . All will die."

"Latin America?"

"But of course. The Arabs ruled Spain for over seven hundred years, remember? After the Reconquista, many Arabs—Muslim and Jew alike—converted to Christianity and stayed. From Spain, their descendents spread out across the New World. If this pestilence is set loose, it won't just devastate the Middle East. It will decimate half the world."

She didn't want to believe him. But his fear was too real, too palpable. Her voice was now a dry, cracked whisper. "So who has it now? Who hired the *Yalena*?"

"You think if I knew, I wouldn't tell you?"

"But you must know something!"

He pushed back his chair and stood. The interview was at an end. "I know what I have told you. That is all."

She followed Amin through the same mean, narrow streets down which they'd walked earlier, only, somehow, everything now seemed changed. She saw a dark-haired little girl in a red skirt jumping rope beside a bullet-chipped doorway, and thought, *If we don't stop what these men have planned, that little girl will die. And so will that boy spinning a soccer ball on his finger, and that young mother laughing at—*

Amin said, "Mind your step," and put out a hand to keep Tobie from stumbling into a muddy puddle in the hollow left by a missing tile.

She jerked her attention back to him. "Thank you."

With the approach of evening, the streets had filled with long blue shadows. Women carrying plastic shopping bags thronged the sidewalks; boys dodged honking rows of cars. Tobie said, "Did you know him? Jasha Baklanov, I mean."

"The Russian?" Amin shrugged. "I've dealt with him. He's—"

The Palestinian broke off, his head turning as the whine of a motorcycle coming up fast cut through the noise of the crowded street. Looking just beyond the hotel, Tobie spotted a dark blue Kawasaki with two black-jacketed, visored riders weaving toward them through the stalled line of dusty cars.

"Shit," she whispered.

As the Kawasaki pulled abreast of them, the rear passenger drew an MP4 from beneath his jacket. Amin shouted, "Look out!" and pushed her down as a spray of bullets ricocheted off the wall beside them.

54

Jax was in their room at the Hotel Offredi, pacing back and forth beneath the watchful eye of Abu Elias when the sudden, staccato burst of machine-gun fire jerked both men to the window.

He saw October hit the sidewalk, saw a line of bullets rip the chest of her kafiya-draped escort even as the young Palestinian drew his MAC10 and returned fire.

"Amin!" cried Abu Elias, pushing away from the window. Machine pistol in hand, he threw open the door, pausing only to shout over his shoulder at Jax, "You stay here."

"Like hell," said Jax, snatching his phone from the litter on the scarred dresser top as he ran.

They tore down the narrow steps and erupted into the street just as the Kawasaki roared around the corner. The body of one of the motorcycle's riders lay sprawled motionless on the blacktop. A throng of shouting, gesturing men spilled from the line of cars blocking the street. Jax pushed through them, his heart hammering in his chest as he neared the spot where he'd last seen October.

She was there, crouched beside the bloodied body of her

young escort. She'd yanked the kafiya from around his neck and was using it to try to stem the flow of blood that darkened his ripped chest.

"October. Thank God." Then Jax saw the blood smeared across her arms and face and felt his stomach tighten. "Are you hit?"

She shook her head, her attention all for her task.

He grabbed her elbow, trying to haul her up. "You need to get inside," he shouted over the wails and excited shouts of the crowd. "They may come back."

She shook her head, hanging back. "No. I need to help him. He saved my life."

"Tobie." Jax tightened his grip on her, jerking her around so that she had no choice but to meet his gaze. "Listen to me. You can't help him. He's dead. Now will you get inside?"

She shivered so violently her entire body shook. Nodding silently, she eased the Palestinian's head to the pavement and pushed to her feet.

When she still hesitated, Jax shouted, "Go!"

Jerking his phone out of his pocket, he punched in the number for Langley, his narrowed gaze carefully scanning the excited, jabbering crowd as he listened to the call go through. "Matt? Your fucking mole almost got October killed! Find him. *Now.*"

Kaliningrad, Russia: Thursday 29 October
6:55 P.M. local time

Andrei Gorchakove stared at the prisoner in the stark, brightly lit cell on the other side of the one-way mirror.

He was a big man, brawny, with the thick red hair one saw sometimes in Chechnya. A couple of militiamen had pulled him over in the southeastern part of the oblast for speeding, then become suspicious when they noticed a photograph of Stefan Baklanov lying on the passenger seat beside him.

Now, seated on a low stool, the Chechen had been stripped naked and doused with cold water, his wrists shackled in a painful position. As Andrei watched, the man shivered violently.

"What does he say?"

Andrei's captain, a stocky man with a thick neck and low forehead and the broad features of an Ossetian, shrugged his shoulders. "He says the boy is alive."

"You believe him?"

The captain, a man named Kokoeva, shrugged his shoulders. "He says what he thinks we want to hear."

"That's always been the trouble with torture. It's a wonderful way to get people to admit they're witches, or heretics, or traitors to the Party. But it's worse than useless when it comes to collecting real intelligence."

"We tried being nice to him. It didn't work."

Andrei grunted. "What else does he say?"

"We asked him what they took off U–114. He said he didn't know. He said it's not his business to know. When we pressed him, he said it was an atom bomb."

"After you suggested it was an atom bomb?"

The captain frowned. "Yes. Why?"

"Who does he say he's with?"

"Al-Qa'ida."

Andrei studied the man on the other side of the glass. Beneath the steady onslaught of the air conditioning, the man was slowly turning blue. "Did you suggest that, too?"

"No. We suggested Chechen separatists."

"Did you run his fingerprints?"

"No."

Andrei turned toward the door. "Do it."

55

"I shouldn't have let you go by yourself," said Jax, for something like the tenth time.

They were walking along Beirut's famous Corniche, the darkening waters of the Mediterranean lapping the beach beside them. A cool breeze blowing in from the sea brought them the scent of salt and fish, and fluttered October's hair across her face. "If I were a man," she said, putting up a hand to catch her hair, "would you still feel that way?"

He thought about it. "Probably not."

"Then stop patronizing me."

He laughed softly as she turned away to stare out over the broad stretch of sand, deserted now in the gathering gloom. She said, "I always thought 'Semitic' was a linguistic division, not ethnic. Arabic, Hebrew, Aramaic . . . they're all Semitic languages, right? Although I have to admit, I don't know much about Aramaic."

"Aha. A language she doesn't speak."

She took a swipe at his head. "It's extinct."

He ducked. "Actually, it isn't. Christ spoke Aramaic, and so did the authors of the biblical books of Daniel and Ezra, which I suppose is why a lot of people think the language is extinct. But there are still populations in the Arab world that speak Aramaic, particularly in places like Syria, Iraq, and Lebanon."

"But if it's just a linguistic division, then it wouldn't have any effect on someone's susceptibility to a disease, would it?"

Jax shook his head. "Not necessarily. Language is turning out to be a pretty good reflection of the genetic relationships between different peoples. You need to remember that the division between 'Arabs' and 'Jews' is something new—and, some people would argue, artificial. Up until the twentieth century, people talked about 'Arab Jews,' the same way they talk about 'French Jews,' or 'Spanish Jews.' For well over a thousand years, some Arabs have been Muslims, some have been Christians, and some have been Jews. The original Jews—the ones from the Holy Land—are basically the same, genetically, as the Arabs. They're all Semites."

"So if George Farrah is telling the truth . . ."

"If Farrah is telling the truth and U–114 really was carrying a pathogen that is lethal to anyone of Semitic origin, then Homeland Security has this thing all wrong."

She glanced over at him. "You mean, because no Arab terrorists are going to unleash a biological weapon that kills Semites?"

"Exactly."

"So who are we dealing with?"

Jax let out a long breath. "I don't know. At this point, there's only one thing we do know for certain: whoever these guys are, they're not from the Middle East."

He felt his phone begin to vibrate. Once he'd calmed down over the shooting outside the Hotel Offredi he'd given Matt a full report on October's meeting with George Farrah. But Jax had few illusions about the kind of reception their new intelligence was likely to receive.

Matt's voice was gruff. "I passed your information on to the big boys."

"And?"

"And they're not buying any of it. They've got half a dozen detainees in dungeons from Guantanamo to Cairo who've confessed to plotting to set off an atom bomb everywhere from New York to Seattle."

"Under torture."

"Under enhanced interrogation techniques," corrected Matt. "Everyone from the President and Homeland Security to the DCI and the DNI are convinced U–114 was carrying an atom bomb that a bunch of crazy Islamist terrorists are now planning to set off somewhere in the US of A."

"Shit." Jax's gaze met October's. "Those stupid, bigoted sons of bitches."

Matt was silent for a moment. "You sure about this, Jax?"

"Sure? No. But it feels right."

"The problem is, we ain't got no verification."

"I'm working on that."

"Well, work fast, Jax. Halloween is barely twenty-four hours away."

Jax clipped his phone back on his belt and stood staring out over the darkened sea. The last of the sunlight had faded from the sky, revealing a universe of brilliant stars. From the sidewalk tables of a nearby restaurant came the sound of soft laughter and voices, and the scent of fish sizzling in olive oil and garlic.

"What is it?" said October, watching him.

He glanced over at her. "You're sure Farrah was telling you the truth?"

She didn't even need to think about it. "Yes. That man is

genuinely frightened by the possibility of this disease getting loose. I think that's why he agreed to meet me."

Jax said, "Did he tell you anything about himself?"

She shook her head. "Not really. Just that his family was originally from Gaza. Why? Do you know him?"

"Not personally, no. But I've heard of him. He's been on our Terror Watch list for twenty-five years. He originally trained as a doctor in England, but came back here to work in the refugee camps."

"A *doctor*? That man's a doctor?"

"A pediatrician. He was living with his wife and three kids in Shatila back in 1982 when the Israelis first invaded Lebanon."

"Why does that name sound so familiar?"

"We passed it this afternoon."

"So what happened?"

"When the Israeli army reached Beirut, they completely surrounded both Sabra and Shatila. At that point, all the Palestinian fighters had been evacuated under a U.S. guarantee for the safety of the women and children they left behind."

"Oh, no," she whispered. "Don't tell me . . ."

Jax nodded. "The Israelis refused to let anyone—man, woman, or child—leave the refugee camps. Instead, they sent in their allies, the Christian Phalangists." Jax paused, and the silence filled with the relentless drone of the surf beside them. "Rape, murder, mutilation . . . You name it, it happened there. When night came, they lit up the sky with flares so the Phalangists could keep killing. By the time the Red Cross was finally let into the camps two days later, they found thousands of bodies, most of them women and children. No one knows exactly how many Palestinians died. A lot of the bodies were bulldozed into mass graves that have never been opened."

"And Farrah's family?"

"I heard he found his wife's body, and one of his little

girls. His son and the other daughter were never found." Jax hesitated. "What was done to his wife was not pretty."

"Where was Farrah when all this happened?"

"At a nearby hospital, taking care of a sick child."

She was silent a moment. "It explains why Baklanov approached him, doesn't it? Not only does he have a powerful grudge against the Israelis, but as a doctor, he understands diseases."

Jax nodded. "It's Farrah's involvement in all this that makes me inclined to believe we really are dealing with a bioweapon. If Baklanov thought he had an atom bomb to sell, I think he'd have gone after a bigger buyer."

She swung around to stare back at the towers of the city's skyline rising up beside them and ablaze now with lights. "Farrah said both the Israelis and the U.S. have bioweapon programs aimed at isolating ethnic-specific diseases. Is that true?"

"I don't know about the Israelis, but we certainly have one. We have had it, for years."

He was aware of her studying him through dark, troubled eyes. "How many years?"

"I don't know exactly. The bioweapon program itself goes back to the thirties. The Nazi experiments from World War II are the most notorious and well known, but they weren't the only ones doing that kind of stuff. Everyone was into it. The Japanese had the biggest program. They actually used their bioweapons, in China."

"You think that's where the Germans were sending this stuff? To Japan? As part of Operation Ceasar?"

"They were sending the Japanese everything from jet planes and rockets to nuclear material. So I suppose it makes sense they'd ship them bioweapons, too."

"But . . . would something like that still be viable? After sixty years?"

"I remember reading about some archaeologists who excavated the graves of the members of an early twentieth-century North Pole expedition. The explorers had died of the flu, and the archaeologists caught the virus from the bodies they dug up. So I'd say, yeah, it could still be viable."

She blew out a long, shaky breath. "And Homeland Security doesn't believe any of this."

"Nope." He met her gaze, and saw his own growing horror reflected in the stark, drawn features of her face.

She said, "We need to find out exactly what was on that U-boat. But how?"

He turned his back on the darkened sea. "I've been thinking. I know someone who might be able to help us. A guy by the name of Leon Ginsburg."

"Who's he?"

"He's the father of Paul Ginsburg."

"As in, Paul W. Ginsburg, former secretary of defense? How can he help us?"

"For one thing, he's a doctor. *And* he was a prisoner at Dachau for three years."

"Where does he live now?"

"Jaffa."

"Jaffa? As in, Jaffa, Israel?"

"That's right."

"So, how do you know him?" she asked, as Jax flagged down a passing taxi.

"It's a long story."

56

Leon Ginsburg lived in an ancient stone house on a narrow, crooked street that dated back to the days when Jaffa was a prosperous Palestinian port surrounded by the vast orange groves that had made the city famous. The orange groves were mostly gone now, the few that were left disappearing fast beneath the runways of Ben-Gurion Airport and the creeping urbanization that had made Jaffa a virtual suburb of Tel Aviv.

It was nearly midnight by the time their taxi pulled up next to the house's worn, shallow steps. A wrought-iron lamp set high on a coursed stone wall cast a pool of warm, golden light over a heavy, weathered door set into a corbelled arch. As Jax raised his fist to knock, the door swung inward to reveal a small, wizened man half lost in a bulky brown cardigan sweater, with thin white hair and wire-framed glasses he wore pushed down on the end of his bulbous nose.

"James! I wondered when you were going to get here." His liver-spotted, bony hand closed on Jax's sleeve, dragging him inside. "Come in, come in. You too, Miss Guinness."

"*James*?" whispered Tobie, following Jax up the steps.

"That's right. James." Leon Ginsburg closed the old door behind them and gave a soft laugh. "It's his real name. James Aiden Xavier Alexander."

"There are only two people in the world who call me James," said Jax, slinging an affectionate arm around the old man's shoulders. "My mother, and Leon."

The old man huffed another laugh and ushered them down a narrow corridor. "I was Jax's grandfather for two years, you know. Did he tell you?"

The corridor erupted suddenly into a leafy courtyard surrounded by open arcades that loomed three stories above them. "No," said Tobie. "He didn't tell me."

"My son Paul was Sophie's third husband." He frowned. "Or was it the fourth?"

"The third," said Jax.

"I don't know how you keep them straight."

"I remember the earlier ones better."

With a soft chuckle, Leon spread his arms wide, indicating a grouping of chairs nestled in amongst potted palms and ferns. "Please. Sit. You've been traveling for hours. You must be hungry. I've asked my wife to fix us something." The sound of soft footsteps brought his head around. "Ah. Here she is."

A woman bearing a heavy tray emerged from an open doorway beneath the far arcade. Leon rushed to help her, murmuring something to her in Arabic as he took the heavy tray from her. She stood a good half a head taller than he, and was perhaps twenty years younger, with a plump face and green eyes and the discreet headscarf of a devout Muslim.

"Good evening," she said in lightly accented English. "Welcome to our home."

"My wife, Yasmina," said Leon, his face breaking into a broad grin as he introduced them. "She is a professor of biology at Al-Quds University. Sixteen years ago this December, I heard a loud pounding on my door just after sunrise. When I peeked outside, there was this beautiful woman standing on my steps. She shook her fist under my nose and said, 'My grandfather built this house. I was born in this house. By what right do you live here?' "

Yasmina Ginsburg's eyes twinkled with silent laughter as husband and wife shared a private smile. "What chutzpah!" he said, setting the tray with its load of homus and bread and olives on the table before them. "I was hopelessly smitten."

While they ate, they talked of Leon's son, Paul, and the time Leon had spent in Washington. Then Leon drew a pipe from the cavernous folds of his cardigan and packed it with tobacco, his expression growing thoughtful. He said, "I may be old and feebleminded, James, but I'm not so far gone as to believe you came all the way here to visit this *alter kocker* just to talk about old times."

"You're far from feebleminded, and you know it. I'm here because I need information."

Leon cast him a long, steady look, and kept tamping his tobacco. "You're a spy. That's what you people do—you collect information. What kind of information could an old man like me possibly give you?"

"I need to know about the Nazi biological weapons program at Dachau."

"Ah." Leon lit a match and held the flame to his pipe with an unsteady hand. "That's a pretty tall order, James. The Nazis were working with everything from anthrax to smallpox, and God only knows what else."

"Did you ever hear of a disease that kills Jews, but is harmless to gentiles?"

Leon went very still. When his match burned down to the tips of his fingers, he dropped it in a nearby ashtray. But it was still a moment before he spoke. "As a matter of fact, yes."

He leaned back in his chair, one hand cupping the bowl of his pipe. "It was in 1944. The fall, I think. A truck brought in a group of Jews from southern France. They were already very ill when they arrived—some sort of acute respiratory disease. No one knew what. They were put in a barracks where something like half the men were Polish intellectuals, the rest French Jews. Some of the Poles came down with a mild case of the sniffles. But almost every one of the Jews in that barracks died."

He sucked silently on his pipe for a moment. Jax and Tobie waited. He said, "You know, a lot of people think the Nazis only sent Jews to the concentration camps. But the truth is, they rounded up anyone and everyone they thought might be a danger to the State. About a third of us at Dachau were Jews. The rest were a combination of Catholic priests, gypsies, Germans who opposed the Nazis, Communists . . ." Leon shrugged. "Hitler had a lot of different enemies.

"We were all made to wear overalls with color-coded triangles. The Jews, of course, wore yellow badges. The Communists and other political prisoners had to wear red. Common criminals wore green triangles. Jehovah's Witnesses were given purple triangles. The Gypsies wore black, while homosexuals had to wear pink." He gave a soft huff. "All these years, and I still remember."

His wife reached out to lay her hand over his, and after a moment, he continued. "There was a doctor at the camp, a man by the name of Martin Kline. After he heard what happened in that barracks, he decided to do an experiment. He selected fifty Jews and fifty gentiles, and had them deliberately infected with the virus."

"It was a virus?"

Leon flattened his lips, his bushy white brows drawing together in a thoughtful frown. "That's what we thought it was. No one had heard of retroviruses in those days. But looking back on it now, it's hard to say."

Jax said, "Where did the disease originally come from?"

"Who can say? Those were terrible times, with vast populations in motion under wretched conditions. The miracle is that it never spread outside the camp."

Tobie leaned forward. "So what happened?"

"Many of the gentiles came down with what I guess you might describe as a cold: sniffles, sore throat—that sort of thing. All but one survived. But half the Jews died. The doctors in the camp took to calling it *die Klinge von Solomon*."

"The Blade or Sword of Solomon," whispered October.

Leon nodded. He drew on his pipe, two streams of smoke leaking out the corners of his mouth. "Kline was ecstatic. He'd been hoping for a higher death rate, but still . . . fifty percent was promising. So he tried it on another group of a hundred prisoners, half Jewish, half not. That time, two of the gentiles died, and about twenty of the Jews. That's when Kline realized it made a difference where the Jews were from."

Tobie shook her head, not understanding. "Why?"

Leon smiled. "Ever hear of the Khazars?"

"No."

"They were a semi-nomadic people who ruled a huge empire across the Russian steppes and the Caucasus, all the way to the Crimea. During the eighth and ninth centuries, they converted to Judaism. A lot of scholars think that many European Jews—particularly those from Russia and Poland—came from the dispersal of the Khazars, rather than from the original Diaspora."

"Is that true?"

Leon shrugged. "Truth and politics make uncomfortable bedfellows. Just to suggest such a thing is enough to send certain people into fits. But there are two professors here at Tel Aviv University who refuse to be silenced—one a historian, the other a linguist."

Pushing up from his chair, Leon shuffled off, to return a moment later with a small stack of well-thumbed books he set on the table before Tobie. "Recent genetic testing of mitochondrial DNA has been very suggestive. But who knows? Future testing may show something else."

"What do you think?"

Leon shrugged. "I think there has to be some reason why I'm alive today to tell you about all this."

"You were one of those exposed?"

He lowered himself stiffly back into his chair. "Yes."

"This Dr. Kline," said Jax. "What happened to him at the end of the war?"

"It's hard to say. The last days were so chaotic. Everyone was starving. Not just the people in the camps, but the villagers and the soldiers, too. There was a terrible outbreak of typhus in all the camps, but because of the Allied blockade, we had no medicine to treat it. As the Russian army advanced, the Germans started moving inmates from the eastern camps, sending them to Dachau. New trains were arriving every day, but their boxcars were full of dead or dying prisoners."

"From the typhus?"

"Mainly, yes. It was horrible—like something from the Apocalypse." He tightened his grip on the bowl of his pipe, his gaze lost in the distance. "At that point, there was no one left to bury them. The bodies just piled up. I still remember the day the American infantry liberated the camp. They took one look at those piles of emaciated corpses, and rounded up every German guard in the camp—about five hundred of them—and shot them."

"The Dachau Massacre," said Jax.

Leon nodded. "Some of those guards were sadistic *bulvons*. But most of them were just kids. Scared kids, drafted into the army and doing what they were told. The ones the

Americans should have shot—men like Martin Kline—are the ones who got away."

Jax leaned forward. "You've no idea what happened to him?"

"I heard he fled east, to the Russians. But who knows?"

Jax met Tobie's gaze, but said nothing.

Leon glanced from one to the other. "Why are you asking me about all this, James?"

"You know I can't tell you that, Leon."

Leon let out a long sigh that shook his narrow chest. "It's still out there, isn't it? That pathogen . . . whatever it is. It's still out there, and someone has it. Someone who's planning to use it."

When Jax didn't answer, Leon raised one shaky hand to rub his eyes, and his voice broke. "God help us all."

57

The call from Andrei came through about ten minutes later.
Excusing himself, Jax retreated to a small chamber on the
far side of the courtyard.

The Russian came straight to the point. "Remember that
boy you were interested in?"

"Stefan Baklanov?"

"That's him."

"You found him?"

"Not exactly. But we picked up someone who appears to
have been looking for him. A Chechen by the name of Borz
Zakaev."

Jax glanced toward the courtyard, where October was
drinking peppermint tea with Ginsburg's Islamic wife. He
said, "Has this guy told you anything?"

"Not yet. But we're working on him. It shouldn't take
long."

Jax knew what that meant. Once, the Russian use of
"enhanced interrogation techniques" had helped brand the
Communists as bad guys. But after the last few years, the
West had kinda lost the high road on that subject.

He said, "Listen, Andrei: have you ever heard of a Nazi doctor named Kline? Martin Kline? There's a good possibility he was picked up by the Russians at the end of the war."

"Kline." There was a pause. "Never heard of him. Why?"

Jax didn't even hesitate; he needed the Russian's cooperation, which meant that now was not the time to pussyfoot with the truth. "I'm beginning to think U–114's hazardous cargo wasn't exactly what we thought it was."

Andrei's voice sharpened. "This Kline . . . what was his specialty?"

"Biological warfare."

"I don't like the sound of this, Jax."

"Neither do I."

Andrei said, "There's an Aeroflot flight leaving Ben-Gurion Airport for Moscow at two A.M., with connections on to Kaliningrad. Be on it."

"What makes you think we can trust this guy?" asked October as their flight backed away from the terminal at Ben-Gurion. Around them, the lights of the airport lit up the night with a sulfurous glow.

Jax looked up from tightening his seat belt. "You mean Andrei? What makes you think I trust him?"

She made an incoherent noise deep in her throat. "Then why are we going to Russia?"

"Because Halloween is less than twenty-four hours away, and we're running out of options."

"You can't seriously think the Russians are behind this?"

"The Russian government, no. Some other interests in Russia, very possibly."

She was silent for a moment. "I don't understand how anyone could do something like this. How could you deliberately unleash a plague you know is going to kill millions? Who could hate that much?"

"A lot of people hate that much. Look at what the Russians did to Kaliningrad. What the Turks did to Izmir. What Hitler did to the Jews."

"But that all happened a long time ago."

"Not that long ago. Remember Sabra and Shatila? There's been a lot of anti-Arab and anti-Muslim bigotry whipped up in the last few years. Not just in the States, but in Europe and Russia and China, too. That kind of stuff turns ugly in a hurry."

"But this disease won't just kill Arab Muslims. It'll kill Arab Christians, and Jews."

"Another perennially favorite target. And as for the Arab Christians—" He pushed his carry-on bag further under the seat ahead of him. "Most people don't even know they exist." He paused. "I suppose it's one way to solve the Middle East crises."

"By wiping out everyone in the area? That's a little extreme, isn't it?"

"More extreme than nukes? Do you know how many good Christian Americans have been calling for the United States to nuke the entire Arab world?"

She stared across the runway to where a long row of planes was already lined up, waiting for takeoff.

Jax said, "From a practical standpoint, the problem with nuking the Arab world has always been contamination, right? No one wants to set off a bunch of atomic bombs in the midst of the richest oil fields in the world—oil fields everyone has been trying to get their hands on for years. But if you could get rid of the population . . ."

"Then you could just walk in and take over the oil fields, no problem. You think that's what this is about? *Oil*?"

"It's a possibility," said Jax. "The United States isn't the only country that'd like to get its hands on the Middle East. Everyone's going to be running out of oil eventually. Europe, China—"

"Russia."

"Russia," Jax agreed. "They might be a big exporter of oil now, but it won't last forever. Think about it: of the five things we know for certain about these bad guys, at least three of them are clustered around Russia."

She frowned. "Five things? We know five things?"

"At least. We know that whoever these bad guys are, they're neither Jewish nor Arab."

"Obviously. But that still leaves a hell of a lot of options open. What else?"

"We know that our bad guys command some serious resources in terms of money and personnel."

"You mean, as in a government?"

"Once, I'd have said so. But there are some very rich crazies out there. And with the way everyone hires mercenaries these days, there are private 'security companies' all over the place. Not just in the U.S., but in places like Britain and South Africa and Russia, too."

"That's two," said October, holding up her fingers. "But as links to Russia, they're both pretty shaky."

"I wasn't counting those as the Russian links." He held up his own fingers. "Three, the last time this Dr. Kline was seen, he was headed toward Russia. One of the questions we haven't addressed in all this is, How did our bad guys find out the pathogen was on that U-boat?"

"You think Kline told them?"

"It seems like a pretty good possibility." He held up another finger. "Four, out of all the salvage outfits operating around the Baltic Sea, our bad guys decided to hire the *Yalena*, a Russian ship. And five, our bad guys have people in Russia. They were there last Saturday, when they killed Baklanov and his crew. They were there when they killed Anna Baklanov. And they're still there, looking for this kid—presumably because he can identify them."

"Which is why we want the kid," she said.

"Which is why we *need* that kid."

October leaned back in her seat, her hands curling around the ends of the armrests as the plane hurtled down the runway toward takeoff. "We know something else," she said.

He swung his head to look at her. "What's that?"

"We know that if they find that boy before we do, they'll kill him."

"If we don't figure out who's doing this and stop them, tens of millions of people are going to die."

"You say that like the boy doesn't matter."

Their gazes met, and Jax knew they were both remembering the same thing: a dark-headed, gangly boy with one arm thrown across the shoulders of a happy, panting mutt. "No," said Jax softly. "The boy matters."

58

Stefan awoke cold and tired and hungry. He'd passed a rest-
less night, startling at every loose board banging in the
wind, every furtive rustling from the unseen creatures of the
dark.

Just before dawn he abandoned all attempts at sleep and
crawled out of the ruined stable where he and the pup had
sought shelter from the snow. He was digging for old potatoes in a snow-dusted field when he noticed a boy of perhaps
ten or twelve staring at him from beneath the bare branches
of a nearby chestnut.

Wrapped in a warm navy jacket, the boy was small and
skinny, with large teeth and freckles and straw-colored hair
that peeked out from beneath a woolen cap. He said, "You're
not supposed to be here."

"Neither are you," said Stefan, straightening slowly.
"What'd you do? Sneak out of your room last night?"

The boy's head jerked back. "What's it to you?"

"Nothing." Stefan squinted at the distant walls of the school, an idea forming in his head. "If I gave you a message for Father Alexei, could you get it to him?"

The boy kicked aimlessly at the snow around him. "Maybe. Depends on how much you're willing to pay me."

Stefan hesitated, then reached in his pocket. "I have this piece of amber."

Rodriguez stood at the window of the small farmhouse they'd commandeered on the outskirts of Yasnaya Polyana. Wrapping his hands around a mug of coffee, he blew softly on the hot brew, his gaze on the light fall of snow that blanketed the surrounding fields.

They'd left Zoya and Nikolayev watching the farm for the night. But Borz had never shown up, and their attempts to raise him had met with a troubling silence. Rodriguez looked at his watch and frowned. *What the hell had happened to him?*

At the kitchen table behind him, the SAS guy, Ian Kirkpatrick, was sipping a cup of tea while Salinger adjusted his equipment and yawned. Suddenly, he sat forward. "The mother's getting an incoming call."

Rodriguez swung around. "Record it, and put it on audio."

A man's gruff voice boomed out. "Nadia? It's me. I wanted to let you know I've heard from Stefan. He's alive!"

"Stefan? You spoke to him? Oh, praise God." There was a moment's silence, during which they heard the woman blow her nose. "Where is he?"

"Hiding. He's afraid to come home. He thinks the men who killed his uncle may be watching your house."

"Hiding? What has my Stefan done that he has these bad men after him?"

"Nadia, Nadia. I don't know everything yet. I'm leaving

now to take him some food and clean clothes. I'll come to you after I've seen him. Have patience."

The woman said something unintelligible, and hung up.

"*Fuck*," said Rodriguez. "Who the fuck was that? Play it again."

They had to listen to the recording three times before Rodriguez finally caught the woman's last words.

"*Thank you, Father.*"

Kirkpatrick pushed up from his chair as Rodriguez reached out to snap off the recorder. "It's the village priest. The little shit contacted his priest." He reached for his jacket. "Call Zoya and Nikolayev. Let's go."

The flight from Moscow touched down in Kaliningrad in a swirl of billowing snow. They were met by the familiar unsmiling Tatar, who drove them across a stretch of empty runway to where Andrei was waiting for them in a blue-and-gray Ansat helicopter, its main rotor stirring up an eddy of biting snow as it beat the air.

October took one look at the Ansat and froze halfway out of the car. "A chopper? I *hate* choppers."

Jax gave her a sharp nudge toward the helicopter's open door and shouted over the roar, "Get over it."

"You're late," yelled Andrei, handing them each a headset as they clambered aboard.

"I need to stop flying Aeroflot." Jax slipped the headset over his ears and adjusted the mike. "Where are we going?"

Andrei nodded to his pilot. "Yasnaya Polyana."

The Ansat lifted off the ground, its tail kicking up and nose dipping as it flew forward. Jax glanced over at October. She'd put on her headset and was sitting stiffly upright, her hands clasped together between her knees, her gaze fixed straight ahead.

Andrei said, "You don't like helicopters, Ensign?"

"No."

"Given what happened in Iraq, I'm not surprised."

She swung her head to stare at him. "How do you know what happened in Iraq?"

"He's a spy," said Jax. "Probing into people's deep dark secrets is what he does for kicks." To Andrei, he said, "Why Yasnaya Polyana?"

"That's where Stefan Baklanov's mother lives. It's also where the militia picked up Borz Zakaev."

"You say he's Chechen? That doesn't sound good. Any chance he has ties to al-Qa'ida?"

Andrei shrugged. "Not that we know of. But it's possible. He worked with the CIA and American Special Forces in Afghanistan back in the eighties, when you Americans and Osama bin Laden were allies, supporting the mujahedeen against us."

"Don't remind me," said Jax.

Andrei showed his teeth in a smile.

"So what did you learn from this guy?" said October.

"Unfortunately, very little." Andrei shrugged. "He had a weak heart."

She frowned. "What does that mean?"

"It means he's dead," said Jax.

Her eyes widened. "You mean you tor—"

Jax brought his heel down on her instep, hard, and said to Andrei, "What can you tell us about the kid?"

"We sent someone out to talk to the mother this morning. She still thinks her son died with the others on the *Yalena*. If the boy is alive, he hasn't contacted her."

Jax grunted. "He's obviously being careful."

"He needs to be careful. When my men were leaving the mother's farm, they noticed a black Durango parked up the road."

They were coming in low over a village, the blades of the

chopper flattening the long grass that thrust up through the new snow. Jax said, "Someone's staking out the mother's house?"

"So it would appear. We've set a couple of militiamen to watch the watchers."

"Why didn't you just pick them up for questioning?" said October.

"Because I have no more use for small fry. I want the big fish. If we leave them alone, the minnows in the Durango will lead us to him."

Adjusting his field glasses, Carlos Rodriguez watched as the old priest came out of his cottage to load two bundles into the sidecar of a rusty Ural motorbike.

Ugly and ungainly but fiercely sturdy, the Urals had been the workhorses of the Soviet Union. This one still bore the stamped star that showed it had come off a military assembly line, although the machine-gun mount had been cut off and a spare tire mounted on the back of the sidecar. The priest himself looked like some latter-day Rasputin, only bigger and broader, with long, flowing black robes and a wild gray beard that tumbled down past his belly.

Tucking up the hem of his robes, he swung one leg over the old Ural and gave it a hard kick. Rodriguez lowered his field glasses.

"Keep him in sight, but don't get too close."

Salinger nodded and eased their silver Range Rover into gear.

They trailed the priest through bleak fields of winter wheat edged with scrub and sodden earth streaked with snow. A few kilometers out of the village, he turned in beneath a soaring arched gate of white stucco and red brick topped by a narrow roof of red tiles. A stylized rendition of a seven-pointed elk antler decorated the arch's keystone.

"Think the kid is hiding here?" said Kirkpatrick as they followed the priest into a neglected court. The two Russians, Zoya and Nikolayev, turned in behind them in a black Durango that was a twin to the one the little shit wrecked.

"Maybe. Or maybe not. The guy's a priest. He could just be visiting some parishioner."

They watched the priest's Ural thump along a rutted dirt lane that wound behind a big, dilapidated old house, then passed into a stand of pines. Through the branches of the trees they could see the ruins of row after row of what looked like stables, their red brick walls crumbling where stretches of the ancient tiled roofs had given way.

"What the hell is this place?" said Kirkpatrick.

"I don't know." Rodriguez signaled to the Russians in the Durango to pull over. "But I think we've just found our boy."

59

The chopper came down on a grassy helipad beside a dreary Soviet-era building of dirty glass and rust-stained concrete. Two blue-and-white militia vans stood at the ready, their idling engines belching clouds of white steam into the cold air.

A tall, lean militia captain with high cheekbones and a tight mouth snapped to attention and delivered a stuttering report.

"What do you mean you lost the men watching the widow's farm?" Andrei bellowed.

"They just . . . left."

"And your men didn't follow them . . . why?"

The militia captain swallowed hard enough to bob his Adam's apple up and down. "One of them was taking a leak."

"And the other was—what? Asleep? Screwing his girlfriend in the backseat?"

A rush of scarlet darkened the militia captain's face before slowly draining away to leave him a sickly white.

Jax said, "I can think of only two reasons they'd leave.

Either they've given up trying to find the boy and are pulling out, or . . ."

Tobie finished for him. "Or they found him."

Andrei stood with his fists on his hips, a muscle bunching and flexing along his tight jaw as he stared through the silently drifting snow at the distant cluster of wooden houses. "If you were a sixteen-year-old kid too scared to go home, who would you turn to?"

From a distant barn came the lowing of a cow and, nearer, the disgruntled *caw-caw* of a crow perched on a nearby electric pole. Looking toward it, Tobie saw the spire of an ancient church thrusting up above the bare, snow-covered branches of a stand of willows.

"The priest," she said suddenly. "Remember when Anna Baklanov was showing us Stefan's picture? She said Jasha used to make fun of the boy for being so devout."

Andrei swung toward the nearest militia van. "It's worth a try. Let's go."

Stefan sat with his knees drawn up to his chest, his spine pressed against one of the iron columns supporting the stable block's soaring roof. Tipping back his head, he could see a giant hook hanging from the center of the beam above. He craned his neck, following the line, hook after hook, disappearing into the gloom. It seemed strange that the hooks should still be here, long after all the blood stallions and broodmares had disappeared.

He shivered. The interior of the stable block was starkly empty and open, the fine polished oak that had once formed the stalls having long ago been ripped out and carted off for firewood. The row of small, arched windows set high on each side wall let in little light. He shivered again, and reached over to draw the dog closer. The pup let out a little whimper and licked his face.

"It'll be all right once Father Alexei gets here," whispered Stefan, his voice echoing eerily in the vast, hollow chamber. "You'll see."

He heard the whine of the priest's motorbike long before he saw it. Scrambling to his feet, he was standing in the broken archway at the end of the stable block when the priest brought his old Ural to a coughing standstill and cut the engine.

Stefan bolted out the door. "Father!"

Climbing stiffly off the motorbike, the old priest turned to open his arms wide. "Stefan. My boy."

Stefan flung himself against the priest's broad chest. "Father," said Stefan again. Pressing his face into the habit's scratchy wet wool, he breathed in the familiar, comforting scents of incense and vodka and cooked cabbage.

"Come, come," said the priest, drawing back to cup Stefan's cheek with one big, work-worn hand. "It's all right. Tell me what has happened."

"They want to kill me!"

"Who? Who wants to kill you?" said the priest, just as the dog at Stefan's side let out a growl that rumbled low in his chest.

Looking up, Stefan saw a shadow, heard the crunch of snow beneath a heavy boot. He took a step back, whispered, "It's them. It's the men who killed Uncle Jasha and the others."

Turning, Father Andrei shoved Stefan behind his big body and shouted, "Run, boy!" just as the men across the clearing opened fire.

60

Stefan dove through the broken archway, his shoulder explod-ing in pain as he hit the litter-covered concrete floor and rolled to one side, his arms coming up to wrap around his head. A cascade of gunfire chipped the brick walls of the stables and pinged off the rusting iron columns. Scrambling to his hands and knees, he screamed, *"Father!"* Then, *"Pup!"* and provoked another volley.

Pushing to his feet, he sprinted down the long stables, beneath high-arched windows that showed patches of dull white sky overhead. He heard the voice from his nightmares shout in stilted Russian, "Nikolayev, stay outside and take the left perimeter. Zoya, you take the right. Kirkpatrick and Salinger, come with me."

"Jesus, Mary, and Joseph," whispered Stefan, flattening against the nearest wall with a shaky gasp.

The hollowed-out shell of the stables stretched before him, long and narrow and totally empty except for the two marching rows of iron columns and the silent line of hooks that marked the center of each overhead beam. He could see a side door about halfway down the far right wall that had once opened to the pasturelands beyond. But if he tried to make a run for it, the Russian named Zoya would cut him down in an instant.

He was trapped.

The militia vans were just turning under the stud farm's high gateway when Jax heard the distant crackle of gunfire. "Shit," he whispered under his breath.

They'd learned from the priest's housekeeper that the old man had bundled up some clean clothes and a slab of roasted pork, fresh bread, and apples, and set off on his motorbike for the ruins of some abandoned royal stables. But from the sounds of things, they were too late.

"Step on it!" yelled Andrei. He hit the siren, the wailing notes blaring out as they bounced and swayed over the rutted lane.

They fishtailed around a stand of pines, breaking out of the trees into a stretch of abandoned pastures with row after row of stable blocks of red brick and stucco walls and collapsing red-tiled roofs.

"There," said Andrei, pointing to a rusty Ural motorbike with a sidecar parked in front of the relatively intact stable block at the far end. A dark mound of faded black lay halfway between the motorbike and the arched entrance to the stables.

As the wailing militia vans bore down on them, a man in a heavy gray sweater broke away from the near side of the stable block. Leaping the tumbled remnants of a fence, he bolted across the abandoned pastures toward a thicket of willows edging a distant small stream.

"Give me a gun," Jax shouted to Andrei.

"Here." Andrei tossed him a Makarov pistol, military issue, with a special twelve-round detachable box magazine.

Sliding on leaf mold and snow and mud, their van skidded to a halt beside a silver Range Rover and a black Durango, heat radiating off their engines to melt the surrounding snow. Andrei handed a second Makarov to October. She took it without comment.

They piled out of the vans, Andrei shouting orders, directing half the militiamen after the dark figure heading for the creek, the others around the far side of the stables.

Jax charged his pistol by pulling back the slide, then pushed down the side-mounted safety lever. "Stay here," he told October as he and Andrei and the militia captain headed for the broken arch of the entrance in the end wall.

"Why?"

"In case they slip past us and double back around to the cars."

A distant shout jerked their gaze toward the fields, where a second man could now be seen running toward the old riding school. "Oh."

Jax sprinted for the stable entrance, tinglingly conscious of what a great target black leather made silhouetted against white snow and sky. He ducked left; Andrei went right.

The militia captain was a little slower.

Jax saw a flash, heard the pop of a pistol from halfway down the stableblock. Looking back, he saw a hole like a giant cigarette burn appear above the captain's left eye. He dropped just inside the doorway.

Flattening on the cold concrete floor, Jax tightened his grip on the Makarov and willed his eyes to adjust to the sudden gloom.

Despite the row of small high windows on each long wall, the stable block was a vast haze of dusty shadows. He heard a rustling from farther down the block, but didn't dare shoot in case it was Stefan.

Levering up on his elbows, he crept forward, the Makarov

held at the ready. As his pupils dilated, features began to solidify out of the murky gloom. Rows of rusting iron columns. Three vague, rectangular shapes near the back wall. A gaping patch of white where once had stood a side door.

A light whimpering sounded at the far end of the building. From some ten feet up ahead to his left came a muzzle flash and the popping of an automatic, fired in rapid succession.

Jax fixed on the shadowy outline of a man with his gun hand stretched out, and fired. He nailed the shooter once, twice, three times. The figure cried out. Lay still.

A voice from somewhere to the right shouted, "*Salinger!*"

Andrei opened up, his automatic belching fire and the smell of burnt powder. Jax heard the sound of bullets striking flesh.

Then all was quiet.

His throat dry, Jax held his breath, every fiber of his being straining with the effort of listening.

A faint rustling drew his attention to the right. The indistinct shape of—a man? a boy?—rose up to make a dash for the side doorway. Without knowing which, Jax couldn't shoot. He yelled, "*Stefan?*"

The figure kept running, a black silhouette that showed for an instant against the white of the fields before darting to the right, footsteps crunching snow as he headed toward the front courtyard. Then came the thunderous boom of what sounded like a Colt 45, and the answering *pop-pop-pop* of a Makarov.

October.

Heedless of whoever else might be lurking in the gloom, Jax shoved up. Racing toward the entrance, he heard another exchange of shots followed by a sputtering cough as the Ural roared to life.

He burst through the crumbling archway, the Makarov

held in a tight two-handed grip, his body crouching into a shooter's stance. He saw October standing in the center of the road, firing over and over at the disappearing whine of the Ural.

Jax straightened slowly.

"Who the hell taught her to shoot?" said Andrei in disgust, coming up beside him.

"The U.S. Navy." Jax glanced at the militia vans. The guy on the Ural had shot out all the front tires. "Shit."

He walked to where October still stood in the center of the dirt road, the Makarov held in a tight grip. "You all right?"

She nodded. "It was him. The one I saw before, in the garden."

"Saw? Saw *when*? What garden?"

She glanced at Andrei, and shook her head in warning. Straightening slowly, she let the gun dangle in a loose grip at her side. "Sorry I missed."

Jax reached out to clasp her shoulder and squeezed. "Hey. You kept yourself alive. That's a good thing."

A volley of shots sounded from the direction of the creek, followed by a shout, and another thunder of murderous fire.

"Think there's anyone left alive to talk?" said Jax.

Holstering his gun, Andrei turned back toward the stables. "Let's go see."

61

The two Russians the militia shot down near the creek were dead. So was the militia captain, and the village priest, and a blond, blue-eyed shooter wearing a camouflage jacket and a turtleneck sweater hiked up to show the U.S. Special Forces tattoo on his side.

"Somehow, I don't think we're dealing with al-Qa'ida," said Andrei, studying the elaborate depiction of a snake swallowing a sword.

Jax shook his head and went to hunker down beside the body of the second shooter, a tall, thin man with brown hair and gray eyes and a pale, faintly freckled face. "Doesn't look like it, does it?" He pushed to his feet. "Any chance I can get these guys' fingerprints?"

"I'll have them faxed to Division Thirteen."

"Oh, Matt'll love that."

They found Stefan Baklanov huddled beside an old feed bin at the far end of the stable block, a half-grown black-and-tan pup cradled in his arms.

"He's hurt," said the boy.

Crouching beside him, October ran one hand over the

pup's rear flank. Her fingers came away sticky with blood. "If you'll carry him outside," she said in her flawless Russian, "I'll take a look at him and see what I can do."

The boy hesitated, then swallowed hard and pushed to his feet.

Their attempts to get anything out of the boy were next to useless until some three hours later when, freshly showered and fed, and in clean clothes, Stefan Baklanov sat on a sofa in his mother's home, the bandaged pup at his side.

"The men who hired your uncle to raise the U-boat," said Andrei, "who were they?"

The boy hugged the dog tighter and threw a questioning glance at Jax.

"Don't worry about him," said Andrei. "Who shot your uncle?"

"Americans," Stefan whispered.

"How do you know they were Americans?" said Jax in English.

Tobie started to translate for him, but Stefan answered easily, "I heard them talking." He turned his head to meet Jax's hard gaze. "They sounded like you."

"That doesn't make any sense," said Jax.

Andrei snorted. "You mean, you don't want it to make any sense." To the boy, he said, "Do you know why these Americans wanted your uncle to salvage that particular U-boat?"

Stefan sank lower on the sofa, his gaze on the worn carpet at his feet.

"It's all right," said Tobie, ignoring Andrei's frown. "No one is blaming you."

Stefan fiddled with his dog's ears. "They said the U-boat carried a weapon."

Andrei's voice sharpened. "What kind of a weapon?"

"A disease. I don't know what kind."

"Do you know why the Americans killed your uncle?"

Stefan nodded. "They found out he was planning to double-cross them. I don't know how."

Jax said, "The man in charge of the Americans—do you know his name?"

Stefan drew the pup up to him in a tight embrace and shook his head. "I only ever heard Uncle Jasha call him 'Major.'"

"What will happen to the boy?" asked Tobie. They were in another militia van on their way back to the helipad.

Andrei took a new pack out of his pocket and shook out a cigarette. "I'll leave a couple of militiamen at their farm for a few days, just in case. But I don't think anyone will bother him. He's told us what he knows."

"They could be mercenaries," said Jax, his thoughts obviously running along a different track entirely.

"They could be," Andrei agreed.

A lot of Special Forces people left the service as soon as they could, taking their training and selling it for big bucks to private 'security companies.' Often they worked for the U.S. government. But sometimes they didn't. Tobie said, "How do we find out who these guys were working for?"

"If they really were in the American military, their prints should lead us right to them."

Tobie felt her stomach clench as the Ansat came into view, its main rotor slowly beating the air. "And if they weren't? We're at a dead end, aren't we?"

The militia driver braked beside the waiting chopper. Andrei drew the smoke from his cigarette deep into his lungs and said, "Not necessarily."

Jax paused with his door half open. "What's that supposed to mean?"

Andrei dropped the half-smoked cigarette in the snow and

ground it beneath his heel. "It means there's someone I think Ensign Guinness might like to meet."

Carlos Rodriguez rode the Ural to within two hundred meters of the Polish border. Abandoning the motorbike in a ditch, he cut through a nearby stand of birch until he came out on a Polish road. He thumbed down a trucker, then caught a series of rides that brought him to Gdansh—which had once been the German city of Danzig but was now very, very Polish.

He booked a flight to Washington, D.C., then found a quiet coffee shop and put in a call to Boyd.

"The Russians have the kid," he told Boyd without preamble.

There was a moment's tense silence. Boyd said, "Tell me what happened."

Rodriguez stared across the concourse to where a woman in a short skirt and high black boots was helping a toddler take off his coat. "They had his house staked out. It was a trap." It wasn't exactly the truth, but it was close enough. "They got my entire team."

"Dead?"

"Yes." It was important that every man be dead; dead men don't tell tales. "No one captured. And they were all sterile."

Boyd's voice was a gravelly rasp. "You must be losing your edge, to fall into a trap like that."

Rodriguez tightened his jaw. "It was an FSB operation. They had their first team in there."

Again, a fierce silence. Boyd said, "When can you get back here?"

"My flight leaves in an hour."

"We'll talk when you get here," said Boyd, and hung up.

Rodriguez glanced again at the woman. As if conscious

of showing too much leg, she'd crouched down. He turned away.

The failure to kill the boy was a concern, but not too much of a problem at this point. If the boy had found someone to listen to his tale earlier in the week, he would have done some real damage. But now? No one would have time to put the pieces of the puzzle together before Saturday night.

It was the loss of Salinger and Kirkpatrick that really stung. Rodriguez didn't like to lose men. He didn't like to lose, period. He still wasn't exactly sure what had gone down in the stables of Yasnaya Polyana. But he knew who to blame for it. And once Boyd's little operation was over, Rodriguez would see that they paid for it.

Both of them.

62

Her name was Dr. Svetlana Bukovsky. A small, slim woman with gray-streaked brown hair and fiercely intelligent gray eyes, she might have been anywhere between forty and sixty. Dressed in a brown tweed skirt, brown sweater, wool tights, and sensible shoes, she met them at the doorway of her office at Immanuel Kant State University in Kaliningrad.

"What a pleasure it is to actually meet you, Ensign. I've been following your career with interest for months."

Tobie found her hand seized in an unexpectedly firm grip. "You have?"

Andrei said, "Dr. Bukovsky teaches here at the University, now. But before that, she spent more than twenty years working with the KGB. Her specialty is remote viewing."

"How did you—" Tobie broke off, her gaze flying to meet Jax's.

"How did I know you're a remote viewer?" Andrei gave

an enigmatic smile and turned to Jax. "Come. Let us leave them to their work."

Tobie said, "I don't really need a tasker."

They sat across from each other at a table made of golden oak. Tobie's chair was comfortably padded, the room dimly lit and soundproofed.

A perfect RV room.

Dr. Bukovsky said, "I know. But it is always easier for others to accept one's results, don't you agree, when one has the mechanics of a more controlled viewing in place?"

"Somehow, I can't see the United States government giving much credence to a viewing I did with a KGB scientist in Kaliningrad."

A soft smile touched the older woman's eyes. "Is that so important at this point?"

Tobie hesitated, aware of the clock ticking relentlessly toward Halloween. She blew out a long sigh. "All right."

She closed her eyes, let her breathing slow and deepen as she relaxed down into her Zone. When she was ready, she opened her eyes.

The Russian rested the palm of one hand on a plain envelope that lay on the table before her. "The target is written here. Tell me what you see."

Tobie closed her eyes again. After her experience in Bremen, she knew a moment of uncertainty, a worry that her gift had somehow deserted her. But this time, the images came. Faint at first. Blurred flashes that slowly solidified. She said, "I'm getting the sense of something rectangular. It's like a box, or a case. A metal case. It's . . . shiny. Like an aluminum case."

"What's in the case? Can you see?"

"Something cylindrical. Yellow." She began to sketch the images on the pad that lay before her. "It's a bright, almost fluorescent yellow. The cylinder is also metal. But I get the sense . . ." She hesitated. "It's as if it's not real. It's an illusion."

It made no sense, but now was not the time for analysis. The Russian said, "Can you back away from it?"

"Yes."

"Now tell me what you see."

"The aluminum case is lying on a desk. A wooden desk. Well polished. The room is rather small, paneled in the same wood as the desk. I get the impression of comfort. Luxury."

"Move above the room, then look down and tell me what you see."

"A railing. White. White walls. It's like a house, but it's not a house. There's water. Sunlight." She started a new sketch, the outlines of a sleek bow and decks slowly taking shape. She said, "It's a boat."

"Can you move around it?"

Tobie shifted her perspective again. Coming around the stern, she could see the name of the boat written in a flowing script. "There's an 'h.'" She frowned. "No. Maybe it's an 'l,' or an 'f.'" She shook her head. She always had a hard time with script. "I can't read it."

"That's all right, October. Back away from the boat now and tell me what you see."

Tobie took a deep breath and smelled the briny bite of the sea. "Water. Calm water. Reflections of lights. City lights. There's a stretch of silvery wood. A dock."

"Keep moving back."

"I'm getting a sense of a wide-open area. Grass. Beyond that are trees. No. Not trees. Columns. A row of columns. Pavement. It's a building, or a house. A large house." She sketched it quickly. An Italianate villa with a terrace overlooking the water. She went back over her drawing, adding arched windows, wide French doors, the feathery fronds of palm trees.

Dr. Bukovsky said, "Can you move back more?"

Tobie tried to focus on the surrounding houses, the street. But the farther she moved away from the boat, the more indistinct and disjointed the images became. She managed to draw a rough sketch of a bridge. But in the end, she shook her head in frustration and leaned back in her seat.

"The target," she said, pushing her hair off her forehead with one splayed hand. "What was it?"

Wordlessly, Dr. Bukovsky held out the plain envelope.

Tobie ripped it open. On a single sheet of white paper, someone—Andrei?—had written, "The current position of the pathogen from U–114."

"I guess that explains why the viewing I tried in Bremen didn't work," said Tobie, pausing on the sidewalk in front of the university building. The snow had stopped, but a bitter wind had kicked up, stinging her cheeks and making her eyes water. She turned up the collar of her jacket. "I was trying to RV an atom bomb that didn't exist."

Jax squinted over at the Tatar, who waited, unsmiling, next to a sleek silver Mercedes S-Class drawn up at the curb. They were booked on the next flight to Washington, D.C. "I suppose we can take this as some kind of proof that the pathogen does exist. Even if we don't have a clue where it is."

"You know it's someplace that has palm trees and boats," said Andrei, a smile tightening the skin beside his eyes. "That should narrow your search."

Jax studied the Russian's enigmatic face. "You're being way too cooperative, Andrei. Why?"

"Can you think of a better way to find out if that pathogen has left Russia?"

"Are you telling me you believe in remote viewing?"

Andrei shook a cigarette from a nearly empty pack. "Why? Don't you?"

When Jax didn't answer, the Russian huffed a soft laugh. Resting the cigarette on his lower lip, he reached inside his jacket for a sheaf of papers folded into thirds. "Here. Some light reading to pass the time on your flight."

Jax took the papers. "What's this?"

Andrei struck his lighter, his eyes narrowing against the smoke. "You remember you asked about Martin Kline?"

"You found something on him?"

"Who told you he came to Russia?"

"Someone who was at Dachau."

Andrei nodded to the papers in Jax's hand. "Those are copies of some old World War II intel reports from the field, including a transcript from the debriefing of one of the Communists liberated from Dachau. According to his report, the Americans took Dr. Kline."

"What makes you so sure your Dachau survivor was right, and mine was wrong?"

"Because this man wasn't just repeating a rumor. He says he helped load Kline's papers and medical samples on a truck. A U.S. Government truck."

"He could have been mistaken," said Tobie.

Andrei glanced over at her. "He might have been. Which is why I've also included a report from an agent we had at Fort Strong, where your government processed the high-value Germans it took to the States after the war."

"Operation Paperclip," said Jax, his fingers tightening around the papers.

Tobie looked from one man to the other, not understanding. "What's Operation Paperclip?"

Miami, Florida: Friday 30 October 10:30 P.M. local time

The 110-foot Hargrave yacht Walker's ex-wife had christened the *Harlequin* rocked gently against the private dock at the base of Walker's Miami garden.

Lifting the aluminum case onto the master stateroom's

built-in desk, he eased it open. Nestled within the gray foam padding lay a fluorescent yellow steel tank, thirteen inches long, of the kind normally used as an emergency air supply by SCUBA divers. Within it waited six cubic feet of deadly air under 3,000 dpi.

Walker didn't often smile, but he smiled now. There weren't many men in history who could truly be said to have changed the world. But he was about to join their ranks.

He snapped the case shut and left it there, behind the locked door of the *Harlequin*'s stateroom.

63

Early that morning, General Gerald Boyd took the train up to Boston to visit his daughter, Taylor, now in her second year at Harvard Law School. They had lunch, and a fudge sundae at Billings and Stover, then went for a walk along the Charles. They were sitting on a bench in Harvard Yard when he got a call from Colonel Lee.

"There's a new development," whispered Lee.

"Excuse me, honey," Boyd told his daughter, smiling apologetically. "This'll just take a minute." Standing, he strolled away some fifteen feet and said to Lee, "Now what?"

"I thought you should know the Russians have sent the fingerprints of Rodriguez's team to Division Thirteen. If they start looking into Rodriguez's files and see—" The man's voice cracked.

"Calm down, Colonel." Boyd squinted up at the banks of heavy white clouds ripe with the promise of snow. Lee was rapidly becoming more of a liability than an asset. If Rodriguez would get his ass back to the States—

"We need to talk," said Lee.

Boyd glanced over at Taylor. She was slim, like her mother, with fine light brown shoulder-length hair and a dimple that appeared in one cheek as she watched a squirrel grab an acorn and run. Whenever he thought of her, he still pictured the little kid in pigtails he used to take fishing. He had to keep reminding himself she was all grown up now. He said, "All right. I'm tied up the rest of the day, but I can meet you at the Boulder Bridge in Rock Creek Park at 0730 tomorrow morning." If Rodriguez wasn't back by then, Boyd would just have to take care of the Colonel himself.

"I'll be there."

Boyd slipped his phone away, then walked back toward Taylor, a smile on his face. "How'd you like to drive your old man to the train station?"

Kaliningrad, Russia: Friday 30 October

Jax barely managed to send Matt an urgent request to look into possible links between Kline and Paperclip, before the flight attendant's warning voice crackled over the intercom and their plane pushed away from the gate.

"Operation Paperclip," said October, watching him put away his phone. "Tell me about it."

He glanced at the staid German businessman sitting in the aisle across from them, and kept his voice low. "Paperclip was the code name for a project dreamed up at the end of World War II by Allen Dulles."

"Who was . . . ?"

"Dulles? He was the first civilian Director of Central Intelligence. Basically, the idea was to sneak Nazi scientists into the United States."

"Why would the United States want to import Nazis?"

"Because we were already gearing up for a fight with our new rivals, the Russians."

"Ah. I see."

"Even before the war was over, both the Americans and the Russians had competing intel teams ready to fan out over the German countryside and grab any kind of scientific booty they could get their hands on. And the biggest prizes of all were the German scientists themselves. At first the U.S. government just took the guys they nabbed back to places like Fort Hunt in Virginia, with the idea of interrogating them and then sending them home. But the more they learned about German advances in everything from rocketry to aeronautics, the more they wanted to keep them."

"Isn't that, like, slave labor or something?"

"Sort of. But a lot of these guys had wives and kids in the parts of Germany taken over by the Russians. They struck a deal: they'd work for the Americans if the U.S. government would get their families out of harm's way."

"That doesn't sound so bad."

"The problem was, some of the people they wanted to keep had been real Nazis—I mean Party members. And the U.S. had laws against the immigration of former Nazis. So Dulles and his boys basically drew up fake dossiers on those guys. The really, *really* bad Nazis had to be smuggled in through the ratlines and given false identities. The program went on for years, even after presidents like Truman and Eisenhower thought it had been shut down."

"How many scientists are we talking about?"

"The official number is sixteen hundred. But who knows? A lot of the relevant documents are still classified."

"After sixty years? But . . . why?"

Jax gave a soft laugh. "The government likes to pretend it classifies stuff for 'national security' reasons. But the truth is, most of that shit is kept under wraps because it's embarrassing—either to some very important people or to the government itself."

"But Kline wasn't a nuclear physicist. He was just a doctor. Why would they want him?"

"Because we had a huge chemical and bioweapons program going ourselves. It wasn't quite as crazy as what happened in Germany under Hitler, but there was some pretty ugly stuff going on."

He expected her to say, *I don't believe it.* Instead, she was silent for a moment, her gaze fixed on the thick white clouds on the other side of the window. When she spoke, her voice was a hushed whisper. "This is starting to sound really, really scary."

"No shit."

Washington, D.C.: 31 October, 6:25 A.M. local time

Rodriguez pushed through the doors from Customs and Immigration into a nearly deserted corridor, and put in a call to Boyd.

"It's about time you got here. Colonel Lee is becoming a problem," said Boyd, his voice gravelly with annoyance. "He'll be at Boulder Bridge in Rock Creek Park at 0730. Can you make it?"

Rodriguez glanced at his watch. "I can make it."

64

By the time their connecting flight from Berlin touched down at Dulles Airport in Washington, D.C., it was Saturday, October 31.

Halloween.

A Company car whisked them off to Langley, where Matt handed them mugs of steaming coffee and said, "I know you guys are tired. But we're running out of time."

Jax leaned back against Matt's steel table and blew on the vile brew in his cup. "Have you looked at the calendar? I'd say we're out of time."

"And the DCI and Homeland Security still aren't buying any of this." Matt's mop of curly, gray-streaked dark hair looked wilder than ever, and dark circles ringed his eyes. "I even went to the VP with the report you sent from Berlin on Tobie's last viewing. But without something more definite . . ." He shrugged. "I'm afraid we're on our own. Everything we do from here on out is off the Company clock."

Tobie took one sip of her coffee and quietly set it aside. "What did you find out about Martin Kline?"

"Looks like the Russians were right: from what I can

figure, the U.S. government brought Dr. Kline over here in the fall of 'forty-five. But after that, he just disappears. Everything related to him is still classified. Even the DCI couldn't access it if he wanted to. That kind of clearance needs to come from the Secretary of Defense, and he's not playing ball."

Tobie said, "I can't believe they brought that guy over here. He was a war criminal!"

Matt let out his breath in a harsh huff. "Ever hear of Arthur Rudolph? He built the V–2 rocket for Hitler at the Mittelwerk factory, where something like twenty thousand prisoners they used as slave labor died. We brought him over and put him to work designing the Saturn V rocket we used in the Apollo moon landings."

Jax rubbed his forehead. "So where did Kline go?"

"That's anybody's guess." Turning away, Matt picked up a sheaf of papers. "I had better luck with this stuff."

Jax looked up. "What's that?"

"I ran the fingerprints your buddy Andrei sent. Do you have any idea how much shit I'm taking around here for receiving a fax from the Russian SVR?"

"Andrei is not my buddy."

"Maybe. But you owe him on this one. Turns out we had all four sets of prints in our files. The shooter with the Special Forces tattoo was a guy from Nebraska named Ben Salinger, while his buddy was an SAS vet, Ian Kirkpatrick. Both left the service several years ago for the big bucks to be had in the private warfare sector."

"And the Chechen?"

"He was on the CIA payroll up until about eight years ago, when he went private." Matt reached for another file and held it out. "All three of them worked with this guy."

Peering over Jax's shoulder, Tobie found herself staring at a photograph of the lean, dark-haired man she'd originally remote viewed standing in a dark garden in Kaliningrad. "He's the one who got away. How'd the Russians get his prints?"

"Off one of the cars."

"Major Carlos Rodriguez," read Jax. "U.S. Army Rangers. Retired."

"Let me guess," said Tobie. "He's gone private, too."

"You got it," said Matt. "These guys were all mercenaries."

"So who are they working for now?"

Matt scratched the beard under his chin. "I don't know. But this guy Rodriguez has been doing a lot of contract jobs for the U.S. government lately. His last assignment was to put together a twenty-man team to train some Ukrainian Special Forces guys."

Tobie said, "What do you mean by 'contract' jobs?"

"Basically, they're no-bid contracts executed at the specific direction of the commanding general in charge of an operation. But here's the interesting thing: in the last two years, Rodriguez and his boys have worked on six contracts. And five of those contracts were all for the same guy: Lieutenant General Gerald T. Boyd."

Jax swore softly under his breath.

Tobie said, "Who's General Gerald Boyd?"

"The Deputy Commander of SOCOM—the U.S. Special Operations Command."

She sank into one of the battered chairs beside the table. "Are you telling me we've stumbled into some kind of black U.S. military project?"

Matt shook his head. "Not necessarily. Most people don't realize how little accountability there is on what these black ops people do. Once they slap a project 'Top Secret,' there's no oversight. They've always had trouble with this kind of shit—Special Forces guys running their own secret projects without any authorization from above. Even the men working for them didn't know their dirty little tricks weren't really authorized."

Jax's eyes narrowed. "Hang on there. Just because Boyd used Rodriguez in the past doesn't mean he's the one using him now."

Matt tossed him another file. "I've been looking into our general. The guy's a real loose cannon. He's been linked to everything from coordinating the activities of unauthorized assassination squads to funding black ops that were off the books. He also has a bad habit of shooting off his mouth in public. It was mildly embarrassing when he was going around calling the 'War on Terror' an Apocalyptic Crusade against the forces of the Antichrist. But then he came out with a few statements that teetered on the edge of anti-Semitism, and some key people in Washington decided that enough was enough. They're retiring him at the end of the year, which means no fourth star for our man Boyd. From what I understand, he's pretty bitter about that. He's been making noises about finally doing what he says should have been done a long time ago."

Tobie said, "What's that supposed to mean?"

Matt shrugged. "The guy's not stupid. He hasn't spelled it out."

Jax leafed through the General's file. "Have you asked him about Rodriguez?"

"I tried to make an appointment to get in to see him, but his aide, Phillips, basically told me to take a flying leap."

"So how do we talk to him?" said Tobie.

"We don't make an appointment," said Matt. "Fortunately, he's here in D.C. right now. He's supposed to be a guest of honor at a charity breakfast at the Renaissance Washington being given today by Paul Ginsburg."

Tobie glanced over at Jax. "He's one of your mother's ex-husbands, right?"

Matt grinned. "Number three."

"Jesus," said Jax. "You keep track of them?"

"Are you kidding? Of course I keep track of them. They're great contacts. I already talked to Ginsburg. He's arranging to get you a ticket for the breakfast. All you need to do is get cleaned up."

"Gladly," said Jax. Straightening, he pulled out his travel wallet and dumped Jason Aldrich's passport, driver's license, and credit cards in a pile on the table. "Here. Do me a favor, would you? Burn this shit."

Matt laughed, but shook his head. "You know I can't do that. If we don't turn that stuff back in to ODIS, two dozen bureaucrats are gonna get their collective tits in a wringer."

Jax scooped up the documents and turned toward the door. "Then I'll burn them. One of these days, some lazy idiot in ODIS is going to get me killed."

He suddenly froze.

"What?" said Tobie, watching the smile that spread slowly across his face. "What is it?"

He turned, the offending documents held up in one triumphant fist. "AODIS. That's it."

She shook her head. "What is AODIS?"

"The Archives for the Office of Documentation and Identity Support," said Matt. "They're the guys who supply field agents with their legends."

"Their whats?"

"Their legends. You know—their cover stories. Life histories, documents, pocket litter. That stuff. They do the same thing for defectors and anyone else the Government wants to bring in on the sly. They've been around since the days of the OSS and TSD."

She knew what the OSS was—the Office of Strategic Services, the forerunner of the CIA. But . . . "What's TSD?"

"Technical Services Division," said Jax, shoving the

debris of Jason Aldrich's legend into the pocket of his jacket. "That's what ODIS used to be called. Their name might have changed, but that's about it. Hell, I wouldn't be surprised if Mudd inked our man Kline's name into those old leather-bound ledgers himself."

"Mudd?" Tobie looked from one man to the other. "Am I missing something?"

"Herman Mudd," said Matt. "Otherwise known as the Bowling Ball. He's in charge of the legend archives. And Jax is right: if the Company manufactured new IDs for the really dirty guys they brought in through the ratlines, then you can bet fifty miles of red tape that some bureaucrat made a record of it."

Tobie said, "But that information would be classified, too, right?"

Matt shook his head. "All the operational files and documents are classified. But the receipts they made Kline sign for his new birth certificate and social security number? That's pure administrative shit."

Tobie pushed up from her chair. "So all we need to do is go to this legends archive, and we'll be able to track down where Martin Kline went, right?"

She watched the excited animation drain from Matt's hairy face. "There's a problem," she said. "What? They're not open on Saturday?"

Jax squinted up at the buzzing fluorescent light overhead and said nothing.

It was Matt who answered her. "Oh, they're open. Mudd practically lives down there. The problem is, Jax had a little run-in with the Bowling Ball a couple of years ago."

"A little run-in? What kind of a little run-in?"

"Let's just put it this way: if anyone from Division Thirteen goes near Herman Mudd with this request, we can kiss our information good-bye."

"So how do we get our hands on this stuff?"

She realized both men were now looking at her. "Me? Why me? I'm with Division Thirteen, too. Remember?"

"Yeah, but the Bowling Ball doesn't know that."

"Why do you keep calling Mudd 'the Bowling Ball'?"

Jax smiled, and turned toward the door. "You'll see."

65

By the time Rodriguez reached Rock Creek Park, the first flakes of snow had begun to drift down from the heavy sky. He cut quickly through the trees, to where the wide arch of Boulder Bridge soared over the rocky stream, the bridge a swath of hard gray against a quickly whitening backdrop of slender, snow-covered beech and gently rolling hills.

The snow did not please him. But the flakes were big and wet, and would soon melt. He would like to have arrived sooner, to set up an early watch; but Colonel Sam Lee had not yet arrived.

Stationing himself in the shadow of the bridge's abutment, Rodriguez had not long to wait before the Colonel came hurrying down the path toward him. Reaching the bridge, Lee looked around nervously, his shoulders hunched, his hands thrust deep into the pockets of his parka. Rodriguez watched the man pace nervously back and forth, and decided the General was right: Lee was becoming a danger.

Rodriguez stepped from behind the stand of dogwood that grew near the end of the bridge. Colonel Lee was about to become the victim of another mugging in Rock Creek Park.

Jax stood at the entrance to the Grand Ballroom of the Renaissance Washington Hotel, where a myriad of tiny white lights sparkled above linen-draped round tables set with gleaming white china. Emaciated women in *haute couture* and wicked high heels mingled with self-satisfied men in hand-tailored Italian suits or ribbon-encrusted uniforms, their voices a low roar of polite chitchat or earnest networking. Vast urns of peach-colored roses and orange lilies filled the air with a heady perfume and served as an unwelcome reminder that today was Halloween.

Jax paused next to his former stepfather. "Don't you get tired of this sort of thing?"

Paul Ginsburg laughed. "Some people enjoy getting shot at. I enjoy . . . this."

Jax's gaze fixed on the far side of the room, where Sophia Talbot, luminous in Armani green silk, laughed with the current secretary of the treasury, who just happened to be ex-husband number five. "Isn't it awkward, constantly finding yourself in the same room with your ex-wife and her various other ex-spouses?"

"Actually, we've formed something of a club."

Jax made an incoherent sound deep in his throat and said, "Better introduce me to the General, quick, before she sees me."

General Gerald T. Boyd turned politely at their approach. He was a big man, well over six feet, with the brawny torso and tan, weathered face of a man who believed that just because he'd reached the rank of lieutenant general was no reason to stop jumping out of airplanes and charging over obstacle courses with the toughest of his men.

"It's a privilege to meet you, General," said Jax, shaking his hand. "A real privilege."

"Excuse me," said Ginsburg, moving on.

"I ran into an old associate of yours the other day," said Jax, when the General made as if to turn away. "A mercenary by the name of Carlos Rodriguez."

The General swung back to face him. The faint, polite smile of a politician never left his lips, but his eyes were cold and hard and decidedly hostile. "I think the Major prefers to think of himself as a private military company contractor."

"Any idea who's contracting his services these days?"

"Right now? No."

"What can you tell me about him?" said Jax, lifting a mimosa from the tray of a circling waiter.

"Rodriguez? He's a fine soldier, and an outstanding American. I've never known him to take on an assignment he couldn't accomplish. Why do you ask?"

Jax took a slow sip of his drink. "I'm afraid Rodriguez and his boys have been involved in some recent incidents that weren't exactly laudable."

"Oh? Where was this?"

"Kaliningrad."

Jax watched the General's face. Boyd had obviously learned long ago to control every muscle of his face, every gesture, every nuance of stance and movement. But he couldn't hide the gleam of lethal rage that flashed in the depths of his steel-gray eyes. "You must have him confused with someone else."

"I don't think so." Jax raised his glass and took another swallow. "You're certain you've no idea who he might be working for?"

"Sorry. I can't help you." Boyd shifted his gaze to the far side of the room. "Excuse me."

Jax was still standing there, sipping his mimosa, his gaze following the General's determined progress across the crowded room, when Ginsburg walked up to him.

"Think he's involved?" said Ginsburg.

Jax drained his glass. "He's involved."

66

Like Division Thirteen, the archives of the ODIS lay deep in the basement of the Old Building at Langley. The air was dank, the false ceiling of stained acoustical tiles low, the fluorescent lights humming an endless, maddening note. Tobie walked up to a high, battered counter and peered over it. From here she could see rows and rows of ladened metal shelves that stretched endlessly into the gloom. No one was in sight.

She cleared her throat. "Hello?"

A man who had been bent over at the far end of the counter straightened with a jerk, and she understood why Matt and Jax called Herman Mudd the Bowling Ball. Short, and as round as he was high, the archivist had a shiny bald head with sparse, nearly invisible eyelashes and eyebrows. His skin was pale and pink from a lack of sunlight, and while she doubted he'd been around since the days of the OSS, he was doubtless coming up rapidly on retirement age.

He rushed toward her, pale plump hands waving, tongue clucking in annoyance. "No, no, no! You are not allowed to lean over the counter! Get back, please."

Tobie jerked back. Not exactly an auspicious beginning. She gave the angry man a broad smile. "You're Mr. Mudd, right? How do you do? It's such a pleasure to meet you. I've heard you're very particular about the way the legend archives are run. It's always a pleasure to work with a professional."

Herman Mudd cleared his throat and blinked at her rapidly, like a man who wore contact lenses but had never quite gotten used to them. "Yes, well . . . what do you want?"

She breathed a long, troubled sigh. "I'm hoping you can help me. I need to see the file on the legend given to a German processed in late 1945. A man by the name of Dr. Martin Kline."

"1945? Those records aren't computerized, you know. I'd have to look him up in the ledgers."

She parodied surprise. "Oh?"

He stared at her solemnly. "May I see your authorization?"

"Authorization? But . . . These records aren't classified, are they?"

"No. But you can't expect me to show these records to just anyone who asks to see them."

Since Langley was hardly open to the public, she didn't see how she could be described as "just anyone." But she swallowed a rising spurt of frustration and said, "The problem is, I need this information *now*."

Mudd turned away. "Without authorization, I'm afraid I can't help you. Good day."

Tobie resisted the urge to reach out and grab him and haul him back. Instead, she huffed another sigh. "I guess this means Jax wins."

Mudd paused to look back at her. "I beg your pardon?"

"That dirty rat. He bet me I wouldn't be able to get the information I need."

Mudd blinked ten times in rapid succession. "Who are you talking about?"

"Jax Alexander. I know it's not your fault. It's just that he's such a sneaky, lying cheat, I was hoping I could show him up for a change. Give him a taste of his own medicine. But . . ." She let her shoulders slump. "I guess he wins."

"Jax Alexander wants this information?"

"Not exactly. He just doesn't want me to get it." She started to turn away.

"Wait!" Mudd flung out one of his pale, plump hands. "What did you say this German's name was?"

"According to the records in the archives, Dr. Martin Kline was officially processed by the OSS in September of 1945," said Tobie. They were sitting around the battered old table in Matt's office. Tobie had a stale roll and a cup of lukewarm tea from the cafeteria; Jax was still in a suit that looked as if it cost as much as the entire contents of Tobie's closet.

"I can't believe you got all this out of Mudd," said Matt.

"Using Jax's name worked like a charm." She flipped open her notebook. "Kline's new identity was Dr. Marvin Clark. You're right about the time-honored tradition of bureaucratic red tape. He signed for everything from a new birth certificate to a social security number and fake degrees. And then, in November, they issued new birth certificates for his wife, who changed her name to Caroline, and to his baby daughter, Hannah."

"That must have been part of the deal he struck," said Jax. "The U.S. government got his family out of Eastern Germany, and he went to work for them. When and where did he die?"

"He didn't. He's still alive. I Googled him. He's ninety-three years old, and he published an article in *Scientific American* just last year."

"An article? On what?"

"Colony Collapse Disorder in bees."

"Bees?"

"Bees. They're his hobby." She frowned down at her notes again. "He worked at Fort Detrick until 1967, then moved to Boston and became a professor of biochemistry at MIT."

Matt said, "But he didn't have a degree in biochemistry."

"He did by the time the OSS got through with him. That's what they gave him, rather than an MD."

"Nice."

"When he retired from MIT in 1988, he moved back to Maryland."

"Any particular reason?"

"That's where his daughter and grandchildren live. She works at Fort Detrick herself, although for a while she was assigned to the human genome project for the Department of Energy." Tobie looked up. "What I don't understand is why the genome project is under the Department of Energy."

"For the same reason the Manhattan Project was," said Jax. "Because this is not about making people's lives better. It's about killing them more efficiently."

Matt said, "Kline's daughter is a scientist, too?"

Tobie nodded. "Dr. Hannah Clark. She has a Ph.D. in biochemistry. A real one."

Jax loosened his tie and unbuttoned the collar of his dress shirt. "I wonder how much she knows about what Daddy did in the war."

"She may not know anything."

"Maybe. Maybe not. You remember what that Communist from Dachau said in those old reports Andrei gave us? About helping load Kline's files and medical specimens on an American truck? Somehow, I can't see Kline shipping all his discoveries off to the Far East on U–114. He must have kept some of the pathogens with him at the camp."

Tobie stared at him. "You think the U.S. government brought the Dachau pathogen back to the States with Kline??"

Matt said, "It makes sense."

"But . . . Then why would Rodriguez and Boyd—or whoever we're dealing with—need to salvage U–114?"

"Maybe they tried to get their hands on the government's stock and couldn't." Jax pushed to his feet. "See if you can get someone at Fort Detrick to talk to us—preferably Kline's daughter. October and I will head up to Maryland and see what we can get out of Kline."

Matt glanced at the clock. It was already a quarter past nine. "You'd better hurry."

67

General Gerald T. Boyd settled back into the comfortable leather seat of the aircraft provided for his particular use by the United States government, and nodded to his aide, Phillips. "Let's go."

Phillips looked at him in surprise. "We're not waiting for Rodriguez?"

"Rodriguez has some business to attend in Maryland."

After thirty years of special ops, Boyd knew that the success of an operation always depended upon the ability to improvise and remain flexible. Which was why he'd decided to send Rodriguez up to Maryland today.

Originally, they'd planned to quietly eliminate the German, Kline, in a few weeks, when the old man's death—and any possible speculation that might arise from it—would be lost in the chaos of the plague sweeping the world. But the situation had changed. The man needed to be silenced, now.

Boyd was not pleased with Rodriguez's recent performance. It was bad enough the way he'd screwed up with the Russian kid. But by letting that asshole from Division Thirteen slip through his fingers again and again, he'd seriously jeopardized the operation.

The most critical segment of the operation—the actual release of the pathogen—would be carried out by Walker himself, with Boyd and Phillips as backup. That segment was simply too crucial, and too delicate, to delegate. Besides, Boyd had learned long ago that the best way to run a black op was to keep each stage carefully compartmentalized, with the men working on one stage kept ignorant of both the details of the other stages and the big picture.

Rodriguez knew about the U-boat and about the pathogen it carried. He now knew about the German, Kline. That was it; the rest of the operation was outside the parameters of his briefing. But Boyd had decided that once the project was completed, Rodriguez would need to be eliminated, too. The man had outlived his usefulness.

Only three people knew the scope of the entire operation: Boyd, Walker, and Phillips. And even Phillips, as Boyd's aide, was clueless about the origins of the venture. The man sincerely believed he and Boyd were working on another dirty but legitimately authorized black op. That was the nice thing about secret projects: they were so easy to keep hidden from everyone—the public, the press, Congress, even the president. Phillips was Boyd's creature and always would be. But Walker . . .

This whole brilliant project had originally been Walker's idea, although he'd lacked the expertise and the dirty contacts required to pull it off. That's why he'd come to Boyd. It didn't matter. Once the pathogen was released, Walker would be silenced, too.

Boyd didn't believe in loose ends.

Frederick, Maryland

Turning off the Interstate at Frederick, Jax drove through idyllic farmland of gently rolling fields and quiet canals.

Here, away from the city, the sky was a cold, crisp blue. The home of the man once known as Dr. Martin Kline turned out to be a neat white Federal two-story with green shutters and acres of pasture that sloped down to a stream edged with beech and white oak.

"Nice place," said Tobie as Jax parked his 650i BMW on the broad gravel sweep before the door. They had not phoned ahead.

A thickset housekeeper with sleek black hair and a heavy accent pointed them toward an almond orchard, where a tall, bone-thin man in a white boiler suit with a veiled hood was tending a hive of bees.

"Dr. Marvin Clark?" said Jax as they walked up to him.

"Yes?"

Jax drew his real, genuine, official CIA ID from his pocket and held it up. "I know you've seen one of these before, Dr. Kline."

The man behind the veiled hood stood very still, a frame crawling with bees gripped in both hands. "What do you want?"

"The answers to some questions. Last Saturday, someone salvaged a World War II-era U-boat that sank off the coast of Denmark in March 1945. Amongst its other cargo, U–114 carried samples of a pathogen you isolated at Dachau and called *die Klinge von Solomon*. The Sword of Solomon."

The old man slid the frame back into the hive and carefully replaced the inner and outer covers. Only then did he take a step back and shove the hood off his white head. His face was long and bony, with deeply wrinkled flesh and dark brown eyes that blinked several times.

"Who?" he said, his voice husky, his German accent still there despite the long passage of years. "Who has it now?"

"We don't know," said Tobie, carefully watching his face. "That's what we're hoping you can help us with."

His gaze shifted to her. "You think I had something to do with this?"

Jax said, "Who else knew the pathogen was on that U-boat?"

Kline shook his head. "How would I know? Surely there have been many with access to the records over the years."

"All official records related to U–114 were lost in the war," said Jax. "As far as we can tell, the only person with any knowledge of the submarine's cargo is you."

Kline stared off across the rolling pastureland to where a stand of oak turned a vibrant gold and rust beneath the pale blue autumn sky. As Tobie watched, a quiver moved across the sunken features of his face.

She said, "Has anyone approached you recently? Someone interested in your research at Dachau?"

He shook his head, his lips pressed into a thin, flat line. "No. No one."

"No one?" said Jax.

"No one." Reaching down, Kline picked up his hive tool and smoker. "I know what you think when you look at me. You see a monster. You judge me by what I did in Germany, in the war. You think I should have been hanged at Nuremburg, with the others."

When neither answered him, he began to walk across the field, toward another stand of hives near the creek. "You tell me this: Why is the work I did for Hitler wrong, and what I did for your government acceptable?"

Keeping pace with him, Tobie said, "You deliberately exposed men to a disease you knew would probably kill them."

He swung to face her. "I did, yes. And what of the American doctors who infected four hundred prisoners in Chicago with malaria in 1940? Or those who exposed African Americans in Virginia to a fungus they hoped to develop into a race-specific weapon? Do you think they should be hanged, as well? How about the presidents who authorized their experiments?"

He glanced at Jax. "And you. Your CIA released Type Two dengue fever in Cuba, and supplied Saddam Hussein with West Nile Virus, sarin gas, and anthrax to use against Iran. And now? Now the United States is spending billions to develop a new generation of genetically engineered bioweapons with no possible cure." He swiped the air before him, as if brushing away a bee. "Don't talk to me about war crimes."

"Is that true?" Tobie whispered to Jax as Kline took off across the pasture again with the long-legged stride of a man half his age.

Jax said, "I'm afraid so."

"You think what some madmen are doing now makes what you did sixty years ago all right?" said Tobie, stomping after him. "Maybe you think it would be a good thing if that pathogen were let loose on the world."

At the edge of the second set of hives, he turned to face her again, his smoker billowing a cloud of fragrant wood smoke around them. As she watched, all the anger and aggression seemed to leach out of him, leaving him looking older than before. "No. In that, you are wrong. I am not proud of the work I did when I was younger—either for Hitler or for your government. We were vain, foolish men, ignorant of so many of the secrets of life and human diversity. I understand now what the Sword of Solomon would do to the world. You think I want that to be my legacy? My gift to my grandchildren?"

"Then tell us who salvaged that U-boat."

He slipped the veil over his head again and turned toward the new hives. "What I am about to do is likely to agitate my little friends. If you are averse to being stung, I suggest you leave."

"Think he's telling the truth?" said Tobie, leaning against the side of Jax's convertible.

Jax stared off across the fields, to where they could see Kline gently prying the cover off a new hive. "Not entirely."

"So what do we do?"

Jax pushed away from the car. "We go talk to his daughter."

68

Dr. Hannah Clark received them on the wraparound porch of her gingerbread-draped Victorian, where she was carving a pumpkin with crescent-moon-shaped eyes and a sad mouth. She was a tall woman, with her father's bony frame and haunted brown eyes. Born in the last years of the Second World War, she was in her sixties now, white haired but still slim and vigorous. According to Matt, who had set up their meeting, she had retired from Ford Detrick the previous year.

She listened without interruption, her hand tightening around her small paring knife, while Jax told her of the salvaging of U–114 and the plot by unidentified agents to release the pathogen known as the Sword of Solomon. When he finished, she said, "Why are you telling me this?"

"Because we're hoping you can help us figure out who's behind it."

Laying aside the knife, she went to stand at the railing, her gaze on the canal that ran placidly beside the distant road. Despite the sunshine, the air was crisp and heavy with the scent of burning leaves. "It's because of my father, isn't it?

You think he's somehow involved." When Jax didn't answer, she said, "Well, you're wrong."

"Am I?"

She swung to face him again. "Last December, shortly before I retired, the security guards at Fort Detrick caught one of the lab technicians trying to smuggle a sample of DP3 out of the facility."

"DP3?"

"The pathogen was never called *die Klinge von Solomon* in this country. When brought here, after the war, it was given the name Dachau Pathogen III—DP3, for short."

Jax and Tobie exchanged quick glances. Dachau Pathogen *Three*? How many of Kline's other nasty diseases had the U.S. imported?

Jax said, "What happened to this technician? Can we talk to him?"

"Unfortunately, no. He was arrested and turned over to the local authorities for prosecution. Two days later, he was found dead in his cell. It was ruled a suicide."

Tobie said, "Do you believe it was?"

A faint, ironic smile touched her lips. "After thirty years of working on secret projects for the government? Hardly. I heard they discovered that a hundred thousand dollars had been transferred into his account the week before the incident."

"Did they trace the source of the funds?" said Jax.

"They tried. It came from a bank in the Cayman Islands." She looked from one of them to the other. "You need to remember that DP3 has been is this country for sixty years. There are probably dozens of people who know about it."

"Perhaps. But how many of them would know that when their attempt to bribe someone to steal the pathogen from Fort Detrick failed, there was more available on a U-boat that sank off the coast of Denmark in 1945?"

Dr. Kline's daughter stood very still. A breeze kicked up, rustling the dying leaves of the beeches along the canal and fluttering the fine white hair that framed her lined face.

Tobie said, "According to what we've been told, this DP3 is some sort of respiratory virus that is only lethal to those of Semitic origin. Is that true?"

Dr. Clark put up a hand to push the windblown hair from her face. "It's a retrovirus, actually, not a virus—which means it replicates itself by using its host's cells to transcribe its RNA into DNA, which is then incorporated into the host's own genome. At first we didn't understand how the pathogen could kill some people so quickly while hardly affecting others. But with the advent of DNA testing, we were able to determine that many Europeans and Asians produce a series of three hormonelike substances called chemokines, which block the DP3 retrovirus from slipping into their T-cells. Those of Middle Eastern descent typically lack those three protective chemokines."

"What about Africans?" said Jax.

"The results there have been mixed. It seems that those from certain areas frequently share the genetic sequence; others don't."

"It's fatal?"

"For those who lack the necessary protective sequence, yes. Nearly always."

"So it really is an ethnic bioweapon," said Tobie softly.

"In a sense. But I'd hardly describe it as a smart bomb."

"Why's that?"

"Because the concept of race is a social illusion—not a scientific construction. The truth is, there is far more genetic variation *within* a group than *between* groups."

Jax said, "Meaning?"

"Meaning that if this pathogen were let loose, millions of those who consider themselves 'white' would also die.

Anyone who sees DP3 as an easy way to rid the world of Jews and Arabs is not just evil; he's a bigoted fool."

Tobie said, "Is there a treatment for it?"

Dr. Clark shook her head. "The U.S. never had any plans to pursue DP3 as a weapon, so there was no need to develop a vaccine." She must have seen the shock in Tobie's face, because she gave another of her wry smiles and said, "The United States gets around the Biological Weapons Convention by saying our bio programs are purely defensive, which technically makes them legal. Unfortunately, knowledge that is developed for 'defensive' purposes can all too easily be used for a different purpose entirely."

Tobie studied the woman's even features. She looked like someone's gentle, white-haired grandmother, not a mad scientist who had devoted her life to devising new and more lethal ways to kill. "That doesn't bother you?"

Dr. Clark turned to look toward the canal, where a fat brown duck waddled complacently across the lawn, its feathers ruffled by the growing wind. "It bothered my father. He long ago decided that all such work is morally indefensible, since we never know how our discoveries will be used by others. It's why he left Fort Detrick and went to MIT."

When neither Tobie nor Jax said anything, she added, "I know you're remembering what he did at Dachau, during the war. But if you think he's involved in any of this, now, you're wrong. He's not the same man. I'm sorry I can't help you more."

It was obvious that as far as she was concerned, the conversation was at an end.

She walked with them to the road beside the canal, where Jax had parked his car. Jax said, "Your father claims he never told anyone about the shipments sent out of Germany under Operation Caesar. But he may have told someone he's hesitant to betray—someone he trusts and doesn't want to believe could be involved in this."

She pressed her lips into a thin line, and after a moment said, "I could try driving out to see him. He may be willing to talk to me."

Jax handed her a card with his cell number. "Please."

He started to get in the car, but paused to say, "If I wanted to expose a group of people to this pathogen, how would I do it?"

She thought about it for a moment. "Probably the best way would be to release it into a subway, or the air-conditioning system of a building—a hotel, perhaps, or a large office building. No one would ever know. That's the terrible beauty of a biological weapon. With a bomb, there's never any doubt that a deliberate attack has taken place. But if an epidemic suddenly sweeps across an area . . . who can say that it was the result of a deliberate biological attack?"

Jax's gaze met Tobie's, and she saw her own dawning horror reflected in his drawn features as the same thought occurred to them both: they might already be too late. The pathogen could have been released that morning, anywhere in the country.

And they would never know it.

69

"Maybe we've been going at this all wrong," said October. They were walking along the banks of Carroll Creek in the historic district of Frederick, waiting for Hannah Clark to call. "Maybe we should be focusing on the kinds of people most likely to do something like this. Or the sites they'd be likely to select."

Jax shook his head. "They could have picked any one of a thousand sites—anywhere from the subways of New York or Washington, D.C., to the Sears Tower in Chicago. And as for the kinds of people most likely to do something like this . . ." He let his voice trail off.

"Where do you start?" she finished for him.

They walked on in silence, October's head turning as she watched two laughing, shouting boys on bicycles run the makeshift obstacle course they'd set up in a nearby driveway.

Following her gaze, he said, "The problem is, wherever it is released, this thing is going to spread like wildfire. Not just here in the States, but across the world. That's always been the problem with biological warfare: the world has grown too small. A disease targeted at one country will circle the globe within a year."

"But that's what these people want, isn't it?" said October, turning toward him. "So it seems to me they'd be likely to pick someplace with Arabs and Jews from all over."

"What are you suggesting? Disney World? Or how about—" He broke off as his phone began to vibrate.

Unclipping it from his belt, he hit Talk and heard Hannah Clark's hushed, troubled voice. "Mr. Alexander? I've had a long discussion with my father. He says he had a visit last winter from one of his former graduate students at MIT, someone from Florida. They've kept in touch over the years, so the visit didn't strike my father as unusual at the time. But it seems this former student asked a number of questions about DP3 and the samples that were sent out of Germany on U–114."

"Who?" said Jax. "Who was it?"

"He won't say. His concern is that the man's questions were unrelated to what is happening, and that by telling you about this former student, my father will be implicating an innocent man. If you could somehow convince him—"

"We'll be right there."

On the way to Kline's house, Jax put in a call to Matt. "See if you can get a printout of the personnel who've accessed the Navy's files on U–114 in, say, the past two years. That might help verify that Boyd's really our man. And while you're at it, you might take a look at the flight records for the General's jet. Maybe we can get something from his travel patterns."

"I'll get on it," said Matt.

October said, "They have boats and palm trees in Florida."

Jax clipped his phone back on his belt. "They what? Oh," he said, remembering the viewing she'd done with Dr. Bukovsky in Russia. "Florida is also a very big state." He shifted down for a curve, then punched the gas again, hard. "We need this guy's name."

"And if Kline won't give it to us?"

Jax shifted rapidly back up through the gears. "He'll give it to us."

Jax was slowing for the turn into Kline's long drive when he spotted the white commercial van parked on the gravel sweep, beside the green-and-white Mini Cooper that he'd seen parked at Hannah Clark's house. He hit the gas and kept going.

"What?" said October. "What's the matter?"

"The Acme Cleaning Service van."

"What about it?"

"See the guy standing next to the front door? The *open* front door?"

"The one in the Tyvek suit?"

"Yeah, that one. The one who's just *standing* there." He pulled off the road in the lee of the oaks down by the creek and reached over to pop open the glove compartment. "Here," he said, handing her a Smith and Wesson 9mm. "Present."

"Why do people keep handing me these things?"

"Because bad men keep shooting at you." Easing open his door, he slipped his own Beretta from the holster he'd clipped inside the waistband of his slacks. "Let's go."

Following the tree line, they swung around until they reached a thick privet hedge that ran down to an arbor-shaded patio with a French door that looked as if it opened off the kitchen.

"Got the safety off?" Jax whispered as they edged close to the patio.

"Yes," she answered with some annoyance.

"Just checking."

Keeping low, they crept to the door. In the room beyond they could see an old round oak table, white beadboard cabinets, the gleam of a stainless steel fridge. No one was in sight.

Carefully reaching out, Jax turned the knob. The door

popped open. The pungent odor of spilled petroleum wafted out to them.

"Why do I smell gasoline?" whispered October, following him into the house and across the kitchen.

"They're probably getting ready to torch the house," said Jax, just as a big black dude wearing a Tyvek suit and carrying two red plastic gas cans walked through the doorway from the hall.

"*Fuck!*" cried the guy. Dropping the gas cans with a sloshing *thump*, he reached for the Glock he wore in a shoulder holster.

October grabbed a giant chef's knife from the pine block on the counter beside them and drove the blade deep into his chest.

"Christ," said Jax. He snatched the guy's silenced Glock 21 as his eyes rolled back in his head and he tumbled to the floor.

Pausing for a moment, Jax listened to the sounds of the old house stretching out around them, but heard nothing.

Taking a deep breath, he nodded to October to follow him. At the entrance to the hallway, they had to step over the body of the dead housekeeper. His gaze lifted to October's. This wasn't looking good.

They crept down the hall, treading warily on the old heart-of-pine floors, past the arched entrance to a shadowy dining room and the living room beyond. To their left, a staircase with an elegant turned banister swept up to the second floor. The front door to the porch still stood open. Through it, Jax could see a trio of pumpkins lined up at the top of the porch's steps.

The sound of footsteps on the stairs from the second floor jerked his head around. He turned, the silenced Glock coming up, just as the man in the Tyvek suit they'd seen waiting outside walked in the front door.

70

"Take him!" shouted Jax. Dropping to the floor in a roll, he pumped three rounds into the dude coming down the stairs.

He heard the *crack-crack-crack* of October's Smith and Wesson. Looking over, he saw the guy in the Tyvek suit stumble backward.

October yelled, "Behind you!"

He swung around just as Carlos Rodriguez came charging through the doorway of a book-lined room at the front of the house. Jax fired both the Glock and his own Beretta at the same time. Slamming back against the wall, Rodriguez hung for a moment, then slid to the floor, leaving a bloody trail down the plaster.

Jax realized his ears were ringing. A blue haze filled the entry; the stench of burnt powder and spilled gasoline stung his nostrils. He waited, his heart pounding, his grip on the two sidearms tight. He heard the wind scuttling dry leaves across the gravel drive, the drip of gasoline from the cans dropped by the man on the stairs.

Jax pushed to his feet. The guy hanging upside down on the stairs was missing half his head. His Tyvek-suited buddy on the front porch was a red, pulpy mess. From the looks of things, October had landed at least half a dozen rounds in him.

"You hit him," said Jax.

She was leaning against the entry wall, her breath coming hard and fast. "He was five feet away and I emptied the gun into him. I should hope I hit him."

Walking over to Rodriguez, Jax hunkered down to lay two fingers against the guy's carotid artery and felt nothing. "He's dead."

She said, "Good." Swiping the sleeve of her sweater across her eyes, she paused in the doorway to the study. "Oh, no," she whispered.

Jax went to stand beside her. Kline was sitting in a chair beside the empty hearth, his ankles and wrists duct taped, his eyes wide and sightless. A line of blood trickled down his chin. His daughter lay facedown on the rug beside him.

Crossing to her, Jax gently turned her over, then pushed up to grab October before she got any closer. "Don't look," he said, pulling her back toward the hallway. "You can't help her. Did you touch anything?"

She thought about it. "The chef's knife. And you touched the back doorknob."

He turned toward the kitchen. "Come on. Let's get out of here."

"I hope you've got something," Jax told Matt as they headed back toward the beltway, "because we just ran out of luck."

"Your idea to check out who might have accessed the Navy's report on U–114 turned up something interesting: a colonel by the name of Sam Lee. He's one of Boyd's protégés—in fact, Boyd got him assigned to the CIA two years ago. He may be our mole."

"Have you talked to him?"

"That would be difficult. He was found in Rock Creek Park about an hour ago. Dead."

"Shit. Sounds like they're cleaning up their loose ends. I hope this doesn't mean the operation's over."

Matt let out a harsh sigh. "I stumbled across something else while I was digging around. Somehow or another, the U.S. government knew U–114 went down with a mysterious weapon called *die Klinge von Solomon* on board. That's why they sent the Navy looking for it when the Brits authorized their Operation Deadlight Expedition. They thought the Sword of Solomon might be the German A-bomb, and they were afraid the publicity surrounding the plans to raise the old U-boats might give someone ideas."

"But that doesn't make sense," said October when Jax relayed Matt's information to her. "The U.S. government had all Kline's nasties at Fort Detrick. They should have known what the Sword of Solomon was."

"You've gotta remember they didn't have computerized databases in those days. *Kline* knew DP3 used to be called the Sword of Solomon, but I doubt anyone else did. Why do you think they renamed all his nasty little bugs? Because they didn't want anyone to know they were carrying on where the Nazis had left off. I've no doubt all the original records were destroyed decades ago. Even if they weren't, you need to understand that the kind of guys playing with plagues up at Fort Detrick don't regularly communicate with the guys down in Washington who worry about Nazi A-bombs and sunken subs. No one in Washington talks to anyone else, remember?" He paused for a moment, then reached for his phone again and hit Matt's number on his speed dial.

"What now?" she said.

"I've got an idea." To Matt, he said, "Did Boyd ever go to MIT?"

"Nope. He's a West Point man."

"Then I think we may have a lead to the guy who's bank-rolling this operation. Get onto the university and see if you can get a list of Kline's former graduate students. We're looking for a male with ties to Florida."

"I'll see what I can do."

"And Matt?"

"Yeah?"

"Hurry."

71

They were on I-270 headed toward the Virginia state line when Matt called back. "You need to turn around. I've got a plane waiting at Frederick Airport to take you to Miami."

"A Company plane? I thought we were off the clock?"

"Yeah, well, I found a way to get creative when I looked at Boyd's flight schedule. He's made a bunch of trips to Miami in the last ten months that don't seem to correlate to anything he was doing for SOCOM. And he left Washington for Miami this afternoon at twelve thirty."

Jax glanced over at October. *Boats and palm trees.*

"And get this," Matt was saying. "You remember that viewing session Tobie did in Kaliningrad with the Russian?"

"Yes. Why?"

"I've been comparing her drawings of that bridge with all the bridges in the Miami area. I think it's the Venetian Causeway. You'll find a boat waiting for you at Bayside Marketplace. The way I figure it, the only way to find that house is to have her look for it."

"Let me get this straight," said Jax. "You want us to cruise around Biscayne Bay looking for a house October saw in her head?"

"You got any better ideas?"

Jax thought about it. "No."

The boat was a Speedboat Marine V-drive with a Shepiro-craft inboard rear-mount 350 Chevy. By the time they reached Bayside Marketplace, the sun was a big ball of fire sinking low behind the city. The heat was beginning to go out of the day—or maybe that was just the effect of the long shadows cast by all those skyscrapers crowding up against the water.

Jax caught the keys tossed by a dark-skinned man in shorts and a white T-shirt, who said, "The hardware's in the lock-box up under the bow."

Jax waited until they were well away from the quay before hauling it out: a Beretta Cougar for himself, and another Beretta he held out to October. "Here. The Smith and Wesson must be out of ammo."

She hesitated, then slipped the pistol in her bag.

"You need to get a holster."

She just looked at him. "Oh, right; and where am I going to hide it?"

He swung around Dodge Island and cut under the Mac-Arthur Causeway, the small, light Speedboat soaring over the sparkling blue waters of the bay. "That look like your bridge?" he said as the Venetian Causeway rose before the boat's bow, the elegant white guardrail sweeping from one man-made island to the next.

Her head tipped back, she put up a hand to catch the hair fluttering around her face. "Yes."

"So which way do we go? Left or right?"

She glanced around her. "I guess that depends on whether or not my brain reversed things."

"Great," said Jax. "We'll try north first."

They ran up the island, past dozens of palatial villas with indoor and outdoor pools, squash courts and tennis courts, fleets of Mercedes and BMWs, Porsches and Bentleys.

"When I see this kind of stuff," he said, eying the hundred-foot, gleaming white Chedyek rocking gently beside the nearest private dock, "it reminds me of this book I read about the French Revolution when I was a kid."

She turned to stare at him. "You read books about the *French Revolution* as a kid? Why Jax, who'd have thought you're really a secret nerd at heart?"

He spun the wheel, hitting the throttle as he brought the Speedboat in a wide arc and headed south under the bridge again. "I was never a nerd. I just liked history."

"Okay. So what about the French Revolution?"

"I just remember reading about those noblemen in their chateaus, with their carriages and their jewels and their velvet gowns, and wondering how they could look at all those starving peasants and not realize they were being really, really shortsighted."

"This from the guy with a BMW convertible and a town-house on the Potomac?" she said. "If you're not careful, someone's going to get the idea you're a—" She broke off.

He cut back on the throttle. "What is it?"

They were coming up on a pale pink Italianate villa with an arched arcade and a wide terrace overlooking an Olympic-sized pool and meticulously maintained lawns that swept down to a private dock. "That's it," she said, leaning forward.

Jax studied the massive fiberglass Hargrave yacht with a raised pilothouse tied up at the dock. "Is that the boat you saw?"

She shook her head. "I honestly couldn't say. All big white yachts kinda look the same to me. But this is the house. I'm sure of it. Now what?"

Jax turned the Speedboat in toward the dock, spinning the wheel and cutting the engine so they drifted in to bump gently against the pier. "Now we look for a fluorescent yellow cylinder in an aluminum metal case," he said, tossing her the bowline, "and hope to hell we're not too late."

72

Jax was tying the stem line to a cleat on the dock when he heard a man's shout. Looking up, he spotted a big, blond-headed security guard loping down the lawn toward them. The guy was wearing tan slacks and boat shoes with no socks and a Hawaiian shirt that flapped open as he ran.

"Hey!" the guy shouted again, waving one beefy tanned arm as he jogged out onto the dock. "This is private property. You can't tie up here."

October straightened. "What do we do?" she said quietly.

"We look at the Hargrave," said Jax, turning toward it.

They'd almost reached the yacht when the security guard caught up with them. He grabbed Jax's left arm and jerked him around. "What the fuck do you think you're doing, man? This is a private dock. Get out of here."

Jax reached behind his back and came up with his Cougar. He stuck the muzzle in the guard's cheek hard enough to pucker the guy's mouth and said, "Look. I've had a bad day. In fact, I've had a bad week. We're going on this boat. We can either climb aboard *with* you, or we can climb *over* you, if you get my drift. The choice is yours."

The man's eyes widened, his splayed hands creeping into the air beside his head. "Who the fuck are you?"

Jax found the Glock in the holster at the small of the guy's back and tossed it off the edge of the dock with a splash. "I'm the guy with the gun. Now move." To October, he said, "Where'd you see the pathogen?"

"The stateroom."

Jax prodded the security guard in the back with the Beretta. "Show us."

"Which stateroom? There's four."

"Start with the master stateroom."

They followed the guard to a cherry-paneled room with a king-sized bed, his and her walk-in closets, a 26-inch HD TV, and en suite his and her heads that gleamed with polished marble and gold-plated faucets. An aluminum case lay open on the bed. Empty.

"Sonofabitch," said Jax. From the looks of the slot in the molded foam interior, the case had once cradled a cylinder just over a foot long and maybe six inches across.

He rested the Beretta's muzzle against the security guard's temple and pulled back the hammer with a click that echoed in the sudden stillness. "Who owns this boat?"

"Mr.—" The man's voice broke. He cleared his throat and tried again. "Mr. Walker. James Nelson Walker."

The name meant nothing to Jax. "Where is he now?"

"I don't know!" The man's voice rose in near hysteria. "He left maybe twenty minutes ago."

"Jax," said October softly.

He glanced at her. "What?" His gaze fell to the sheaf of blueprints she was unrolling. "What are those?"

"It says 'Heating, Ventilation, and Air Conditioning System.'"

"Shit. It's an HVAC plan. What building?"

"The Intercontinental."

Jax swung back to the security guard. "Where's that?"

The man's nose quivered. "Chopin Plaza. On the bay. Right next to Bayfront Park."

Jax shoved the guy into the nearest closet and turned the key. "Bring the plans," Jax told October. "Let's go."

By now the sun was only a rosy memory on a darkening horizon. October took the Speedboat's helm while Jax spread the HVAC plans out on the floorboards.

"Anything?" she asked as the Speedboat skimmed over the smooth black waters of the bay.

"Someone's circled the section of the system that serves the grand ballroom," he said, straightening. "I'd say that's their target." He snapped his penlight closed and punched in a call to Matt. "Ever hear of some fat cat named James Nelson Walker?"

"As a matter of fact, yes," said Matt. "He's the head of Walker Pharmaceuticals. I was just looking into him."

"Why's that?"

"Because he studied biochemistry at MIT when Kline was there. From what I can discover, he's quite a closet bigot. He keeps it quiet for the sake of business."

Jax squinted across the bay, to where the lights of the Manhattan-like skyscrapers twinkled out over the water. "Do me a favor, Matt: look on the Intercontinental website and see what function they're holding in the grand ballroom tonight."

After a minute, Matt said, *"Oh, man."*

"What is it?"

"The hotel's hosting the People of the Book Conference."

"The what?"

"It's a kind of religious peace conference. The idea is that all three of the big Western religions—Judaism, Christianity, and Islam—respect the same holy book—what Christians call the Old Testament—and share many of the same beliefs. So they've brought together rabbis, priests, and imams from all over the world to try to find a way to work for interracial and interreligious peace. Their grand banquet is tonight. In the ballroom."

73

Turning the wheel hard, October slammed the side of the Speedboat into the *U*-shaped wooden walkway that curved out into the bay at Chopin Plaza and cut the engine.

"Hey," shouted a dark, stocky bellboy, starting toward them. "You're not allowed to tie up your boat there!"

"Catch." Jax tossed him the bow line and grabbed October's hand to haul her up onto the boardwalk. "It's yours."

They sprinted across the pavement and burst through the hotel's massive glass entrance doors into a soaring space of tan marble turned to gold by the subtle gleam of light. A swashbuckling pirate in a black eye patch careened into them, said, "Excuse me," and stepped back into an Arab in flowing *bisht* and a *ghutra* and *igal.* The Arab was real. The pirate wasn't.

"What the hell?" said Jax, turning in a circle. The lobby teemed with curvaceous Little Bo Peeps and Naughty Nurses, Orthodox Jews with black slouch hats and curly ringlets, Klingons and Vulcans, caped vampires and hairy werewolves and Catholic priests in white collars and befuddled expressions.

October touched his arm and pointed to a discreet black sign with white letters that read, HIGHGATE HALLOWEEN CHARITY BALL, RM B12; PEOPLE OF THE BOOK BANQUET, GRAND BALLROOM. "Where's the ballroom?" she shouted over the roar of voices and the splash of the fountain.

"We don't want the ballroom," he said, pushing though a coven of witches. "We want the floor above it. That's where the HVAC unit is. According to the plans, the building's entire system runs next to the service-elevator shaft. This way."

They found the service elevator in a quiet hallway to their right. The indicator was stuck on the third floor, and it wasn't moving.

"They're probably holding it there," said Jax, punching open the door to the nearby stairwell. "Come on."

They raced up the bare concrete steps, the only sounds the clatter of their footfalls and the echoing rasp of their breath. At first, she kept pace with him. But as they were turning toward the second flight, he heard her let out a gasp as she hunched over to brace one hand against her knee. He slowed. "You okay?"

"Don't wait for me! Keep going."

He was maybe five seconds ahead of her when he slapped open the heavy firedoors on the third floor, his Beretta in his hand.

Rigged out in a Crusader costume with fake chain mail and a white surcoat marked by a giant red cross, General Gerald T. Boyd stood in the center of the hall, his hands on his hips, his attention focused on a closed gray door marked MAINTENANCE. A second man—younger, leaner, with a military buzzcut that clashed badly with his medieval squire's costume—had one foot wedged in the partially open doors of the service elevator.

At Jax's catapulted entrance, both men jerked around. The squire had a 9mm Glock half out of the holster hidden beneath his hauberk when Jax pumped two bullets into his chest.

The force of the impact knocked the squire back into the elevator. The doors slammed shut and the elevator whirled away with a ding.

"You bastard," roared Boyd. Arms spread, he plowed into Jax and enveloped him in a deadly bear hug, just as October burst through the firedoor from the stairs.

With the General's beefy arms squeezing the air out of his lungs, Jax wheezed, "The HVAC room. Quick."

Arms pinned to his sides, lungs bursting, Jax pointed the Beretta's muzzle vaguely in the direction of Boyd's foot and pulled the trigger. He heard the bullet ricochet off the floor and smelled burned leather, cloth, and flesh. Boyd roared again and squeezed harder.

Jax pulled the trigger again and missed. The pressure on his lungs tightened. He could hear his ears ringing. His vision dimmed. He looked up into the General's furious red face and knew a moment of disbelief. He was being crushed to death by a giant crazy general just feet away from where a mad scientist was unleashing a plague that could wipe out a good quarter of the world's population.

Bending one knee, he braced his foot against the wall behind him and pushed. The General staggered back just enough to enable Jax to shift the angle of the Beretta's barrel and fire again.

This time, the bullet found a more sensitive portion of the General's anatomy. The steely gray eyes widened in shock and pain and disbelief. The pressure on Jax's chest eased and he slammed the top of his head into the General's face.

Boyd staggered back. Jax brought up the Beretta and fired point-blank into the red Crusader's cross.

74

Tobie thrust open the gray door and fell into a hot musty room with exposed I-beams and pipes and a massive rectangular steel box that filled the dusty space with a loud roar. The HVAC unit stood on a concrete pad that raised it some ten to twelve inches off the floor. Crouched beside it, a lean man with short curly hair and wire-framed glasses was working a pry bar beneath one edge of the heavy sheet metal that formed the unit's locked hatch. In honor of Halloween, he was dressed in a black wetsuit. A small fluorescent-yellow SCUBA tank known as a pony bottle rested on the edge of the concrete pad beside him.

When the heavy door slammed shut behind her, the man— Walker?—swung around, the pry bar still gripped in his fist. "Who the hell are—"

She kicked the pry bar out of his hand, the iron rod spinning across the room to hit an exposed pipe with a clatter.

Walker might be small and wiry, but a lifetime of racquetball and sailing had made him lithe and strong. Surging up, he snatched the metal pony bottle from the concrete plinth and swung it at her head.

She ducked, but the momentum of his swing carried Walker on around. Before he could catch his balance, he smacked the pony bottle into one of the exposed I-beams. The impact sheared off the bottle's valve and knocked the container from his hands. It hit the concrete pad under the HVAC unit with a sudden release of deadly contaminated air that sounded like an explosion.

With a whoosh, the bottle took off like a rocket, a missile driven by six cubic feet of weaponized DP3 under 3,000 pounds of pressure. It clattered against a pipe, ricocheted off another I-beam. Walker hit the floor, his arms coming up to protect his head. Tobie dove behind the HVAC and dug frantically in her shoulder bag for the Beretta.

The empty pony bottle whacked against the far wall with a hollow clang and tumbled to the floor beside the pry bar. Walker scrambled toward it, fingers groping toward the iron rod. Tobie's fist closed around the pistol's barrel. Yanking the gun from her bag, she slammed the handle into Walker's temple.

He went down and stayed down.

She was breathing hard, hideously conscious that with every breath she drew a noxious cloud of death into her lungs. A thump jerked her gaze to the door. The handle was turning.

"Shit." Stumbling over Walker's prostrate body, she leaped for the door and threw her weight against it.

From the far side of the panel came Jax's shout, "October?"

"Don't come in here!" she screamed, sliding down to her haunches with her back pressed against the door. Half sobbing, she dug her cell phone out of her pocket and punched in 911 with shaking fingers.

"Hello? This is Ensign October Guinness. I have an emergency situation involving a biological hazard at the Miami Intercontinental."

75

Jax stared through the wavy plastic barrier at the young woman in a hospital gown on the inside of the isolation bubble.

"How is she?" he asked.

Beside him, the young Latino doctor in green scrubs glanced down at his chart. "She's doing great. It's basically like a bad cold. But she'll need to stay in there until they're sure she's no longer contagious."

"Can I talk to her?"

The doctor tapped the microphone beside him. "Through the intercom system."

Jax cleared his throat. "Hey, October. You look like shit."

"Thank you." She blew her nose. "They haven't told me anything. What's going on?"

"You did it, Tobie; you stopped Walker before he'd managed to break the seal on the HVAC system. They're monitoring everyone who was in the hotel, just to be safe, but so far the only two people showing any signs of exposure to the pathogen are you and Walker. Not that anyone knows what really happened. The official line is they're worried about an outbreak of Legionnaires' disease."

"So how's Walker?"

"Not good, actually. The arrogant SOB obviously never thought to check his own DNA. They've had him on life support for the past twelve hours, but they're about ready to pull the plug. How's that for poetic justice?"

She sniffed. "What about Boyd?"

"Well, according to the press, the General died a hero, saving a young Naval ensign from an unknown assailant. That's you, by the way. The ensign, I mean—not the assailant."

She stared at him with wide, red-rimmed eyes. "That's not poetic justice."

"No. That's the government covering its ass."

"And the guy in the elevator?"

"Boyd's aide, Captain Syd Phillips. He's downstairs in the ICU, too, but he's expected to make it. Says he thought the entire operation was a legitimate, authorized black op."

"You believe him?"

"Actually, yes. That's one of the problems with black ops. They're all dirty, and they're all secret. So how was he supposed to know this one wasn't actually authorized?"

"What'll happen to him?"

"He can kiss his military career—and his pension—good-bye."

"That doesn't seem fair."

Jax rubbed the side of his nose with his knuckles. "He was up to his captain's bars in a plan to kill millions—including you and me. And his defense is, 'I was just following orders'? Excuse me while I don't feel sorry for him."

October blew her nose again. "How'd those two ever get together in the first place?"

"You mean Boyd and Walker?" Jax shrugged. "Who knows? They probably met at some political fund-raiser for the neofascistly inclined. I suspect Boyd said something like—" Jax pitched his voice into a gravelly Texas drawl. "'You know what we need? Some new plague that'll wipe out all these damned A-rabs, and maybe take out the Jews, too.' And Walker probably said" —Jax switched to a Boston twang—"'Funny you should mention that. I had this old professor at MIT who told me once about a nasty little pathogen he used to play with back when he was a Nazi . . .'"

She laughed softly, then shook her head, her smile fading. "It's terrifying to realize how close a handful of men can come to killing tens of millions of people."

"That's exactly what makes bioweapons so scary. All it takes is one nut case with a mission—or even a careless mistake—and half the people on this planet could die. Look at the anthrax scare of 2001. And anthrax is actually pretty hard to weaponize. There are plenty of nasties in the world's laboratories that would be a lot easier to disperse. And a hell of a lot more deadly."

She stared at him through the wavy plastic, her face pale.

He said, "You doing okay in there, October?"

She rubbed her forehead. "Yeah. The isolation is just starting to get to me, that's all."

"How about if I send you some books? What would you like?"

She thought about it a minute, then smiled. "Got anything on the French Revolution?"

AUTHOR'S NOTE

Wondering what's real and what isn't? Here's a quick rundown, along with some sources for those interested in doing further research.

- The bioweapon "Sword of Solomon" is a figment of our imagination.

- Operation Caesar, Germany's last-ditch effort near the end of the Second World War to supply its ally, Japan, with war material and weapons technology, was real.

- The Type XB submarine described here did exist and was used as part of Operation Caesar. One of these massive submarines, U–234, surrendered at the end of the war and was found to be carrying uranium and a variety of other war material to Japan. Another Type XB, loaded with a cargo of mercury, sank off the coast of Norway at the end of the war and is indeed causing serious problems. Four keels for an even larger U-boat, the XI-B, were indeed laid down in the shipyards of Bremen. There are no records of these giant subs ever having been completed, although rumors persist that one was built and launched on a secret mission at the end of the war. The Deutsches U-Boot Museum-Archiv in Cuxhaven-Altenbruch, Germany, is real, and is an invaluable source of documents on German submarines and their crews. For more detailed information on the U-boats of World War II, see the excellent publications of Rainer Busch and Hans Joachim Röll. The book Jax is reading, *Iron Coffins: A Personal Account of the German U-boat Battles of World War II,* by Herbert Warner, is real, and is a fascinating memoir written by one of the few German submarine commanders to survive the war.

- At the end of World War II, over one hundred U-boats surrendered to the Allies and were scuttled off the coast of Britain in what was known as Operation Deadlight. These submarines are now being salvaged for their pre–1945 steel.

- The demolition of ships, or shipbreaking, has now moved almost exclusively to third-world countries and entails serious health and environmental concerns. For more information, see *End of the Line*, a photo essay on shipbreaking in Bangladesh by Brendan Cor at en.wikipedia.org/wiki/Ship_breaking, and Greenpeace's *Platform on Shipbreaking*, www.shipbreakingplatform.com.

- The history of the United States government involvement in remote viewing is much as described by McClintock in Chapter 4. For more information, we suggest Jon Ronson's *Men Who Stare at Goats* (2005), and Joseph McMoneagle's *Mind Trek* (1997).

- The history of Kaliningrad Oblast, formerly part of the German province of East Prussia, is essentially as described here. Because Western access to Kaliningrad was, until recently, prohibited, little has been written about the modern oblast. By far the best easily available study of Kaliningrad today is "Between East and West: a study of the Kaliningrad Region as a Russian exclave in the EU," a masters thesis by Fred Balvert at the Faculty of Social Sciences of the Erasmus University Rotterdam, 2007.

- On the massacres and ethnic cleansing of Germans after World War II, little has been written in English. Probably the best look is still *Documents on the Expulsion of the Germans from Eastern-Central Europe*, volumes I–III, translated into English and published by the Federal Ministry for Expellees, Refugees, and War Victims, Bonn, in the 1950s. Be warned, it makes haunting reading.

- For the tragic history of Izmir/Smyrna, see Margorie Housepian Dobkin, *Smyran 1922: The Destruction of a City* (1972).

- The number of Palestinian refugees massacred at Sabra and Shatila in 1982 is disputed. Between six hundred and eight hundred bodies were recovered; another eighteen hundred civilians were reported missing and never found. Most are believed to lie buried in mass graves, many of them beneath Beirut's Cité Sportif. See "Sabra and Shatila 20 Years On," *BBC News*, 14 September 2002, and Leila Shahid, "The Sabra and Shatila Massacres: Eye-Witness Reports," *Journal of Palestine Studies*, Vol. 32, No. 1. (Autumn 2002). You can also watch the eyewitness account of British journalist Robert Fisk in *The Martyrs Smile, Part Two*, at www.youtube.com/watch?v=_JAmZCLhaoQ&NR=1, although be warned that the images are gruesome.

- Historians continue to argue over the true extent of the German atomic program during World War II. Recent discoveries in Russian archives and what was East Germany are much as Wolfgang describes them in Chapters 42–43, and have made many earlier studies out of date. See Mark Walker, *Nazi Science: Myth, Truth, and the German Atomic Bomb* (2005), and *Hitlers Bombe*, by Rainer Karlsch and Heiko Petermann (2007).

- Much has been written about the Nazi concentration camps and medical experiments. See *Doctors from Hell: The Horrific Account of Nazi Experiments on Humans*, by Vivien Spitz, a correspondent at the Nuremberg War Crimes Trials (republished 2005), and Harold Marcuse, *Legacies of Dachau: The Uses and Abuses of a Concentration Camp, 1933–2001* (Cambridge University Press, 2001).

- For the Dachau Massacre of German prisoners of war by the U.S. 3rd Battalion of the 157th Infantry Regiment, see Colonel Howard Buechner's *The Hour of the Avenger* (1986). Again, the numbers vary, from fifteen to more than six hundred; Eisenhower is said to have put the number of German prisoners murdered at around five hundred.

- Politics has turned the subject of the ethnic origins of modern Jews into a potential mine field. For two opposing views, see Tel Aviv University historian and Holocaust survivor Shlomo Sand's book, *Matai ve'ech humtza ha'am hayehudi? (When and How the Jewish People Was Invented*, 2008, in Hebrew), versus the article "The Khazar Myth and the New Anti-Semitism" by Steven Plaut, an American-born economics professor at the University of Haifa. For a history of the Khazars, Kevin Alan Brook's *The Jews of Khazaria* (republished 2006), is considered a classic. For more on the Arab Christians, see Charles Sennott, *The Body and the Blood: The Middle East's Vanishing Christians and the Possibility for Peace* (2002).

- Operation Paperclip was a very real program that brought German scientists to the United States at the end of WWII to work on various projects for the government, from NASA to the CIA. Not all were Nazis. Those who were Nazis were brought in illegally and without the knowledge of either Truman or Eisenhower. See Clare Lasby's *Operation Paperclip* (1975), and Christopher Simpson's *Blowback: America's Recruitment of Nazis and Its Effects on the Cold War* (1988).

- For a look at American black ops, see Tim Weiner, *Legacy of Ashes* (2007). For American operations run against Cuba from Florida, see Don Bohning, *The Castro Obessession: U.S. Covert Operations Against Cuba* (2005). On U.S. biological and chemical warfare projects, see Seymour Hersh, *Chemical and Biological Warfare: America's Hidden Arsenal* (1969), and William Broad, Stephen Engelberg, and Judith Miller, *Germs: Biological Weapons and America's Secret War* (2001). On modern ethnic biowarfare, see the British Medical Association Report, *Biotechnology, Weapons, and Humanity* (1999); the article reported in the *London Sunday Times* by Uzi Mahnaimi and Marie Colvin, "Israel Planning 'ethnic bomb'" (November 1998); and "Lethal Legacy: Bioweapons for Sale," an article by Joby Warrick and John Mintz in the Sunday, April 20, 2003 *Washington Post* on the sale of apartheid-era South African manmade pathogens to the private sector.

- The "People of the Book Conference" draws upon various references in the Qur'an, where Christians and Jews are referred to as "People of the Book," i.e., those who have received and believe previous revelations of God's prophets, including the Jewish Torah, the Book of Psalms, and the Four Christian Gospels. In Islam, the Qur'an is seen as the completion of these earlier scriptures. See, for instance, "Surely those who believe, and those who are Jews, and Christians, and the Sabians—whoever believes in God and the Last Day and does good, they shall have their reward from the Lord. And that will be no fear for them, nor shall they grieve." (Qur'an 2:62, 5:69, and many others) In Judaism, "People of the Book" tends to be applied specifically to the Jewish people and the Torah.

The theft of an ancient and valuable artifact from the Baghdad Museum . . .
The convening of the richest and most powerful men on earth . . .
The sudden, mysterious death of the vice president . . .

From the Middle East to Europe, remote viewer Tobie Guinness and disgraced CIA agent Jax Alexander race to uncover a deadly plot to subvert America's freedom and destroy the world as we know it.

Don't miss the next thrilling adventure by C.S. Graham,

THE BABYLONIAN CODEX

Coming soon from HarperCollins

1

By late afternoon the clouds had gathered low in the valley, and snow began to fall. The soft flakes drifted across the icy streets of the exclusive Alpine ski resort and dusted the cashmere coats and fur hats of the wealthy, powerful men assembled there.

Sheltered in the lee of a picturesque shop selling rock climbing equipment, Noah Bosch studied the tan, confident faces of the men hurrying past him. Despite the cold, he was sweating, his throat dry with fear and anticipation. These were the men who ruled the world, although no one had elected them. They were the richest of the rich, a superclass of hedge fund managers and international bankers, corporate CEOs and venture capitalists. They gathered together here, at the World Economic Forum in Davos, to network and schmooze and set the agendas that would determine the lives and in many cases the deaths of the other six billion inhabitants of the planet.

The official pass dangling around Bosch's neck identified him as an outsider, a journalist admitted only to observe and report. But no one needed to read his nametag to know that he wasn't one of these captains of the universe. He was marked by his ratty parka, by the clumsily-cut brown hair worn a little too long, by the lanky, narrow-chested body of a twenty-something geek without a private gym or the leisure to schedule regular workouts. A tall, long-legged woman in a cropped mink jacket, her gloved hand tucked into the elbow of a man three times her age, glanced over at Bosch, her lips twitching with amusement. Bosch ignored her.

Narrowing his eyes against the thickening snow, he anxiously scanned the growing crowd on the Promenade. The sessions at the Congress Center must have ended. Bosch was looking for one man: the newly inaugurated vice president of the United States, Bill Hamilton.

Where was he?

He spotted the tall, silver-haired Southerner a moment later. Flanked by two Secret Service men, Hamilton was pausing to read the blackboard set out in front of a fondue restaurant when Bosch pushed his way through the crowd toward him.

"Excuse me, Mr. Vice President?"

One of the Secret Service agents moved to block him, but Hamilton turned with a politician's ready smile and waved the bodyguard back. He was a handsome man, with an open, tanned face and brilliant blue eyes. "I know you," said Hamilton with the affable charm that had helped win him the number two slot on his party's ticket. "You're that journalist—Bosch, isn't it? The one who thinks someone is planning to kill me."

One of the Secret Service agents—an ex-footballer with small dark eyes and a neck as thick as his head—laughed.

Bosch set his jaw. "Please, Mr. Hamilton; you've got to listen to me. I don't know how they'll do it, but they're going to make their move *here*. At Davos. And I tell you, this is meant to be just the beginning. They're going to kill the President next!"

Hamilton's smile was still in place, but the vivid blue eyes had hardened. "Look, Noah— You don't mind if I call you Noah, do you? I appreciate your concern. I really do. But take a look around. No place is more secure than Davos. You can't walk half a block without running into a Swiss police check. No one could touch me here."

"Mr. Vice President—"

Hamilton reached out to pat Bosch's shoulder. "Son, I don't know who's been jerking your chain, but you can't believe ninety percent of what you hear in this business." He nodded to the restaurant beside them. "Why don't you go sit down, have a nice cup of hot chocolate, and relax?"

"But—"

"Good day, Mr. Bosch."

The Vice President moved on up the street, his deep, drawling voice raised in cheerful greeting to a man Bosch recognized as a defense contractor from Texas. Bosch stood chewing his lower lip in frustration. Maybe what he needed was to—

Even though he was watching, Bosch couldn't understand what happened next. One minute, the Vice President was striding energetically up the street. Then he went down, and Bosch heard the thump of Hamilton's long, solid body hitting the ice. A woman let out a soft gasp. Someone shouted, "Quick! Is there a doctor? Someone get an ambulance. *Oh, God.* I think he's dead!"

A shocked, jabbering crowd of expensively dressed men and women converged on the fallen man. Over their heads, the Secret Service agent's dark gaze met Bosch's. Bosch felt a chill run up his spine.

He took a step back, then another, and another. When he reached the snowy alley beside the restaurant, Bosch turned and ran.

2

Two men strolled side by side along the C&O Canal towpath in Georgetown. Despite the rare winter sunshine slicing down through the trees to cast a green glow on the slow-moving water, they had the path largely to themselves. One man, tall and muscular and dark haired, was the head of the FBI's Criminal Investigative Division; his companion—younger, smaller, fairer—was the personal assistant of one of the richest men on earth.

"Things didn't go down exactly as planned in Davos," said the slight blond man, adjusting the sleeves of his soft gray Italian suit so that they lay just so against the cuffs of his crisp, hand-tailored white shirt.

The FBI director, Duane Davenport, glanced over at the man beside him and swallowed a spurt of irritation. "Operations rarely go precisely as planned. We succeeded; that's what's important. Now we're ready to move on to the next phase."

A strange smile tightened the other man's lips. He had

bland, forgettable features and straight, corn silk-fine hair that had a tendency to fall forward. He swept it back now in a quick, fastidious gesture. "There could be repercussions."

Davenport snorted. To listen to the guy, you'd think he had some kind of experience running field operations, when in truth he was just a lousy suit. A very powerful suit, maybe, but still a suit.

His name was Casper Nordstrom and for the past ten years he'd served as personal assistant to Perry Kane, an investment banker who'd taken advantage of all the deregulations pushed through back in the eighties to amass billions. Being a personal assistant might not sound very powerful, until you realized that Kane made all of his moves through Nordstrom. One whispered suggestion from Nordstrom was enough to send everyone from senators and congressmen to judges and generals scrambling to do his bidding. To cross Nordstrom was to cross the powerful, shadowy figure who stood behind him, and that was something few men dared to do.

"There won't be any repercussions," said Davenport. "Everything is under control."

Unlike Nordstrom, who'd been bred in the rarified atmosphere of Andover and Princeton, Davenport had grown up on the streets of Trenton, New Jersey, the son of an out-of-work longshoreman and an alcoholic mother. He'd started out as a cop walking a beat in Trenton, then joined the Bureau as a Special Agent assigned to Organized Crime while he was still finishing up his law degree at night school. In the twenty-two years since then, he'd risen rapidly through the ranks so that he was now one of the top men in the Bureau. And he owed much of his advancement to Perry Kane's influence. Kane was very good at identifying promising individuals in politics, law enforcement, the judiciary, and the military, and shepherding them through to positions of power.

"I'm more concerned about this woman the Art Crime

Team is bringing in here to try to help recover some of the items missing from Baghdad," said Davenport.

"You mean, the remote viewer?" Nordstrom gave a sharp laugh. "Don't tell me you believe in that hocus-pocus nonsense?"

Davenport paused to let a slim, fair-haired woman on a red bicycle zip past them. "There is much on God's earth we don't understand," he said, watching the cyclist disappear around the bend.

"Then eliminate her," said Nordstrom matter of factly.

"If I have to, I will. I've detailed one of my men to work with the Special Agent involved in the project. If this woman somehow accesses information that could be dangerous to us, he has orders to take them all out."

Nordstrom cleared his throat and glanced at his watch. "We've got just over a week. It's critical that you not let yourself get distracted."

Davenport huffed a soft laugh. "By Ensign October Guinness? Are you kidding? I've looked at her records. The woman's a real whack job. The Navy gave her a psycho discharge just months into her tour in Iraq. The only reason they brought her back to active duty was because T.J. Beckham insisted on it."

Nordstrom frowned. Until last month's inauguration, T. J. Beckham had been the vice president. Now he was back in Kentucky raising coon dogs. "So she no longer has a sponsor. Why not simply have her called off the case?"

Davenport shook his head. "This isn't an assignment. It's a personal favor to an old friend, through unofficial channels. I could have shut it down with strongarm tactics from my end, but now is not a good time to draw unwanted attention to the codex."

"You think taking out a couple of Navy personnel and an FBI agent isn't going to draw 'undue attention'?"

Davenport smiled. "I told you, Guinness is a certified whack job. If my man has to eliminate them, he'll fix it so it looks like a classic murder-suicide. Nothing could be simpler."

3

October Guinness was scanning the arrival and departure terminals in the New Orleans airport when she felt a strange sensation steal her breath, leaving her shaky and hot.

She didn't realize her reaction showed on her face until Colonel F. Scott McClintock, who'd driven her to the airport, said, "What is it, Tobie? What's wrong?"

She gave an unsteady laugh and turned away from the terminal bank toward the security lines. "I don't know. Maybe somebody walked on my grave." Remembering where she was, she cast a quick glance around and lowered her voice. "Can I say that here without getting arrested?"

McClintock smiled. "Last I checked." Standing well over six feet tall, with a thick shock of white hair and a weathered face, the Colonel had spent more than thirty years as a psychiatrist in Army Intelligence. Although officially retired, he still saw VA patients on a volunteer basis, in addition to working with Tobie to set up a small, hush-hush remote viewing program at the Algiers Naval base across the river from the French Quarter.

Now, his smile slowly faded as he continued studying her face. "Are you worried about flying?"

"In a jet? No. I'm fine—as long as it's not a helicopter." Tobie had had a really bad experience with a Kiowa helicopter in Iraq.

He laughed. "I can promise, no helicopters on this assignment."

She was on her way to Washington, D.C., to work on a project for an old friend of the Colonel's at the FBI's Art Crime Team. The ACT was still trying to track down thousands of artifacts looted from the National Museum of Iraq during the 2003 fall of Baghdad, and the expert in charge of the project, Special Agent Elaine Cox, had asked for Tobie's help in locating a dozen or so of the rarest items.

Unfortunately, the Colonel himself had had to back out of the trip at the last minute. Mary, his wife of forty years, had been slipping away into the fogs of Alzheimer's for several years. But recently she'd contracted a bad infection that had settled in her lungs. He paused beside Tobie at the end of the security line and said, "I wish I was going with you."

She reached out to press his forearm, gently, in a gesture of sympathy. "Mary needs you. Hopefully she'll be better soon. Peter and I work together just fine."

McClintock nodded. Peter Abrams, McClintock's assistant, had flown up to DC the night before and would be taking McClintock's place in the project for the Art Crime Team.

From the TV in the bar beside them came a reporter's lightly accented voice. "*The world is in shock today following the sudden death of United States Vice President Bill Hamilton. Preliminary reports suggest Hamilton could have hit his head after slipping on the ice, although it is possible the sixty-two-year-old Vice President may have suffered a heart attack. We should have a more information available in half an hour."*

McClintock nodded toward the TV set. "That might be what has you unsettled."

Tobie followed his gaze to the screen, where a reporter huddled in a heavy hooded coat could be seen against a backdrop of steep, snow-covered slopes. And she felt it again, that swift sensation of what she now recognized as disembodied fear. "Maybe," she said softly.

"Listen, Tobie . . . If you think this might be a bad idea you can still back out. I'll just tell Elaine—"

She jerked her gaze away from the snowy scene. "Are you kidding? We couldn't ask for a better chance to show all the skeptics in D.C. just what remote viewing can accomplish. I wouldn't miss this for anything."

She was almost at the front of the line. McClintock said, "Just . . . be careful, you hear?"

"I'll be fine. I'm going to be sitting in a soundproofed room remote viewing a bunch of dusty old artifacts." She pulled her boarding pass out of her carryon bag and fumbled for her ID. "How dangerous can that be?"

From C.S. GRAHAM writing as C.S. HARRIS

The acclaimed Sebastian St. Cyr mysteries

AVAILABLE NOVEMBER 2009

London, 1812. The brutal murder of eight young prostitutes
leaves one survivor—and one witness: Hero Jarvis, who turns
to Sebastian St. Cyr for help. Working in an uneasy alliance, they
follow a trail of clues leading from the seedy brothels of London's
East End to the Mayfair mansions of a noble family with secrets
to hide. Risking both their lives and their reputations, the two must
race against time to stop a killer whose ominous plot threatens to
shake the nation to its core.

"Harris delves deep into the mores of Regency England,
    but hers is a darker, more dangerous place."
                        —*Kirkus Reviews* (starred review)

csharris.net

⊙ Obsidian Mysteries
A Member of Penguin Group (USA) • penguin.com

NEED SOMETHING
NEW TO READ?

Download it Now!

Visit www.harpercollinsebooks.com
to choose from thousands of titles
you can easily download to your
computer or PDA.

Save 20% off the printed book price.
Ordering is easy and secure.

HarperCollins e-books

Download to your laptop, PDA, or phone for
convenient, immediate, or on-the-go reading. Visit
www.harpercollinsebooks.com or other online
e-book retailers.

Visit www.AuthorTracker.com for exclusive
information on your favorite HarperCollins authors.

Available wherever books are sold or please call 1-800-331-3761 to order.
HRE 0307